THE BORODINS
BOOK III
FATE and DREAMS

LESLIE ARLEN

A JOVE BOOK

First Jove edition published September 1981

First printing

Printed in the United States of America

Jove books are published by Jove Publications, Inc.,
200 Madison Avenue, New York, N.Y. 10016

"WOULD YOU LIKE TO MAKE LOVE TO ME?" TATTIE SAID, SMILING.

"What?" He sat back in his chair.

"Well, I supposed you must, since you invited me out," she explained. "And since you watched most of my performances."

Bullen finished his wine.

"I would like you to," she said. "In fact, Mr. Bullen, you are the very first man in all my life that I have actually wanted to make love to me."

He leaned forward. "I would very much like to make love to you, Tatiana Nej. I have dreamed of nothing else since that first night in Berlin. You must forgive me for being absurd just now."

"Not at all. I suppose English girls do not speak as I did."

"No," he said. "They don't. But Russian girls do?"

"I don't know," she said. "I am not a Russian girl, Clive Bullen. I am Tatiana Nej. Shall we go, and make love?"

TATTIE...
She was a Borodin princess, Lenin's friend, and Ivan's wife. But she belonged to no one.
ILONA HAYMAN. *Safe in America, she is yet drawn into the web of terror spun by her sister's husband, Ivan.*
PRINCE PETER BORODIN. *Steeped in the glories of the family name, he looked ever more coldly on Tattie's wild ways—and plotted to stop her.*
JOHN HAYMAN. *Ilona's son shares the prince's dangerous dreams—and becomes the bait in a Soviet trap.*

FATE AND DREAMS

By Leslie Arlen
from Jove

THE BORODINS

Chapter 1

THE LAND UNDULATED, IN SLOW WAVES, LIKE THE SURFACE OF A calm ocean. In years gone by it had indeed suggested a sea, of wheat. In the autumn of 1921 it resembled a desert, disturbed only by the long, slender, glimmering steel track, and today by the train that slithered across the landscape beneath its shroud of black smoke.

But now the train was halting, the boxcar doors were being opened, the horses and their riders were disembarking; rifles were slipped into holsters, and swords slapped thighs. Suddenly the track became a khaki-colored antheap.

Captain Ashcherin stood on the platform of the single passenger car and surveyed the empty plain. "We are wasting our time, comrade commissar," he suggested. "This is a dead country. What the White armies did not destroy, your brother destroyed. And what he missed, this drought has killed."

Commissar Ivan Nej took off his glasses, and slowly polished them before replacing them on his nose. Beneath the platform, men were mounting their horses, and a stallion waited for him at the foot of the steps. He was a surprising choice to

1

be in charge of so many husky Russian soldiers, being no more than medium height and appearing smaller since he habitually hunched his shoulders. His features were narrow and pinched, dominated by his heavy mustache; the glasses struck an incongruous note for a soldier. His khaki peaked cap seemed too large for his head, his shoulders too narrow for the khaki jacket, dragged down by the heavy holster attached to his belt. His boots were dusty.

Now he took his binoculars from their case, surveyed the distance, and pointed. "The river," he said.

Captain Ashcherin peered in turn at the slow-moving trickle of water that felt its way down the bed of the deep ravine. Even in the basin of the Don it had not rained for several months.

"I lived here as a boy," Ivan Nej said, half to himself. "At a place called Starogan. The home of the Princes Borodin, you know. It is gone now, destroyed in the fighting. But before the war—why, it was the richest country in the world, comrade captain. It will be again. This soil is black. Black. And there will be survivors. There are always survivors. The Brusilovs are survivors. There." He had been using his binoculars as he spoke, and now he pointed at a just-visible cluster of buildings, close by the river.

"They must have seen the train, comrade commissar," the captain said.

Ivan glanced at him. "And will resist? No, no, comrade. These kulaks are tired of fighting. They are even more tired of dying. They will wish to live. And we represent the Soviet."

He mounted, kicked his horse into a canter, and led his men down the slope and away from the railway line, the captain just behind him. Now they could clearly see the farm, seeming to grow out of the river bank. Even here the fields were brown and parched, but there had been an attempt at cultivation during the spring and summer. And here some animals had survived; the cattle were securely penned in a heavy wooden corral and guarded by two armed men. The house itself, and the outbuildings, were arranged so as to suggest a fortress, any gaps between wall and wall filled in with rubble and earth. No doubt the place had been defended before, and could be defended again; as the cavalry approached more men appeared in the farmstead, every one armed with a rifle, each taking up a previously selected position to face the intruders. Ivan Nej held up his hand again, and the soldiers clattered to a halt, rifles still in scabbards, machine guns still slung behind saddles.

"Wait," Ivan said, and walked his horse forward.

The captain pushed his cap back on his forehead and scratched himself. He had been a regular soldier, a corporal, before the revolution. He hated requisitioning patrols, just as he had always hated tax gatherers. He hated Bolshevik commissars. And of all the Bolshevik commissars, he hated Ivan Nej most of all, as did everyone in Russia. But he was forced to admit that the man, however detestable his methods, had courage.

"Stop there," someone called from the barricaded front gate.

Ivan Nej reined in his horse, surveyed the people in front of him, reached into his saddlebag, and produced a dog-eared notebook. "You are Feodor Petrovich Brusilov," he said to the man who had spoken. He looked at the woman standing beside the farmer. "You are Alexandra Nikolaievna Brusilova." His teeth showed as he smiled at the little girl, perhaps ten years old, waiting on her father's other side. "And you are Natasha Feodorovna Brusilova." He put away his notebook, raised his cap. "I am Commissar Nej."

The men at the barricades exchanged glances.

"Look around you," said the peasant named Brusilov. "There has been no rain in six months. Half my cattle are dead. And the rest will surely die this winter, as I have no hay. There is no wheat. There is nothing."

"There are those who are even more unfortunate than yourself, Comrade Brusilov," Ivan said. "It is the duty of the government to care for all. I will take half your store of grain, half your cattle."

"You cannot," Brusilov said. "Comrade Lenin has said we are to be allowed to keep our grain and our cattle. Only the surplus must go to the state. And this year there is no surplus."

"You have more than anyone else in this district," Ivan said quietly. "That is a surplus. I will also take half your wagons, to transport the grain. My men will commence now."

He wheeled his horse, but the click of a safety catch being removed sounded above the scuffle of the hooves. He paused, his side to the farmers, his head turned towards them.

"If you resist me, comrade, I will burn your farm and give

your women to my men." Once again he smiled at the little girl. "You too, Natasha. If you resist me." He raised his hand, and the machine-gun squads dismounted, erecting their weapons and taking their positions with the ease and efficiency of long training. Ivan continued to look at the men lining the barricades. "My men will come in now," he said. He walked his horse back to stand beside the captain. The soldiers rode forward.

"Are you never afraid, comrade commissar?" asked Captain Ashcherin.

"Of a kulak?"

"Of a desperate man."

"Men are only *that* desperate when they are about to lose all," Ivan said. "And these peasants—especially the rich ones, the kulaks—have no intelligence. They cannot make themselves realize that they *have* lost all. Comrade Lenin allows them to exist only because the country needs their food. When our victory has been consolidated, he will give the word, and I will come down and destroy them like the vermin they are."

"You enjoy destroying people, comrade commissar," Ashcherin observed.

"Oh, indeed," Ivan agreed. "People I hate. I hate kulaks. Just as I hate all bourgeois. I hate them even more than I hate tsarists." He smiled as he watched his men breaking down the barricades. Except for one tsarist, he thought, and that was Prince Peter Borodin. There was no one he hated more than Prince Peter. Unless . . . What of George Hayman? And Ilona Hayman? But he hated her only because he had never been able to possess her.

And who knows? he wondered. The day may yet come when even Peter Borodin and George Hayman will be there to be destroyed, like the kulaks. Perhaps it was only a matter of being patient.

And Ilona Hayman? There was a dream.

Mrs. Killett knocked briefly, then held the door ajar as she smiled at her employer. "Mr. Hoover to see you, Mr. Hayman."

George Hayman stepped from behind his huge mahogany desk and strode across the lush Oriental carpets to welcome his guest. The office stretched the width of the eighteenth floor of the Hayman Newspaper Building, sixty feet of polished elegance that overlooked the East River. "Herb," he said, shaking his hand. "Good to see you. Have a cigar."

Herbert Hoover nodded, sat in the leather armchair in front of the desk, and selected a Corona from the box Hayman offered to him. The two men made a considerable contrast. Hoover, only a few years the elder, was heavy-shouldered and bulldog-faced. Hayman, at forty-four, was still slim and exuded energetic health; his long features and serious mouth were enlivened by dancing brown eyes.

"You don't seem to grow any older," Hoover complained, and frowned at him. "Hair receding a bit?"

George ran his fingers through the still thick brown hair. "The beginning of the end." He retrieved the clipper from his friend and lit his own cigar, settling again behind his desk. "How's Europe?"

"Grim." Hoover blew smoke at the ceiling. "You know why I'm here?"

George leaned back, continuing to smile. "Haven't a clue."

"Newspaper business prospering?"

"It's a living."

"Oh, sure." Hoover allowed his gaze to encompass the graphs on the walls, tracing the rising sales of not only the *American People*, but of all the other papers, in England and France and Japan as well as in the United States and Canada, owned by Hayman Newspapers. "I suppose people have to read."

"I'll say amen to that."

"Just as they have to eat."

George leaned forward and placed his elbows on the desk. "Russia?"

"George, there are going to be something like ten million people dying over there this winter, of sheer starvation. Add to that those who died last winter, and those who were killed in the civil war, and those who died in the Great War itself, and you have the worst human catastrophe in history."

"I was there," George said. "I saw some of it. Okay, so we'll launch another appeal. But I'm not hopeful. You know as well as I that the people of this country are just a little bit fed up with Europe. We helped them out of their mess in '17, and now they seem anxious to get themselves into another mess as rapidly as possible. As for the Russians—well, you know my opinion of the Bolsheviks. And I have always believed a country gets the government it deserves."

"I'm not looking for money," Hoover said. "My organization has money. So it can buy food. But that's only the beginning of the story. I thought you were quite friendly with some of the Soviet leaders."

"I *know* them," George said. "Not the same thing."

"Some fellow called Nej. Didn't you save his life once?"

"I saved Michael Nej from being hanged," George said. "Since then he and I have not always seen eye to eye. And when I left Russia eighteen months ago, I was forced to make use of his brother, Ivan Nej."

Hoover at last smiled. "Didn't you kidnap the man?"

"Briefly. Long enough to make sure he hates my guts. And Ivan Nej, in case you didn't know, is one of the commanders of the Cheka. That's Lenin's secret police."

Hoover nodded. "I know. Still, since he's married to your sister-in-law, George, I shouldn't think he'd shoot you on sight. And anyway, if you were to meet him again, it wouldn't be just as George Hayman, Jr., newspaper correspondent, it would be as George Hayman, soon to be president of the *American People*, and God knows how many other things besides. How is the old man, anyway?"

"He survives. Because I'm here to run the papers for him. Just what are you driving at?"

Hoover leaned forward in turn, and placed his elbows on the desk. "As I said, I have the money, and I have the food. But dealing with the Soviets..." he shook his head. "They seem *willing* to let millions starve, rather than allow any outside force to muscle in. And the situation isn't helped by the State Department not being prepared to recognize the regime. What I want is someone who knows Russia, who speaks the language, who's acquainted with the bosses over there, and maybe someone who loves the country, as well. That person is going to have to cut through all the red tape, get permission for our people to move in and do their stuff."

George leaned back. "You must be out of your mind."

"Ten million lives, George. And that's a conservative estimate, with God knows how many more to follow if we don't do something by next summer. And you *do* love Russia. Everything you've ever written or said on the subject makes me sure of that. For God's sake, you're married to a Russian. George, sitting here and making ten million dollars turn into twenty million dollars is fine. It's good for you, it's good for the country. Maybe it's good for the world. But there are ten million men, women, and children over there who aren't going to benefit from your success, because they're going to die soon."

George pushed back his chair, got up, and walked to the window. From here he looked east across a sea of roofs and a river towards Long Island. And beyond Long Island, there was the ocean. And beyond the ocean, Europe. And beyond Europe, Russia. Where he had spent the most exciting, the most memorable, the most traumatic moments of his entire life. And from where he had extracted the greatest prize any man could ever achieve, the love of Princess Ilona Borodina.

"I'd like you to go back, George," Hoover said, "as representative of the American Relief Administration. I'll give you carte blanche, and I'll arrange it with Lenin himself. No one is going to interfere with what you want to do. Not even Ivan Nej. I give you my word on that. Just put Lenin in the picture, tell him we want to help. For God's sake, if he intends to lead his people, he's got to accept that."

George continued to stare towards the distant sea.

"The paper will manage for a month or two, George," Hoover said. "If necessary, I'll talk to the old man myself."

George turned. "I'm not worried about the old man. Sure he can manage. I was thinking of Ilona."

"Talk to her, " Hoover said. "You talk to her, George. It's her people."

"Russia?" Ilona Hayman asked. "He wants you to go back to Russia?" She spoke quietly, as always. Her calmness had always been remarkable; George had been attracted by it seventeen years before, when they had first met in the doomed city of Port Arthur, with the Japanese guns thundering in the background. It was a result, he supposed, first of her beauty. Ilona Hayman was a tall woman, and at thirty-five the only visible results of her somewhat tempestuous life were an increased firmness of the flawless mouth and chin, a deepened thoughtfulness in the huge, wideset blue eyes. The long straight nose, the high forehead, remained unchanged. So did the golden hair that was her glory—she had resisted the current mania for bobbing. "A Russian princess," she had remarked to her hairdresser, "does not cut her hair."

And this was the second element that had created the essential Ilona. She *was* a Russian princess, and no one could look at her and not understand that simple fact, which had not changed despite the destruction of her family, of its fortune and its titles and its palaces and its prerogatives in the mad onrush of the revolution sparked by Lenin. That she should have decided to become George's wife was to him one of the great miracles of all time.

Now she gazed at him in that delightfully surprised fashion that she had, mouth slightly open, fingers delicately cradling the sherry glass provided by Harrison, their English butler, her figure only accentuated by the pink voile dress with its flower design on skirt and bodice. Whenever he came back to such a vision he was surprised at his carelessness in leaving home at all.

And yet they both knew there remained that even stronger magnet, drawing him away from the individual magnificence of the woman, towards the collective magnificence of that strange, brooding country and its teeming millions, so empty of hope, so consumed with passion.

"There are some pretty good arguments," he suggested mildly.

"For *you* to go?"

"Well, sweetheart, there's nobody else quite in the position I am, as regards the Soviets. Since the State Department has withdrawn diplomatic recognition of the regime, why, I'm probably the *only* American they'll listen to. And besides, there's Tattie."

Ilona looked over at the silver-framed photograph of her younger sister. Tatiana Borodina had been twenty-one when that picture was taken in 1914, just after her birthday party, in fact. The very last time the entire family had been united, before being torn apart forever. The remarkable thing was that the lovely laughing girl represented there had hardly changed at all in the next six years, as George, who had seen her less than two years ago, well knew.

"Tattie made her choice," Ilona said. "She married Ivan Nej. That . . . that yardboy."

"The commissar for internal security," George reminded her.

"That raping, murdering bastard," Ilona said, still speaking quietly. "I'm sorry George, but—"

"But she is your sister."

"She made her choice," Ilona said again. "She's a Communist, George. She's a Bolshevik. You saw her last. You told me, remember? She wasn't even interested when the Steins were executed. She's interested in nothing but her absurd music and her obscene dancing. She—well, she's a Bolshevik."

"She married Ivan," George said, "because it was that or starve, at best. And she made what she could of it. That's to her credit. And she's a Bolshevik, *if* she is one, simply because your family kept trying to bully her into being something she was not. So she wants to dance and write music to her own taste. She can do that over here just as well as in Russia. I'd like to talk to her again."

"You mean you'd like to see Russia again. You'd like to get involved. You're still a newspaper correspondent at heart. Oh, my darling . . ." she took his hands. "I don't blame you, believe me. Maybe I'd like to go back too. Just to see Starogan again, one more time."

"Now, my sweet—"

"Oh, I know what you're going to say. That it would be dangerous for me, because I'm a Borodin? But what of all the things you were going to do here? You were going to campaign against Prohibition, you were—"

"Prohibition is a *fait accompli*, my darling. I don't approve of interfering with any man's liberty, whether it's to drink himself to death or not. Man has always drunk and he always will, and to make it a crime will just be to hand the business over to the underworld. But no one is going to listen to me now. They'll have to learn for a year or two."

"And Mr. Harding?"

George shrugged. "I campaigned for his election because he's the man the party chose. But I don't think he's the best choice, and I certainly don't like all his choices for the cabinet. I imagine Warren can run the country without me. Besides,

Hoover squared it with the White House in advance."

Ilona sighed. "I still think . . . what does Peter say?"

"We'll find out this evening," George said. "I've suggested that they come back here for supper after the party. It's certainly a matter for a family discussion."

Peter Borodin was an elegant man. Tall and blond like his sisters, he possessed in full the Borodin good looks, the perfect, somewhat large features, the wideset eyes; the face, in his case, was enhanced by the little blonde mustache that adorned his upper lip. He dressed flawlessly, usually in a light gray suit; his tiepin was a pearl. Only in his slight air of defiance could any trace of his history be discerned: the family squabbles and the tragedies that had dogged his brief princedom; the disappointments of the Great War against the Germans; and then the disasters when, as General Denikin's chief of staff, he had led the White armies against the Bolsheviks, who were commanded by the man who had been his own valet, Michael Nej. Endless defeats had culminated in the horrifying evacuation of Sevastopol, nearly two years before. And now, George supposed, there was the final tragedy of all; that Prince Peter Borodin of Starogan should finish his life working for his American brother-in-law.

They had also met in Port Arthur, and liked each other. But Peter's friendship had turned to anger when the brash American had had the temerity to ask for Ilona's hand in marriage. So they had quarreled, only to be reconciled nine years later, after Ilona's elopement with George had made further quarreling pointless. That reconciliation had taken place amid all the splendor of Starogan, with liveried footmen at their elbows, with the entire Borodin family gathered for Tatiana's twenty-first birthday, with all the glory of autocratic Russia displayed in its imperial immutability—and with the war which would sweep it all away already rushing upon them. Now George Hayman remained, as he had been in 1914, a millionaire and the son of a millionaire, taking his power and his influence from the network of newspapers he had created around the globe, while Peter Borodin was a penniless émigré with an empty title, forced to earn his bread as Russian-affairs editor on the *American People*.

But he was still able, on occasion, to regain just a whiff

of his past glories. He *was*, after all, a prince, and to Harriet Maclain that one word eclipsed all faults and all misfortunes. And since Harriet was New York's premier hostess, Peter was able, at parties like this one, to remind the eager throng of just what the word prince stood for. He occupied the center of the room, entirely surrounded by jeweled women who smoked their cigarettes, if they smoked at all, from long holders and pressed forward for a touch of his arm, for some contact with the most exciting thing that had happened in New York society since Lily Langtry's visit. To them he talked, so casually, about his three hundred thousand acres of wheat, his stable of horses, his three cars, the Petrograd town house, the tsarina's habit of looking down her nose when she was displeased, the tsar's diffidence, the tsarevich's constant illness . . . all trampled into dust by the boots of Trotsky's legions, and all totally beyond the comprehension of his audience except as represented in the person of this tall, distinguished, handsome man.

And his equally exciting sister. For as the Haymans entered, he managed to extricate himself from his admirers to cross the room, kiss Ilona upon each cheek, and shake George's hand. "We are to have a family conference," he said. "I am quite excited. Rachel thinks there is some crisis."

He smiled at his wife across the room. The Princess of Starogan was also the center of an eager crowd of admirers, mainly men. Like her husband, she dressed in the height of fashion, indulging her fondness for black silk. Presumably, George thought, they were busily running themselves into debt; but as George Hayman's in-laws, they would always easily obtain credit in a booming America. He wondered what Rachel had to tell her audience. She had only briefly known the prerogatives of being a Princess of Starogan. Hers had been a wartime marriage; she had nothing but her title to which she could now cling, and she used that with relentless determination, even with Ilona. Having received her husband's signal and joined him by the door, she allowed her sister-in-law to kiss *her* on the cheek, a privilege that was then extended to George.

She could be indulged. Because George knew she remained what she had always been, a terrified little social climber from Petrograd Island, amazed and confused by the society in which her sister Judith had involved her. That she had picked the plum out of the pudding, the plum that had always been Judith's by right, was merely an example of the unpredictability of fate.

But Judith Stein had learned her place. While the Prince and Princess of Starogan scintillated, she stood in a corner quietly conversing with a bespectacled young man, and looked up with a relieved smile when she saw George coming towards her, about half an hour after he and Ilona arrived. The sisters were very alike, tall without matching the Borodins in height, slender and willowy, with bold features and black eyes that could sparkle—but had not, in some time. Yet George thought that Judith had fitted more easily into the pattern of American life, perhaps because she had expected less, having left less behind; perhaps because she had actually fled here in the company of her benefactor, George Hayman. Unlike either Rachel or Ilona, Judith had cut her hair, leaving her face and neck strangely exposed. Yet this, George thought, as he took her hands and kissed her cheek, had been her most important act. Of them all, Judith, with her background of arrests for terrorism, her three years in a Siberian labor camp, the child she had lost and the family who had been murdered, wanted only to forget. She was thirty-two, and surely her life had just begun. If only he could be certain where it was she wished to go, and with whom. It was widely accepted that Peter Borodin had fallen in love with her way back in 1907, had only married her younger sister because he had believed Judith dead. But now all three of them were alive and living in New York. And should Judith's dreams and desires in any way interest a man who was married to Ilona Borodina?

"Must you leave so soon?" Harriet Maclain cried. "Oh, George, you've only just come."

"I'm sorry, Harriet," George said. "But—"

"And you're taking the prince and princess with you? Oh, *George!*"

"Business," George said firmly. "But it's been a lovely party, Harriet." He escorted them downstairs to the waiting Rolls.

"So boring," Rachel said, sitting beside Ilona. "I really can't imagine why we attend."

"We attend," Peter remarked, "because you accept every invitation we receive." He fitted a cigarette into his holder as the car drew away from the curb. "Well?"

"Briefly," George began, and related his conversation with Hoover. But they were through Glen Cove before he finished.

"That is madness," Judith Stein said quickly, and flushed, as if realizing she should have been the last to offer an opinion.

"Exactly what I said," Ilona agreed. They had been friends as young women, and invariably took the same side.

"I don't think so at all," Peter said. "Lenin, whatever his crimes, is no fool. He knows he needs American help. He'll never risk harming someone like George. I'd say you'll get the red-carpet treatment, George."

"Except that Lenin may no longer be in control over there," Judith said.

"I wanted to talk to you about that, Peter," George said.

"Ah, well, there is no doubt that he has been ill," Peter said. "It is difficult to be certain, because of course they are not advertising the news, but he has been seen at very few functions this winter, and there is a report that at one where he did appear, he had to be helped to walk, and his speech was hesitant. Now that sounds rather like a stroke to me. Which is why you *must* go back, George. If Lenin were to die, or even become permanently incapacitated, that whole rotten house of cards would come tumbling down."

George frowned at him. "I'm not sure I understand you."

"Listen to me. There are hundreds, thousands, no doubt millions of Russians who loathe Communism as much as you or I. Once Lenin goes, and the others, Trotsky and Stalin and Nej and the rest, start quarreling among themselves, then will be the opportunity for a counter revolution. I can put you in touch with several people—"

"You *are* mad," Judith said. "You want George to involve himself with some sort of White group? That would be committing suicide."

"Now, really, Judith, one would suppose you didn't *want* to see the Bolsheviks overthrown."

The car was pulling into the driveway.

"I think," Ilona said, "that we should forget about Russia, until after the children have said goodnight. I told them to wait up especially."

George Hayman III bubbled. At nine years old he already gave promise of the handsome size he had inherited from both his parents. His sister Felicity, a year his junior, was one of the prettiest little girls imaginable, possessing a remarkably pleasing mixture of her mother's coloring and her father's features. But they exuded so much more than the mere healthy vitality of lively children. They were Haymans. If they had adventured, been caught up with their mother in the terrors of a Bolshevik prison, they had been too young at the time to remember it as anything more than an adventure. And besides, they had been able to repeat to themselves, as Ilona had repeated endlessly to their guards, that they were not Russian, whatever their ancestry; they were Haymans, and Americans, and had no more than accidental parts to play in the hate and mistrust and greed and anger that had swept across Russia in the summer of 1918. And in time, as they had never doubted, they had been released to regain the safety of their sunlit land.

Now they flitted from guest to guest, with a kiss here and a hug there. George wondered if they would ever be able to understand how great an upheaval there had to have been in the affairs of the world, the ordered structure of things, for them to be calling two middle-class Jewish women "aunt," to be acknowledging one of those women as the Princess of Starogan.

But their brother knew. John Hayman waited in the doorway while his half-brother and half-sister completed their greetings and farewells. His quiet dignity was more than the conscious gravity of being the eldest, and of being thirteen years old. He knew, so much more than they. He knew that he did not belong here, that his father was presumably dead, one of the casualties of the Revolution. He had been conceived while his mother had been married to Sergei Roditchev; his youthful innocence could take him no further than that, and besides, there was clearly no Hayman blood in his veins. Thus he thought he knew that his father had been murdered by Dora Ulyanova in an act of bloody revenge—and of bloody justice too, the history books would say; there could be no other fitting end for the commander of the tsar's secret police.

But there was a burden of guilt for a young boy to carry. And the tragedy was that if he ever learned the true identity of his father, he would merely exchange one burden for another, even heavier and more confusing.

Now he came into the room, and slowly circulated, shaking

hands, presenting his cheek for a kiss. His Uncle Peter addressed him in Russian, as he always did, and John replied in kind.

"And what will you do when you leave school?" Peter inquired.

"I shall play chess," John replied.

"Ha ha," Peter shouted. "A good old Russian game. Yes, you will play at chess, Ivan Sergeievich. And be a champion. A second Tchigorin, eh?"

"No, sir," John said. "A second Frank Marshall."

Peter frowned at him for a moment, then gave another laugh. "Well, and why not? They were both great attacking players."

"Mr. Marshall is still a great attacking player." John Hayman continued on his way, reached his mother last, and gave her the only truly warm embrace of the evening.

"A boy who knows his own mind," Peter declared as the adults sat down to a late supper. "He will go far."

"Of course he will go far," Rachel said. "He is a Borodin. Just as my Ruth will go far. They are the very last Borodins." She gazed around the table with those huge black eyes of hers, daring anyone to doubt her statement.

George found Judith watching him, as she often watched him, and shivers of suppressed emotion ran up and down his spine. Why? He had not even known she existed, until the day in 1911 when Sergei Roditchev, already suspecting perhaps that George had again become his wife's lover, had taken him on a tour of the hideous underworld of the Okhrana prison. Prime Minister Stolypin had been assassinated, and Prince Roditchev had been given carte blanche to arrest and torture to his heart's content, in order to discover the conspirators. Michael Nej had been in that jail, a beaten and bloody hulk. So had many others. And so had Judith Stein, a naked sliver of cane-wealed flesh. It was a sight George would never forget, a sudden, horrifying glimpse into the realities both of rebellion and of police work, a suggestion of the ghastly intimacy that must arise between interrogator and victim—for him made worse by the reflection that the woman he loved was the wife of this monster, and equally subject to his vicious brutality.

At least he had been able to free Ilona. And he had supposed Judith Stein would remain nothing more than a memory. That he should meet her again, and at Starogan, as a guest of the

Borodins *after* she had spent three years in a Siberian prison, had been just another example of the chaos into which the world of 1914 had collapsed. Then they had met again, often, in Petrograd during the Great War, and at the end of it all, after her mother and father had been executed by Ivan Nej, who seemed determined to show that the Bolshevik Cheka could be every bit as vicious as tsarist secret police. After their deaths George had taken her with him from Russia, using Ivan himself as a hostage. There would be no forgiveness there, any more than there would be forgiveness from Michael Nej; he too had known and loved this strange, passionate, strong-willed Jewess. Their relationship had ended with her flight from Russia.

And so George and Judith had crossed the Atlantic together, their cabins adjoining. They had eaten together and they had walked together, and they had talked together. She had told him of her life in Siberia, of the men, and the women she had loved there, of the child who had not survived one winter. She had told him how she felt the night she had lured Rasputin to his doom. Things, he supposed, she had never discussed with anyone before.

And she had told, him, too, of her feelings for Peter Borodin. Without being explicit, she had suggested those feelings were over and done with, especially since Peter was now married to her sister. But the reminder had been enough, quite apart from the fact that he was on his way back to Ilona, to restrain even a handclasp. Yet they had looked at each other, and known what the other was thinking. That the Atlantic crossing had been a fast one was probably equally fortunate for both of them.

As if his thoughts could possibly have ended with the mere fact of their arrival in New York. She was destitute but for his charity. But she was also an accomplished writer, and Hayman Newspapers was interested in the Russian scene. She was worth every cent he paid her. But what did she think, what did she do, when she was not at the office? Or not, as now, dining here in their Long Island home?

He loved Ilona. There was no argument about that. To know Ilona was to love her; to be loved by her was the most remarkable emotional experience any man could dream of.

But to look at Judith Stein was to *want* her, without ever

understanding why. And now she was looking at him. "You won't really go back to Russia, George," she said softly, from her seat at his right hand. "Promise that you won't."

"I worry about Peter." Ilona Hayman sat at her dressing table and brushed her hair. She preferred to do this herself, waited until after her maid had undressed her to sit in her nightdress, brush in hand, and slowly draw it through the long golden strands. She always waited until George was already in bed to perform this ritual; it was a moment of special intimacy, relished by them both. A time for speaking their minds.

"He still dreams of returning to Russia, of rebuilding Starogan and hanging the Nej brothers," Ilona said.

George put down the newspaper he had been surveying, a copy of the London edition, and took off his glasses. "I suppose it's inevitable. When you remember what he lost . . . what you all lost."

"But it is so futile, to keep looking over your shoulder," Ilona said. She put down her brush and turned to face him. "To spend your time hating. Mama is dead. Aunt Anna and Uncle Igor and Xenia and Tigran are all dead. Nothing we can do is ever going to bring them back to life. To remember why and how they died . . ." she gave a little shudder. "I do not even want to remember why and how his majesty died, and the tsarina, and those girls. And that little tsarevich."

"Did you know I have had a report from Germany that a woman over there claims to be Anastasia Romanova?"

Ilona frowned. "That is impossible."

"Nothing is impossible in this life, my darling. It could just be. Nobody knows for certain what happened down in that cellar."

Ilona came across the room and sat beside him. "Well, then, I hope and pray it may be she, however terrible the memories she will carry for the rest of her life. But she will know, as well as any of us, that there can never be an imperial restoration in Russia. You and Peter are so excited because this Lenin is ill, because you think there may be another revolution. But even if there is another revolution, it is not going to turn back the clock for us or for the Romanovs."

He held her hands. "I agree with you. But it may yet be possible to rescue *something* from the mess. If everything

Hoover told me is true—and from what I saw before I left I'm
inclined to believe him—the Bolsheviks really have no government at all. The entire country has degenerated into a vast
no-man's-land, run by brigands *for* brigands. It is extremely
likely that it may split up into what it was only a few hundred
years ago, a lot of separate khanates and princedoms."

"And you suppose Peter may have a chance of finding his
princedom again?"

"It's not beyond the bounds of possibility. He is a very
capable man, a brilliant soldier. Had he fought for a more
limited objective, instead of attempting to reconquer the whole
country, he might even have succeeded last year."

"And Russia will be thrown into another ten years of civil
war, with people dying like flies."

"They are doing that anyway, according to Hoover."

She gazed into his eyes. "But you would like to go and
see."

"Well . . ."

"To act as Peter's agent? You?"

"Good Lord, no. I have no intention of getting mixed up
in his politics. But I would like to see, that I admit. And if I
could also help—"

"Then you would be helping Bolshevism, would you not?
They will certainly take the credit for any improvements that
result."

He kissed her on the mouth, and a moment later she was
in his arms, rolling over him to find herself on her back, her
hair scattered about her, his lips tight on hers as his body
covered hers, as his hand went down to lift her nightgown. She
loved with a silent, consuming passion that had not diminished
a whit since that first unforgettable night together, on a settee
in her father's house in Port Arthur, with the Japanese shells
creeping closer and closer. The knowledge that but for that
looming debacle he would not even have been accepted as a
guest in Count Borodin's house, much less be finding himself
sharing an evening with the count's eldest daughter, that she
would not have considered addressing an American journalist,
much less surrendering herself to him, had sparked their love
for all those seventeen years, as much as the pleasure he felt
in kissing those eager lips, in possessing those swelling breasts,

in seeking the splendor of that thick-forested groin. He had once thought that in Ilona Borodina four hundred years of Russian aristocracy had found their most splendid representative. And she was his, utterly and without reserve, the mother of his children, the support of his every decision. And the sensual companion of his every lust.

Then why was he wondering if Judith Stein would be similarly silent as she loved, similarly convulsed at the moment of orgasm, similarly everything a man could ever dream of?

He sat on the edge of the bed, stared at himself in the full-length mirror on the opposite wall.

"Oh, my darling," Ilona said. "You make me so very happy."

Surely no woman would ever equal Ilona, much less Judith, whose very existence was a mass of tortured hopes and fears and memories, who carried the seeds of death within her, who could *hate*, as he had seen, in a fashion that made Peter Borodin's dreams of revenge no more than childish.

Ilona's nails slipped up and down his back. "But you are not happy tonight."

And even if Judith could, in some unimaginable way, equal Ilona, did it matter? Ilona was his, and he was hers. No one else had any part in their world.

But it was not the first time he had thought of Judith when making love to Ilona, since his return from Russia.

"You will not be happy until you have gone back to Russia," she said, and sighed, and released him to lie down once more. "I sometimes think that it means more to you than to me."

He turned and lay on his elbow beside her. "It gave you me."

She smiled sadly. "But one should not love the mother more than the daughter one has married."

"There are people dying over there. Millions of people dying, simply because they do not have enough to eat. If I can help them—"

"Do not ever lie to me, George. You just want to go back to Russia. It is like a drug to you. That you can find a reason, a good reason is to your advantage. But you just want to go back to Russia."

I do want to go, he thought. Almost the most criminal act

he could imagine himself committing—willingly to leave yet
again, the newspaper and the financial empire and his family.
To leave Ilona? No. That was not what he wished. But to leave
Judith, the sight of her and the sound of her—and most important of all, the thought of her—just for a while. To attempt
to sort out the tangled mess the war had made of his emotions.

"Then you must go, my darling," Ilona said. "But we will
not be separated again. You will take me with you."

"Now that _is_ madness," Peter Borodin declared. "You? You
are a Borodin. You are proscribed. You are regarded as an
enemy of the state."

"Nonsense," Ilona declared, standing in the center of her
living room—rather, George thought, like someone on trial.
"Mr. Hoover has promised that I will have a carte blanche
from the Soviet government. And I can help. I actually have
met Lenin. I know I can help."

"We have tickets to _Blossom Time_," Rachel Borodina said,
scrutinizing her nails. "Isn't that splendid? I'm told it's absolutely marvelous. Why don't you come with us, Ilona?"

The family regarded her as if she were a beetle.

"Well," she said sulkily. "All this talk about Russia. I don't
see why you _want_ to help them, Ilona. All they ever did was
murder your family. And mine." She gave an entirely artificial
sniff. "I can't see how you can even _think_ of going back."

Ilona gazed at her for a moment, while pink spots gathered
in her cheeks. "It is my home," she said quietly. "And I would
like to see Starogan again."

Now she gazed at George. Her feelings about returning to
Russia could be no secret to him. He knew she wanted to see
more than Starogan, do more than renew an acquaintance with
Lenin. You could not love a man, and bear his child, and never
again wish to see him. So, was he jealous? Or afraid of what
might happen? He did not think so. Ilona's affair with Michael
Nej had been born of desperation, of misery at her existence
as Roditchev's wife, of hopelessness at the supposition that
she would never see George again. No, he was neither jealous
nor afraid of the future. For Ilona Borodina, turning her back
entirely on the past had never been a possibility.

"I think Ilona will be a great help," he said. "And I have
no doubt at all that she will be quite safe." He looked at Peter.

"Always assuming we do nothing stupid. We are going there as guests of the Soviet government."

"But it's almost Christmas!" Rachel wailed.

"We shan't leave until January," Ilona said reassuringly.

"And the newspaper? The children?" Peter demanded.

"The newspaper will continue to run itself. Crowther is an excellent editor, and Dad can still look after things for a month or two. I've spoken with him. As for the children, well..." He looked at Judith.

She had hitherto said nothing, had sat in a corner and merely listened to the arguments. Because *she* was afraid? Or because she knew the real reason he was going, the real reason he was glad to take Ilona.

"Of course I would be happy to look after them for you," she said. "If you really wish me to."

"Oh, would you, Judith?" Ilona hurried across the room to sit beside her, kiss her on the cheek. "That was my only worry. Isn't that going to be fun, Johnnie? Aunt Judith will be moving in here with you."

John Hayman had been allowed to join the discussion, since it was so important. Now he held his mother's gaze with his own. "I would like to come with you, Mother." He looked at his stepfather. "I also would like to see Russia again."

"That's quite impossible," George said.

"But if it is safe for Mother and you—"

"In a political sense it is perfectly safe, Johnnie. But there is no doubt that Russia is in a dreadful state, and that we are going to have to visit places where you could say there is no government, no civilization at all. Besides, there's your school." He smiled. "You will go to Russia, Johnnie. I give you my word on that. But when you're older and Russia has decided which way it's going to go."

John Hayman continued to stare at his stepfather for a moment, then glanced at his Uncle Peter.

Peter Borodin got up, walked across the room, and clapped him on the shoulder. "George is right, you know. You are too young. But I will tell you about Russia, Johnnie. All about Russia. And maybe one day I'll take you back there myself."

"Well, then," Ilona said, getting up and squeezing Judith's hand. "That's all settled. I'm so glad we're all in agreement. And we're only going to be gone a month or two, I promise you. Do you know, I'm quite excited. I really never thought I'd have the chance to go back. I think we should open a bottle of champagne."

"And drink to the downfall of Lenin and all his crew," Peter said.

"And drink to Russia," George suggested. "May she find her way out of the mess she's in."

"Miss Stein is waiting," Mrs. Killett said.

"Oh, ask her to come in, please, Mrs. Killett." George found his fingers were tapping nervously on the desk. Now why was he nervous? She was being placed in charge of his children—indeed, of his home—for several months, so it was entirely proper, even necessary, for them to have a private chat. "Judith," he said, getting up. "Close the door, will you?"

She hesitated, then gently pushed it to. George came round his desk to hold the chair for her.

"I'm afraid we rather sprang our decision on you, the other night."

She sank into the seat; the sleeve of her fawn suit brushed his arm and he could inhale her scent—a natural one, not the product of perfume. "Of course you didn't. I had anticipated it."

"Despite my promise?" He went round the desk and sat down.

"You didn't promise. I asked you to, but you didn't. I knew then you were going back."

He gazed at her. Her face was a remarkable combination of strength and weakness. Strength, in the firmness of mouth and chin, indicating an obvious ability to survive. Or was that only because he knew that she *had* survived, in ways he would probably have found impossible? But there was vulnerability, too, in the softness of the huge brown eyes. Judith Stein had been raised to be the wife of a prosperous Jewish merchant or lawyer, the mother of a tribe of children, the arbiter of a host of lives, of hopes and dreams. And at thirty-two she remained unmarried.

"But I was wondering if you might not have changed your mind," she said. "I meant about my staying with the children."

"Why should we do that?"

"Well...I don't think my background really makes me everyone's idea of a nanny."

"Now Judith..." He leaned across the desk. "We aren't thinking of you as a nanny."

"But you know what I mean. For heaven's sake, George, I've been to a labor camp in Siberia. I've killed a man!"

"That is nonsense."

"I lured Rasputin to his death. There's not a lot of difference between that and pulling the trigger."

"For a lot of your life you've been in the position of a front-line soldier. There's nothing disreputable about that."

"A front-line soldier for Communism, George."

"Now really—"

"It's true. I may not have realized it at the time. What did we use to call it? How many names we had. Some were Social Democrats, some were just plain socialists, some were Social Revolutionaries, some were Mensheviks, and some were Bolsheviks. But the Bolsheviks won. And besides, we were all revolutionaries."

"Against the tsarists, who were a pretty dreadful bunch. And anyway, you've seen your mistake, haven't you?"

"I've realized that Communism, as practiced by the Bolsheviks, is a pretty dreadful thing, if that is what you mean. But there's another thing. I'm a Jew."

"So?"

Judith gazed at him for some seconds. Then she got up, walked slowly to the far window, turned, and walked back again.

"I don't remember your being Jewish ever having made a lot of difference to your thinking, before," George ventured.

"In which case the fault was mine." She shrugged. "Oh, Poppa and Momma played it down. I don't really blame them. Not really and truly. If you wanted to make it, professionally or socially, in tsarist Russia—and oh, how they wanted to make it—you had to play it down. But that's all changed. That entire world has turned upside down, George. I go to the synagogue every Saturday."

"I know that."

Her eyebrows raised.

"Well," he said defensively, "you don't keep it a secret."

"I'm *involved*, George. I want to be involved. I think the only good thing that came out of the Great War was Balfour's declaration. And you don't agree with that."

He smiled at her. "You've been reading my editorials. It's true that I don't think the British government can promise the Arabs a world of their own on the one hand, and take some of it away to give to the Jews on the other, without some trouble involved. Maybe they can smooth it out. The British have a great record at that."

"But you're against the idea of a Zionist state."

"You're trying to put words into my mouth." He got up and walked round the desk to stand beside her. "I think there should be a Zionist state. And I can understand that the Zionists feel that such a state can only be in their historical and religious homeland. I just happen to feel that it's not going to be quite as simple as that. But if you want to get involved in Zionism, that's your decision. I don't see how that affects you as a human being. You're not planning to emigrate to Palestine in the next couple of months, are you?"

Judith flushed. "Of course I'm not."

"Well, then, what brought this on?" Without thinking, his arm had gone around her shoulder, holding her against him. "Not Rachel?"

"Well . . ." Judith shrugged herself free.

"That little vixen. She feels *she* should be moving in while Ilona and I are away?"

"Well . . . she is the Princess Borodin."

"Don't give me any of that stuff. 'The Princess Borodin.' That doesn't mean a damn thing outside of her house and those of one or two title-mad hostesses."

"It means everything to Peter."

"But not to Ilona. The past is past, Judith. Neither you nor I, nor Peter, can bring it back. And Peter's wild dreams about regaining Starogan, or anything else, are one very good reason why I'd sooner have you looking after the children than the two of them."

"Even Johnnie?"

"Johnnie even more than George or Felicity. He needs to turn his back on Russia even more than Peter does. Or you. Or Rachel."

Judith did another perambulation, then came to a stop opposite him. "And Ilona is happy about it? About everything?"

"It was partly her idea."

She gazed at him. "And you've made all possible allowance for . . . well, suppose you don't come back. It has to be thought of. There could be an accident . . ."

"I've made all possible allowance."

"But you will come back, George. Say you'll come back?" Her cheeks were pink.

"I'll come back, Judith. I don't know . . ," He bit his lip. "I need to think about things." He paused, waiting, but she did not help him. "I'll come back."

Her turn to bite her lip. "Then I'll wish you bon voyage, George. If by any chance, you happen to run into Joseph, will you give him my love?" She smiled and shrugged. "He's my kid brother, after all."

"I'll do that."

She kissed him on the cheek. "And take care, George. Do, please, take care."

Hats and handkerchiefs waved, foghorns hooted, and the *Mauretania* slowly pulled away from the pier and into the January mist, helped and hurried by her attendant tugs.

"Do you know what I think?" Rachel Borodina dried her eyes. "I think they just wanted a second honeymoon."

"Well, of course they did," Judith agreed. Her eyes were dry.

"I wish they'd taken me," John Hayman said.

"On a second honeymoon?" Rachel asked, and gave a peal of laughter, as she hurried George III and Felicity in front of her.

Peter Borodin put his arm round the boy's shoulders and allowed the others to go on ahead, to be quickly swallowed up by the receding crowd.

"I know what you mean," he said. "Russia is your country. As it is mine."

"Is it, Uncle Peter? Bolshevik Russia?"

"There have been upheavals and revolutions in Russia before, my boy," Peter said. "There have been tsars overthrown before, and even executed before. Why, to be accurate, most of the tsars have either been murdered or executed. Everyone felt very upset about the Romanovs because they ruled for a very long time. Three hundred years. But they came to power because of a revolution themselves. There will be another tsar. Believe me. That is the inevitable destiny of Russia. Democracy will never take hold there. The Russian people do not have the temperament for it."

"Then you don't think Bolshevism is there to stay?"

"Good Lord no," Peter said. "Bolshevism is a temporary aberration. No, no, it will be overthrown. The important question is, who will overthrow it? That means a great deal. To you as well as to me."

"Father does not expect it to be overthrown."

"Your father, Johnnie—your stepfather, I should say—was no admirer of tsarism. Now, I'd be the first to admit that many terrible things were done in the name of the tsar. That is inevitable in any autocratic regime. But you know as well as I that many terrible things are being done in the name of Bolshevism, too. And being an American, if you'll pardon me, your stepfather also believes in government by the people, and I suspect he feels that more of the people, by whatever means, are involved in a government run by Bolsheviks than there were under the tsars. The lesser of two evils, he thinks. So perhaps he is prepared to accept them. To help them, as he is helping them now. But you and I know better. And we know, too, that Bolshevism is unlikely to fall of itself. We have to work to bring it down, to restore Russia to the greatness it once had. I am working to that end, Johnnie."

"Are you, Uncle Peter? But—"

"But I work for your stepfather's newspaper? That is what I must do, and not only to earn a living. Being Russian editor keeps me in touch with every bit of news coming out of the country. I couldn't be in a better situation for what I want to accomplish. But I am working too, with other émigrés like myself. Like yourself, Ivan Sergeievich. For the restoration of Russia as a great power. Would you like to help me?"

They had reached the street, and the Rolls-Royce and the uniformed chauffeur. Rachel and Judith and the children had already got into the car.

John Hayman hesitated. "Father would never let me."

"Sometimes, Ivan Sergeievich, as one grows older, it is

necessary for a man to decide what is right, even if it means going against the wishes of his father. And you would not be going against the wishes of *your* father, you know. If poor Sergei Pavlovich had survived, he would be entirely in favor of what I am doing." Peter opened the door. "As for George Hayman—well, you know, I suspect he is going to find himself helping us whether he wishes to or not. He is helping us merely by going to Russia."

Chapter 2

SEVASTOPOL. THE LAST TIME THEY HAD BEEN HERE WAS IN JULY, 1914, when they landed with their children on their way to Starogan. When the world was an ordered place. When the lunatic fringe, like Lenin and Michael Nej and Judith Stein, were all either exiled or in Siberia, and Ivan Nej was the Starogan bootblack. When Prince Peter Borodin's word was law in this part of Russia, and when to celebrate his youngest sister's twenty-first birthday, he could summon his friends and relations from across the globe.

In the spring of 1922 Sevastopol was nothing more than an indication of how unchangeably mad that apparently unchanging world of the old regime had become.

George had elected for them to travel all the way by sea, not only because they enjoyed ship travel and he wanted this to be a second honeymoon, but because Russia was not the only place he wanted to observe. They had changed ships at Southampton, and had called not only at Gibraltar, an oasis of British calm in the surrounding hurricane, but also at Naples, where he had been able to see for himself the disarray of the

Italian state. The next stop had been Athens, where the
Acropolis did no more than preside in its stately ruination over
the collapse of a Greek state that had too rashly attempted to
recapture the glories of the past. Then came Constantinople,
where the Turks, enabled by that Greek ambition to pluck
victory out of defeat, were busily erecting a modern dictator-
ship, and then at last they had begun to cross the Black Sea.
He had looked on a good deal of despair and ruin and shattered
dreams, and he had no doubt he would see a great deal more
on his return journey, for he intended then to take a train across
Europe, to view for himself the collapse of Germany beneath
the weight of the greatest inflation known in modern times.
And, he hoped, to meet this strange young woman who claimed
to be the tsar's daughter and to have miraculously survived the
horrors of that cellar in Ekaterinburg.

He had found himself wondering if the world had ever been
in such a mess before. Certainly it was being illustrated to him
that the world could never again stand such a holocaust as the
Great War.

And yet, there had been days of sunshine, and there had
been laughing people. There was the Rock of Gibraltar, and
Vesuvius, brooding over the Bay of Naples. There was still
the Acropolis, and there was still the Church of St. Sophia,
however the Turks had renamed it. It had been possible, from
time to time, to forget that they were doing nothing more than
picking among the ruins of a civilization, to pretend that it was
still 1914 and the world was still sane, that one could still say,
I live here now and when I die, it will be *here*, with my children
and my grandchildren and my great-grandchildren around me.

Ilona certainly had embarked upon the entire journey in that
spirit, even accepting his decision that they should travel without maid or valet, or even secretary, cutting themselves adrift
from the life they knew, to be entirely dependent on each other.
He had no means of knowing whether she suspected the real
reason they were here at all. She had fallen in with the idea
of a second honeymoon because she loved him, because it was
a delightful prospect, and because she was undoubtedly curious
to see what changes had taken place in her motherland. He
also suspected that she wanted to get away from New York
for a while, from the whole American scene, because she could
not really understand the Calvinist passions that had led a great

nation, which believed itself to be the last refuge of true freedom in the entire world, to prohibit the use of alcohol. To a Russian this was totally incomprehensible.

But the journey had not been quite what George had anticipated or hoped for. They had certainly honeymooned. But it was the first time in all their eighteen years of knowing and loving that they had been absolutely alone together, separated from servants and family and children, over a long period of time. That, of course, had been his decision, but it had led him to realize that, for all their intimacy, he really understood very little of what went on in Ilona's brain.

He supposed he never had understood, had spent his life being surprised. Delightfully surprised, at least until now. In the shattering collapse of Port Arthur, her first experience of warfare—of anything that limited the prerogatives of being a Borodin of Starogan—it had not been surprising, he supposed, that she should seek emotional and ultimately physical refuge in the arms of a man who, by virtue of his neutrality, stood aside from the catastrophe. Or that having loved, she should continue to do so, despite her family's angry opposition to a presumptuous foreigner. That was the essential Ilona. But that she should have *continued* to love, after their enforced separation and years of an enforced marriage to Sergei Roditchev, he still found difficult to believe. That she should have thrown over husband and family and friends and religion and title and position to elope with him—to be damned by every orthodox Russian aristocrat, to have the mention of her name forbidden by the tsar's court—had left him with an immense responsibility to see to her happiness, to make such a sacrifice worthwhile, for the rest of her life.

But she had never told him *her* true feelings in the matter. The subject had been smothered in her obvious love for him, and he had been afraid to probe, afraid to uncover the raw emotions that must still remain, the horror of submitting to Roditchev, night after night after night, the desperate anger that had driven her into the arms of Michael Nej, her brother's valet.

And then she had visited Russia during the war, had imagined herself safe, as he had imagined her safe, down in quiet Starogan. And when they had realized their mistake, and with her children she had endeavored to escape before it was too late, it *had* been too late, and she had had to endure the misery of six months' imprisonment in Siberia before her eventual release. She had never discussed that either—they had continued to be separated for some time after her release—and later he had hesitated to probe. Some of that imprisonment had been spent with Judith Stein, and they had both eventually been freed by Michael Nej, no longer a valet, but a friend of Lenin, and thus an important man in this new Russia. George conceived of Ilona's life, and memories, as a series of secret compartments, each locked away from the other. He had always supposed that he possessed enough of them for happiness.

Thus if he had been disconcerted by her almost callous disinterest in the things they saw and smelled and heard at their various stopovers, it was impossible to blame her for turning away from the sordid and the sad, especially where, as in Greece or Italy, the people did not concern her. There were too many things that did concern her in Russia. And the moment was here. He glanced at her, standing beside him on the upper deck, mink coat held close against the still-biting wind. She had laughed since leaving New York, and when he would have been serious himself, she had kissed him to bed. But now the honeymoon had to be over. This was Sevastopol, a liquid graveyard, with sunken ships thrusting their rusting masts and funnels out of the windswept waters, with decaying docks resembling the skeletons of long-dead dinosaurs, with roofless houses and empty windows in the background, with the stench of untreated sewage and unwashed bodies drifting towards them on the breeze. Petrograd had been like this, when he and Judith Stein stole away two years ago. What was Petrograd like now?

With consummate skill the pilot navigated the ship between the wrecks. Telegraphs clanged, orders were given, and with a roar the anchor chain plunged into the blue water. George, peering over the side, saw the bloated body of a dead cat drifting by. He looked at his wife, saw her nostrils dilate and her head lift away from the sea towards the sky. But if that was the least pleasant sight they would see in Russia, they would have no cause for complaint.

A motor launch approached the ship, filled with uniformed and armed men. In Russia, the Russia of the revolution, one either wore a uniform, and prospered, or one did not and starved. This rule seemed to apply to both sexes, for now he saw that several of the approaching officials were in fact women, although, with their trousers and their bobbed hair, it required an attentive inspection to establish that fact.

He escorted Ilona back to the upper saloon, where they sat down and waited with the other passengers—a small list; everyone even remotely interested in pleasure had left the ship at Constantinople.

"Mr. and Mrs. George Hayman," remarked the immigration officer, stroking his mustache. "The newspaper magnate."

"I am in the newspaper business, yes," George agreed, and the man raised his head; no doubt he had not expected such perfect Russian.

"And now you have come to write scurrilous articles about Soviet Russia," the man decided.

"Not at all," George said.

But the official was looking at Ilona's passport. "Your wife was born in Russia."

"My wife is an American citizen, as you will see," George pointed out.

"Nevertheless, this must be investigated. You will stay on the ship until this has been investigated."

"We are expecting Mr. and Mrs. Hayman," said a girl who had suddenly stepped forward.

And she was a girl, hardly twenty-one, George estimated. She was slight and dark, with the high cheekbones of a Tartar, and the splendidly clipped features and the seething black eyes of that people.

He smiled at her. "Well, that's a relief."

"Mr. and Mrs. Hayman have come to help us," the girl said. She held out her hand. "I am Catherine Lissitsina."

He shook the strong fingers. Her dark green topcoat, secured with a belt from which there hung a revolver holster, did not make her any less attractive; her fur hat and black boots completed a spectacular and disturbingly erotic picture. But the eroticism was less in the uniform than in the way she wore it, the expression in her eyes. He glanced at Ilona, but she too was shaking hands, her face expressionless.

"Then they are your responsibility, comrade," the immigration officer said.

"Of course," she agreed. "You have a bag?"

"Three," George indicated the pile.

Catherine Lissitsina surveyed them, then selected the largest. "You will have to take the other two. Watch your step on the ladder."

"Give me one," Ilona said. She had never, to his knowledge, lifted a suitcase in her life. Now she revealed surprising strength and agility as she followed the girl. George took the last suitcase, winked at the scandalized steward, and followed them to the rail. Beneath them the launch bobbed on the water; it looked a very long way away. But the girl was already on her way down, the heavy suitcase dangling from her fingers like a handbag. Ilona, in high-heeled shoes, was descending more cautiously. George drew a long breath and followed, staying as close to his wife as possible. But her balance was as good as his.

At the bottom Catherine Lissitsina waited to help them; the crew of the launch watched with interest.

They took seats in the stern. "We had expected several people," Catherine Lissitsina said. "A party."

"And yet they sent you alone?" George chose the middle.

"I would have arranged it," she explained. "I am here to arrange everything for you. But since you are by yourself, it will make it simpler."

"There are people from my organization, waiting in Constantinople," George said. "They have grain, they have money, they have a ship. But they have been refused permission to land here."

"Do you think we wish to be invaded?" Catherine asked. "We have been invaded before. Besides, not everyone is capable of understanding our problem here, or what we must do to succeed in our task. You must tell me what you wish to do."

"We wish to see, in the first place," George said, "and we wish to talk, and to listen. My people wish to help yours, but they cannot if you will not let us."

"Soviet Russia does not need help," Catherine Lissitsina pointed out, "from anyone. There are those who would not have let *you* land. Certainly they would not let you see." She brooded at the approaching dock. "But you have friends, Mr. Hayman."

"Have we?"

"Oh, yes. Mrs. Hayman also. That is fortunate for you. I

will take you to the hotel, and you will tell me what you wish to see. I have authority to show you anything."

Ilona's head turned when even above the launch engine, they could hear the sudden rattle of gunfire. "I thought the civil war was over!"

"It is, Mrs. Hayman. Those are criminals—black marketeers and profiteers. We shoot several every day."

A car waited for them on the dock, a very old Daimler, driven by an armed chauffeur. There were several other men and women standing around, also wearing uniforms, also armed. There did not appear to be any civilians in Sevastopol.

"Do you not shoot criminals in America?" Catherine Lissitsina asked, sitting opposite them as they drove away.

Catherine Lissitsina. Ilona wondered how old she was. Certainly not yet twenty-five. Probably not much over twenty-one. She would have been fourteen when the Great War began, must have spent the last seven years attempting to exist in the eye of the storm. And succeeding. Would I have been like this, she wondered, had I been forced to live in Russia throughout those years? It was not an idle reflection; her own sister Tatiana had undergone that experience.

Tattie. They had last met in the winter of 1917, at Starogan. They had spent the entire war down there, in safety and seclusion, far from the guns and the food shortages, far from the hatred and the hysteria. Until George had wired to say that the Bolsheviks were taking power, and that she must go at once, as had been arranged, across Siberia to Vladivostock, and thence to Japan and home. Tattie, utterly bored by her long confinement away from the bright lights of Petrograd, had asked to accompany her. But Mama had said, What nonsense! and Ilona had not felt able to go against Mama's wishes. So Tattie had stayed, to watch her family be torn to pieces by a mob, to be raped and then appropriated by the same man who had violated her, her former servant, Ivan Nej. How Ilona hated the very sound of that man's name.

But like this girl, Tattie had survived. She had accepted Ivan Nej as a husband with an insouciance that only someone as introverted and as single-minded as Tattie could ever have been capable of. George had seen her, and had said she was happy, a mother, dancing as she had always wanted to dance, laughing as she did at everything, even at death itself.

But this girl did not laugh.

"You are very young," George remarked, echoing her own thoughts. "Why did they send you to meet us?"

"Because I speak the English," Catherine said, in that language.

"Indeed you do. But it is not necessary."

She glanced at him. "Perhaps they did not know." She looked over her shoulder at the driver. "What is the matter with this car, Dimitri Igorovich?" The Daimler, which had not been traveling very fast, was now definitely coasting to a stop.

"There is no gasoline," the chauffeur explained.

"Dimitri Igorovich," Catherine said severely, "that is very careless of you. Did you not get an allocation?"

The driver shrugged. "There was none at the depot when I got there."

"Because you were drinking vodka," Catherine said angrily. "It will go in my report, Dimitri Igorovich. Oh, it will go in my report." She opened the door and got out. "It is not far."

"I'll take that one now," George said to Ilona, and followed Catherine, a suitcase in each hand. Ilona walked behind them. In studying the girl she had not properly been seeing the city. But away from the waterfront it seemed even more decayed, although there was some evidence of life in the occasional passersby stopping to stare at the motor car, and in the faces that appeared at the broken windows and hastily disappeared again when she attempted to return their interest. The surfaces of the streets were cracked, allowing the spring grass to come thrusting through, and the trees lining the boulevards had not been pruned in several years; their branches hung close to the ground.

Would Tattie laugh at this? Did she laugh at this, assuming Moscow was no better? Ilona remembered Moscow as the most boring place on earth. At least, it had been the most boring place on earth, for the wife of Prince Roditchev, until she had met Judith Stein and until Michael Nej had so strangely come back into her life. Was Tattie laughing in Moscow?

And would she laugh in Moscow? Was that why she was here? She was here so that she could be with George, of course. But was that because she felt like a stranger with him, after all this time? They had been separated for six years, between 1905 and 1911. But when she saw him again, she did not doubt for an instant that he was the only man in the world for her. From that moment they had been united until 1915, when his duties as a war correspondent had kept him away from her, but since she herself had been at Starogan, they had communicated by telephone. Then in 1918, she had returned to America while he remained, to see the birth of the new Communist state—the most important event in the history of the world, he had said, since the birth of the United States in 1776. And when he had returned in the spring of 1920, with Judith Stein, she had felt as if she and her husband were strangers. He had become more serious, even brooding. Obviously he had seen some terrible things, although he would not discuss them with her. And his close friendship with Judith Stein had not helped. Judith had always been a deeply sensitive girl, made more so by her ghastly experiences. Ilona actually hoped that on this trip she might be able to witness some of the horrors that had so affected George and Judith. She wanted to understand, to share. With George. But the difference between them had been clear throughout their travels in Europe. She could concentrate only on the immense tragedy that was her own people, and was left to envy George's ability to think about and feel for all humanity.

But was she going to laugh or weep over Russia as the revolution had left it? Didn't she want to see Starogan again? And Moscow? And even Petrograd? And what of Tattie? Tattie was her sister. Whatever Ilona had said in angry reproach, she was her sister. Her little sister. She could not be abandoned forever. Some effort had to be made to persuade her to join her family in the West. And looking around her at this shattered city, Ilona could not believe that much persuasion would be needed.

And then there was Michael Nej. Had she not come back at least partly to see Michael again? She glanced at George, plodding on behind the girl. George understood that, certainly, and had not reproached her for it. George had never reproached her for anything. Therefore, was it not her duty to George never to do anything for which she *could* be reproached?

Besides, after so long, what could Michael possibly mean to her? If only she had not met him again, for that brief hour, in Ekaterinburg. Or if only, on that occasion, he had proved himself to be the brutal doctrinaire Bolshevik that was his reputation. If only he had not shown, then, that he still loved.

For the first time since leaving New York, she wished she hadn't come. But surely that was the effect of Sevastopol.

"I am sorry about the car," Catherine Lissitsina said, marching up the street, the suitcase swinging at her side. "That man is an incompetent. That is our problem, incompetent people."

"I'm enjoying the walk," Ilona said, slightly out-of-breath. "I've confessed in that church."

Catherine Lissitsina glanced at the obviously derelict building. "Confessed," she mused. "We do not confess in church nowadays. The Church is a superstition. Comrade Lenin has said so. The hotel is just here."

They had entered a square in which there had once been a fountain. Now the basin and the spurting lips of the Cupid were dry and dust-caked. The trees here, however, *had* been pruned, and there had been some attempt at cleaning the pavement. And the hotel in front of them, which had certainly once been a palace, was decorated by an enormous red flag hanging from an upstairs window, while there were armed guards on the steps. Catherine Lissitsina produced a pass, and the men stood to attention to let them through. There were several people in the lobby, and even one or two who might have been bellhops, but no one offered to relieve them of the suitcases. Catherine led them across the threadbare carpet to the unpolished mahogany reception counter, and once again produced her pass.

"The Americans," remarked the clerk, looking George up and down, and then giving Ilona a somewhat longer inspection. Predictably, he wore a uniform. "Room thirty-seven."

"Nobody else is to be given that room," Catherine said. "Not before tomorrow."

"That is what is written here," the clerk said.

"You see?" Catherine said, picking up her suitcase once again. "It is all arranged." She jerked her head as Ilona instinctively headed for the elevator. "The elevator does not work. But it is only on the third floor." She climbed the stairs in front of them, at last beginning to breathe heavily. "It will work," she promised. "Soon. But there are more important things to be done than making elevators work, don't you agree?"

"Entirely." George allowed Ilona to go next, and brought up the rear himself. Ilona watched the hips moving beneath the greatcoat in front of her.

"I'm sure I could take a turn with that suitcase," she offered.

"It is not heavy," the girl said.

"What are you thinking?" George asked in English.

"That I'd like a hot bath," Ilona said.

"I'm thinking," George said, returning to Russian, "that that fellow forgot to give us the key. Damnation."

They had reached the first landing, and paused for breath. "There is no key, Mr. Hayman," Catherine said. "Why should you wish a key? You have a secret?"

There did not seem to be any answer to that. Ilona raised her eyebrows at him.

Catherine resumed her climb. "We do not need to lock things away in Soviet Russia. I know you think this hotel is bad, but it is not so bad. There is a restaurant downstairs, and there is food. And there is water in the rooms. You did not suppose so, eh?"

"Well . . . I hadn't thought about it," George confessed.

"Unfortunately, there is no hot water, Mrs. Hayman. But a cold bath is good for the skin. You will be very comfortable here. And it is arranged that they can put no one else in the room with you, eh? You will be comfortable."

"We're not staying here very long, are we?" George asked in sudden concern. "We came to see the country. And to meet your leaders."

"And you will do that, Mr. Hayman. The Commissar for Internal Affairs awaits you in Moscow. And on the way, you shall look at the country. Tomorrow, I have seats booked on the train to Kharkov."

"We wish to stop at Starogan."

She paused on the third landing. "Starogan?"

"It is a village in the Don basin. We wish to go there."

She nodded. "I have been there. There is nothing there now. It used to be the seat of the Borodins. Tsarist princes," she said in disgust. "But they are gone. So is the village. I think all the Borodins have been executed."

"We would still like to go there," Ilona said in a low voice.

They had reached the third floor, and Catherine was pushing a door in with her boot. Then she placed the suitcase in the center of the room and gave a sigh of relief. "Then you shall. We will stop there. But there is nothing to see." She placed her hands on her hips and waited for them to come in. "Do you not like the room?"

It actually was a large and spacious room, and must once have been elegant. Now the paint was dirty and peeling, and the carpet, like all the carpets in the hotel, was threadbare. But the room had a washbasin and all the necessary plumbing for running water, as well as an easy chair and four beds, arranged in a row.

"I think we shall be quite comfortable here," Ilona said. "Where do you sleep?"

"In here with you, Mrs. Hayman," Catherine said. "But there will be nobody else. It is all arranged."

"What was that?" George closed the door.

Catherine took off her greatcoat. "We do not have to sleep in the same bed, Mr. Hayman, unless you wish it. There are four beds."

George stared at Ilona, who suddenly did want to laugh. Soviet Russia had obviously changed even since his recent departure.

Catherine Lissitsina was continuing to undress. She removed her belt and her uniform tunic; she wore nothing underneath, and revealed firm and well-muscled white flesh, heavy and perfectly shaped breasts standing away from her chest, armpits filled with luxurious black hair, which she now proceeded to wash in the basin. "There are not many rooms with running water," she explained. "And it is best to wash while the water is still warm."

George scratched his head. "But where are your own things?"

Catherine raised a soap-covered face. "Things?"

"Your own clothes. Your suitcase."

Catherine rinsed and dried herself. "I don't have a suitcase, Mr. Hayman."

Ilona, amused, sat down in the easy chair and crossed her legs. This was one problem George was going to have to solve on his own.

Catherine had finished drying herself, and was releasing the belt of her breeches, to slide them down to her knees. She wore no underclothes at all, and Ilona was again terribly conscious of silky black hair.

While Catherine soaped, George walked to the window to look out. He was now beside Ilona's chair, but he didn't look at her either. "A change of clothing..." he suggested.

"I am on duty, Mr. Hayman," Catherine said. "I do not need a change of clothing."

Ilona reached across to squeeze his hand. He was nine years older than she, but it suddenly occurred to her that he did not really know a great deal about women, except for herself. She had always assumed that he was very experienced, because of the difference in their ages, because he had had female friends before they had ever met, because during their enforced separation he had been pushed into an engagement with a debutante named Elizabeth Lee. None of that had ever meant a thing to Ilona, compared to his love for her. That was something she had never considered doubting.

But suddenly she wondered if he might want to make love to this girl. And what her own reaction would be if he did.

Catherine dried between her legs and smiled at Ilona. "Will you not wash?" she asked.

"I...I had a bath on board the ship, this morning."

"Ah." Catherine lifted a suitcase onto the nearest bed, opened it, and held up a pair of silk panties. She gazed over them at Ilona, her mouth making an O.

"I wear them," Ilona explained. "Under my dress."

Catherine looked at the garment again, dropped it back into the suitcase, and then produced Ilona's traveling wash case. She opened it and took out Ilona's toothbrush. "May I use it?"

Ilona opened her mouth, and then closed it again. George released her hand as he once again turned. Ilona shrugged. "Be my guest. There's some tooth powder in there, as well."

Catherine picked up the powder, looked at it, and put it back again. "It is not necessary," she said, and took the brush to the basin.

"Are you sure the hotel is full?" George asked. "It doesn't look very full to me. What I mean is, my wife and I would like some time to ourselves."

Catherine spat, and raised her head again. "I have been sent to look after you, Mr. Hayman," she said. "You can do what you wish with your wife. I will not mind. But I cannot leave you by yourselves."

George stared at Ilona.

Ilona smiled at him. "I think Mademoiselle Lissitsina should stay here with us, George. I think it may be rather interesting."

Ilona sat opposite Catherine at dinner and watched her drinking vodka. The large dining room was nearly empty. Each table was full, but there were only six tables in all; four were occupied by Russian officers, one by a group of civilians, obviously German, from their language, and then there was their own group. They were served by an elderly waiter who stopped just short of throwing the plates onto the table. But the sea bass was prepared surprisingly well, there was caviar as an appetizer, and the glass flagon of vodka was constantly replaced.

"I have heard that you were in Russia during the war," Catherine said, filling her glass.

George nodded and drank. He was on his third glass, Ilona observed; she had remained on her first. Clearly he was fortifying himself for what might lie ahead. She wondered if it might not be a good idea for her to do the same.

"So was I," Catherine said. "I was in Petrograd."

"I was there too."

She frowned at him. "I never saw you."

George shrugged.

"I was at the Okhrana building when it was stormed," she said.

"Why, so was I," he said in surprise.

"But you were watching. I helped."

Ilona gazed at Catherine again as she methodically ate. The storming of the Okhrana building in March 1917 was one of the things George *had* told her about; it had been too horrible an experience even for secrecy. She watched Catherine delicately drying her fingers on her napkin, a strange relic of an imperial past, and then drinking some more vodka. She would have been seventeen or eighteen. And had she rushed along those corridors, shrieking and shouting, dragging men and women out to be butchered in the most bestial of ways?

Catherine raised her head and frowned at her. "You do not like me," she accused.

"On the contrary, I find you fascinating."

Catherine rested her elbow on the table, her chin on her hand, and stared at Ilona. "Yes," she said. "You too are fascinating. I have heard that you were born in Russia. Where were you born?"

"I was born at Starogan," Ilona said. "I was a Borodin. I am a Borodin. Or is that thought too horrible to be considered?"

Catherine continued to gaze at her for some seconds. "I had heard all the Borodins were dead," she said.

"Not all."

Catherine leaned back. "They are all dead as far as Russia is concerned. Why did you come back?"

"Because Russia is not dead, for me."

Catherine belched, drank the last of her vodka, then got up and came round the table. She took a strand of Ilona's golden hair between thumb and forefinger and held it up to the light. "We should go to bed," she said. "There is much to be done tomorrow."

"You go ahead," George said. "Mrs. Hayman and I will stay down here for a while."

Catherine looked from one to the other. "I am here to look after you."

"We won't leave the hotel," George said. "I give you my word."

Another hesitation. "You will need your sleep," she said. "Tomorrow is going to be a busy day. I have much to show you."

"Profiteers and black marketeers being shot?"

Catherine gazed at him for a moment. "If that is what you wish to see, Mr. Hayman," she agreed, and left the room.

"I don't think you should be quite so hostile," Ilona suggested.

"Well, for God's sake, I don't think it's going to be much of a trip for us, with her underfoot all the while."

"Perhaps we should recognize that the holiday part of our trip is now over."

"You're right." George snapped his fingers, and after some moments the waiter approached. "Brandy? You have brandy?"

"There is no brandy," the waiter said. "You wish some more vodka?"

"My wife and I would like some brandy," George said, placing a ten-dollar bill on the table beside his plate.

The waiter looked at it for a second, gave a hasty glance around the room, departed, and returned a moment later with two glasses of brandy. These he placed on the table, then swept his hand over the cloth to remove the last of the crumbs, and the money.

"That was cruel," Ilona said.

"It proved, to my satisfaction, that Russia hasn't changed all that much," George said. "Question is, what are we going to do with our mutual lady friend?"

"What would you like to do with her?" Ilona asked wickedly, picking up the brandy glass.

George matched her smile. "So it's funny. She's not a bad-looking girl."

So Catherine's primitive sexuality *had* got through to him. "Yes," Ilona agreed. "Tell you what we'll do about her for a start—we'll share one of the beds. It'll be warmer, too."

Catherine Lissitsina stood in the doorway of the first-class compartment. "We are coming to Starogan," she said. "The train will stop here. It is all arranged."

Ilona got up and peered in the cracked mirror to straighten her hat. Catherine had arranged for them to be alone in a compartment and had thoughtfully spent little time with them. But it really was a poor excuse for a first-class carriage, Ilona thought, with much of the upholstery ripped to shreds and the floor clearly unswept for at least a week.

"Nervous?" George asked.

She shook her head. "Just . . ." She didn't know what to say. During the past twenty-four hours her emotions had become increasingly confused. Undoubtedly it had a great deal to do with the presence of Catherine—her unequivocal sexuality added to the almost aggressive sexual equality she continuously projected. Ilona's first reaction had been that this was nothing more than a manifestation of the new Russia. But might it not be something much more important, to her, than that? Simply youth, and exuberance, and confidence. Qualities she had possessed in ample measure when George had first met and loved her. And which she no longer possessed? Well, youth, obviously not. But the other? It was unusual for Mrs. George Hayman to ask herself such a question, but *did* she still have the complete confidence she had possessed as Ilona Borodina? Had the traumas of the revolution and the eclipse of her family affected her subconsiously in a way not even she understood, or even recognized?

And was that part of the trouble with George? She had no idea how to find out.

And for the moment he was entirely misunderstanding her mood.

"I know," he said, and held the door for her. "But it is something I think we both have to do."

She stepped to the door at the end of the car, to gaze at the fields. Because there had been fields here, once. And before the wheat had started to grow, the earth had been black, the richest soil on earth, Papa had always claimed. The soil that had made the Borodins wealthy and powerful and famous.

Now it was just steppe, mile after mile of tangled bush and shrub. And then the river. Even after the winter it was hardly more than a trickle of water. Tattie had bathed in that river, scandalizing her mother and grandmother. And her sister.

And then, the station, and beyond, the village. Ilona wondered when the train had last stopped here; the boards of the station platform had fallen in, and the stationmaster's office was roofless. But so were most of the houses in the village.

The train wheezed to a stop, some yards short of the platform. Catherine Lissitsina appeared, walking beside the track. "You must get down here," she said. "The platform is not safe. I will help you."

"I can manage, thank you," Ilona said, and waited for George to get down first and hold up his hands for her.

"How long does the train halt here?" he asked.

"Until we are ready to rejoin it, Mr. Hayman," she said. "It is all arranged."

She marched ahead of them into the village, holster slapping her thigh, and stood in the center of what had once been the village square, surveying the skeletons of houses around her. "The White armies destroyed the village," she said. "Your village, Princess Borodina. Because the villagers had attacked your house."

Ilona looked at the crumbling platform. From that platform Peter had addressed the village, at the end of July, 1914, telling them they must send their sons and brothers off to war. All the family had been present on that occasion. And she and George had been in the second Rolls-Royce, parked just about here. She squeezed his hand, and he put his arm around her shoulder.

"I should like to see the house," Ilona said. "If the train will wait."

"The train will wait, princess. It is all arranged. But it is a long walk. Let us go."

Once again she marched in front of them.

"It's incredible," Ilona said. "The people here were so alive. Old Father Gregory, Geller the schoolmaster, and that fat little daughter of his . . . my God, she married Ivan Nej."

"Yes," George said grimly. "Darling, you know—"

"I know they are buried there," she said. "I want to see the grave."

The river was close on their right now, and they could see the trees of the orchard. But not yet the roof of the house. Ilona's heart seemed to constrict. Always the roof of the house had loomed above the trees of the orchard. She began to hurry, and George took long strides at her side; their breath clouded into the still chilly spring air.

"It was burned," Catherine Lissitsina said unnecessarily, as they came in sight of the rotting, blackened timbers. "I do not know which side burned it. But there was much fighting down here, three years ago."

Ilona looked at the remains of the front steps. Always, when visitors had arrived at the house, the family had stood at the top of those steps to greet them. She could see them now, dim shadows from an unbelievable past. Grandpapa, tall and broad and white-bearded, standing beside Grandmama, so small and hunched; Papa, always in uniform, and Mama, her enormous bosom thrust in front of her like a battering ram, always with its rope of pearls; Uncle Igor and Aunt Anna, thin and bitter; and the children. Red-headed Xenia, exuding precocious beauty; sophisticated Tigran, toying with the ends of his mustache; sullen Viktor. And there had always been three other children too, the two golden-haired girls, and the handsome young man. Of them all, only those three survived.

No, she realized with a start of horror: Viktor Borodin had also survived. Or at least, they did not know of his death. He had been swallowed up in the revolution—shouting, if George was to be believed, Death to the tsar. Where was *he* now?

"The grave is at the back," Catherine Lissitsina said, and walked round the house.

Ilona stood in front of the earthen mound. The end of the Borodins, she thought. A heap of moldering, tortured bones, still haunted by the screams that had shrouded their deaths.

"There was also a farm," Catherine said, pointing down the overgrown track. "Down there. Do you wish to see down there?"

Ilona shook her head.

"Are you sure? Two of our great leaders, the Nej brothers, were born down there. And lived there, too. Did you know the Nej brothers, Princess Borodina?"

"I knew the Nej brothers," Ilona said. She turned away from the grave and walked back towards the patient train, George's hand on her shoulder.

"Moscow Central," said the guard.

Ilona sat up straight and looked out of the window, at the houses, and in the background the new buildings, just starting to thrust their steel and concrete skeletons into the sky. And then the Kremlin, perched on a rocky rise overlooking the Moscow River. How often had she heard those words, "Moscow Central," and looked out the window at this sight.

She found that George, seated opposite, was looking at her, and gave him a hasty smile. "I'm a bundle of nerves."

"I suppose I'm excited myself," he admitted, and glanced at Catherine Lissitsina, reading a political tract in the other corner of the compartment. They had now spent nearly a week together, and they were no nearer, Ilona supposed, to knowing the essential girl. She had taken them to ruined farms, and she had taken them to the farms of the wealthier peasants, the kulaks, men who by their knowledge and their confidence had managed to survive the worst of both the civil war and the drought that had reduced this country to a desert. She had allowed them to ask what questions they wished, take what photographs they wished. She had merely reiterated three themes: first, that all had been arranged; second, that Russia did not really require outside help; and third, that all would eventually be well.

And what impression had they gained? Of a country brought to its knees by mismanagement and doctrainaire philosophies. Of people who were desperately trying to make a living, and a profit, within the existing framework, hampered by uncertainty of the future and by fear of the individuals with whom they had to deal; she thought especially of the Brusilovs—contemptuously dismissed as kulaks by Catherine—who had managed to salvage something from the wreckage of the civil war and the drought, and who had been subjected to merciless raids by the tax collectors. They had mentioned the name of Ivan Nej. Everyone seemed to know the name of Ivan Nej. Her grandfather's bootblack, and Peter's bootblack afterwards. The most feared commissar in all Russia.

And Tatiana's husband. Because she had accepted him. Because this was a world gone mad.

Could a world gone mad ever be sane again? And if Russia ever did become sane again, what sort of world would it be? And what would that mean for the *rest* of the world?

Catherine closed her book, stood up, and put on her fur cap. "I will take you to your hotel first," she said. "It is a good hotel. It has all been arranged." She smiled at Ilona. "There I will leave you. You will have a room to yourselves, princess."

"I'm sure we will enjoy that," Ilona said.

"And then, tomorrow morning, I will take you to the Party secretary, who will be pleased to see you, and discuss things with you," Catherine said.

The train stopped, and she hurried on ahead of them to arrange transport.

"Nervous?" he asked for surely the tenth time.

"No," she lied determinedly. But her sense of failure, growing from the moment they had landed in Sevastopol, was suddenly acute. George, magnificent George, stood unchangingly for the essential goodness in life, the virtues of free speech and free trade—for free drinking, as he put it—for freedom from fear or from want, and yet, because of his essentially New England upbringing, for an almost puritanical system of morals. Soviet Russia, as she had observed it so far, stood for regimentation in all things except in matters of sex. And this touched a chord in her. Because I am Russian she thought.

Russians have always been regimented. Russians have been ruled, whether by their princes or the Mongol overlords, or their grand dukes or their tsars, or now, by their commissars. Russians were born to be ruled. In everything. As I was once ruled. She remembered her wedding night, when Sergei Roditchev had turned to her so casually and informed her he intended to beat her. She had not been able to believe her ears, because she had always been the spoiled daughter of the future Prince of Starogan.

She had not been able to believe that it was actually going to happen. But it had happened. Again and again and again. Sergei Roditchev had belonged to the old school. She had hinted to George about what she had had to suffer as Princess Roditcheva, but she wondered if he had ever really understood. Just as she had confessed her relationship with Michael Nej, a servant, a member of that vast amorphous group of Russians who had no hope and no duty, except that of obeying their superiors. But Michael had always hoped, and dreamed, and one of his dreams had been to possess her. Throughout all their childhood, when she had been the young mistress and he had been a male servant only a year older than she, eager and willing to help her in her games and her fantasies, he had been there, a part of the furniture. Life without Michael Nej had been as impossible to envisage as life without food, or drink, or water to bathe in. Until that remarkable night when his dream had come true, and she had found herself in his arms. Did George really understand that?

But she had never told George how, to secure the prison pass for him, which had taken Michael to freedom, she had visited Rasputin in his salon, had submitted to the lecherous caresses of that most evil of men.

It was occurring to her that she had never allowed her husband to know her very well. And now she was about to meet Michael Nej again.

Perhaps *she* did not know herself very well, either.

Catherine Lissitsina had actually managed to secure them a taxi. Or perhaps it was an official car; they seemed to be the same thing. Moscow was a great improvement on Sevastopol, or even on Kharkov. The streets were paved, and they were busy. There were goods in the shops—primitive goods, by American standards, but still goods—and if the people looked threadbare and pinch-faced, they lacked the haunted expressions of those further south.

"Did you ever live in Moscow, princess?" asked Catherine.

"My husband was Prince Roditchev, military governor of the city, at the time of the revolution of 1905."

Catherine turned to stare at her. Clearly this was something beyond her comprehension.

"That was our palace there," Ilona pointed.

Catherine's mouth opened and then closed again. "It is your hotel. We call it the Berlin."

"Why not?" Ilona said.

George's hand strayed over hers and gave it a squeeze.

The car was stopping, and a major domo, complete with Russian hat and Cossack cartridge belts, was coming forward to open the door. Catherine, by now in a fine fettle of Communist arrogance, swept past him, snapping her fingers to summon bellhops to assist with the luggage. Ilona could not recognize the hall of her former home, gutted to create a vast lobby, with its walls repapered in a garish crimson, and an elevator installed within the spiral of the grand staircase. And here the elevator worked, whisking them to the fourth floor, and to an elegant apartment with a grand piano in the sitting room, and a vast double bed in the next room. A guest apartment in the old days. The bedroom she had shared with Sergei Roditchev was now, apparently, a smoking room.

"You will be comfortable here," Catherine said.

"Thank you," Ilona said. "Will it disturb the neighbors if I play?"

Catherine looked from her to the piano, then shrugged. "There are no neighbors. It is all arranged. But do not answer the door, unless I have telephoned from the desk first."

"Why not?" George asked.

Catherine shrugged again. "Because there are many people who know that the American newspaper tycoon is in Moscow. People who are against the state." She might have been discussing exposure to leprosy, Ilona thought. "It is not good for you to talk with them."

"I must only talk with those the state thinks would be good for me." George suggested.

"You are here as a guest of the Soviet, Mr. Hayman," Catherine pointed out with quiet dignity. "Have a good dinner, and a good night. I will come for you at eight o'clock tomorrow morning, when the Party secretary will be waiting for you."

She closed the door behind her.

"So here we are," Ilona said. "Moscow. After so many years."

George held out his arms, and she found herself against his chest. "A bit different from the last time."

"Different for us," she said. "Do you suppose it is different for the people out there?"

"No." He released her, walked to the window, and looked down at the street outside. "That's what disturbs me. You know, I used to think that the tsarist regime was about the worst in . . . well, not in history, but in the current world. People like Roditchev . . . you don't mind my saying that?"

"It's true." She went into the bedroom and sat on the bed.

"Well, what's bothering me is that everything I've read and seen about this Bolshevik regime suggests that it's even worse than the tsars were. You know, Sergei Roditchev may have been pretty sadistic, but he was operating within a certain framework, a framework that had as its ideal the rule of the law and the church, a certain concept of something greater than the state or the individual. Something eternal, if you like, which possessed a soul. Can you understand that?"

"Of course I can. And you feel that this new Russia lacks soul."

"Can you see any evidence of it? Those people, the Brusilovs. They were the backbone of old Russia. Far more so than the Borodins, if I may say so. They were not princes, not aristocrats in any sense. They tilled the soil, and they worked hard, and they attempted to make a profit, and when they had a bad year, a drought, they prayed to God to make it better next year, and they believed that it would be better next year. And now, what have they got? They are told that there is no God, and all they have to look forward to next year is another band of tax gatherers, removing all their profit, or if they haven't made a profit, all their surplus food and stock. Mankind must hope, Ilona. However spurious the hope, they must have it, or there's nothing to live for."

"But you would help them to exist like that. You and Hoover."

"What's the alternative? Do we just let them starve?"

"Oh, God knows." She kicked off her shoes. "I'm more confused now than when I left New York. About what I would like to happen, I mean. About—" She paused, and looked at the outer door. They had heard a gentle knock.

Ilona put on her shoes again, and was on her feet in an instant. George had already turned towards the door.

"Catherine said not to open it," Ilona said.

"Obviously it's not Catherine. Anyway, she'd have walked straight in," he pointed out.

"Well, maybe we should telephone the desk."

"For God's sake, Ilona. *They* may have to live in such an atmosphere. I don't see why *we* should." He crossed the sitting room, and opened the door. "Can I help you, comrade?"

The man wore a beard and horn-rimmed spectacles. Now he looked from left to right up and down the corridor. "Can't I come in?"

"If you'll tell me what you want."

"I should think you'd remember me, George," he said, and pushed his way into the room, taking off his fur cap as he did so. "Good evening to you, Ilona. You haven't changed a bit. Not a single bit."

Ilona stared at him. "Viktor? Is it really you?"

"None other. Would you close the door, George?"

George did as he asked. "But . . . the last time I saw you was the day the Bolsheviks stormed the Winter Palace. You were with them."

Viktor Borodin nodded, took his cousin's hands, and kissed them.

"And according to Peter," Ilona said coldly, withdrawing her hands, "you wanted to have him arrested and shot as a tsarist."

"Yes. Well . . ." Viktor looked around the room. "Do you have a drink?"

"I have some scotch," George said. "No vodka, I'm afraid."

"Scotch whisky. My God, how long is it since I have tasted that!"

George poured some into a tumbler and handed it to him.

"Well?" Ilona demanded, standing in front of him, hands on hips. "I think you owe us some sort of an explanation."

"I made mistakes," Victor said. "We all made mistakes, I

suppose. But Peter and I are friends again now. I work for him. It was he who told me you'd be in Moscow."

"You work for *him*?" George cried.

"Keep your voice down, please."

"And he told you we'd be in Russia? But how?"

"We keep in touch. By courier, from his headquarters in Poland. He has another in Constantinople." Viktor frowned at them. "But . . . aren't you working for him too?"

"Working for Peter?" George sat down abruptly. "Do you seriously mean to say that Peter is conducting some sort of an espionage organization inside the Soviet Union?"

"Well—of course he is. We are. We don't intend to let this regime get away with it."

"Get away with what?" Ilona asked.

Viktor finished his drink and looked longingly at the bottle. George glanced at Ilona, shrugged, got up and refilled the glass.

"Get away with ruling Russia," Viktor said. "It is the duty of all true Russians to work to defeat them. The day will not be long delayed, now."

"Because Peter says so," George said grimly.

"Well . . . because it's true. This government is literally falling apart, and when Lenin dies—You have heard he is ill?"

George nodded.

"Well, then." He was frowning again. "But if you did not come here for Peter, why *are* you here?"

"I'm on a mission for the American Relief Administration," George said. "I'm here to see the Soviet leaders. To make a deal with them, not to bring them down. There are millions of lives at stake."

"Millions. You do not know how many millions. But Peter . . . he said you would wish to see me, to—"

"He did, did he? I'm going to have to have a word with your brother when I get home, Ilona. Well, I'll tell you, Victor. It's been great seeing you again after all this time. And I won't pretend I'm not pleased that you've learned some sense at last. But I have come here to do a job, and it's not going to be helped by hobnobbing with tsarist agents. My advice to you is to clear out. If you want to leave Russia, we'll help you. But anti-Soviet espionage, no."

Viktor stared at him, then got up slowly. "Leave Russia?" he asked. He looked at Ilona. "Leave Russia?"

"It would be the best thing," Ilona said. "Come to America with us. I'm sure George..." She looked at her husband.

"Of course," George said. "I'll give you a job, Viktor. You can replace Peter in my Russian news department, for a start."

Viktor looked from one to the other, and then at the door. George and Ilona's heads also turned to the sound of booted feet. They watched the door crash in, almost coming off its hinges, and stared at the four armed men who stood there, wearing the green overcoats and the fur caps of Russian policemen.

"Now wait just a moment," George said, "What the devil do you want?"

"You are George Hayman," said the first policeman, apparently an officer. He looked at Ilona. "And you are Ilona Hayman. You are under arrest."

"You must be crazy," George said. "What is the charge?"

"Consorting with anti-Soviet criminals," the officer said, and looked at Viktor, who was slowly backing across the room. "If you attempt to get out of that window, Comrade Borodin, my men will shoot you."

One of the policemen took his pistol from its holster.

"I think you had better check with your superiors," George said. "I think you had better get hold of Comrade Michael Nej, or you are going to find yourself in a lot of trouble."

"You will come with us," the officer said. "All of you. If you resist you will be taken by force. Come along now."

Ilona stared at George. Her stomach seemed to have become a terrified mass. This just couldn't be happening.

"What is the meaning of this?" Catherine Lissitsina stepped past the guards, surveyed the room and the shattered door. "Are you out of your mind, comrade captain? These people are guests of the Moscow Soviet."

The captain stared at her. "You are Catherine Lissitsina?" he demanded.

"That is my name," Catherine said. "And I demand to know by what right—"

The captain hit her in the stomach.

Catherine's words exploded in a gasp of pain as she doubled forward and fell to her hands and knees.

"Oh, my God," Ilona cried.

"Why, you . . ." George stepped forward, fists bunched. But the policemen saw him coming, and one of them swung his nightstick. George gave a gasp and fell sideways.

"George!" Ilona screamed, and ran to his side, only to have her shoulders seized to jerk her backwards. She lost her balance and struck the floor heavily, one shoe coming off, and all the breath being forced from her lungs.

"Viktor," she gasped. "Viktor!"

But Viktor remained standing motionless by the settee, staring at the policemen as a rabbit might stare at a snake.

Ilona looked at George, obviously unconscious, a trickle of blood coming from his ear, where the blow had landed. She pushed herself up on her hands and knees. "Listen," she said. "My husband—" She thrust out a hand towards him, and had it seized at the same time as other hands grasped her to pull her to her feet. Her skirt rode up and she stamped her feet to straighten it.

"Take her out," the captain said.

"No," she said. "Listen. My husband—"

Fingers bit into her arms and she was thrust into the corridor. There were some housemaids and one or two men at the far end of the corridor, alerted by the noise; when they saw the policemen they turned and ran.

Ilona found herself being marched towards the elevator, and then she was thrust forward, again to land on her hands and knees, only just stopping her face from cannoning against the wall. She heard the two men come into the elevator behind her, and then the motor whirred as they began to descend.

Think, she told herself. Decide what to do. Obviously there had been a mistake . . . She pictured George, lying on the floor in his blood.

She turned to look up at them. They returned her gaze. They did not look vicious, merely indifferent.

Ilona pulled herself to her feet, pushed hair from her eyes, and straightened her skirt. "Listen to me," she said. "There are letters to Comrade Nej, to Comrade Lenin himself. You are making a terrible mistake. Please take me to my husband. Please."

The elevator came to a halt and the doors were opened. The lobby outside was crowded. Now the men were stepping for-

ward to seize her arms again. But she couldn't be forced across
a hotel lobby, which had once been her own front hall.

"All right," she said. "All right. I'll go with you. Just don't
touch me. I won't try to get away."

The fingers bit into her arms again, and she was half dragged
and half carried across the floor, only then remembering that
she had on only one shoe. She closed her eyes so as not to see
the people in the lobby, opened them again when she stubbed
her stockinged toe on the doorsill, and realized that everyone
in the hotel was far too frightened to pay any attention to her.

The air on the street was like a hand slapping her face. She
found herself at the door of a black limousine. A moment later
she was inside, again on her hands and knees, head banging
against the far door. Hastily she pushed herself up and sat
down, found herself next to one policemen, while the other
had seated himself opposite in one of the jump seats. And the
car was already moving away from the curb.

Suddenly she was angry. She was Ilona Hayman. And before that she had been Ilona Roditcheva. And before that, Ilona
Borodina. Even if Russia had been turned upside down, even
if she had once experienced the terror of imprisonment, she
had never been manhandled like this before in her entire life,
not even by Roditchev. And to hit George Hayman, vice-president of Hayman Newspapers, with a stick . . . "You are going
to suffer for this," she said. "By God, you are going to suffer
for this."

The man sitting opposite made a quick movement. She had
not realized he held his stick in his hand, drooping beside his
boot. Now it came over in an arc, and struck her across the
thigh, a paralyzing blow that for a moment did not even hurt.
Then agony rushed away from the bruise, down to one knee
and up to her hip. She gasped, and half-fell forward. She
caught herself in time to keep from collapsing on the floor,
but could not stop herself whimpering with pain as she nursed
the flesh in both hands. God, she thought. Oh, God, this has
to be a dream.

Had Judith Stein thought that, when Roditchev's policemen
arrested *her*?

The car was stopping. She raised her head and stared. They
were in a courtyard, brilliantly lit by searchlights playing down
on them from above, and containing a large number of uni-

formed men and one or two women. A typical Russian police station, she thought, biting her lip to stop crying because of the pain and the despair.

The door was opened, and one of the policemen got out. "Come," he said.

Ilona thrust her left foot out of the car, pushed her body forward, and discovered to her horror that there was no strength in the leg; she found herself kneeling, while a fresh rush of pain raced away from her knees.

"Get up," said the policeman.

Ilona raised her head, stared at their faces. She expected them to laugh at her helpless humiliation. But they didn't. They merely looked at her, as she might have looked at a cockroach on whom, for some reason, she was not going to step, even though she *could* of course step on the cockroach whenever she wished.

She held on to the car door and pulled herself up.

"In there," said the first policeman.

Ilona gritted her teeth, pushed away from the car, and limped behind him into the doorway. As she looked at more faces and desks, she realized with a start of pure fear that she had never in her life actually been inside a police station before. She had never been encouraged to visit her first husband's cells, nor had she wanted to; and since leaving Roditchev, her life had been lived under the vast umbrella of Hayman Newspapers. She had never supposed that could change.

But George was lying on the floor, bleeding.

They came to a corridor, down which she forced herself, resisting the temptation to seize her leg and rub it, making herself stand straight and walk with only a slight limp. She followed her guard down a flight of stairs, and suddenly entered a colder, damper world, although the electric lightbulbs continued to glow. Then another door was held open, and she stepped inside, to stare at a blank wall, and turn back again as the door behind her closed.

She was alone. She had never before realized just how empty a room could be. There was not a stick of furniture. There was no wallpaper, just stone. And there was no window. The only object in the entire room was a bare electric bulb, in the very center of the ceiling—some nine feet high; she could not possibly reach it.

Why should she want to reach it?

Slowly she sank to her knees, but that was too painful, and she found herself sitting, knees drawn up. Now, at last she could think. Now . . .

The door opened, and her head jerked. A woman in uniform stood there. But this woman was not in the least like Catherine Lissitsina. She was gray-haired and harsh-faced, and she was large, tall and strong. She carried a bunch of keys and a stick, and wore the inevitable revolver.

"Up," she commanded.

Ilona started to respond without thinking, then deliberately checked herself. "I prefer to sit," she said. "My leg hurts."

The woman came closer. "Up," she commanded again, the stick suddenly in evidence.

Ilona pushed herself up, hating herself.

"Undress," the woman said. "Everything. Quickly."

Ilona stepped backwards, and found herself against the wall. "Undress? You must be mad."

The woman stared at her, and then turned her head to look at the door. It was opening again, to admit Ivan Nej.

Chapter 3

IVAN NEJ'S HEART POUNDED SO HARD HE WAS AMAZED THAT HE had found the courage to open the door at all. She was here, as he had planned she would be. As he had dreamed she would be.

And there she was, left hand clutching her dress against her thigh, high forehead creased by a slight frown, golden hair loosed and untidy, flopping across her forehead. And face and body as lovely as he remembered them. Twenty years before, he had managed to see her naked, on that never-to-be-forgotten night when her little sister Tattie threw open the door as he was passing. She was sixteen, then. He was fourteen. And he had dreamed of her ever since. He had dreamed of both the Borodin daughters. And in time, he had gained possession of Tattie. For a man had to make his dreams real, if he was to become anything at all.

But Tattie, for all her beauty, remained only a substitute, because she was unaware of what she possessed. Tattie was concerned only with the wild rhythms that coursed through her brain, sent her limbs into their mad gyrations. Her body was there to be admired, to be possessed, even, by the first to lay claim to it; she asked, in return, only to be allowed to dance.

But Ilona, magnificent, statuesque Ilona, knew just what her body, her face, her hair, and her mind could do to a man. Or for him.

He had last seen her in July, 1914, when she and her husband had come back to Starogan for Tattie's twenty-first birthday, on the eve of the Great War. He, the bootblack, too incompetent even to be made a footman, had hurried forward to greet her, and she had said, "Why, Ivan Nikolaievich, you have not changed at all," and passed on to talk to his mother as if he were not really there.

What did she think now? She stared at him, reached up to push hair from her forehead, and bit her lip as she straightened. "Ivan?" she asked. "Ivan Nikolaievich?"

"Commissar Nej," snapped the jailer, swinging her hand. The blow caught Ilona on the side of the face and sent her staggering forward, to hit the wall opposite and collapse in a heap against it.

"You must show proper respect, Mrs. Hayman," Ivan said, closing the door behind him as he came further into the room. He had not expected to be able to speak at all. But he was pleased. His voice was even, matter-of-fact.

Her head turned. "You," she said, her face bright with outrage. "You will—"

"Pay for this?" He moved closer, to see her better. "I am only doing my duty," he said. "If there has been a mistake—"

She was not that strong. She turned on her knees, once again pushing hair away from her eyes. "Yes," she said. "Yes, Ivan—Commissar Nej. There has been a mistake. You know there has been a mistake. My husband and I were given passports to visit Moscow, to see Michael—to see Comrade Lenin himself."

"But not to consort with known tsarist enemies of the state, I think."

"We did not know Viktor was even *alive*," she shouted.

"If there has been a mistake, Mrs. Hayman," he said again, "be sure that all will be well. Moreover, I promise to investigate the circumstances personally, and if there has been a mistake heads will roll. I give you my word on that. But until then—why, we must do our duty. Try to understand that."

She was following every word, like a small child trying to understand her schoolteacher, her face a mixture of frantic worry and eager absorption. This was Ivan Nikolaievich speaking, her family's old servant. So he had become a Soviet scourge, with a reputation that had spread the width of Europe and America. But he was still Ivan Nikolaievich. And he was her brother-in-law. He was not going to harm her. He was going to help her. He had just promised her that.

Slowly Ilona pushed herself to her feet. "Yes," she said. "I do understand that. There *has* been a mistake."

"I am sure there has," Ivan said sympathetically. "And you may leave it with me. But for now, if Comrade Rutkovsky says you must undress to be searched, why, I am afraid you must undress to be searched. It is the law, you understand."

Ilona gazed at him, then at the woman. Pink spots gathered in her cheeks. But once again he could see her brain working, trying to reason, trying to choose her best course. It was a process he had witnessed so often, in others, that he supposed he could tell exactly what she would say, as well as do.

"If . . . if it is the law," she said at last. "But you could not expect me to undress in front of you. In front of a man."

"Of course not," Ivan said. "That would be barbaric. And we are not barbarians. You understand, however, that Comrade Rutkovsky will have to search you?"

Once again the quick glance from left to right. The pink spots deepened. But she nodded. Once again he could read her mind. Just survive, she was thinking. Go along with them, avoid being hurt, and survive. Because there had been a mistake, and she would be released.

"Well, then," Ivan said. "I will leave you. I will go and investigate what has happened, so that you may be released. If what you say is true."

"My husband—"

"I will attend to him also, I promise you that. I will discover the entire truth of the matter, Mrs. Hayman, and I am sure you will soon be reunited with your husband. Have courage. I shall not be long."

He smiled at her, stepped outside, and closed the door behind him. He climbed a few steps to the observation room, where a policeman was on duty. "Outside," he said. He had no intention of sharing this pleasure with anyone.

The policeman saluted and hurried from the tiny room. Ivan closed the door, sat down, and looked through the observation window. It was shaded brown, and from the point of view of the prisoner appeared to be just another stone in the wall. But vision was perfect.

He watched Ilona Hayman slowly remove her dress and slip, her stockings and her shoes, her panties. With each garment laid on the floor he felt his heartbeat quicken. She was more beautiful, more desirable than he had dreamed, certainly than he remembered. Because he remembered a sixteen-year-old girl, and here was a thirty-six-year-old woman, in all the glory of her femininity. So, he thought, nothing is perfect. This is only a fleeting glimpse, and I cannot touch. But it is as close to perfection as I can get.

Was it? Was he not a coward? He had the right to go in there and search her himself, and rape her himself, again and again and again, and then summon others to do it again and again, so that he could watch. If he were bold enough. But he was not bold enough—either to confront Michael, and then Lenin, with what he had done, or to confront the woman herself. So, nothing was perfect.

He watched Comrade Rutkovsky make her prisoner bend until her long golden hair swept the floor, while she thrust fingers into every aperture of Ilona's body. He could almost hear Ilona's breathing, hear the pounding of her heart, feel the swelling anger that was bubbling through her system and showing itself in the scorching heat of her cheeks. But she submitted. Because she was telling herself that survival, the reincarnation of Ilona Borodina, was only minutes away, could only be lost by the admission of anger and shame.

He went outside because he could not breathe, and signaled with his head for the policeman to return. That young man also would have something to remember for the rest of his life. Some men were just born lucky.

He went along the corridor to the interrogation room, where Captain Ashcherin waited.

"You realize there has been a ghastly mistake," Ivan said.

"I am sorry, comrade commissar." Ashcherin came to attention. "No doubt your orders were based upon good evidence."

"*My* orders?" Ivan's voice expressed mild surprise.

Ashcherin's head started to turn, and then straightened again.

"I knew nothing of this, comrade captain," Ivan said. "I am afraid you have been overzealous. Do you understand?"

Ashcherin licked his lips. "Have you not visited the woman, comrade commissar?"

"To offer her help," Ivan said. "She is distraught, worried about her husband. Mr. Hayman is an important man. A guest of Comrade Lenin, no less. And a friend of my brother. We shall have to make amends. There will have to be punishments."

Now Ashcherin's head did turn.

"Which I will carry out," Ivan said. "You will be sent to Irkutsk, and put in charge of the police there."

"Irkutsk?"

"Oh, you may take your wife, comrade captain. And your family. And it will only be for five years."

"Five *years*?"

"At the end of five years, comrade captain, I swear to you, I will bring you back as my right-hand man. Just five years, comrade."

Ashcherin drew a long breath.

"Providing, of course, you keep our secrets," Ivan said. "And providing you obtain sufficient proof that *you* acted in good faith, here. Which of the two prisoners is the weaker? Borodin or the woman?"

Ashcherin considered; he seemed to have difficulty in concentrating. "The man."

"I thought so. Well, obtain what you wish from him, and then have him shot—but do it yourself, and enter in your report that he escaped custody and disappeared. Make it convincing, comrade captain. Mr. Hayman will certainly be in a very aggressive frame of mind when he regains his freedom."

"Yes, comrade commissar." Ashcherin saluted, turned to the door, and hesitated. "A question, comrade commissar?"

"Yes?"

"These people. You have arrested them, just to let them

go? You knew Viktor Borodin was a tsarist months ago, but you have never arrested him before. Now he must be shot. Surely, if he confesses, we can hold the Haymans?"

"Of course we could."

"But you mean to let them go."

"Yes."

"Why, comrade commissar? Why go to all this trouble, and then just let them go again?"

Ivan Nej put on his cap, making sure it was straight on his head. "I wished to refresh my memory, comrade captain," he said, and left the room.

Michael Nej hummed as he entered his office, and went to the window to look out over the river and the city beyond. It was a beautiful spring morning. And it was going to be a beautiful day. A good day. The best of the year. Ilona was arriving today.

He was a much larger man than his brother. His somewhat harsh features had mellowed over the years of power; in contrast his eyes, once surprisingly soft for a man who had earned himself a reputation as a dangerous terrorist, had hardened. But this morning the eyes were as soft as they had ever been.

Ilona. Of course, she would have George with her. A man he should hate with all the savage intensity of his brother. A man he had, in fact, hated from that night in Port Arthur, when he had seen the pair of them rolling about on the settee together. His princess, with an American journalist. And yet, in a strange way, that hateful night had brought her closer to him, because he had realized, for the first time, that Ilona Dimitrievna, tall, glacial, with the face and figure of a goddess and the aloofness reserved for princesses, was underneath just a bubbling turmoil of emotions. He doubted that even George truly understood that, however much and however often he had benefited from those emotions. But Michael had guessed, from that night, that such a woman was always likely to fall for the person nearest at hand, when the crisis came.

So he had taken care to be at her side when her misery at having to live with Sergei Roditchev had overflowed. And he had fallen in love, the way, no doubt, George had fallen in love. To make love to Ilona Borodina, was to love her for the rest of her life. In pursuit of that love he had thrown up family, and position, and security, to be a vagabond, living by her charity and at her command. In desperation, when George's reappearance had withheld that love, he had become a revolutionary. George had saved him from hanging after Prime Minister Stolypin's assassination—an assassination he had not actually taken part in, for at the crucial moment he had found himself unable to pull the trigger. Undoubtedly Ilona's memory of him had caused George to take the risk of helping him escape from prison. And since then he had survived, to meet and know Lenin, to rise and rise and rise, as the Bolsheviks had risen, and risen, and risen.

So why hate? Even George? Even if George had robbed him once again, of the only other woman with whom he had supposed he could be happy? He would never have remained happy with Judith Stein though; that was the point. Judith had looks and passion, but she had no serenity of spirit. Judith was not out to make the best of the world in which she found herself, as Ilona was. Judith was out to change the world to her own specifications.

But he had no reason to hate. He had loved two remarkable women, and been left by them. To get on with his own business. And to remember. And thus to be happy, that she was going to be here today.

"Comrade Nej." Alla Vasiukova, his secretary, was a tall, raw-boned woman. "A fine day."

"A fine day." Michael sat at his desk. "Is there news from Comrade Lenin?"

"He is well, comrade. He is sitting up and dictating letters."

"Good. Good." Even beautiful days could be saddened by the threat of looming thunderstorms. "Now, Comrade Vasiukova, today is the day the Americans arrive."

"Comrade—"

"I wish to know the moment their train gets in. I do not wish to meet them, you understand. Just to know. Then I will call on them at their hotel. The Berlin, is it?"

Alla Vasiukova drew a long breath. "The Americans arrived last night, comrade commissar."

"Last night? Well, well, the trains must be running on time. Very good. Have my car come to the door in fifteen minutes.

Oh, and telephone Comrade Tatiana Nej and tell her that her sister has arrived, and that I will be bringing her to call, this morning."

Alla Vasiukova stood at attention and stared at the wall above Michael's head. "Comrade, Mr. and Mrs. Hayman have been arrested."

"What did you say?" Michael spoke slowly.

"Mr. and Mrs. Hayman have been arrested, comrade commissar."

"By whose order?"

"By order of the deputy commissar of the All-Russian Extraordinary Commission, comrade commissar."

"Ivan?" Michael whispered. "Ivan?" he shouted, getting to his feet. "They were arrested last night?"

"Yes, comrade commissar."

"Last night. My God—" He checked himself, glanced at the woman, and flushed. But even Lenin used the phrase from time to time, in moments of stress. "Have my car sent round now, and get me Commissar Nej on the telephone."

"Yes, comrade commissar." Alla Vasiukova hurried from the room.

Ivan, Michael thought. Back to his old tricks. Ivan, who had dreamed, aloud, from the time they were boys, of somehow being able to possess the Borodin sisters. Ivan, who had had her in his power for an entire night. Ivan . . .

The telephone jangled. "Ivan," he snapped.

"Good morning, Michael," Ivan said.

"What has happened?" Michael shouted. "Where are the Haymans?"

"I think they are staying at the Berlin."

"At the . . . you had them arrested?"

"A mistake," Ivan admitted.

"A *mistake*?"

"Well, I would have handled it differently. They had a meeting with her cousin Viktor. You remember Viktor Borodin? A known subversive. An agent for Peter Borodin. We have been watching him for some time."

"And do you not think it is natural that Ilona would wish to meet with her cousin again, after so long?"

"I doubt it was an innocent meeting, Michael," Ivan said patiently. "We have evidence. But as I say, *I* would certainly have handled it differently, considering the circumstances. But Ashcherin—you know what a hothead he is. He will be disciplined. Oh, yes, he will be disciplined."

"And Ilona—"

"I am sure she would like to see you, Michael. I'm afraid Hayman resisted arrest and got a thump on the head. But I have sent a doctor over. I am told it is nothing serious."

"They came here under a *carte blanche*," Michael said.

"Indeed they did," Ivan agreed.

"Comrade Lenin will be very angry."

"No doubt. As I have said, Ashcherin will certainly be disciplined. But the poor fellow was only doing his duty as he saw it. He knows nothing of the nuances of the situation. And if he did, he probably would not approve. As I do not approve and Comrade Stalin does not approve. We do not require American help. It is an admission of failure on the part of the Soviet."

"We are fortunate," Michael said coldly, "that neither you nor Comrade Stalin has any part in formulating state policy. Does Tattie know about this fiasco?"

"I told her the very moment I discovered what was going on. She is at the hotel now, I think."

Michael got up, but did not immediately put down the telephone. "And Viktor Borodin?"

"Ah, well, he is most certainly guilty, as he has proved."

"He has confessed?"

"He has escaped. Would you believe it?"

Michael's eyes narrowed. "You expect me to believe that Viktor Borodin has escaped your custody?"

"Not my custody, Michael. Ashcherin's. He has made a botch of the entire thing."

Michael gazed at the telephone in impotent anger. But he knew that it was unlikely he would ever discover what had really happened. Ivan was too good at his job, and his people were too afraid of him. "Was there anyone else involved?"

"An interpreter and guide. A woman named Lissitsina."

"And has she also escaped?"

"She has not been that fortunate, Michael. She is still under interrogation. I am sure she has a great deal to tell us."

And may God have mercy on her soul, Michael thought, as he put down the receiver.

* * *

"Now, Mr. Hayman," said Nurse Bondarevskaya. "If you will drink this, you will go back to sleep, and when you wake up, you will be fine again."

"I've just *waked* up," George complained. "I really have no desire to go back to sleep again."

"But it is good for you," Nurse Bondarevskaya insisted. "Dr. Yudovich said so. It was a nasty blow."

"Can't you explain to her, sweetheart?" George appealed to Ilona, standing on the other side of the bed. "I have too much to do."

"Nothing that cannot wait," Ilona said, "in view of what happened."

It was ten o'clock in the morning. She had returned to the hotel, with George, the doctor, and the nurse, at three that morning. She had had a hot bath, and a sedative, and she had slept deeply. After breakfast and another bath, she had felt almost human again. She did not suppose she would ever forget those fingers poking up her rectum and her vagina, just as she would never forget the hours that had followed, alone in that empty, windowless room with the brilliant naked bulb flooding her brain with searing light. But it was an experience that would help her to understand so many things. Judith, for example. Judith had suffered much worse, under the tsars. To *hear* of Siberia, to hear of children dying, to hear of beatings, meant nothing compared to the simple fact of now having *experienced*. And she had endured only a search. Except for the blow from the policeman, she had not been truly hurt.

But George, who could remember very little of what had happened, could not be expected to react so passively. She smiled at him and bent over him to kiss his forehead. "You cannot conduct any business with a headache."

He shook his head. "I wish I could remember. I wish—" He frowned at her. "Are you sure it was Ivan Nej who set you free?"

"Of course. He was actually apologetic, George. So . . . well, you could almost say *decent* about everything. And if Peter *is* behaving like a lunatic, well, you can't blame him for suspecting Peter's sister."

She was rationalizing, she knew, forcing herself to see

things as they were, instead of as she remembered them. Ivan Nej was a monster, responsible for the murders of her family, the abduction of her sister. She could never have any feelings for him save total loathing. And yet last night he had been a perfect gentleman. So was it possible for even an Ivan Nej to change for the better?

George sighed. "I suppose not. But the others? Viktor?"

"I shall find out. Tattie will find out for me. She's coming here this morning. Ivan was going to send her to take care of us."

"And the girl? Catherine Lissitsina? You'll find out what has happened to her? She surely can't be mixed up in anything against the government."

"I'll find out about that too." Her head jerked as she heard a rap on the door. She wondered if she would ever be able to hear a rap on the door again, without having her heart leap all the way into her throat.

"I will go," Nurse Bondarevskaya said, understanding. She went into the outer room, opened the door, and the apartment was filled with a tempest of effervescent blond beauty.

"Ilona," Tatiana Nej shrieked. "George. Oh, Ilona. Oh, George."

The same height as her sister, Tattie had the more voluptuous figure and somewhat bolder features. She was no less attractive, but in the entirely different manner that was representative of their personalities. Tattie bubbled, like a racing stream. She was dressed as she always dressed, in an eye-stopping pink dress that swirled about her ankles, and was set off by a thick necklace of yellow amber, which, added to the scattered yellow hair, reaching to her thighs, and the enormous pink hat with its yellow flowers, suggested that the morning sun had suddenly decided to make its home in the Hotel Berlin.

"Tattie?" Ilona gasped. "Is it really you?"

"Me," Tattie said, and gave her a hug and a kiss, before half-throwing herself on to the bed beside George, white high-heeled shoes flailing the air. "How could it not be me?"

Because you're not in uniform, Ilona thought. Because you're so obviously healthy, and so obviously happy. Because your face isn't pinched and your clothes are splendid—if a trifle garish—and your shoes are new. Because you aren't afraid.

She decided not to answer.

"Oh, George," Tattie said, smothering him with kisses. "You poor thing! Oh, I was so *angry* when I heard how they'd hit you with a stick. My God, I was angry. I told Ivan that the man should be punished. They are all going to be punished. Are you all right?"

"I think so," George said. "But they keep giving me sedatives."

"And a good thing too." Tattie pushed herself up and gave her dress a perfunctory tug. Tidiness had never been her forte. "Ilona." She held both her sister's hands and kissed her again. "It's so good to see you."

"And to see you," Ilona said. "Tattie—"

"I want you to come with me," Tattie said. "I've so much to show you. So much to tell you. So much to ask you. How are the children?"

"They're fine," Ilona said. "But Tattie—"

"You can spare her for a while, George," Tattie said. "You have a good rest. There's to be a state banquet for you, tomorrow night. You'll want to be fit for that. Vladimir Ilich himself is coming, and he hasn't been very well. But he's coming to meet you. I told him he had to. Now come along, Ilona." She took Ilona's hand and began to drag her towards the door.

"But—" Ilona looked at George helplessly.

"It would be good for Mr. Hayman to sleep," Nurse Bondarevskaya said.

"All right," George said. "All right. I surrender. I'll sleep. Can I come to see you later, Tattie?"

"Of course you can, George," she said, and blew him a kiss from across the room. "I've got so much to tell you. But I'll tell Ilona first."

"And you'll check on Viktor and Catherine Lissitsina?" George reminded Ilona.

"Right away. Tattie—" But she was being bundled into her mink and thrust out the front door. There was an armed guard on the door—for their own safety, Ivan had said, and Ilona was prepared to believe him. She was prepared to believe almost anything at this moment. "Tattie."

"Svetlana and Gregory are at the school," Tattie said, striding into the elevator, which the three people already inside

·hastily evacuated. "It'll be back in a moment," Tattie said, smiling at them.

"But . . ." Ilona stared at the doors as they shut. "Those people—"

"I don't like sharing lifts with people," Tattie explained. "After all, I am Tatiana Nej."

"Oh," Ilona said mildly. "Of course, your husband is deputy commissar of the All-Russian Extraordinary Commission."

Tattie giggled. "The Cheka. Yes. All it means is that he's deputy chief of the secret police. Felix doesn't really do anything any more, although he's the official head. But Ivan isn't really important. How can a policeman be important? *I'm* important."

The elevator stopped, and the doors were opened. There were several people waiting to get in, but they were swept imperiously aside by a uniformed chauffeur, who had been guarding the exit.

"So I thought we'd go to the school first," Tattie said. "I so want to show you the school."

"The school?" Ilona said, wishing the lobby would stop spinning.

"It's all mine," Tattie said. "Vladimir Ilich gave it to me. He didn't approve at first." She gave another laugh. "He's a stuffy old bird, really. But when I explained that my girls would catch the real spirit of Russia . . . He's very keen now."

The revolving doors were turning, and they were out into the sunlit morning, and the sight of more policemen, standing at attention and saluting as the two women emerged. Waiting for them was a brand new Mercedes, and the chauffeur was holding the door.

"Tattie," Ilona said urgently. "I don't really understand. This school—"

"The Tatiana Nej Academy, I've called it," Tattie explained.

"But . . . what do you do?"

"We dance," Tattie said. "And we sing. It's what I've always wanted. And now it's mine. I'll never be able to thank Vladimir Ilich enough."

The car was racing through the streets, out of the city and into the hills to the north.

"This Vladimir Ilich . . . is that Lenin?"

"Of course."

"And he's a friend of yours?"

"Of course," Tattie said. "Vladimir Ilich is my very best friend in all Russia. My very best friend in all the world." She kissed Ilona on the cheek. "He thinks I'm a genius . . . Well," she said thoughtfully, "I suppose I am."

"No, no, no," Tattie shouted. "That won't do at all."

The room was enormous. But then, the house was enormous. Clearly it had once been a princely palace, a summer cottage situated in the hills south of the city. It sat in its own grounds, surrounded by lush green fields and stately pines. Anything farther removed from the eye-burning misery and poverty of the south could hardly be imagined. It was even, Ilona realized with a sudden awareness of disloyalty, more beautiful than Starogan had ever been.

And it hummed with a frenetic energy Starogan had never possessed. It followed the metabolic pulses of its director, who had stridden into the house, past bowing flunkies, ostensibly to show her sister her academy, but who had immediately become involved in the rehearsal being conducted. For what sort of performance, Ilona could not be sure; she sat against the wall and stared in amazement at the fifty-odd young women, ranging in ages between twelve and twenty, who had been cavorting about the polished floor under the supervision of a couple of older instructors. Tattie had looked at them for a matter of seconds, pausing in midsentence to do so, and then had kicked off her own shoes and rushed into the center of the room, bringing the proceedings to a halt with her tremendous shouting.

Now they gathered round, anxiously awaiting whatever she was about to say.

"You are *trees*," Tattie said. "Trees, and the wind is blowing. There is a gale. A storm. Sway, and ruffle, sway, and bend, sway, and straighten, sway, and scatter, sway. Dimitri Dimitrievich?"

A young boy sitting in the far corner before an old upright piano began to strike the keys, and the room filled with rushing, tumultuous music, which *was*, Ilona realized to her surprise, suggestive of a howling, rising wind. But she was more taken with Tattie, who began to dance the movement herself, not shifting her feet, since she was supposed to be a tree, but twisting and contorting her body, throwing her shoulders and head about, so that her hat went sailing across the room, her skirt flew about her, and her breasts surged, all in a tremendous expression of energy and movement, all while she remained standing still—and all amazingly graceful as well as erotic.

The girls about her took up the theme, and the dance chamber became filled with the heaving, tossing, and yet stationary bodies. It was quite remarkable, the amount of energy being expended, the utter beauty of the movements and of the movers—for not one of the girls was less than pretty—the concentration in their faces, the sweat which soon shone on faces and chests, the sensuous cadence of the music. Suddenly Ilona found herself moving to it while still sitting, then stopped in embarrassment as Tattie abandoned the dance and came towards her, pushing hair and sweat from her face.

"Silly things," Tattie said. "I can never get it through their heads that dancing is a matter of movement. They must move with every part of their bodies, even when the piece calls for them to be standing still." She panted for a moment, but she was obviously superbly fit. "And now, the children," she said.

Ilona got up. "Did you write the music?" she asked.

Tattie pouted. "No. I do not write much music anymore. Mine simply isn't good enough." She smiled, sunshine cascading through the rain. "And I haven't the time. Come and meet Dimitri Dimitrievich. He's only sixteen, you know. A student at the Music Academy. But I make him write for our dances." She held Ilona's hand and dragged her round the room to the piano. The young man stopped playing and stood up, and the dancers stopped also. Suddenly the room was full of the sounds of their breathing.

"Dimitri Dimitrievich Shostakovich," Tattie said. "My sister, Mrs. George Hayman."

The young man clicked his heels and bowed over Ilona's hand. "It is a privilege, Mrs. Hayman."

"It—it's a very dramatic piece," Ilona confessed.

"Thank you." He bowed again.

"Back to work," Tattie said, and seized Ilona's hand again. "Come along." They left the room by a door in the far wall, hurried along other corridors, past other rooms, from each of which there came the sound of booming music, unlike anything Ilona had ever heard before, and of panting, straining bodies.

"How many students do you have here?" she asked.

"Oh, about three hundred. But they are not students. They are dancers. Of course, some of them are *students* of the dance."

"But . . . they're very young," Ilona said.

"That has nothing to do with it," Tattie said. "I danced just as well when I was twelve as I do now. Don't you remember me dancing, when I was twelve?"

"I remember Mama sending you to your room for being obscene," Ilona said.

Tattie smiled. "Mama did not understand. Nobody understood then. But Vladimir Ilich understands. He understood from the very first time we talked. Do you know, he has promised me, when I think my girls are ready, that we can go on a tour of Europe? Think of it, my girls, in all the capitals of the world. And it'll be soon. We'll be ready in a year or so. Oh, I'm so looking forward to it." She gave a giggle. "Ivan doesn't want me to go. But Ivan is even stuffier than Vladimir Ilich, really. And anyway, what Ivan Nej says doesn't matter. It's what Lenin says that matters."

She threw open a door, showed Ilona into another vast room, but one entirely filled, except for the half-dozen nurses, with children who all seemed to be under the age of four. They played, and they cooed, and they cried, and they turned with open mouths to stare at the two women, while the nurses hastily stood at attention. Tattie marched through the middle of them, Ilona at her heels. "All my girls who have babies bring them here," she said. "We look after them. I don't like my girls to marry, you see. Husbands confuse them, make them lose interest." She grimaced. "I should know. This is Svetlana."

The girl, in the process of laboriously crawling from one pile of blocks to another, raised her head. She was nearly three years old, as Ilona knew, and already possessed the Borodin blondness, as well as the Borodin features.

"And this is Gregory," Tattie said, leaning over into the tiny bed and lifting up a small boy. Gregory was one, and was dark and small.

"They're lovely children," Ilona said. "Are they both Ivan's?"

Tattie gave a peal of laughter. "Well, of course they are! I don't think Ivan would like me to have one by anyone else. He'd have the man arrested or something."

"Well...I..." Ilona flushed. But it was more than embarrassment at having made an improper suggestion. It was embarrassment at having so entirely misjudged the situation between Tattie and her husband.

Tattie was looking past her to the door, and frowning. "Well, Michael Nikolaievich?" she demanded. "What do you want?"

Ilona turned, heart fluttering.

Michael Nej smiled at her. "I have come to take Ilona to lunch."

"It's years since I've eaten so much," Ilona confessed, popping another piece of caviar-laden black bread into her mouth. She gazed at him with wide, bright eyes. She was aware of having talked almost nonstop for the past hour. Utter nonsense, most of it. Sheer conversational absurdity. But she didn't want to stop, lest she give him a chance to say some of the things that were obviously hammering at his mind.

Yet she would have to stop soon. Or become serious. She could not keep this up forever.

Michael Nej smiled gently. She was remembering that gentleness was his outstanding characteristic. Yet he had signed the warrant which had given the Ekaterinburg Soviet the right to execute the Romanovs. No doubt he had done that gently, too. "Do you not have enough to eat in America? There is a dream ended."

"Oh, of course we do. But I suppose women there are more conscious of their figures."

"In Russia, we do not like our women to be thin," he said, still smiling.

"Then I'm well on the way to qualifying for being liked," she said.

He leaned across the table to hold her fingers. "You—"

"But I guess I'm just feeling guilty," she hurried on. She would have to turn him aside. "Because...well, I suppose it seems wrong, for me to be sitting here..." She looked around her. The well-filled restaurant, the white-coated waiters, the linen tablecloths and napkins, the clink of crystal and the clatter of silver cutlery ... She had dined here often while Sergei was military governor of Moscow. They were in the Kitai-Gorod, the fashionable shopping center of the old city, and just down the road was the square where the abortive revolution of 1905 had taken place, that famous night when she had gone mad and actually worked on the barricades, with Judith Stein and Lenin, before she had remembered who and what she was.

And just down the road, too, was the bookseller's shop where she and this man had held their afternoon trysts and consummated their love. And where she had taken George, thus driving Michael into becoming a revolutionary.

"You have sat here before," he said, also remembering. His fingers were tight on hers.

"I wasn't thinking of the past," she lied, giving a tug without success, and using her free hand to drink some more vodka. She was going to need a bludgeon. "I was thinking of ... of what George and I saw down south. Of Sevastopol. Of ... of Starogan."

His grip relaxed as he leaned back. "I have seen them too."

"Well, then ..." She was leaning forward without meaning to. "How can you? I just don't understand."

"Not two years ago, Starogan and Sevastopol were battle-fields. I entered Sevastopol with my troops the day the last of the Whites sailed away with the British Navy. The day Peter Borodin sailed away, Ilona. Less than two years ago. But Moscow and Petrograd were equally ruined then. We are re-building an entire nation. A start has to be made somewhere. And of course last year's drought did not help. But we are succeeding. There is a great deal to be done. A great deal to be done even here in Moscow. We will get to Sevastopol eventually. And Starogan will be there again. I have that much in mind. But we need time." He smiled. "And despite what others may say, we need help. That is why I am so happy to have George here. And so sorry about what happened."

"Oh..." She shrugged. "We do not blame anyone. But Michael—"

"Tell me about little Ivan."

She drank some more vodka. "He is well. A fine boy. He looks like you. But Michael, his name is John, and he is American."

"How can he be American? He was born in Russia. Both his mother and his father are Russian. How can he be American?"

"Because..." Her own hand had crept across the table, and he was holding it again. "Because that is what America is all about. It's not about where you were born, or who your parents are or were. It's about being what you *are*, what you want to be, what you are capable of being."

He stared at her for some seconds, then he smiled. "He can never be president, you know. You have to be born there to be president. So it is not quite as idyllic as you suggest."

"Nowhere is as idyllic as one would wish," she said. "But his son can be president, Michael."

Another stare. Then another smile. "Will you ever let him visit me?"

"If... if he wishes to."

"Do you talk of me?"

"He doesn't know, Michael. He thinks his father was Sergei."

"Then he is a tsarist, and by definition, a hater of me and all I stand for."

"I am trying to give him a fair picture of what happened here, of what life was like. Then he can make his own decision."

"What happened here. Do *you* approve of what happened here, Ilona? Do you approve of me? Of Bolshevism?"

"How can I? You Bolsheviks murdered my family."

He flinched, and looked down. "Then he *will* hate me, because you hate me."

"No," she said, "I do not hate you. You used the word *approve*. I do not approve. Maybe I hate Bolshevism and all it stands for. But I know there were reasons. I know there were faults. I suffered from tsarism as well as you, you know."

"Yes," he said. "I know. Then I will be content. But now you are happy with George."

She bit her lip. "Yes," she said. "I am happy with George."

He sighed.

"Don't you have a wife? A woman, anywhere?"

"I've walked in the sun. Do you think I could easily choose the rain?"

She smiled, but her mouth was twisted. "Poetry?"

"Is that so unimaginable?"

"Now you are getting angry."

He shook his head. "I am getting sad. And that is no good. I must take you home, to George, and then I must sit down with George and decide how he can help us. That *is* a strange situation. But you . . . if there is anything I can do for you, Ilona . . ."

"Yes. There is Viktor."

Michael sighed. "Viktor has escaped custody."

"Escaped? But—"

"It was a foolish thing to do. He will be caught eventually."

"George will be very upset. And angry with Peter more than anyone. Michael . . ." She took his hand again. "There was a girl, too. Our interpreter and guide. Her name is Catherine Lissitsina. She was arrested too. Did she escape?"

He shook his head. "She is still in custody. But she is equally guilty."

"But she can't be," Ilona cried. "She believes in Communism. My God, she made that plain enough. Find out about her, will you? Oh, please, Michael."

Michael frowned at her. "Is she your friend?"

"I only met her a week ago."

"And you are more concerned about her than about Viktor?"

"Well . . . she was so young. So full of life."

Michael continued to frown. "Was George also concerned about her?"

"Of course. George is wild with worry about her."

"I see." Michael smiled. "Well, then, I will find out about her, I promise you."

"To the American people." Lenin smiled as he raised his glass. "We have so much in common. Only time separates our revolutions."

"I'll drink to that," George agreed, standing, as did the assembled company. He gazed at the Soviet leader. They had met briefly in 1918, and he had read most of Lenin's books, long before they had met, and even before the Revolution. If he had from the first abhorred the ruthless pedantry with which the man had always encouraged his cohorts to carry out his theoretical requirements, he had been forced to admire the enormous mental power, the driving determination, and above all, the unholy energy that had characterized his every movement. What then was he to make of him now? The voice was unchanged, harshly abrasive, surprisingly effective. But this man was ill, and suddenly old, although he could not be more than in his middle fifties. The close-cropped hair was still reddish brown; the red beard still jutted aggressively from the square chin; the mouth still resembled a steel trap. The complexion, however, was sallow, and the eyes were dull, and every so often the quick, definite movements were halted by a hesitation.

George glanced at Krupskaya, who had been seated beside him. She had changed too. The remarkable features, beautiful in their contrast of small nose and pouting lips, had tightened as she watched her husband's strength dwindle. And Krupskaya, as he remembered, was every bit as dedicated a Communist as Lenin had ever been. She had shared his exiles and his miseries, his dreams, and eventually his triumphs. Now she must share his fears for the future of this ramshackle state they had created between them.

He looked around the table. Ilona stood on Lenin's right. She had been welcomed cordially; he remembered that night working on the barricades together, in 1905, before he had discovered her true identity and sent her away. Ten years later he would have had her shot.

Next to Ilona there stood Lev Davidovich Trotsky. Trotsky had created the Red Army, a force of uncertain quality, to be sure, but one which, alone, had enabled this group of desperate men to hold on to their hastily seized power. And it was a force which, if properly commanded and inspired, could defeat even hardened professionals. Tonight Michael Nej stood next to Trotsky, and it had been Michael Nej, himself driven by Trotsky's genius, who had completed the defeat of General Denikin and Prince Peter Borodin, and had conquered the south for Bolshevism. Was each a contender for Lenin's post?

But there were others who had shared Lenin's Swiss exile with him. Men like Lev Kamenev, or Nikolai Bukharin, or Joseph Stalin, smiling benevolently behind his enormous mustache. Stalin was a Party man through and through, George estimated, one who would go as the Party decided, and one, moreover, who was clearly not that interested in politics; his gaze kept drifting to the lovely, quiet features of his wife, Nadezhda Alliluyeva. A happy man. But probably not leadership material—at least, not the leadership material this motley crew would demand.

He wondered what the others, the intellectuals, thought of it all. For instance, there was Maxim Gorky, who had embraced the revolution in his writings, and stood unchallenged at the head of the Russian literary tree. And Tatiana Nej . . . was it possible to describe Tattie as an intellectual? In her breathtaking décolletage she put every other woman in the room, even her own sister, to shame. Tattie, he supposed, represented the Bolsheviks' greatest triumph. Gorky had come from the lower class, Lenin from the middle. Tattie was an aristocrat who had embraced the new religion, despite the murder of her family, despite her own experiences, and who, in her almost regal beauty and splendor, raised the whole proceedings above a tawdry gathering of desperate men.

Or did Tattie truly embrace anything, except the necessity of being Tattie? From their first meeting, when an eleven-year-old girl had burst into his bedroom in Port Arthur, bubbling with laughter and excitement and sheer animal femaleness, he had found her fascinating. He had watched her progress with an almost fatherly affection. Not love, though. He wondered if there was a man in the world who could dare *love* Tattie, without being consumed in the fires of her volcanic spirit. But there was hardly a man could meet her and not adore her, not be prepared to forgive her every excess—except, perhaps, Ivan Nej, standing rigorously at attention, entirely the policeman, yet unctuous in his deference. George assumed he had seen the man often during his stays at Starogan. Indeed, he could remember meeting him, too, in Port Arthur, and commenting then, to himself, on the way the bootblack had looked at his master's youngest daughter. Ivan had watched and waited, and in time, triumphed. Ivan owned all that beauty and all that energy and all that surging humor. Or did all of those things own him? Certainly he remained a tortured and twisted man.

But that Ivan Nej and Tatiana Borodina should be married at all! He thought that in that single remarkable fact was condensed the entire consequences of the World War and the revolution, here in Russia.

"My toast was sincere, Mr. Hayman." They sat together after dinner, puffing their cigars, surrounded by the hum of conversation, but still aware that there was no one in the room, except possibly Tattie, who was not straining an ear to hear what the two of them were saying. "I see our people," Lenin went on, "as the ultimate arbiters of world society."

"Don't you suppose England and France would have something to say about that?" George asked.

Lenin chuckled. "England, and France, and Germany have had their day. Western Europe—the Europe of aristocrats and kings, of capitalist exploitation—has had its day." He raised a finger. "I know you claim your country is one where any man at all can become a millionaire, at whatever cost to his fellows. In time you will learn that even that is wrong. But at least you have prevented the crime of allowing a man to have power merely because his grandfather also held power, regardless of his own qualifications. The coming era is the era of the common man, Mr. Hayman."

"I won't argue with that."

"Then why do you hate us? I am not speaking of you personally." He allowed his gaze to settle on Ilona, talking animatedly with Krupskaya. "Perhaps *you* have some reason. But your people—why will they not grant us diplomatic recognition, send us an ambassador, allow our two nations to go forward hand in hand?"

"That's a tough one," George admitted.

"I would like to know."

"Well, of course there's been a change of government since the end of the war, and the new administration believes that Europe is Europe and America is America, and each should be left to get on with its own affairs."

"The world is too small for such an attitude. But I have heard that you support this new administration."

George grinned. "I voted Republican, yes. That doesn't mean I agree with their every policy. The way I see it, we did become involved in Europe back in 1917, and we should stay involved. But I'm not the president."

"Which is a pity. You said there were other reasons."

"There's also the financial one. Our government believes in honoring its debts. It expects others to do the same."

Lenin gazed at him for several seconds. "Those were tsarist debts," he said at last.

"But if you claim to be the legitimate heirs to the tsarist government, comrade, then you have legitimately inherited its debts as well."

"And not their assets? Is there not a vast hoard secreted in a London bank, sent there by the tsars, just so it could never fall into the hands of the Russian people, to whom it rightfully belongs?"

"I've no information on that," George said.

"But it is true. I will be frank with you, Mr. Hayman. We cannot pay our debts at this moment. You have traveled through Russia this last week. You have seen. There is nothing. We are fighting for our survival." He held up his finger again. "Do not mistake me. We shall win our fight, with or without assistance. But Russia must come first. Anyway," he smiled, "I cannot believe your people take money quite so seriously."

"I'm afraid they do."

"Yet there must be other reasons as well."

"I guess there are."

"But not ones you are prepared to discuss."

"I'd rather not."

"Then shall I tell you what they are? Is not the main one that the American government will not deal with a government it has dismissed as a pack of murderers?"

"Well . . ."

"That is a hypocritical and unhistoric point of view. Your English ancestors once chopped off the head of their king. And tell me truly, Mr. Hayman, would the first Americans not have done the same to George III, had he had the misfortune to be in New York in 1780?"

"Maybe. We wouldn't have touched his wife and children, though."

"That is specious. I can tell you that Alexandra Romanova was a far more dangerous enemy of the Russian people than her husband ever was. But I will not quarrel with a guest. I am grateful to you for coming, to see and listen, and help. You must remember to tell your president, however, that just as the English eventually had to deal with the Jacobins, so will your people eventually have to deal with ours. The sooner it is done, the better, because..." He paused, and allowed his gaze to wander about the room. "I shall not always be here."

He smiled at his wife, who came towards him, Ilona at her side. "And now I must retire. My wife thinks I stay up too late." He kissed Ilona's hands. "You have made Russia look that much brighter, Mrs. Hayman. You must visit us again. Mr. Hayman." He shook hands. "Michael Nikolaievich knows my thoughts on most matters. I will leave it to him to discuss details with you. Good night."

All the guests stood, respectfully, as he went around the room to shake hands, moving slowly and deliberately, exchanging a word or a quip with everyone. Then he was gone, and Michael sat beside George.

"He *is* grateful, believe me, George," Michael said. "He is well aware that we need help, that those"—he looked around the room much as his leader had done—"who would oppose the idea are narrow-minded theorists. Starting tomorrow, we shall get down to the details of the matter. Would you like that?"

"That's why I'm here," George said. "And I wouldn't say you have time to waste."

"Things are improving," Michael said. "There is evidence that this will be a normal summer, with enough rainfall to ensure a crop. Oh, don't misunderstand me, things will remain difficult for a year or two; but Comrade Lenin's decision to halt the march towards total collectivization of farming as well as industry will make a difference. It already has made a difference, and that difference will be felt this year." He smiled. "It grieves me, as a good Marxist, to have to say it, but men are such poor creatures that they will always work harder when they are told there is some profit in it for them rather than merely for the prosperity of the entire state, the entire people. Now, with help from your relief administration as well—"

"I was thinking," George said, "that you might not have much time before a change of leadership."

Michael glanced at him and took another sip of brandy. "You have observed?"

"That he is ill? Yes."

"He has had a stroke," Michael said. "A very minor one, to be sure. It has impaired his powers only in the slightest degree. But he needs to rest. When one has had a stroke there is always the possibility of another. But how may Comrade Lenin rest, when there is so much to be done?"

"Who will replace him as leader?"

Michael shrugged. "Who knows?"

George frowned at him. "You mean he has not appointed a successor?"

"Comrade Lenin is not a king, George. Or a dictator. He is a great man who has chosen to lead his country. We are his friends and his supporters. But he cannot choose one of us to follow him. We must do that for ourselves."

"He must have a preference."

"As to that . . ." Michael gave a quick glance across the room to where Trotsky was in laughing conversation with Tattie. "Trotsky is the most brilliant, the best equipped mentally, to follow. But . . ." He grimaced.

"I'm interested."

"This is off the record, George."

"Okay."

"Our revolution has just begun. Even Comrade Lenin knows that. And he is disappointed, of course. We thought that it would have traveled further, have consumed all Europe—certainly Germany and Austria-Hungary. And that has not happened. So you can imagine there is a continuing debate as to the course we must pursue in the coming years."

"I can see that."

"Well, Comrade Trotsky, I suppose because he is a soldier, is for carrying on as we have begun. He is astonished that we should have pulled back from Europe, to concentrate on Russia alone. He is sure that had we pressed our objectives, we would have had that German revolution. He cannot conceive of a Soviet Russia in a capitalist Europe."

"So he'd be a difficult man to live with."

"Indeed. Do not misunderstand me. I know, as we all know, that Communism is the future salvation of the entire world. Even of America, George. But the question is, should it just be allowed to happen, in the course of inevitable events, as Comrade Bukharin suggests, or should it be undertaken by force, if necessary, with the prospect of more destruction and more bloodshed?"

"I see. And where does Comrade Lenin stand in this debate?"

"Comrade Lenin stands for Russia first. He refuses to contemplate any international advance in the revolution until Russia is once again strong, economically and militarily."

"Which makes sense to me. And Comrade Nej?"

"I agree with Comrade Lenin."

"Well, then . . ."

Michael flushed. "That would be quite impossible."

"Tell me why."

"I am a peasant."

"Oh, come now."

"It is true, my friend. I am a peasant and the son and grandson of peasants. Of serfs, in fact. I have never even been to a proper school."

"Common sense is more important for leadership than book learning, surely."

"One needs both. No, no. Never Michael Nej."

"Well, then, perhaps the power behind the throne, if you'll pardon the simile. There must be someone who thinks as you do."

"Oh, yes." Michael gazed at Stalin, drinking by himself.

"I wouldn't have thought *he* was leadership material."

"Do not underestimate him. He has a ruthless streak, and is a capable man. He organized several of the raids that kept the Party in funds, before the war. And led them himself. He is a bold and resourceful man, beneath that sleepy exterior. In fact, if I had a reservation . . ."

"Go on."

"Well, perhaps he is a shade too self-contained, too much his own man, to lead the Party. We will not be bullied."

"Yes. Well, we must hope your Comrade Lenin manages to hang on for a while yet. Michael, I meant to ask you, have you done anything about that girl?"

"What girl?"

"Catherine Lissitsina. Ilona said she mentioned her to you."

"Ah, the guide. Why does she interest you so much, George?"

"Because she's innocent, for God's sake."

"No other reason?"

George stared at him. "No," he said, "no other reason. I'm here with Ilona, remember?"

"Of course," Michael said. "I have been very busy. I had forgotten about this girl. But I will look into it, I promise you, since she means so much to you."

"Comrade Commissar." The guards came to attention.

Michael saluted. "Comrades. You have a prisoner here. Comrade Lissitsina?"

"We have a prisoner named Lissitsina, comrade." The jailer consulted his list. "A tsarist, undoubtedly."

"She has confessed to this?"

"She has confessed to nothing. She is very stubborn. But she was arrested with the man Borodin, and in the company of the Americans. She had spent a week in the company of the Americans."

"Comrade," Michael said patiently, "she was given that duty by the Party secretary, Comrade Stalin himself. That is not a crime."

The jailer exchanged glances with his inferiors. "Commissar Nej himself ordered her arrest, comrade."

"Of course he did. Commissar Nej is a policeman. Has *he* interrogated her?"

"Not yet, comrade."

Michael allowed himself a brief sigh of relief. "Then I will see her."

The jailer frowned. "You, Comrade Nej?"

"Me," Michael said. "And I am in a hurry."

"Of course, Comrade Nej." The jailer hurried in front of him, one of the guards falling in behind. They walked along a corridor, and down a flight of steps. In the glow of the electric bulbs, the freshly painted white walls and ceilings were brilliant. Ivan kept a clean prison, Michael thought. It was the first time he had entered the place. He preferred not to know the methods by which the tsarists and other subversives were kept in check. He had spent enough of his life in tsarist jails, and he did not suppose these were any different.

Then what was he doing here now? This girl, this Lissitsina, was a nonentity. And yet, she interested George. Could she be his mistress? Michael sometimes wondered if every woman whom George looked at twice would immediately become his mistress. Certainly Ilona Borodina had been happy to do so. And what of Judith Stein? She had fled Russia in the company of George Hayman. Had left him to go with George.

It occurred to him that he envied George Hayman. Well, of course he did. He envied him his confidence. He envied him his money and his place in the world. For people like George Hayman there was no need for revolution. They could take the world as they found it, reshape it to their own specifications, not by violence or by rhetoric, but just by being. And most of all, he envied him his relationship with the two most desirable women in the world, Ilona Borodina and Judith Stein. That he should have either the time or the inclination to look at any other woman was incredible.

They had reached another office and entered a world of women. Big, strong women. Women used to ruling by violence.

"We wish to see the woman Lissitsina," said the head jailer.

The woman behind the desk raised her eyebrows. "She is in number seventeen."

"Take me to her," Michael said.

The woman stared at him. Michael wondered if she ever emerged from this unholy mole hole of hers to discover what was going on in the world outside.

"This is Commissar Nej," the head jailer said.

The woman got up.

"Do you need me, comrade commissar?" asked the head jailer.

Michael shook his head. The men saluted, and withdrew. The woman was waiting just inside the next corridor. Michael followed her down another flight of steps. They were certainly beneath ground level by now, in a cold place, a place without hope. There were no windows in the corridor, just a succession of closed doors. He did not imagine there were any windows in the cells, either.

What would she be like, this girl who had so interested a man who had possession of Ilona and probably of Judith? And whatever she had once been like, what would she be like now, after several days in Ivan's cells?

The wardress was unlocking the door numbered 17. "She is stubborn," she remarked.

"So I understand."

The door was thrown inwards, and the woman stepped inside. Michael followed her.

The girl—she was hardly a woman—was in the far corner. She was naked, her legs drawn up against her body, her arms arranged so as to guard her face from the brilliant light of the bulb above her head. There were red weals on her back and her thighs. At the sound of the door opening she had lifted her head, and now she hastily ducked it down again, only to lift it again as she sneezed.

"What have you done to her, so far?" Michael asked, keeping his voice soft and calm. He had once lain in a cell just like this, naked, just like this, with whip marks on his back and legs. But Roditchev had done more than just whip *him*.

"We have caned her," the wardress said. "And we have kept her without sleep. And we have used cold water. But she is stubborn. She says not a word."

Michael walked across the room and stood above her. She was not in the least like either Ilona or Judith. Her hair was black like Judith's, but it was cut short. And her figure was short and slight, though voluptuous enough, with strong legs and wide thighs. But her face was not in the least elegant, as she raised her head again, looked at him as a cat might look at the man who has just kicked her, and sneezed once more.

"You will release her into my custody," Michael said.

"Comrade commissar?"

"I will sign the necessary authority."

"Yes, comrade commissar," the wardress said, doubtfully.

The girl sneezed again. But her head remained up, watching him, and listening, too.

"You will come with me," Michael said. "You have caught a cold, Catherine Lissitsina. You will come to me, and we will put you to bed, eh, and make you well again." He snapped his fingers. "Bring her clothes."

"Yes, comrade commissar." The wardress hurried from the room.

Michael stooped, the better to look into the girl's black eyes. Tartar eyes. Eyes that could hate. But eyes that could also love. Had they ever looked on George Hayman with love?

"You will come with me, Catherine Lissitsina," he said again. "And together we will walk out into the sun."

Chapter 4

MRS. KILLETT OPENED THE DOOR. "PRINCE BORODIN. MR. HAY-MAN."

"George!" Peter strode into the room, arms held wide. "My God, but it's good to see you. I'm amazed they let you out, really I am. I wrote that in my letters, remember. If only you'd cabled which ship you were catching, we'd have been there to meet you."

George gazed at his brother-in-law for some seconds. Clearly a rehearsed entrance, he thought, as they shook hands. "Sit down."

"Children all well? They were when last I saw them," Peter said.

"They appeared to be."

"And Judith?"

"I haven't really had a chance to speak with her," George said. "But she looked all right. Have you seen much of her while we've been away?"

"Some," Peter said. "But I've been very busy. There's a

great deal of news coming out of Russia. Well, you know that. You were there."

"Yes," George agreed. "I was there. With Ilona. Your sister."

Peter nodded. "I was terribly worried," he said. "But of course I need not have been. They would never dare lay a finger on Mr. and Mrs. George Hayman."

"You think so," George said grimly.

"Well . . . they didn't, did they?"

"We were arrested on March 17," George said, speaking very slowly and distinctly. "I was hit over the head with a night stick. And Ilona was forced to submit to a strip search."

"My God," Peter said, leaning back in his chair. "I heard nothing of this."

"I'm wondering if you hear anything of the truth of what goes on inside Russia. Or only what you want to hear."

Another quick frown, then Peter smiled. "I can understand that you are angry. My God, what an experience! Then all that talk—about your having secured the necessary permission for Hoover's people to ship in food and machinery for an unofficial exchange of diplomatic representation—was just a ruse to get you out."

"It was not," George said.

"But . . . now you *know* what these people are like. Now that you have had the wool pulled away from in front of your eyes, how can you possibly consider helping them?" He leaned forward. "The Russian government, George, is composed of a band of thugs and murderers. I have told you that often enough. Well, now you have seen with your own eyes. Men like Michael and Ivan Nej—"

"It was Ivan Nej who got us released from prison," George pointed out.

"Ivan? He is virtually chief of police in Moscow. You mean it was he who had you arrested in the first place."

George shook his head. "That was the work of some over-zealous underling, who has since been exiled to Irkutsk. We were arrested because of our meeting with Viktor. A meeting planned by you, Peter, and without my knowledge. I resent that. I resent that very deeply. The moment Ivan Nej learned of what had happened, he had us released."

"You *believe* that?"

"It happened. And no twisted imagination can make it any different. Ilona and I were arrested at about six o'clock in the evening. At three o'clock the next morning Ivan appeared and released us. He had been to see Ilona earlier. Okay, so he assumed we had to be guilty. I can't blame him. He's got no love for me, and there we were having a secret meeting with an apparently well-known tsarist agent. But as soon as Ilona told him we knew nothing about it, he checked out our story and then released us. Those are facts, Peter."

Peter leaned back. "I think they have made a fool of you, George."

"Really? Well, I was sure made a fool of, I'll agree with that. But I have my own ideas as to who was responsible. Peter, I don't consider that you have the necessary objectivity to remain as head of this paper's Russian section. I think you're too bound up in your own private vendetta against the Russian leaders. I'm going to ask Judith to take over your desk."

Peter's frown slowly gathered. "You are dismissing me?"

"I am moving you to another department. Don't worry, you'll get the same salary."

Peter thrust back his chair and got up. "I am no office boy to be kicked from desk to desk. If I am not to be head of the Russian section, I quit."

"That's up to you. You'll collect three months' severance pay. And you can take it from me that Ilona feels the same as I do."

Peter stared at him for some seconds. "If only I could make you understand," he said, "what those people are really like."

"If only I could make you understand," George said, "just what sort of damage your silly spy games can cause. Okay, so Ilona and I can survive. As you said, nobody's really going to harm either of us. But thanks to you our guide, a perfectly decent girl—who is, incidentally, a dedicated Communist— has apparently had to be sent to a psychiatric hospital to recover, and your own cousin is on the run, a wanted man. What do you think is going to happen to him when they catch up with him?"

"They told you that? You accepted it?"

"It happened."

"And on the strength of that you again abandoned Tattie?"

"Don't be absurd. Ilona suggested to Tattie that she might wish to come over here, and Tattie laughed. Why should she leave? She has everything going for her, in Moscow. Believe me, Peter, you have it all wrong about the Soviets. Okay, they are revolutionaries, and in revolutions people get hurt. But now they are doing their damndest to get Russia back on its feet, and I think they should be given a chance."

"A chance." Peter placed his hands on the desk. "As you say, I have my people inside Russia, and they manage to get most news out to me. Well, for your information, George Hayman, Viktor Borodin was shot in the courtyard of the Cheka Building in Moscow on the night of March 17, 1922. The very same night you were arrested. Now, who do you think ordered that? Some underling? Or the man my sister's married to? One of those you say should be given a chance?"

George Hayman strode through the corridors of the Hayman Building, while people hastily got out of his way. It was not a very usual sight to see Mr. Hayman in a bad mood, but the rumor had it that he had entered the building this morning, for the first time in three months, in a towering rage, which had not abated at all in the couple of hours he had been at his desk.

George saw the apprehensive expressions people were giving him. Well, he thought, they were damned right. Had Viktor been shot? Had he really been made a fool of, by Ivan Nej? And by Michael? Or were there countercurrents running deep and fast beneath the surface of Russian politics? Of course there were, and he had to decide that Lenin and Michael, at least, were attempting to be honest men.

But he was not pleased. Going to Europe at all had been disillusioning. Apart from what had happened in Russia, he had not liked what he had seen, what he had heard, and what he had calculated. He had never had any doubt that the war was probably the greatest catastrophe the world had known since the Flood, but he had hoped for more positive signs that the leaders of Western Europe, and that meant the intellectuals and the labor leaders as well as the politicians, would have decided that now was the time to make a break with the past and look forward to a future where survival and prosperity would be guaranteed by cooperation and understanding. Instead they seemed to have slipped back into the same bitter squabbles that had been so alarming in the years before 1914.

He had not been able to believe in Anastasia Romanova.

And he had not been able to solve his marital problem, whatever it was. No doubt, he thought bitterly, no marriage has ever been held together by a trip, no matter how many couples have attempted to find that way out. But in his case things had got worse. The tragic thing was that Ilona still loved him; he was sure of that, just as he was sure that he still loved her. He did not suppose she had ever been unfaithful to him since their marrige, any more than he had ever been unfaithful to her. Certainly nothing physical had happened, in Russia. But something else had. They had sat together and drunk together and talked together and made love together, and in fact they had shared nothing. Their thoughts never occupied the same plane. Where everything he had seen or heard during the past few months, just as everything he had seen or heard during the war, had made him more anxious, more pessimistic about the immediate future of civilized mankind, and most of all about Western Europe and North America, Ilona seemed to be more and more determined to shed *her* normal seriousness in favor of laughter and drink and amusement. He would have guessed she was consciously aping her sister, had she not shown all the signs before ever being reunited with Tattie. But undoubtedly Tattie had a lot to do with it. Probably she had expected to see in Tattie a bedraggled waif, miserably tied to a man she hated, the epitome of all the misery which had swept over Russia. And instead they had found a glowing, exuberant, utterly confident woman who was living the dream she had always cherished.

Tattie was a survivor, in the most triumphant sense. So where did that leave George and Ilona Hayman, who also appeared to have everything they most wanted in life?

He reached the door he sought and hesitated, fingers already on the knob. Then he squared his shoulders, opened the door, and stepped inside.

Judith, as usual, was surrounded by papers and books and pens and half-completed paragraphs. Her secretary, a small, dark, intense girl, was equally submerged beneath an ocean of paper and ideas. They both stared at their employer as if seeing a ghost.

"May I have a word?"

"Of course, Mr. Hayman. Lucy, would you leave us?"

The girl scrambled to her feet, gave George a hasty nod that was half a salute, and scurried from the room. George closed the door behind him.

"I didn't have a chance to say thank you, last night," he said.

"It was my pleasure," Judith said. "They really are wonderful children. If only you'd let us know when you were coming back, we'd—"

"Forget it. We weren't in the mood for celebratory parties, last night." He sat in the chair just vacated by Lucy. "What are you doing now?"

"It's an analysis of the various political speeches made by Lenin over the past year. I thought it might be the basis for an article."

"Sounds interesting."

"Not half as interesting as some of the stuff you're going to give me, I hope. I was thinking of something like, say, Moscow Diary. Or is that corny?"

"I don't see why it should be. Except that I didn't keep one, and I only spent three weeks of the entire trip in Russia."

"Well, then, European Diary. And it doesn't have to be real. If you'd let me have your impressions, I'll work something out."

He smiled. "You're becoming quite a novelist in your spare time. Well, it's a good idea. But you can hand it on to someone else. I have a job for you."

"Yes?"

"I want you to take over the Russian section from Peter." She frowned. "But . . . he won't like giving that up."

"He's quit."

"Peter?"

"For the reason you thought he wouldn't want to. He's too highly involved in Russian affairs to be the objective editor this newspaper requires. Did you know that?"

"Well . . ."

"Did you know he was maintaining some sort of espionage system inside Russia?"

"I knew he had some pretty unusual sources of information."

"You can say that again. And the Bolsheviks know all about it. So he and I had some words... Ilona didn't mention anything of what happened to us?"

Judith shook her head.

"Hm. Well, we'll talk about it later. But I want you up there right away." He stood up and smiled again. "You don't look very pleased. It'll mean an increase in salary."

"George... are you sure?"

"Of course I'm sure. You have the talent, the background... You're very much more suited to the job than Peter ever was. And despite all that's happened, you're objective."

"Maybe because Russia doesn't mean all that much to me anymore. George, may I think about it?"

"I don't think that's necessary. I have no doubt you are going to be a success. Move upstairs today, will you? We'll be able to see more of each other."

Her head rose to stare at him. Now, why did you say that, George Hayman? he wondered. Because that trip to Europe solved nothing at all?

Rabbi Yanowski had been born in Brest-Litovsk and had spent his early years there. He had not emigrated to America until the great pogrom of 1906, which had followed the failed revolution of 1905, and he had departed not because he was a revolutionary or a socialist, but simply because he was a Jew. Because he was more Polish than Russian, and because he did not approve of Bolshevism or Communism in any guise, and because he clearly knew a great deal about her own background, Judith Stein had felt uneasy with him when they first met. She had, indeed, considered discovering another synagogue at which to pursue her new interest in her religion.

She had soon changed her mind. Menachem Yanowski had the gift of understanding. True, he could become angry. There were certain aspects of life which made him very angry indeed. But he could also listen, and he could soothe. And since Judith desperately needed someone to talk to, someone who might understand without becoming involved, they had soon become fast friends. Without Rabbi Yanowski, Judith sometimes thought she would have gone mad long ago.

It all had to do, she supposed, with loneliness. Her mother

and father had been executed by the Bolsheviks for briefly harboring Prince Peter Borodin. Her brother was presumably still somewhere in Russia; but Joseph had embraced the very principles of his parents' murderers; she did not suppose they would have much in common even if they managed to meet again. It was quite impossible for her to talk intimately with her sister; even if they had had anything at all in common, Rachel was married to the man who had first wished to marry *her*, and they were both too aware of that fact. Ilona was too remote. Peter, having realized he had married the wrong Stein, was thinking only of making amends in the most masculine manner. And George, the rock on whom she had built so much of her hopes for the future, was now moving in the same direction—she had seen enough of life to know what a man meant when he looked at her in that fashion—even if she could not possibly understand why he should want to, with Ilona waiting at home.

All of which contributed to hardening her decision. It was a decision she had taken just before Christmas, and had confided only to Rabbi Yanowski. Thus it was to him that she now turned to bolster any weakening of her resolve.

"It's no use my just telling him I'm not taking the job," she explained. "George is a very forceful man. When I tell him, I have to tell him what I am doing instead, where I am going, and what's more, I have to be actually doing it." She gave a guilty smile. "I'd be happier to leave a letter for him and actually be on the boat."

"That would be the coward's way out," Rabbi Yanowski said. "And you have never been a coward, Judith."

"Haven't I? You don't know me as well as you think."

"I know you better than you know yourself. Cowardice has nothing to do with being afraid. Any man, or any woman, who has never been afraid has never lived. Cowardice is when you let your fear get the better of you."

"You're not going to bog me down in semantics, Menachem," she said. "I want you to find me a boat leaving this weekend. It doesn't have to be going directly to Palestine. Just Europe."

Rabbi Yanowski got up and took a turn up and down the floor, hands clasped behind his back. "Are you sure you want to go?"

"For heaven's sake—"

"Oh, indeed, I am thinking of heaven, as well as one or two other things. I would like you to listen to me for a moment. There are practical difficulties in getting you to Palestine at all. Certainly if you have to go by way of some other country. You are not a Russian anymore, Judith, and you are not yet an American. You have no passport."

"I got here without a passport."

"Because Mr. Hayman was with you, and he is a powerful man with powerful friends. Getting out again may not be so simple. But far more important than that, *why* do you want to go to Palestine?"

"Because . . . because that's where all Jews should be. Don't you see, if we're going to build ourselves back into a nation—"

"We are going to need all the help we can get. Now, what are you going to do, in Palestine?"

"Work."

"At what? Building roads, starting farms, hoeing fields? I suppose there will be a newspaper, soon enough."

"I am not going to Palestine to look for anything easy, Menachem. I am going to play my part in creating a Zionist state."

"And do you suppose that Zionist state is going to be helped forward in the slightest fashion by your presence there, working in a field? Or hindered in the slightest if you are not working in that field?"

She stared at him. "Don't you *want* a Zionist state? If everyone thought like that, no one would go."

"There will be a Zionist state, Judith. But it will come about quicker if everyone does his or her *best* to make it happen. And that means putting one's talents to their best use. Now, in Palestine we need mechanics and artisans and farmers and engineers. We need laborers, too—that is, men and women who have no other talents. And we need soldiers, to be sure, because the Arabs will very soon react to our presence. All these things we need in Palestine. Have you any of those talents?"

"I can learn. Anyway, you just said there is room for those without talent."

"But you *have* talent, Judith. More than that, you have

experience, and you have importance, in fields no one else knows anything about. I cannot believe you were put on earth to till a field. You saw Rasputin die. You have rubbed shoulders with the highest in Russia, whether they be tsars or Bolshevik leaders. Do you know that there are still five million Jews in Russia?"

"I know that."

"Don't you suppose they are going to need help, and organization, if we are ever going to get *them* to Palestine?"

"If the Bolsheviks will let you. They've abolished God. Hadn't you heard?"

"So did the Jacobins in France, a hundred and thirty years ago, not very successfully. Judith, listen to me. You are being given a chance to be very important indeed in our hopes for the future. You have the support and the sympathy of America's leading newspaper publisher. You are being given a job that will keep you in touch with Russia, which you can use to further our cause and the cause of Russian Jews. From your position as editor of the Russian desk you will be able to raise funds, influence opinions, put across our point of view. To my mind that is far more important than digging a field outside Jerusalem."

Judith gazed at him, crossed and uncrossed her legs, suddenly felt like having a cigarette—another bad habit she had acquired since coming to New York.

"And when this powerful, sympathetic newspaper magnate invites me to his bed?"

Yanowski frowned. "Is that likely?"

"It's looking that way. It's been looking that way for a long time. But I think we're getting to a critical stage."

Yanowski continued to stare at her for some seconds. Then he said, "Have you encouraged him?"

"Of course I haven't. Well . . ." Judith could feel her cheeks burning. "We have known each other a long time. We have . . . we've adventured together."

"And you like him."

"Of course I like him." She found herself nearly shouting, and made herself speak quietly. "I think he is the first man I have ever really known."

"Are you in love with him?"

She raised her head. "How can I be? He's married to my oldest friend."

"That is not an answer."

"For God's sake, what are you trying to make me say?"

"Judith, I am trying to make you come to a decision. As you say, this man is the husband of your close friend, and he is your employer. Do you suppose his wife could remain your friend and that you could continue working for him, if you became his mistress?"

"Are you telling me how to live my life?" Judith demanded, suddenly angry, because of course he was right, in every way.

Rabbi Yanowski shook his head. "No, Judith, I don't think anyone could tell you how to live your life. I am only asking you to think of everything you have to offer to a far greater cause than that of casual love. Think, Judith. For God's sake, think."

"Don't you like the color?" Rachel Borodin paraded before her sister, swirling her hips to send the organdy skirt flaring, a kaleidoscope of gold and red. The brilliant colors did no more than match the splendor of the room itself, the heavy cloth-of-gold draperies over the windows, the brass ornaments that covered the little tables, the thick carpets on the floor. The entire apartment was furnished in this same lavish and incredibly expensive style. Presumably, Judith thought, they had run themselves into debt.

"It's very bright," Judith said. "Pretty, but bright. Don't you think the hem is a bit high?"

"Skirts are getting shorter," Rachel pointed out. "Up and up and up. One must keep abreast of the times." She giggled. "Even if it means showing your knees. Now you . . . those suits are positively dowdy."

"Well, I have no great desire to be a clothes horse," Judith said. "Isn't that Ruth crying?"

"Ruth is always crying," Rachel explained. "Anyway, Miriam is there to look after her. Now listen—" She sat beside Judith on the settee. "You simply must get yourself a new dress for the party."

"Are you still having the party?"

Rachel's eyes became enormous. "Why shouldn't we?"

"Well . . ."

"You mean because Peter is changing positions? What difference does that make?"

"Well, I had thought that until he does get another position—"

"For heaven's sake, Judith. He is Prince Peter Borodin of Starogan. You're worrying about money again. Just as Poppa always used to worry about money. Judith, things are different. Princes don't worry about money."

"Perhaps," Judith said. "I suppose, because I've never had any—"

"It's the most marvelous feeling in the world," Rachel said, getting up and doing another pirouette. "To be a princess. Never to have to worry about money, about anything. Here he is." She faced the door. "Peter, darling, Judith's here. *Worrying*."

Peter Borodin was, as usual, faultlessly dressed in a pale gray suit with matching socks and tie, and his pearl tiepin. His face was composed, but cold; he regarded his wife as if she were a favorite cat that had soiled the living-room floor. "Really, Rachel, my love, whatever is that you're wearing?"

"It's my new dress," Rachel said, doing another spin.

"Your *new* dress?"

"From Lord and Taylor. I had four sent up, but this is my favorite."

"*Four*? Isn't that Ruth crying?"

"Ruth is always crying," Rachel explained. "But Miriam is there to see to her."

"I have just given Miriam notice," Peter said. "And she has left the house."

Rachel came to a halt before her husband. "You have done *what*?"

"I have given Miriam notice," Peter said again, speaking slowly and carefully. "Simply because I don't have the money to pay her. Nor do I have the money to pay for four dresses from Lord and Taylor. So I'd be obliged if you'd go and see to Ruth, and then take off that outlandish garment. No," he said. "On second thought, take off the dress first, just in case you damage it."

Rachel stared at him. "You wouldn't," she said. "You

wouldn't fire Miriam." She started to cry. "You wouldn't make me send these dresses back!"

"I have and I can and I will." Peter seized her shoulders and thrust her through the door. "Go and see to Ruth." He kicked the door shut behind himself.

"That was cruel," Judith said, getting up. "In front of me, it was cruel."

"It was cruel for me," he said, "if the rumors are to be believed."

"That I have been offered the Russian desk?"

"That you have accepted it. I had not expected to be stabbed in the back by you, Judith."

"It's a job that has to be done," she said. "But I *am* concerned about you."

"Don't worry about me."

"And Rachel's dresses? Rachel's parties? Rachel's servants?"

"Rachel is going to have to learn that there are more important things in life than parties and dresses and servants."

"And food?"

"We shan't starve."

"Tell me why not."

He glanced at her, went to the liquor cabinet, and poured himself three fingers of straight whiskey. "Editing the Russian section was never full-time work for me. Oh, it was well paid, and I shall miss the money. But it was not a matter of life and death. My real business in life is far more important."

"Running a tsarist counterrevolutionary society."

"I wouldn't put it quite that way. I am dedicating my life to the eventual downfall of Bolshevism, the eventual restoration of the tsars to the throne of Russia. And there are thousands, even tens of thousands, of people who agree with me and are prepared to work with me."

"And are they going to support you?"

Peter flushed, and sipped his drink. "They are going to support the cause. As the mainspring of that cause, I am entitled to pay myself a salary. Would you like a drink?"

She shook her head.

Peter took her hand and guided her back to the settee, where he sat beside her. "But I would be lying if I pretended I am not upset at losing my job, more for the job itself than the money. Yet I was pretending just now when I appeared to be angry with you, because I can think of no one I would rather have as editor of the Russian section than you. It is the information that I need, Judith. Without the international correspondents that Hayman Newspapers provide, I am working in the dark. But with you there—"

"Why should I help you?"

"Because we are working for the same thing, because I am your brother-in-law, because I saved you from execution once, and because I love you." His hand slid over hers and up her arm to squeeze her forearm and continue further, to her elbow. "Judith, you know that Rachel and I really have nothing in common. Judith, my dearest, dearest darling, I married her because I thought you were dead. You know that. Judith—"

"Peter, *please*," she said, pulling away.

He shrugged. "Be that way, be foolishly feminine. One day you will know how much I love you. One day. My God, I have been trying to tell you so for fifteen years. Do you imagine I will wait forever?"

"As you have just reminded me, you are married to my sister," Judith said, getting up. "I really must be going."

"All right," he said. "Be offended. But at least admit that there are more important things in life than love and hate. There are great things happening in Russia. Even George admits that. Lenin is dying. Who will succeed him, eh? Will anyone, with his power? Will it be Trotsky? That should interest you. He is a Jew."

She frowned at him, her hand on the door. "Trotsky? I didn't know that."

"Well, he is. What would you make of that, eh? Russia ruled by a Jew."

"I would find that very interesting," Judith said thoughtfully.

"I'm sure. Will you help me? Will you bring me what news you can, about Russia? Will you come to see me, Judith?"

Judith considered. But Menachem Yanowski had given her her orders. A Russia ruled by a Jew. Could any Zionist ask for anything better than that?

Was there any chance, however, that Peter Borodin could actually support a Bolshevik, whether Trotsky or anyone else? He had vowed to wipe them all out of government. Judith had little reason to doubt that Peter had only mentioned Trotsky as a lure.

She had another reason for meeting with Peter and his émigrés, though. She, more than any of them, knew just how dangerous clandestine politics could be. She cared for Peter, and for her sister, and she would continue to keep an eye on them.

"Yes," she said. "I will come to see you, Peter. But be nice to Rachel. For God's sake be nice to Rachel."

Chapter 5

"GREAT PARTY, GEORGE. GREAT PARTY." WEBSTER MACLAIN peered across the smoke-filled room, past the cocktail dresses and the bright ties, the clinking glasses and the circulating waiters. The room was enormous, occupying the entire width of the Fifth Avenue apartment. George maintained a New York apartment not only for his own use when work required that he spend the night in the city, but because it was so much more convenient for Ilona's parties, which she enjoyed throwing, and which New York society enjoyed attending; there was no more glamorous hostess in the city than the beautiful Russian princess so romantically married to the nation's favorite newspaper publisher. "First I've been to since the funeral."

"For us too," George said. "Either funeral."

"Yes," Maclain said. "He was a great man."

"The president? Or Dad?"

"I was thinking of your dad, actually. Still, he had a good life, didn't he? And he must have died happy, knowing the House of Hayman is in such good hands. Life must go on, right, old man?"

"I suppose it must," George said. "And it is Ilona's birthday."

"Well, well. I won't ask how old the little lady is today. I'll just go across and give her a big kiss when the crowd thins a little. You're a lucky man, George. A lucky man. I've never known a luckier."

"I'll drink to that," George said without conviction. He watched Judith talking to the new president. She was taller than Calvin Coolidge. But then, he supposed, almost everyone was taller than Coolidge, in every way. However, he was not going to start brooding on politics tonight. He had too much else to brood on. Like Judith, wearing an elegant dark-green cocktail dress, and even a necklace—she did not usually dress very well. For over a year now they had worked closely together; she was required, as Russian editor, to bring the news from Moscow to his desk every morning and amplify any points that required it. Together they had discussed the reports of Lenin's repeated strokes, of the power struggles that were going on behind the scene, of the slow economic recovery of Russia, and of its growing rapprochment with the new German republic—even though that republic seemed to be collapsing into a wastebasket of worthless marks.

And in all that time he had never touched her, even though she might well have been expecting a touch and bracing herself to receive it. Perhaps that was the point, more than his concern over the sudden collapse of his father's health, which had so preoccupied him over the past year. He did not know whether Judith was bracing herself or not. Whether she *had* to brace herself. He was her benefactor. How could she possibly say no? But what sort of a man did that make him, to take advantage of a woman in a difficult position?

And never a thought of Ilona's place in this? Ilona, the most beautiful woman of all the beautiful women in this room tonight, Ilona, celebrating her thirty-eighth birthday as if it were her twenty-first. If only . . . but if only what? Theirs was a perfect marriage, in the estimation of everyone in the room. Even Judith must think so, as she must think this was the reason that he never allowed his obvious feeling for her to get beyond a feeling. And was it not a perfect marriage? He was handsome, she was lovely. He had money, she had background. They possessed three handsome and brilliant children, a magnificent home, three cars, seven dogs, and four cats, as well as a retinue of servants. Their parties were the most popular on Long Island.

And they even, lest anyone penetrate that far in their appraisal, still enjoyed making love together. There could be no marriage in the entire United States of America as blessed. And yet... he thought of Judith. Then why not do it, and be done with it?

Because Ilona was blameless? Of course she was. And yet... she too had her reflective moments, moments when he would catch her staring into space, her mind obviously miles away. Six thousand miles? There was no way of knowing, and there was no way of getting her to discuss those secret areas of her mind just as she would not dream of entering into any discussion of his deepest thoughts. He had never been sure whether or not she felt he had been too hard on Peter. From all accounts, Peter was finding the going tough, and when he had encountered Rachel on the street the other day, she had cut him dead. But neither he nor Peter was the sort to shake hands and apologize. And Ilona had been just as angry with Peter on the European trip, especially after she had been told of Viktor's death.

But oh, to know what went on behind those huge blue eyes.

Maclain had been following the direction of his gaze, even if he had misunderstood the object. "How do you think Calvin is shaping up?"

"Very well," George said. "It's a hell of a business, being pitchforked into the presidency."

"And at such a time," Maclain agreed. "Between you and me, George, old Warren died at just the right moment for him, or we might even have had an impeachment. The papers were really after him. Not that I include yours, of course. You handled that Teapot Dome mess with proper restraint. But some of these rags—"

"Not birthday-party talk, Webster," George said. "Warren Harding is dead, and there's an end to it. As you say, Calvin is doing a fine job. Now come and circulate. Who'd you like to meet?"

"Someone said that Russian character is here."

"Petrov? Yes, that's him over there."

"Is it true the wheat dealing is just a cover, and that he's

really representing the Soviet Government as some sort of
unofficial ambassador?"

"That's hardly cocktail-party talk either," George pointed
out.

"But didn't he come over at your invitation?"

George winked at him. "In a manner of speaking. But come
on over and I'll introduce you. He speaks perfect English."

"How does it feel to be thirty-eight?" Judith asked. For this
brief moment they were alone in the bedroom.

Ilona carefully etched the line of her eyebrow, lips pursed,
pencil poised between thumb and forefinger. "Not a lot different than being thirty-seven. Although I suppose I'm living
on borrowed time."

"Aren't we all!" Judith touched up her lipstick.

Ilona glanced at her. "You've a year or two to go yet."

"That's not a lot. Not when you're a bachelor girl."

"Judith." Ilona took her hands. "Why *don't* you get married?"

Judith shrugged. "Maybe I'm too busy."

"Or maybe you've just not found the right man," Ilona said.

"Or maybe he's already married," Judith said, and flushed;
one glass too many of champagne.

"Yes," Ilona said thoughtfully. "It's funny how things turn
out." It was her turn to flush. "I don't mean comical, I mean
odd. And sad. How is he, by the way?"

"What?" Judith's head jerked.

"Well, I haven't seen him since he left the paper. I've
invited them round several times, but they won't come. I invited them to come tonight, and Peter refused. I suppose he's
mad at George. I suppose that's inevitable. And I know George
was mad at him. But you see them, don't you? I mean, you
and Rachel haven't quarreled?"

Judith was busy getting her breathing under control; but
why hadn't she immediately known Ilona was referring to
Peter? "I see them about once a week. They're managing. Not
as the Prince of Starogan should, perhaps, but they're managing. He's secretary of this émigré organization."

"I know that. It all seems so futile." Ilona sighed and got
up. "Give him my love, anyway, and tell him if either he or

Rachel, or both, feel like dropping by here for a chat, I'd be happy to see them."

"I'll do that," Judith agreed, and waited, because she suspected Ilona wasn't finished. A confidence from *Ilona*?

"It gets so lonely out on Long Island," Ilona remarked, picking up her handbag.

"Lonely? You?"

Ilona gave her a quick glance. "Why not me?"

"I'd have thought, running that place—"

"Oh, I have plenty to do. But it *all* seems so futile. A competent housekeeper would be better at it than I am. You know, when the children were smaller, it didn't matter so much. They were there to be looked after. But now that George and Felicity are away at school . . . As for Johnnie . . . I worry so about him. All this bad liquor these children are trying to get hold of, all the hoodlums that are mixed up in that business . . ."

"Johnnie doesn't drink," Judith said, far too definitely. That damned champagne again.

"I wish I could be sure. He always seems so far away, so preoccupied. And if he doesn't drink, where does he *go* in the evenings? If he has a girl, a decent girl, he'd tell us. But nobody knows." She gave a half-smile. "I guess I'm not a very good mother. Every time I look at him I see . . . well, I see his father, I suppose. And I think George does too. We've neither of us ever been very successful at maintaining discipline. But I didn't bring you in here to moan."

"I think you need a job," Judith said.

Ilona stared at her.

"I don't mean for the money, goose," Judith said. "I mean to have something to do, apart from running the house."

"Yes," Ilona said. "Something worthwhile. To tell you the truth, I've thought about it. I've thought about it ever since coming back from Russia. There was so much there that . . ." She gave another shrug. "George would never hear of it, anyway."

"What about Russia, Ilona? That was over a year ago, and you've said so little."

Ilona walked to the window and stared out at the December night. "Sentimentalism, I suppose. You know, going back at all, seeing Starogan again, what was left of it, seeing . . ." She gave a little shiver and hugged herself. "But it makes you think." She turned. "Don't misunderstand. They're existing in the most miserable of conditions, ruled by a set of thugs. When I remember that cell, and that woman . . . ugh! I mean, suppose it hadn't all been a mistake? Suppose I *had* been guilty of anti-Soviet activities? It was the most horrible experience of my life."

She flushed, because one really did not discuss horrible experiences with Judith Stein. "But at the same time, they're . . . well, they're aware of being alive, because tomorrow they may be dead. That's not as ghastly as it seems. I think it must be rather the way it was over here, a hundred years ago. You didn't have time to sit back and be bored, or wonder whether you should change your hairdresser, or which frock to wear for tea. Your biggest crisis wasn't whether to leave out Mrs. Smith from your next dinner party because she might possibly offend Mrs. Doe. You . . . oh, I don't even know what I'm saying myself. But even Tattie! Well, you should see her. She—she just bubbles."

"She never did lack energy," Judith said.

"Yes, but now it's a directed energy. It's . . ." She laughed. "Here I am, lecturing you, and you know more about Russia than I ever did. We must rejoin the party. And I've just the person for you to meet. Boris Petrov."

"I've heard of him."

"Of course you have. He's over here to buy wheat. It's all part of the setup George did for Hoover. But between you and me, he's having an occasional chat down in Washington too. And he's nice. You'll like him."

"Boris Petrov." Peter sat at his desk, wrote the name down in his usual neat, careful writing, and underlined it. "And?" He raised his head to smile at Judith Stein.

"He seemed very nice."

"Oh, yes? I'd like some physical details."

"Well, thirtyish, I suppose. Clean-shaven. Medium height, average build, good-looking in a heavy sort of way. Quite sophisticated."

"For a Bolshevik, you were going to say. Because he is a

Bolshevik. You'd do well to remember that. Did he know who you were?"

"I'm not sure. His eyes flickered when Ilona introduced us."

"Yes, well, I have an idea he may prove useful."

"He's here with the blessing of the State Department. As well as George."

Peter smiled. "I don't propose either to assassinate him or kidnap him, dear girl. I merely suggested that he might prove useful. Especially with that other news you've given me. Let's join the meeting."

He held open the study door for her, and she went into the living room, where about a dozen people were already gathered, drinking either coffee or vodka, talking among themselves, but rising deferentially as the Prince of Starogan came into the room. Several of these people laid claim to the title of count, and more than one had been a field officer in the tsarist army. Now they were pinch-faced, and their clothes were threadbare. Yet their faces glowed with the intense determination they shared, with the fierce loyalty that was their sole reason for living, the dedication to the restoration of the tsars and the autocracy under which they had all grown to adulthood and which they considered the only sensible form of government. Judith found it impossible not to admire them, however much she might disagree with their point of view. And of course it was their monthly contributions that kept Peter and Rachel looking as elegant as ever, and maintained this Manhattan apartment, not the cheapest form of housing in the world.

"Now, then," Peter said. "Let us have your reports. Colonel Stepinov?"

Judith found herself a seat at the back, next to John Hayman. She could understand Ilona's feelings of helplessness with this boy. At fifteen he was already virtually a man, with his mother's height and his father's breadth. His father's? No one knew for certain about that. But Judith had been in Ekaterinburg when Commissar Michael Nej had come there on his dreadful duty, to exterminate the tsar and his family. Ilona had been there then, and had promptly been released, with her family, to board the train going east to safety. Simple to say that she had become an American citizen and the Bolsheviks had no legal right to hold her; the Bolsheviks had never been overly concerned with legality. Equally simple to say that George Hayman had saved Michael's life, and he was simply repaying the debt. But *why* had George Hayman risked his life to save Michael's?

Having seen Michael and Ilona in conversation that day, just for a moment, Judith was sure she knew the answer, even if it was something she dared not discuss with this boy.

Besides, Michael's love for Ilona had rebounded on to her. Unable, from his odd sense of honor, to take advantage of his former mistress, the commissar had sought another. Judith had struck a bargain with him, and had thought herself to be doing the sensible thing: the lives and the comfort of her mother and father in exchange for her body. It had not seemed so terrible then, for a girl who had been sent to Siberia, mothered a child, been loved and then deserted by Peter Borodin, taken part in the murder of Rasputin. Perhaps, in those days, she had even thought of herself as a *femme fatale*.

The execution of her parents by Ivan Nej had ended that episode. Michael had known nothing of the murders; she was sure of that. But to remain in his bed for a day longer would have been impossible, and it had so happened that at that very moment George, himself sickened by the Bolshevik savagery as they enforced their rule, had decided it was time to cease being Russian correspondent for his father's paper, and go home.

What had she thought when she had fled with him, as the train chugged its way across Sweden to Göteberg, as the liner had ploughed its way across the Atlantic? She had expected him to make an advance, certainly. Would she have fallen into bed with him without hesitation? The war had left her emotions in too jumbled a state for reason, and besides, from the moment she had first met him, in Starogan in that so strange summer of 1914, she had thought him a remarkable man.

But nothing had happened, and in New York, so sane and sensible and *moral*, after the frenzy of war-torn Europe, adultery had not appeared so simple a matter, especially when it would involve Ilona, her oldest living friend. New York had made her think about something other than politics for the first time she could remember. New York had driven her to Menachem Yanowski, given her life purpose.

And would give it more. Dedication. To a people and a religion. What if she did turn her back on everything she held dear? As if that were truly relevant! In the year and more since that conversation with Rabbi Yanowski, not a thing had happened. She and George had worked well together. He still looked at her, from time to time, with that hunger. But he was, after all, Ilona's husband. There was absolutely nothing more to be said.

Except that, at this moment, she felt more than ever a part of the Borodin family. And thus more than ever responsible for their weaknesses and their ambitions.

"I had no idea that your mother doesn't know you attend your Uncle Peter's meetings," she remarked.

John, listening to the speaker in front of him, turned his head in surprise.

"I was talking to her the other night," Judith said. "I know she worries about you. Don't you think it might be a good idea to tell her?"

"She wouldn't understand," John said.

"Why not?"

"Well . . . she and Uncle Peter aren't exactly on the same side anymore, are they?"

"And you are on the same side as Peter?"

Once again he turned to look at her. "Uncle Peter stands for the overthrow of Bolshevism and the restoration of the tsars. He salutes the Grand Duke Michael as the true ruler of Russia. I must stand for that, since my father died for that cause. I must wish to fight for it, and if need be, to die for it, too."

Judith sighed. There was no answer to that point of view. Not for her to make.

"I still think it is something you should discuss with your mother," she ventured. "I do know that she's very unhappy, worrying about you."

"I will discuss it with Mother," Johnnie said. "In a few years."

"A few years?"

"Well, right now, she could forbid me to come here,

couldn't she? George certainly would. He's a rabid anti-tsarist."

"Do you hate him for that?"

"Hate him? Good Lord, no. He just doesn't understand. Nobody could understand who isn't Russian. But you understand, Judith. Despite everything, you do understand."

Despite everything, she thought. The arrogant simplicity of youth. He assumed his father was Sergei Roditchev. He knew a great deal about Russia, so he must know what Roditchev did to those unfortunate enough to fall into his clutches. And he certainly knew that she had been one of those unfortunates.

Fifteen years old, and his mind was consumed—or as Peter would have it, dedicated.

His attention was lost, for Peter was addressing the meeting.

"And now for some truly great news, my friends," he was saying. "I have just heard that Lenin has had a third stroke." He held up his hands as there was an outbreak of clapping. "He still lives. But just. He cannot speak, and he can hardly move. He is a cabbage. I tell you, my friends, that Soviet Russia lies paralyzed at this moment. And for many moments to come, in my opinion. Who will succeed the wretch? Trotsky? A Jew, my friends. Will the rest of that unholy crew support a Jew? Bukharin? He lacks decision. Nej? Perhaps he is the most likely candidate. But he is a peasant. I know Michael Nej, my friends. His father was my father's serf, and he was my valet." This brought a roar of laughter. "We have nothing to fear from Michael Nej."

Which by implication means that you have a great deal to fear from Lenin, Judith thought, as she slipped from her seat and through the door into the kitchen, where Rachel was buttering bread for sandwiches.

"Still at it?" Rachel asked.

"I'm afraid so. I'm going to sneak out and go home. Tomorrow is a long day."

Rachel sighed, and shrugged, and nodded. She looked tired. But then, she always looked tired.

"You know," Judith said, "Ilona would love for you to go and see her."

"Ilona? You've seen Ilona?"

"Well, of course I see Ilona. Quite a lot of her, in fact. I was at a party there the other night, just before Christmas, in fact."

"You were at Ilona's birthday party? Oh, Judith, was the president there?"

"As a matter of fact, yes."

"Oh, I wish I'd been there." Her huge eyes filled with tears. "We're not living. We're just existing."

"Living doesn't mean going to parties, Rachel."

"It doesn't mean existing on a dream either. The Bolsheviks aren't going to give up Russia, and Peter knows that. He's just deluding himself, while we starve."

"Do you?"

This time Rachel's shrug was defensive. "Well, we don't starve. But he won't let me spend any money. There's plenty of money, but he says we must keep every penny we can to finance the campaign against the Bolsheviks. Sometimes I think hate has turned his brain. Judith . . ."

"Why don't you go and see Ilona?" Judith suggested. "Talk it over with her. I'm sure it would help." She kissed Rachel on the cheek. "I have to rush."

She hurried down the stairs and out into the freezing January night, coat held close, nostrils dilating against the air which was filling her lungs. But she felt strangely free, too, as she always did when leaving Peter's. Rachel was right: the atmosphere *was* riddled with hatred.

But could any Borodin or any Stein ever be utterly normal again? They had seen the world torn apart, and none of them had any idea how to put it back together again. Only how to widen the tear.

She found a cruising taxi without difficulty, drove back to her apartment deeply preoccupied, paid the cabbie, stepped into the front lobby of her building as she took out her key, and stopped in alarm as she discovered a man standing there.

He raised his hat. "Miss Stein? Forgive this intrusion, but I should so like a word with you."

It was Boris Petrov.

"Well, you'd better come up," Judith said. Was she afraid of him? She had it always in mind that there were people in Russia who hated her, who might even attempt to strike at her in some way. But she did not really suppose that an envoy of the Soviet government, allowed into the United States by courtesy of the State Department, would ever consider attempting to harm her physically.

She supposed that, like everyone else in America, she found the mere fact that he was an openly confessed Bolshevik the most upsetting thing about him. Certainly he was an attractive man, somewhat heavily built, like so many Russians, but with a surprisingly lean, intelligent face and features that were strong without being aggressive. Add to that his distinct charm, the ready way in which, as she had observed at Ilona's party, his conversation disarmed those who approached him either to tease or to inquire, and he added up to a very capable man.

Or a very dangerous one?

"That would be very kind of you," he said.

"Yes, well . . . the elevator's over here."

They faced each other as the car slowly climbed the floors.

"It was a great pleasure, meeting you at Mrs. Hayman's reception," he said. "You are so famous that I had been looking forward to it. And may I say, Miss Stein, that you are everything I supposed you would be."

"Famous? Me?"

"But of course. The accomplice of Mordka Bogrov and Michael Nej in the assassination of Stolypin—"

"I was never their accomplice," Judith said.

"You were sent to Siberia."

"Unjustly." The elevator stopped, and she stepped out. lobby.

"But you will admit to having assisted in the execution of the monster Rasputin?"

Judith sighed. "I suppose I must. I was there."

"And then, you were Commissar Nej's military secretary during the campaigns against Denikin and Wrangel and Borodin?"

"Is that what they call it? Military secretary?" Judith took out her key, unlocked the door, waited for him to enter. "You've been listening to too much propaganda, comrade."

Petrov was looking about the room, walking to the window to admire the view. "New York is such an elegant city."

"Would you like a drink?" Judith asked. "I have vodka."

"I would rather have a scotch."

She poured two glasses of whisky and held one out. Their fingers touched.

"And now you are Russian-affairs editor of Hayman Newspapers," he said. "You have had a remarkable career, Miss Stein. Greatly to be envied."

"Do you know, I have never considered that?" She smiled. "I suppose when one is living something, the fact that other people might find it enviable, or even interesting, isn't very obvious." She sat down and crossed her legs. "Did Michael send you to me?"

"Michael? Oh, you mean Commissar Nej." Petrov gave a brief shake of his head and sat opposite her in a rocking chair. "No."

"Well, then?"

"We are both Russians, far from the Motherland. Could that not be a reason?"

It was her turn to shake her head. "No, Mr. Petrov."

"Because I represent the Soviet," he said, and sighed. "Well, then, I will tell you that your name was among those given to me by Commissar Ivan Nej. Names of people who might be useful to know. I knew your name before, of course, but I did not know you were living in New York." He sipped his drink. "It is also a pleasure to be able to speak with so beautiful and so famous a lady."

"But you would like me to help you."

"Well, I certainly need help. Secretary of State Hughes has made my task very difficult."

"By saying that the State Department would never deal with a government that repudiated its debts and expropriated property. He didn't say the half of it, Mr. Petrov. Do you know why I left Russia? Why I gave up my position as military secretary to Michael Nej, as the history books seem to have it?"

"No. But I would like to know."

"I left Russia, Mr. Petrov," Judith said, speaking very carefully, "because I could no longer stomach the murder and deceit, the sheer brutality, of the Bolsheviks. Do you really suppose I am going to help them towards recognition by the American government?"

She gazed at him, watched his cheeks pinken, waited for

him to get up and go. Instead he merely finished his drink.
"May I pour myself another?"

"Be my guest."

He moved easily, and confidently, poured his drink with
a seasoned hand, glanced at her and raised the bottle. She
shook her head.

"Revolution is a nasty business," he said, and came back
across the room to sit beside her. "There are those who consider
that Russia is still in a state of revolution, and therefore that
nasty methods are still acceptable. I do not happen to be one
of them."

"Come, come," she said. "You've just told me you were
sent here by Ivan Nej."

He shook his head. "I was briefed by Ivan Nej. That went
with the job, I'm afraid. I don't approve of his methods." He
met her gaze. "But you don't believe me."

"If, for example, Mr. Petrov, I didn't approve of the methods Mr. Hayman used to operate his newspapers, I wouldn't
be working for him."

He smiled. "We are not exactly in the same position, Miss
Stein. Mr. Hayman is not the American government. And in
America you are reasonably free to choose what you will be-
lieve and what you will do with your life."

"And you are saying that in Russia you are not free to
choose what you will believe? There's an admission I had never
expected to have from a Bolshevik."

Petrov continued to smile. "As I said, we suppose that we
are still living in a revolutionary society. Miss Stein, I apologize."

"I should apologize to you. I've been awfully rude."

"But I was equally rude, in coming here at all. In asking
you to help me. I made a mistake, based upon Commissar
Nej's doubtful information. But that does not mean I would
not like to be your friend. Will you have dinner with me?"

"What on earth for?" She had to smile. "I mean, I'm not
likely to change my attitude, you know. And I can think of
a hundred and one reasons why you'd be throwing money
away."

"Bolshevik money, Miss Stein. So, does it matter? But it
does matter to me why you think I would not enjoy an evening
with you."

"For God's sake. I'm against everything you stand for,"

"Everything I represent, Miss Stein. There is a difference. And I have just promised to abstain from political conversation."

"I'm older than you," she said.

"Is that important? Age is a man-made invention."

She finished her drink and got up. "I'm a Jew, Mr. Petrov. I've recently realized that I'm not Russian at all. I'm a Jew. That I was born in Moscow is an accident of history. I don't want any part of Russia, anymore, except that there are still a great number of Jews there. Everything we say to each other is going to be a disaster."

"Then I promise not to say anything at all," he said. "I shall just look at you, Miss Stein, if that will not offend you. Now, shall we dine?"

She gazed at him for some seconds. Then she shrugged. "I think you should call me Judith."

Judith shuffled her papers together and closed the file. "So you see, there's not a lot to go on. Obviously the Bolsheviks aren't going to broadcast just how ill he is. And there's no way of finding out what is actually happening inside the Kremlin, until they tell the world *something*. As soon as I hear anything, anything at all, about Comrade Lenin, be sure I'll let you know."

George smiled at her. "I'll be patient." He looked at his watch. "Five-thirty already. Not much point in starting anything else. Get your coat and I'll drive you home. Then we can stop somewhere and have a drink."

"Aren't you afraid of getting caught up in a raid?"

"We don't take Prohibition as seriously in New York as in some other states, or hadn't you noticed? Anyway, the place I'm going to take you has never been raided, and will never be raided."

"Because you, and others, contribute to the police pension fund. It really does shock me."

"No, because it's a private club."

She got up. "Well, I can't, anyway, George. I'd love to, really, but I have plans tonight."

"The fact is," George said, still smiling, "that Ilona is having a meeting of some sort tonight—one of her charities. She takes her responsibilities seriously, you know. I actually think she prefers not to have me around. So I promised to get home reasonably late. I'm not very good at eating alone."

She gazed at him. "Oh." He was nervous, for all his smile; his fingers were drumming on his desk.

"So, unless your plans are terribly important . . ."

"Oh," she said again. Oh, Menachem Yanowski, where are you now? After all these months. All these years, when she really came down to it.

But Ilona. And Boris, dear, sweet Boris who was trying so hard to convince her he was not a Bolshevik, after all, but merely a patriot with a job to do. And herself? For very nearly ten years she had wanted this man to take her in his arms, to shroud her with the strength of the Hayman personality no less than the Hayman background. Suddenly she felt sick.

"Well?" George invited, leaning forward.

Boris was picking her up after Peter's meeting tonight. He didn't know, of course, that she would have come straight from an émigré discussion on how best to combat the Soviets. But she had been uneasy about it, anyway. Partly because of the deceit involved, and partly because, for all his charm—and, she believed, his honesty—she had lived her entire life in such an atmosphere of double-dealing that she could not be quite certain that he wasn't merely using her to get at Peter, in due course.

How easily sweet reason can make it appear that what we want to do is the best thing to do!

But did she want to do it? Oh, how she wanted to do it, as she had wanted to do it ever since that day in 1914 when she had been expelled from Starogan, and this man had come to the station to see her off.

And Ilona? But if he was in this mood, and she turned him down, and he was staying in town for several hours in any event, there was going to be *someone*.

"I'll have to make a telephone call," she said, suddenly breathless.

He nodded. "I'll meet you downstairs in ten minutes."

"Yes." She got up. If it was going to happen, she didn't want to miss a moment of it. "And . . . why worry with clubs? I have some gin at home. Imported. I'll even boil you an egg, or something."

* * *

Judith unlocked the door and led him inside. He had only been here once before, when she had thrown a small party to which the boss and his wife had of course been invited.

"New curtains, I see," he remarked as she switched on the living-room lights.

"Well, I just got a raise, remember." She stood by the door, waiting. It was all up to him, now. It had to be all up to him. Because she wasn't a *femme fatale*, after all.

George took off his hat and coat. "You mentioned imported gin."

"In the sideboard."

He stooped and opened the cupboard. "And all the right mixes, as well." He expertly concocted two martinis while Judith took off her own coat and hat, and laid her gloves on top of them. I should hang them up, she thought, absently. But suddenly the apartment wasn't hers anymore.

He held out her glass, and she went closer, and took it from his hand. He was no longer nervous. He knew why he was here as well as she did.

"Well," she said. "Here's to 1924."

"Here's to us," he said, and took her free hand to draw her closer. They kissed, each holding a glass away from the other. She realized that it was the first time she had been kissed since leaving Michael Nej. Peter's occasional fumblings and Boris's correct goodnight pecks on the cheek really didn't count, in this context. Here was gentleness, and depth, and above all confidence. He might have taken a long time to make up his mind, but once the decision was taken, there could be no further uncertainty. But this, she realized, was the character of the man.

She found herself moving backwards, carrying him with her. She reached the table she sought, put down the glass, and he followed her example. Then at last he released her lips. She stepped away to look at him, wondering if he would speak. But he had more sense than to do that. She turned her head to look at the settee, still not sure what he actually wanted, still unable to *believe* that after very nearly ten years this moment was at last at hand. He put his arm around her shoulders, walked her through the bedroom door. My God, she thought, suppose he doesn't like my underclothes, or my bed linens, or—

He turned her into his arms and kissed her again. He still had taken not a single liberty with her body, but now his hands closed on her shoulder blades, then slid up to hold her neck, fingers thrust into her hair. And now, for the first time, she felt him.

She lay on her back across the bed, and he knelt beside her, gently unbuttoning her blouse. She kicked off her shoes, watched his head lower, remembered that in January she wore a woolen camisole, and hated herself for it. But he merely smiled, and kissed her suddenly erect nipple through the thin wool, then held her hands and pulled her into a sitting position.

She understood what he wanted, removed jacket and blouse and camisole in quick movements, sat and waited, flesh faintly chilled although the apartment was well heated. Her eyes started to close, and she forced them open again. She wanted to be able to remember every aspect of this moment, this evening. He knelt beside the bed, hands sliding up her stockings and under the skirt while his lips came forward to kiss each nipple in turn. She put her arms round his head to hug his face into her breasts. It felt so good, after so long. And the certainty of what was going to happen was so good. It would not matter about orgasms and mutual moments of ecstasy. That was kid stuff, born of uncertainty. There would be those, in the course of time. But just to feel him inside her, feel his body covering hers . . .

He had released her, and was undressing. She stood as well, dropped skirt and panties to the floor, sat down again to remove garters and stockings, watching him, enjoying the sight of him, the body of a man in the very prime of life, thickening at the waist, certainly, but none the less magnificent in his perfect health, his obvious strength . . . and his looming desire. She found herself breathing heavily as she pushed herself back up the bed to reach the pillows, and she lay there, on her back, waiting as he knelt beside her again, leaned down to kiss her mouth. Now she felt him on her thigh, the softest of caresses, and instinctively spread her legs. There was no haste, no anxiety, only gentle probing and the easist of entries, while his face came down to hers again, to kiss and hold her mouth while he moved, one arm round her neck, using his elbow to keep the main part of his weight from her, the other hand gently massaging her breast.

She knew she was not going to climax. She was far too excited, far too unsure of her own emotions, far too eager to feel every thrust, every movement, far too eager to be utterly aware of the man on top of her. But how she wanted *him* to come, to have the best moment of his entire life, to want to come back to her again and again and again.

And then it happened, quickly and easily, and now he did let his body come down on hers, and she could feel him, from shoulder to toe, while his cheek lay against hers. No time for moving, now. A time for lying absolutely still, and feeling each other. A silent time.

But a time, suddenly, for thought, for responsibility, where before there had been no room. Ilona! Entertaining her charity committee, no doubt with a pang of conscience that George might be having a sandwich alone. But he would be going home to Ilona. Again and again and again, he would be going home to Ilona. Ilona might have to lend her husband, from time to time, even without her knowledge. But she would never lose him. Losing things which she wished to keep was not in Ilona Hayman's stars at all. There was no real reason to be sorry for her.

Thus conscience, busily making itself ready to deal with the coming days and weeks and months.

But his conscience was working as well, and not quite so adaptably.

"Ilona worries," he said finally, "about Johnnie."

Judith sighed. "She mentioned it to me."

"He's a strange boy. Well, I suppose he would be, with such a background. But it's nearly impossible for her to get through to him, and quite impossible for me."

He had slipped off her. She got up and pulled on her dressing gown. "Would you like some coffee?"

"I'd rather finish those martinis."

She went into the living room and came back with the glasses. "I said something about eggs, didn't I?"

"Sounds great." He sat up, back against the pillows pushed against the headboard, sipped, and smiled at her as she disappeared again.

But his smile was uneasy. What had happened had perhaps

been inevitable, in view of everything else that had happened, over the years, but now the thought, the actual anticipation, had given way to the deed. And now he was remembering Ilona, all the joys and adventures they had shared, and all the moments of sexual ecstasy, too.

Just as Judith was remembering everything she had set out to do with life, and which had now, as Menachem had prophesied, come tumbling into a simple matter of wanting a man.

And because it was *this* man, there could be no turning back now.

She reappeared and sat beside him, placed the plate of food between them. "Scrambled okay?"

"My favorite." He kissed her on the nose. "I feel I should make it clear..."

She shook her head. "Don't. Don't make anything clear, George. Just let it be you and me, here, because we want it to be you and me, here. From time to time, maybe."

"And this date you broke?"

She shrugged. "He's just a friend." She got up, and he caught her hand.

"You don't happen to know anything about Johnnie's habits, do you, Judith?"

She looked at him. "Why should I?" But she was flushing.

"Because he and you always seem to have a secret understanding."

"Do we? You left me in charge of them all, remember? I thought then you might be making a mistake."

"I doubt that. But I wish you'd tell me."

She hesitated. But to refuse him would be to erect a barrier between them, and she was more afraid of that, now, than of anything else.

"He goes to see Peter."

George frowned at her. "Every week? Twice a week?" The frown deepened. "My God. You don't mean he attends those émigré meetings?"

"You know about those?"

"Of course I do. The State Department got in touch with me to see if I thought they were all right. And I said yes, fool that I am. I suspect they're actually subsidizing him, to a certain extent. But you mean Peter has been corrupting my son?"

"I wouldn't go so far as to say that," Judith protested. "Johnnie thinks of himself as Russian, so it stands to reason that he's interested in the Russian scene. Peter is his uncle and Sergei Roditchev was his father, so it stands to reason he's anti-Bolshevik."

"There's a hell of a lot of difference between being anti-Bolshevik and being mixed up in Peter's madcap schemes. Do *you* go to those meetings?"

Judith sighed. "Sometimes."

"You?"

She sat down again. "I go partly to see Rachel, because she *is* my sister, George. And partly because I'm your Russian editor. I get quite a lot of information from listening to them." She did not mention that Peter also considered *her* to be a source of information. So, she thought, immediately the deceit has started, between us and Ilona, and even between George and me.

"Yes," he said. "Yes, I can see that. But Johnnie . . . when is the next meeting?"

"There's one tonight. I was supposed to be there."

"Was that what you were canceling?" He didn't wait for her reply, but got out of bed and began pulling on his clothes. "Well, I'll go along there, if you don't mind, and tell them a few truths they don't yet appreciate. And if Johnnie is there—"

"George." She caught his hand. "These people have nothing else to live for."

"Johnnie sure as hell has."

She lay down. "I'm sorry. Believe me, I'm so terribly sorry. Don't be hard on him, George."

"No harder than I have to be." He knelt on the bed, knotting his tie, and leaned forward to kiss her. "And you have nothing to be sorry about. You have made me very, very happy. And I'm going to do my best to make you very, very happy in return. Now you—"

The telephone jangled. They gazed at each other for a moment. Ilona? Clearly they were both thinking the same thing. But why on earth should Ilona telephone here?

Judith picked up the receiver. "Hello?" she said. "Judith Stein."

"Miss Stein?" It was her secretary, voice breathless with

excitement. "Oh, I'm so glad I caught you. Miss Stein, it's just come in on the wire. Lenin is dead."

The ripple of the drums was submerged in the thunderous rumble of gunfire, the measured tread of nearly a hundred thousand boots striking the cobblestones of Red Square, the shuffling of many more times that number of feet surrounding the parade.

They honored an empty coffin. It had been a unanimous decision of the Presidium that the founder of the Soviet state could not be allowed merely to disappear into the earth, or into a niche in the Kremlin wall, but must lie forever in his own mausoleum, so that all the faithful, and even those yet to be converted, might look upon his face and understand his greatness.

But that was for the distant future. Even as the embalmers got to work, and as this tribute was made to Lenin's memory, thoughts were turning to the immediate future, to tomorrow. Those who had inherited that great burden stood in a group together. Trotsky, as befitted his rank and reputation, was a little to the fore, wearing his uniform as commander of the Red Army, and standing strictly at attention, perhaps consciously seeing this occasion less as a tribute to Lenin than as a salute to his most likely successor. Bukharin, Kamenev and Kalinin made a separate group just to his right, watching him as closely as they watched the parade. Stalin and Sergei Kirov were to his left, immediately behind them Felix Dzershinsky and Ivan Nej, the commanders of the OGPU, the latest manifestation of the secret police. But this need not be significant; it was natural for the policemen to take their places close by their immediate superior, the General Secretary of the Party.

Michael Nej stood by himself, behind Trotsky. Again, no reason for comment. Michael Nej was well known as Lenin's closest friend, his constant companion in exile since 1911. Besides, Michael Nej was the man who had participated in the assassination of Prime Minister Stolypin. Like Trotsky, he needed no supporting group.

The marching feet died away, the crowds also started to melt into the snow, which, having miraculously held off during the actual procession, now started to cloud down quite thickly. Flanked by·the guards, the Presidium also moved off, to hot tea and vodka, and conversation with their wives, who had watched the proceedings from curtained windows.

"A great man," Kalinin said, sitting beside the black-clad Krupskaya.

"The greatest in the history of the world," Bukharin agreed, sitting on her other side.

"The founder of our state," Trotsky said, standing before her. "His name will live for all time. We have decided, with your permission, Krupskaya, to rename Petrograd Leningrad, in Vladimir Ilich's honor. Why should the greatest of the tsars be remembered at the expense of the greatest of all Russians?"

Michael stood at the back, beside Catherine, who gazed at the scene with huge, wide Tartar eyes. They had been married for eighteen months now, and yet she seemed lost in a world beyond her understanding, a world of which, as a guide-interpreter, she had heard but had never expected to join. He suspected that she had counted herself dead, once she found herself inside the OGPU headquarters. He knew now that under torture she had told them nothing because she had nothing to tell. The most unfortunate position anyone can possibly be in, when one's adversaries are convinced of the opposite. Thus composed, with all the stoicism that the Tartar can command, it had taken her several weeks to unfreeze her brain, and for him to convince her that she was going to live, and prosper. She had lain, and submitted. A far cry from either Ilona Borodina or Judith Stein. But his in a sense that neither of those had ever been. He had only just realized how lonely he had been, in the years since Judith had abandoned him, in not having a woman.

And however great her wonder, however total her submission, she was slowly coming to terms with her new situation. When he had taken her before the court to declare her his wife, she had stared at him throughout the ceremony, perhaps only then believing that it was really true, that at the whim of one man she had been raised above the common herd, given security and position. She still found it difficult to respond to him, still lay and allowed him to love her rather than ever venturing to love him. A strange relationship, perhaps, and yet he was happy in it. Happier, certainly, than his brother Ivan was, even though Ivan's marriage had united him with the woman with whom he had always been obsessed. But would certainly never possess. It was, in fact, impossible to imagine Ivan and Tattie making love at all. Which might, he realized, account for a good deal of Ivan's misanthropy.

Today it was impossible to imagine Tattie ever laughing, or even dancing again. She also wore black, from head to toe, and a veil to conceal her obvious tears. Lenin had been her friend. Her best friend, as she never tired of telling anyone who would listen to her. He had encouraged her music and her dancing school, had promised her greater support in the future. Now, like everyone else, that future was clouded.

For some more than most.

"The testament," Bukharin was saying. "We must come to a decision on the testament."

All heads turned to look at Stalin, since everyone knew that in his last dictations, Lenin had heavily criticized the General Party secretary, mainly on personal rather than public grounds, but the criticism was nonetheless damning. So, were they the ramblings of a dying man on the point of losing his faculties, or the reasoned conclusions of the greatest man in Russian history, drawing his thoughts together before his demise?

"The day he wrote that," Stalin said, in his quiet, almost diffident manner, "I had been rude to Krupskaya. I apologize, Krupskaya."

"Nonetheless, it is written down," Kamenev said, "for all the world to see."

"All the world?" Ivan Nej asked softly.

"My husband certainly meant his testament to be made public," Krupskaya said, meeting Stalin's gaze.

"It would harm the party," Trotsky said. "Now, more than ever before, we who control the Party must be seen to be standing shoulder to shoulder, facing the future without fear and with the utmost confidence. In the course of time, out of our deliberations, out of our circumstances, I have no doubt, a new leader of measurable, if not comparable, stature will emerge. Until that happens, we are all leaders." He stood straight, spectacles glinting as he looked at each of them in turn, and then at Michael Nej longer than any. "I must attend my office. Krupskaya." He nodded in acknowledgment to Lenin's widow.

The door closed behind him.

"He already counts himself chosen," Kamenev muttered.

The entire room looked at Michael, with the exception of Tattie, who was staring out the window.

"I also have work to do," Michael said. "You'll excuse me. Krupskaya." He went to the door, and Catherine, who had been listening and watching in confused amazement, collected herself and started to hurry behind him.

Once again the men in the room exchanged glances.

"Wait," Stalin said. "I'll go with you. Krupskaya!" He escorted his wife, Nadezhda Alliluyeva, to the door. "Why don't you take Catherine Pavlovna for some coffee?" he suggested.

Nadezhda glanced at him, nodded, and took Catherine's hand. "Come along, my dear. The men wish to talk."

Stalin walked beside Michael, hands clasped behind his back, lips and mouth almost concealed beneath the heavy mustache. "Life is a matter of decisions, is it not, Michael Nikolaievich? Some easy, most difficult. All important decisions are difficult. Would you not agree?"

"I would agree," Michael said.

"The decision that now lies ahead of us is probably the most difficult any of us has ever had to make," Stalin mused. "Partly because we have not made many important decisions in recent years; Vladimir Ilich made them all for us. And partly because they must necessarily, at this juncture, involve personalities. Involve deciding about men who have always been our friends. Yet we have a greater responsibility than friendship, Michael Nikolaievich. We have a duty to Russia, to the countless millions who have placed their trust in us."

"I won't argue with that."

Stalin paused at a window in the long corridor and looked at the snow settling in the courtyard outside. "You are a friend of Trotsky's."

Michael nodded. He had guessed this was coming. "He placed me in command of an army during the war, Joseph Vissarionovich. And when I was defeated, he confirmed me in that command."

"And eventually you won your war, and are a hero because of it," Stalin agreed. "Loyalty is a great quality. But loyalty to one's country is always the greater quality. Lev Davidovich Trotsky already imagines himself sole leader, Lenin's replacement. He considers himself qualified for that position because of his military genius, because of his personality, because he is the best known of us to the people at large. All true. But he is not Lenin. He has no calmness of spirit. And he is a soldier. Do you suppose this country could stand a war, now, so soon after the last?"

"It would be a disaster," Michael said.

"Quite. But Trotsky is committed, by everything he has ever said, to carrying Communism abroad, by force, if need be. Do you suppose the democracies would stand by and watch us, just for example, renew our invasion of Poland—his idea, in 1920—or carry our red flags into Rumania?"

"The democracies are just as weary of war as are we, and even less able to afford it," Michael said.

"Which is not to say they would not *go* to war. In any event, it would hamper our own recovery, here at home. We have an immense task ahead of us, building Russia. It is a task that is only half completed. It is surely our duty, sacred to the memory of our leader, to complete that task before undertaking any other."

"I am sure even Lev Davidovich will appreciate that, when it is put to him," Michael said.

"I doubt that," Stalin said. "I doubt that very much."

"In any event," Michael said, "he cannot become the sole leader unless we all vote for it. So there is nothing to worry about."

"It is not so simple as that, Michael Nikolaievich. We are united now. But Lev Davidovich will surely work away at each of us in turn, to convert us to his point of view. He will start with you."

"And I will resist him."

"Others may not be as strong. Even you may not be as strong, over a period of time."

Michael frowned at him. "Just what are you suggesting?"

"It is my opinion that the only safe way is to remove Trotsky from the Presidium."

"Are you serious?"

"I am very serious indeed, where the welfare of Communist Russia is concerned."

"Will he accept such a decision?"

"That is a point. Normally, a man would have to. But when that man is also Commissar of the Army—"

"You would not dare."

"It is not I, Comrade Nej. It will be a joint decision. Comrade Trotsky is a dangerous man. A very talented one, to be sure. A man to whom the state owes an enormous amount of gratitude for his brilliant efforts on our behalf. But a man who, at this precise moment in our history, it would be unwise to trust with the great powers he has wielded in the past, when overseen and controlled by the will of our leader. Believe me, Michael Nikolaievich, there is not one of us who seeks such a position of authority for ourselves. We are determined to rule by committee, to reach unanimous decisions, jointly carried out. I give you my word on that. Things will change. Things will improve. And in the fullness of time it may be possible for us to invite Comrade Trotsky back to take his place at the head of our armies. At this moment it would be highly dangerous to leave him there."

Michael chewed his lip.

"So we ask you, as his friend, as his loyal supporter, to join us for the good of Russia."

Or to be eclipsed with him, Michael thought. Was that important? The important thing *was* Russia. Lenin's view of Russia. A Russia once again to be ranked among the great nations of the world. And Lenin himself had recognized that Trotsky needed a firm hand on the rein. With Lenin dead, there was surely only one way to exercise that control.

He sighed, and held out his hand. "I will support the majority decision, comrade," he said.

Chapter 6

"YOUR VODKA, COMRADE." CATHERINE HELD OUT THE GLASS.

Michael Nej shook his head. "I do not feel like vodka tonight."

"It was a long meeting," she remarked, still standing before his chair, holding the glass.

"A long meeting," Michael said. He raised his head to glance at her. "Why do you not drink the vodka yourself?"

"I do not feel like it either." She put the glass on the table and turned to face him again. "I am to have a child."

His head jerked.

"I am sorry, comrade," she said, "so to disrupt your household. I have been careless. I should be punished."

"Punished?" He got up and took her into his arms. "You should be rewarded. Russia needs babies. And I...I need babies more than anyone else."

Her head tilted back as she looked up at him. "You have not had a baby, before?"

He sighed. "Yes, I have had a baby before. But he is far away, now. Far, far away." His face cleared, and he squeezed her against him and then kissed her on the lips. "Now I will have another. We will call him Nikolai, after my father. Nikolai Mikhailovich. Catherine, I am delighted." He released her, went to the table, and lifted the glass. "As I hope you are also delighted."

"If you are, comrade." She bit her lip. "But suppose it is a girl?"

Michael's frown flashed briefly, then his smile reappeared. "I shall be equally delighted. Well, not equally. But I shall be delighted." He finished his drink. "We must tell Ivan and Tattie."

"Oh, but—"

"It is not a secret, Catherine. It is a great occasion for the Nej family. Come on." He seized her hand, dragged her out of the door and across the landing to the apartment opposite, and paused with his hand on the bell. From inside they could hear the sound of Tattie shouting.

"Sometimes I am very sorry for my brother," Michael said. "But he brought it on himself." He pressed the bell, and the noise from inside died.

The door swung back, and Tattie glared at them. "Have you come to complain?" Behind her, little Gregory whimpered.

"We have come to celebrate," Michael said.

"Ha," she snorted. "Comrade Trotsky's disgrace? Vladimir Ilich has been dead only a year, and see what has happened!"

"He has not been disgraced, Tatiana Dimitrievna, and you should not use careless expressions like that. We are celebrating the fact that Catherine is pregnant."

"Pregnant? Oh, you darling." Tattie's ill humor disappeared as if a switch had been pulled, and she embraced her sister-in-law. "I am so happy for you." Still with her arms round Catherine, she pulled them both into the small living room, where Ivan Nej was standing, looking at once hangdog and defiant. "Ivan, Catherine is to have a baby. Now, if you were able to go on giving me babies, we wouldn't be quarreling, would we?"

Ivan opened his mouth, then closed it again. Michael glanced at Catherine. What did she think of his domestic circumstances? He wondered how much any of the thousands of miserable prisoners held in the OGPU cells would give to see Ivan being browbeaten by his wife.

"Is that what you were quarreling about?" he asked.

"What are you standing there for, you silly little man?" Tattie demanded of her husband. "Vodka. Aren't we going to drink to Catherine's health.

Ivan hurried to the table and poured four glasses.

"He won't let me tour Europe," Tattie said, throwing herself into the settee with such force that it moved several inches back across the floor; there was no carpet. "Shut up," she shouted in the direction of the bedroom. The crying stopped. "And he won't get us a larger apartment," she growled. "What is the point in being almost a member of the Politburo if we have to live in a two-room apartment? It is ridiculous."

"Tour Europe?" Michael asked.

Ivan presented him with a glass. "She has this absurd idea that she and her girls should go on a tour of Europe," he said.

"It is not absurd," Tattie declared, signs of volcanic eruption once again evident. "Vladimir Ilich said I could. He said I could go as soon as I thought the troupe was ready. Well, it has been ready for months. The bookings are assured. But Ivan says I can't go."

"She will make herself the laughingstock of the world," Ivan said.

"I will put Russian dancing on the map," she shouted angrily.

"I know where you got your ideas," Ivan said, growing in courage because of the presence of Michael and Catherine. "It is from that Duncan woman when she was here. It is obscene. Obscene!"

"Vladimir Ilich thought Isadora Duncan was the most talented dancer he had ever seen. And she thinks I am almost as talented as she," Tattie said, speaking in measured tones. "It is Miss Duncan who has arranged the tour. We have bookings in Berlin, in Vienna, in Prague, in Rome, in Paris, and in London. Russian culture. So it may be different from what the West regards as culture. Our whole revolution is different from how they think. Vladimir Ilich gave me permission. And," she said, lowering her voice but sounding even more menacing, "I am going. You will have to lock me up if you want to stop me."

Ivan raised an eyebrow, as if that idea was the best that had yet come up.

"If Lenin actually gave permission . . ." Michael suggested.

"Have you seen her dance?" Ivan inquired. "Her and her pupils? They cavort about with next to nothing on, showing everything they possess . . ."

"I think it's rather beautiful," Catherine ventured.

They all turned to look at her. She had never offered an opinion on anything, before.

"And I can't help but feel that Comrade Lenin's wishes should be followed," Michael said. Don't you suppose it's about time we did something to revise the world's view of us?"

Ivan snorted.

"It is important," Michael insisted. "We wish to see Russia again take its place among the great nations of the world. How can we do that when everyone in the world thinks of us as a nation in the last stages of collapse, at the mercy of a secret police. Oh, yes, Ivan, you must take your share of the blame for that disastrous fiasco over the Haymans. To invite America's foremost newspaper magnate to the country to see for himself, beat him up and put his wife in prison—"

"Only for one night," Ivan said sulkily.

"For one minute was too long. No, no. I think we have to do a great deal of work to restore people's idea of what we stand for." He paused, and looked at the door as they heard heavy footsteps outside. A moment later the doorbell rang.

"Not some of your people coming to dinner," Tattie said in disgust.

Ivan glanced at her and opened the door. Leon Trotsky stood there.

"Forgive me, Comrade Nej. I am looking for your brother. He does not appear to be in."

"I am here, Lev Davidovich," Michael said.

Trotsky looked at Ivan, who stepped aside to allow him into the room.

"I have come to say good-bye," Trotsky said.

"You're leaving Moscow?" Tattie asked.

Trotsky's smile was twisted. "I am going to the Caucasus, Tatiana Dimitrievna. I am being *sent* to the Caucasus. To inspect farming methods." He gazed at Michael. "I am told it was by unanimous vote of the Politburo, in my absence."

Michael bit his lip. "The future of the nation depends on the success of our farming, Lev Davidovich. It is hoped that you will have the success there you did with the army."

"With farming," Trotsky said bitterly. "I suppose you are now commissar for war."

Michael shook his head. "I am going to the commissariat of foreign affairs, with Litvinov. It is felt that this too is important."

"And the new secretary?"

"Why, Joseph Vissarionovich, of course. He knows more about party organization than any of us."

"Stalin," Trotsky said, "who hides behind his mustache, says little, and thinks a lot. And plans even more." Now he looked at Ivan. "And is well supported. Beware, my comrades. The man who sits at the center is like a spider. He has all the threads in his hands, and the day may come when you will find that they are wrapped around *you*." He glanced at them each in turn. "All of you."

He stepped outside, and the door closed behind him.

The room was silent for some moments.

"If he doesn't want to go," Tattie said at last, "why didn't he say so? Why didn't he attend the meeting and say so? He is Trotsky. Why didn't he say so?"

"He didn't attend the meeting because he knew how the vote would go," Michael said. "And he is obeying the vote just because he is Trotsky. For the very reason that he agreed to suppress Lenin's criticism of Stalin. He believes in the unity of the Party."

"You make him sound like a hero," Ivan sneered.

"I think he is a hero, a Soviet hero," Michael said. "Whether he will always so meekly abide by the majority decision remains to be seen."

"Without the army at his back, he is nothing," Ivan said. "Comrade Trotsky has stepped off the stage of history for the last time, Michael. And should he attempt to step back on— why, that is what I am here for."

Michael gazed at him. "I should not like to take that literally, brother," he said. "Save your thuggery for those who cannot fight back. But in all the circumstances, I would say that it is more important than ever for us to allow a little pro-Soviet propaganda. As deputy commissar for foreign affairs, I intend to give Tatiana and her troupe the permission to tour Europe."

"Ten minutes, Frau Nej," said the stage manager, half opening the door, taking a quick peek. He was at once nervous and excited. Nervous because while the Berlin of the Weimar Republic was a very relaxed place, in which it was said most moralistic points of view had gone the way of the old mark, into the wastebasket by the truckload, this was a very new and very daring departure on which the theater was embarking. And excited because the whole concept was exciting, just as the woman herself was the most exciting creature he had ever seen. And if she was really meaning to go on stage wearing a pair of harem trousers and a bolero jacket, equally sheer, and not another thing . . . Damnation. The maid had moved between himself and the mirror in which Tattie was reflected.

"Thank you, *mein Herr*," she said. "You may close the door."

"He is like a dog with two tails," Olga confided.

"Like a dog with two pricks, you mean," Tattie pointed out. "And he is not at all sure that either of them is going to wag properly. I must get out there." She pushed back the stool and stood up, inhaled. When she did that the jacket fell away to either side, allowed just a glimpse of nipple. But the secret was to keep moving, so that everyone caught only a glimpse, and never anything more than that.

"Are you nervous, Comrade Nej?" Olga asked.

"Nervous? Why should I be nervous? This is the greatest moment of my life."

She stepped outside, into the corridor that led to the backstage area, and her knees touched even as she was suddenly aware of a gigantic heat, seeming to cover every inch of her body. Why should she be nervous? She was Tatiana Nej. People thought she was mad, in a pleasant and uncertifiable fashion. As mad people can never do anything wrong, or even unusual, by the standards of their madness, what did she have to be nervous about?

Her mother, she recalled, had thought her mad, or at least soft-headed, almost from the moment of her birth. It was not so uncommon for the last child to be weak-brained, and there

was that lengthy gap between herself and Ilona. Mama had had
a hard time with Ilona, and had not intended to have any more
children. Tatiana had been the result of an oversight.

When she was only four years old, the family had been
whisked off to Port Arthur, where Papa was to take up a
military position. Papa had been a career soldier, an uncommon
occupation for a count who would one day be the premier
prince in all Russia. Thus he had been the only one of such
rank in Port Arthur, and his children had not been allowed to
make friends with the common herd. Ilona and Peter had had
each other; they were only two years apart. And they had had
the Nej boys, sons of Papa's steward, to help them in their
games. Tattie had been left to grow up as best she could, with
only her French governess for company. So she had had to
amuse herself. But when her amusements had led her into
utterly happy and uninhibited dancing and piano playing, she
had been punished. Not severely. "Soft in the head, you see,"
Mama had said.

Then George Hayman had drifted into the Borodin world,
so strangely, so unexpectedly, a breath of an outside society
that did not depend on rank or birth or custom alone, a place
where she might be able to dance and sing and play to her
heart's content. Getting to America had become her entire
dream. She had even tried to escape with Ilona, when Ilona
had determined to elope, and like Ilona, she had been punished.
Since she was only twelve at the time, she could not be married
off, as Ilona had been. But she had been sent to a convent in
St. Petersburg, her only relief her cousin Xenia and her sister-
in-law Irina, Peter's wife. But what splendid companions. They
had introduced her to Father Gregory, and Father Gregory had
let her dance for him. He had encouraged her to dance for him.

Of course she now knew—she supposed she had known
then—that Xenia and Irina were two of the most corrupt women
in all Russia, that Gregory Rasputin was a charlatan from the
steppes who added to his other crimes that of being an un-
principled lecher. She had been told so, often enough, since
the revolution. But he had let her dance, and he had never,
ever, scolded her. In return all he wished to do was to sit her
on his lap and stroke between her legs and finger her growing
girlish breasts. That she had enjoyed his caresses, she supposed, was merely another aspect of her weak-mindedness.

But they had not harmed her, and she *had* enjoyed them. More than once Father Gregory had induced a feeling that promised to burst into an ecstasy she had only hitherto felt when dancing. She had known it would happen . . . but Peter had found out about it and carried her back to Starogan, to utter imprisonment in the center of thousands of acres of wheat, until the time she could marry.

From that moment she had hated Peter, as she had hated Mama, as she had hated the very name Borodin. It was a symbol of her imprisonment. And through her it seemed to be a symbol of the imprisonment of every idea in all Russia that was worth having. When, on that unforgettable day in 1918, the entire village, it seemed, had come boiling up the road— led, amazingly, by Ivan Nej, who had gone off to war in 1914 and never been heard of again—she was terrified. But the seven years of imprisonment were coming to an end. She had expected to die, but she knew that she was about to live, even if briefly, for the first time since 1911.

No doubt Mama would have said that was another example of her weak-headedness. But she had survived, when Mama and Xenia and Irina and Grandmama and everyone else had died. She had been concerned entirely with survival. When Ivan had carried her into her own bedroom and thrown her on the bed, she thought he was about to kill her. When instead he had torn the clothes from her body before tearing off his own, she had realized that she was, after all, going to survive, because, apparently, Rasputin had been no more lecherous than any other man. Afterwards it had seemed the natural thing to do to go with him when he left, before the advancing White armies. Judith Stein, at that time living with Michael, had not understood. She had offered to exchange her, send her back to her own people, her own brother, then chief of staff to General Denikin. And like everyone else, Judith had not understood when she had said she would rather stay. Even with Ivan Nej, she would rather stay.

What, go back to Peter? Go back to being a prisoner? Go back to worse. She had been raped by a bootblack who was now a Red revolutionary. There could be no place for such an outcast in polite society. It would have meant a convent for her, for the rest of her life. If it was a choice between that and lying under Ivan Nej for the rest of her life, even if he had led the mob that had murdered Mama and the rest, well, life was a matter of living.

But no one had understood. Not even George, then Moscow correspondent for his father's newspaper, had understood. It was merely another example of Tattie's weak-mindedness.

What had confused them most was that she should be happy. But it had not taken her long to discover that Ivan was far more afraid of her than she ever had been of him. Ivan Nej, with his whips and his ice-cold baths and his execution squads, entered her bedroom in utter terror, whenever she unlocked the door. Because Ivan, for all his pretense, was a sexless man. He was afraid of the very act. And if he had never even come near arousing her as Father Gregory had done, she could simulate such passion easily enough, which reduced him to a cowering wreck. She had triumphed over him, and thus over the entire revolution, and out of her triumph had come an even greater one. Lenin had visited one day, and found her dancing, and been entranced. Poor little weak-minded Tattie, she thought. Survival, there was the key. The key to the Berlin Opera House. It might have taken her twenty years, but that was a little price to pay.

And Ilona wanted her to emigrate to America. When she had the entire world at her feet.

What did she have to be nervous about?

Wave after wave of applause cascaded through the auditorium, rose to the high ceiling, tinkled the chandeliers and then flooded back down onto the stage. People stood, partly to clap and shout, partly to gain a better view of the dancers, at last motionless. The audience was suddenly released from the spell under which it had been held for the previous hour. After its first polite applause, it had sunk into an utter silence as the fact had slowly penetrated its mind that the twenty young ladies on the stage, any one of whom would have been fit for a sultan's bed, were each and every one apparently dressed for that bed. Then there had been a few nervous titters, and several people got up and walked out. But the rest had stayed, fascinated by the uniqueness of what they were seeing as well as by the beauty of the performers, exhilarated by the tremendous pace and rhythm of the music, and at last captivated by the sheer grace and excellence of the dancing.

Now the stage was a place of flowing sweat, of gasping breaths, while the audience cheered themselves hoarse, even applauding old Yuri Bogdanovich, fat and fifty, who played the Sultan, and who had nothing at all to do but sit in the center of the stage on his cushion and occasionally clap his hands.

But the shouts were all "Nej," or "Tatiana." She rose from the kneeling position in which she had finished the dance, advanced to the edge of the stage, gazed out into the theater, and made her curtsey while the applause renewed itself even louder than before. She blinked back her tears, smiled at Isadora Duncan, sitting in the front row, and at the people sitting beside her, shouting "bravo," and at one man in particular. She did not usually notice any members of the audience when dancing; there was no time and her movements too fast. But she had noticed this man, drawn to him by the intensity of his stare. She had supposed there was nothing different about him than any other man present. He wore a black dinner jacket, had wavy dark brown hair, neatly brushed, and gold cufflinks that only supported the certainty, as he had a seat in the orchestra section, that he was a man either of wealth or importance. His features were aquiline, his eyes dark, so far as she could make out. It was a strong face, with prominent nose and chin. But there was something more, which had her noticing him. He was not shouting. He was not even clapping anymore. He was just staring at her, and she could almost *feel* his stare, completely embracing her, so that for a moment it was as if there was no one else in the theater at all, just the two of them.

The descending curtain cut him off for a moment, then it rose again and she blinked at the fresh outburst of noise. Again he, and they, disappeared, and when they reappeared again, she realized that she was alone in the center of the vast stage, her troupe having stolen away to let her have the honors she deserved. Now ushers came up the side stairs with bouquets of flowers, which she gathered in front of her as she curtsied for the last time, gave him a last glance, and then hurried off.

"There will be people coming backstage," said Nikoyan, the head of the OGPU escort Ivan had insisted must accompany her. "We do not want that. If you will put on a wrap, Comrade Nej, we will take you back to your hotel."

"But I do want that," Tattie insisted. "I am not running off. Bring me my robe."

Already more flowers were arriving, and behind them people, hurrying past the stage manager, surrounding her, wishing to kiss her and shake her hands and hug her, filling the backstage area with a hum as great as that which remained inside the theater.

"Was it all right?" she asked Isadora Duncan.

Isadora laughed brilliantly and held her close. "It was magnificent. Superb! It will set all Europe alight. All Europe? What am I talking about? The world. I danced like that once, my darling. A long time ago. But I never had your beauty. Oh, I am so happy for you, my dearest girl. So happy. And so happy for Russia."

She too had known and been accepted and admired by Vladimir Ilich. But he was dead. Suddenly, on this triumphant night, the fact came home to her with a force that had previously been lacking. Vladimir Ilich was dead. And who in all Russia now admired her dancing, whatever the rest of the world might say?

She shook her head as if she would clear her mind of such dismal thoughts, and found herself staring at the man from the front row. Slowly he raised her hand to his lips, while once again she felt utterly shrouded in his gaze, and his admiration.

"I wish to present Mr. Clive Bullen, Frau Nej," said the stage manager. "Mr. Bullen apologizes, but he does not speak Russian."

"Does . . . does he speak French?" Tattie asked in that language—haltingly, for it was a long time since she had been allowed to use it.

"A little," Bullen said. His voice was low, but quick, suggesting the surging impulses of his personality.

Tattie found herself as breathless as she had been at the end of the dance.

"Then, Mr. Bullen," she said, "it is my pleasure."

"The pleasure is mine, Madame Nej," he said, and was swept to one side by the press of people. "Endlessly mine."

"Well?" Tattie stretched the full length and width of the double bed, toes thrust as far as they could go beneath the

sheets, arms hurled as wide as she could. Stretching was a
daily ritual, and a daily pleasure as well. All the more because
she was alone in the bed. No Ivan. Not even little wailing
Gregory. She loved the boy dearly, but he was a nuisance.
Now she had had neither of them for three months. Three
whole, gorgeous, delightful, triumphant months.

But this morning she was not happy. She sat up, throwing
back the covers. "Well?" she demanded.

Olga had been waiting patiently, the newspapers piled before her. "The usual, Tatiana Dimitrievna," she said. "Let me
see, the bad ones first: vulgar posturing . . . obscene . . . should
be banned . . . a disgrace to the theater . . . That is from Serge
Diaghilev. Now, is he not a disgrace to Soviet Russia?" She
chuckled. "But the good ones: Slav goddess . . . goddess from
the steppes . . . unequaled grace . . . delicious eroticism . . .
splendid pageantry . . . original choreography . . . a triumph
. . . a delight . . . an experience to be remembered . . . Tatiana
Nej, we love you . . . all France is entranced . . . Paris goes
wild . . . no occasion ever like it before . . . Isadora Duncan
reincarnated . . . She lives here, you know? Or she used to."

"I know all that," Tattie said, getting out of bed and stalking
across the room to the window, where she threw back the lace
curtains to look out at the street. Paris, she thought. Throughout
the entire tour she had dreamed of coming to Paris. And Paris
was dead.

"Tatiana Dimitrievna," Olga complained, hurrying forward
with a robe. It might be possible, or even correct, for Tatiana
Nej to appear on the stages of Europe with almost nothing on,
but she could not possibly stand at a window with nothing on
at all.

"Have you discovered anything?" Tattie demanded.

Clive Bullen had been there almost every night in Berlin,
almost every night in Vienna, almost every night in Rome, and
every night there had been flowers. Nothing else. He had not
even come backstage after that first night. Perhaps because he
was an Englishman; she had often been told that they were
very shy, incoherent men. But she preferred it this way. It was
the most beautifully romantic thing she had ever heard of, far
more romantic than anything in the English novels she had read
as a girl. No doubt he had discovered she was married, just
as she had discovered that he was not. And perhaps he was

being restrained by the supposition that she was a Communist, since she was Russian, just as she had also learned that he was very much a capitalist, the managing director of a vast engineering firm. But in any event, she did not wish it to become anything physical. She had known sex with only two men, and technically only with her husband. And if either Rasputin or Ivan was representative of what men were like when searching for sex, then the whole thing was an overrated pastime. She gloried in her own sexuality, her obvious ability to make men drool with desire and women snarl with envy. She really didn't need anyone to maul her about and in doing so upset their image of her—or hers of them.

But she had come to rely on seeing his face out there, certainly on the first night of each performance. Throughout the two weeks in Paris he had not been there once, and there had been no flowers. And Paris had been perhaps the greatest triumph of the entire tour. Because, as Isadora had said, the French could appreciate these things far more than the Germans or the Austrians, or even the Italians. Paris was bound to be the highlight of the entire tour, Isadora had pointed out, because the English were quite incapable of appreciating anything not blessed by having been there for five hundred years. Isadora was in fact amazed that the troupe intended to take in England at all, and in fact the London season had been in doubt because of some stupid letter written by Gregory Zinoviev, which had apparently upset the British government.

But that had been smoothed over, and she had expected London to be *her* triumph, because it was Clive's home. At least, she assumed so. Then he had not come to see her at all, in Paris. Of course he was ill. But if he was ill, why had Olga not been able to find out anything?

Was it nor far more likely that as he, and she, approached his home he was beginning to realize, since he was English, that those critics who found her dancing obscene were probably right, after all?

"Well?" she demanded, again.

"There is no trace of Mr. Bullen at any hotel in Paris, that I have been able to discover, Tatiana Dimitrievna," Olga said. "But I have the most exciting news. You'll never believe who is downstairs now, wishing to see you!"

"Who?" Tattie turned.

"Your brother," Olga shouted. "Peter Borodin."

"Peter? Here in Paris?"

"Comrade Nikoyan is very worried. He wishes a word. He is outside now."

Tattie shrugged. "Tell him to come in. And ring down and tell Peter to come up, since he's here. I thought he still lived in America."

"He does live in America, Comrade Nej," Nikoyan pointed out; he had obviously been listening at the door. "And he is well known to us—to your husband, comrade—as a subversive and an anti-Bolshevik campaigner, a tsarist agent in the worst possible sense. It is my duty to forbid you to see him."

"My own brother? Nikoyan, you are a fool. Go back to bed."

"I am acting under orders from Commissar Nej, comrade. Your husband. He has told me to use my own judgment to keep you away from subversives and undesirables. And I am bound to say that I shall have to make a report on our return about your infatuation with this Bullen. This sending two of my men to make inquiries at all the hotels in Paris—"

"Comrade Nikoyan," Tattie said. "Get out. If you have to make a report I suggest you get on with it. And if you think I am not going to receive my brother, when I haven't seen him in nine years, you need your head examined. Olga, where is Prince Peter?"

"He is here now, Tatiana Dimitrievna."

"Then show him in."

"*Prince* Peter," Nikoyan sneered.

"Out," she said, pointing, and since he was as afraid of her as Ivan, he left, casting a narrow-eyed look at Peter in the doorway, as he passed.

"Tattie." Peter stepped into the room, arms wide, and stopped to stare.

"Good morning, Peter," she said, and sat down. "Will you take coffee?"

"But . . ." He came closer, kissed her hands and then her cheeks. "I saw your photograph in the newspapers, of course, and then last night—"

"You saw me dance?" she cried in delight. "Did you like it?"

"Well, perhaps it is a shade too modern for me. A shade too revolutionary. But I was right at the back and could not see clearly. I had no idea you were so . . . well, so . . ."

"I am a Slav goddess," she pointed out, accepting a cup from Olga's tray. "I think I must always have been a Slav goddess, even if there were people, my own family included, who did not agree with me." She looked at him, but he did not even flush.

"Of course I realize," Peter said magnanimously, "that you had to concoct something like this to get out of Russia at all. But now that you *are* out, it is all prepared."

"What is all prepared?"

Peter glanced at Olga. "Isn't it possible to be alone with you?"

Tattie waved her hand, and Olga left the room, closing the double doors behind her.

"What is all prepared?"

"Your escape from these people. Listen, you will go to London, as planned, and there it will happen. You may leave it all to me. I just wanted you to know, so you won't be frightened. Just continue to dance and act naturally, and in no time you'll be safe in New York."

"Safe?" Tattie inquired. "In New York?"

"Yes. That's where we all are, you know. Rachel and little Ruth, Judith Stein—you remember Judith Stein? And of course Ilona and George, and the children. You want to see Ilona and George again?"

"I am going to see Ilona and George again, anyway," Tattie pointed out. "I have had a letter from her. She and George, and the children, are on their way across now. They are going to see me in London, and we are going to have the most wonderful get-together. I don't have to go all the way to New York."

"But . . . don't you want to leave Russia?"

"Why should I want to do that?"

"For God's sake," he shouted, "it's Communist! And you're tied to that dreadful Ivan Nej. We'd get you a divorce. You'd start a whole new life."

"Would I have a dancing troupe? A dancing school? Would I be a friend of this president person?"

Peter scratched his head. "Well...I suppose you could dance. I suppose George could even finance you in a school, if you wanted one. I'm not sure he'd approve. I don't approve. As for the president—well, I suppose it's possible. It might take a little time."

"Time," Tattie said. "I don't have any time. I am thirty-two years old. I can't afford the time. Why should I leave Russia? I have everything I want right there. My children are there. My friends are there. I'm looking forward to seeing George and Ilona again, but I have no other friends in America. You were never my friend, Peter. All you wanted to do was lock me up. And that's what you'll do all over again. Lock me up. I'd have to be mad." She got up and opened the door. "Prince Borodin is just leaving."

"If this is London in the summer," Olga grumbled, peering out of the train window, "give me Paris."

Tattie supposed she was right. It was raining, a slow and steady drizzle. But even had the sun been shining, she would have found the scene depressing: the close-huddled houses, the grime everywhere, the clouds of coal smoke hanging on the still air. She had thought her first glimpse of the city would be of the Tower, with St. Paul's in the background, and Buckingham Palace rising on the right, and the river...and there it was, the river, iron-gray and sluggish, coursing under the railway bridge. She couldn't see much else, except to her left the towers of the Palace of Westminster, she realized, and the clock tower of Big Ben. But the rest was there, to be seen. And none of that mattered anyway. Everything that was interesting or exciting about London was waiting for her.

She opened the note and read it again. It was written in Russian. He had spent the three months of the tour not only in watching her, but in learning Russian. Of all the darling, romantic men.

She chewed her lip. But that aspect of things was coming to an end. He had not been in Paris because he was already in London, arranging things. He wished to come to see her. He wished to take her out to dinner. He wished...he would wish a lot more than that.

"I absolutely forbid it," Nikoyan said. He sat in the far corner of the compartment, watching her, and watching her read. He knew what was in the letter; he insisted on opening all her mail.

His statement just about settled the matter. She wasn't at all sure whether or not she wanted to go out to dinner with Clive Bullen. She was quite sure that she didn't want him to get to the physically serious stage. But if Nikoyan was going to forbid it—

"You listen to me, Comrade Nikoyan," she said, speaking in very even tones. "If you even attempt to interfere with Mr. Bullen, I am personally going to take your balls and twist them right off."

Nikoyan gazed at her and blinked, while turning crimson. It was not merely that her language continually shocked him. He suspected she was quite capable of carrying out her threat.

"We seem to be stopping," Olga said, anxious to pour oil on the troubled waters.

A station named after some dead queen, and as grimy as all the rest of London. A bowing reception committee, and then taxis, very odd-looking cars like contracted buses. A drive through the rain, and all the while a growing excitement. A hotel overlooking a park. Quite a large park, beautiful even in the rain. A hot bath and a cup of English tea, which was apparently de rigueur. Nikoyan, sitting in the outer room and glowering. And Olga, slowly taking out the dinner gown she had bought for her mistress in Paris.

It was black lace, with a black crêpe-de-chine lining. Its chiffon top was flesh-colored, and with Tattie's bust this was apt to be both disturbing and confusing. Her stockings were also flesh-colored and there was an awful lot of them on display, for the hem ended just below the knee. Nikoyan had been scandalized, but this, according to the Parisian saleswoman, was all the current rage. Her shoes were silver, her necklace pearls, and her bracelets silver, also all bought in Paris.

"You look enchanting, Tatiana Dimitrievna," Olga said. "Fit for the stage."

"And for nowhere else," Nikoyan growled from the doorway.

"Mr. Bullen is here, Madam Nej," said the girl on the house telephone.

The elevator seemed to travel terribly slowly. But eventually she reached the lobby and stepped out. She could not see him.

"Mr. Bullen?" she asked the bellboy.

"He went outside, Madam Nej, with two gentlemen."

"With—" Tattie brushed him aside, ran to the revolving doors, and burst into the open air, looking left and right. She saw Clive standing by a huge potted palm that half-concealed him from the street, between the two OGPU men, who were each holding one of his arms and talking to him. She had not even known they spoke English.

But to see Clive so bullied! She started forward, and then stopped, because did she really wish to be wined and dined by a man who could be so bullied. And yet she couldn't just let them beat him up, as they were so fond of doing. And then she realized that he wasn't going to be beaten up, after all. She couldn't be sure what had happened, but suddenly one of the Russians was sitting in the flower pot, and the other was holding his wrist with an agonized expression on his face, while Clive was walking towards her, smiling.

"Clive," she cried. "What—"

"I didn't hurt them," he said. "I merely explained to them that we don't behave like that in England." He dusted the sleeve of his dinner jacket. "My car is right here."

It occurred to Tattie that she had never seen him wearing anything other than a black dinner jacket. But did she wish to see him in anything else? It was clearly a decision she was going to have to make very soon. And suddenly she felt curiously unexcited, almost detached. The excitement was there, lurking just beneath her consciousness. She could feel it, knew that in time, in a very short time, it was going to take over her entire personality. But knowing that, she felt no need for either impatience or apprehension. It was like beginning a dance, knowing from the beginning how it should end, how she wanted it to end, but not knowing how good her performance was going to be, this night, how much applause she would receive, how happy or how miserable she would be at the end of it. She could only dance, and wait to find out.

But while dancing, she must always be Tattie.

"I hope I didn't cause any trouble with your people," he said, kissing her hand.

"They bring their troubles on themselves," she said. "Your Russian is very good."

"I actually did have a word or two of it when we first met,

Madam Nej, but I didn't regard it as good enough for conversation. My firm does a lot of business with Germany and the Balkan states. We have considered attempting to come into Russia, without very great enthusiasm, I may say. But I intend to change that."

They sat together in the back of his Rolls-Royce.

"What does your firm do, Mr. Bullen?" she asked.

"We are engineering consultants," he explained. "If you wish a factory built, we will come along, if invited, and tell you where and how would be best. We'll even supervise the whole thing for you."

"And in Russia," she said, "we need a great number of factories."

They dined at the Café Royal; she refused caviar in favor of snails.

"I imagine this is your first visit to London," he said.

"It is the first time I have ever left Russia, this tour."

"That is amazing."

"Not so amazing. I was regarded as the black sheep of my family, then there came the revolution, and they were all killed. Except for my brother and sister, who got away to America. Although Peter is somewhere in Europe now, and my sister and her husband are arriving here the day after tomorrow, to see my performance."

"But you stayed in Russia."

"Well, I got married." She smiled at him. "To a Bolshevik. I suppose Mama is turning in her grave, especially as it was Ivan who put her there."

"Who . . .?"

"Don't let me shock you, Mr. Bullen. You have to take me as I am. Even Ivan has to do that."

"Ivan being your husband?"

She nodded, and drank some wine. She realized she was going to have to take the lead, if she wanted anything from this man. He might be able to take care of himself with impressive ease, but he remained an English gentleman, and that meant he was positively humble in regard to women. But suddenly she did want a great deal from him. The elegance of the car, of the surroundings, of the man himself, as much as the strength that rippled beneath that so-well-groomed exterior, was causing her excitement to grow. And he had not even attempted to touch her hand, merely sat opposite her and devoured her with his eyes. But that he wanted her could not be doubted for a moment.

"Yes," she said. "Ivan is my husband."

"Is it true that he is deputy chief of the OGPU?"

She placed her elbow on the table and rested her chin on her knuckles. "Does that frighten you, Mr. Bullen?"

"It intrigues me, if half of what one hears is true."

"All of what one hears is true, Mr. Bullen. Ivan is a monster."

It was his turn to drink some wine.

"Which makes you suppose that I must be a monster too, to live with him." She shrugged. "Well, perhaps I am. I have been called a monster often enough. Are you disturbed at being out to dinner with a monster?"

"If you are a monster, Madam Nej, then meet Bluebeard."

She smiled at him. "You are taking me at my face value. You do not know what I am really like. Perhaps I do not know myself. Do you know you are the first man who has ever taken me out to dinner?"

"The—" He frowned at her. "I can't believe that."

"It is true."

"But . . . on this tour . . ."

She shook her head. "There have been invitations, but none I have accepted. And anyway, Nikoyan frowns on invitations."

"Nikoyan being your watchdog?"

"He works for my husband."

"And he approves of your going out with me?"

"Oh, no. He disapproves of you more than anyone else."

"Then I don't understand."

"*I* approve of you, Mr. Bullen. So I accepted the invitation."

"But . . . won't you be in trouble?"

"I am never in trouble, Mr. Bullen. I am Tatiana Nej."

"Ah. Would you like to dance?"

She surveyed the floor, where an assortment of men and women were doing the Charleston.

"No," she said.

"It was a silly question. What would you like to do?"

"It is up to you. Would you like to make love to me?"

"What?" He sat back in his chair.

"Well, I supposed you must, since you invited me out," she

explained. "And since you have watched most of my performances."

Bullen finished his wine.

"I would like you to," she said. "In fact, Mr. Bullen, you are the very first man in all my life that I have actually wanted to make love to me. Otherwise I wouldn't have accepted your invitation."

Well, now, she thought. Are you a man or a mouse, Clive Bullen?

He took out a handkerchief, looked at it, and put it back in his pocket.

"But if you don't," she said. "Then I think we should go back to the hotel. I have to rehearse tomorrow."

He leaned forward. "I would like very much to make love to you, Tatiana Nej. I have dreamed of nothing else since that first night in Berlin. You must forgive me for being absurd just now."

"Not at all. I suppose English girls do not speak like that."

"No," he said. "They don't. But Russian girls do?"

"I don't know," she said. "I am not a Russian girl, Clive Bullen. I am Tatiana Nej. Shall we go, and make love?"

Chapter 7

IT SHOULD BE LIKE DANCING.

Dancing while standing still. One of the first lessons she always instilled in her girls. If they could move, sinuously and erotically, but also gracefully and with rhythm, while never moving their feet, then they must do better when allowed to hurtle about a stage. And to dance when lying on their backs had been the next lesson. It was one of her favorite occupations.

She had never tried it under a man before. Before tonight the man had not existed.

Now desire, mounting ecstasy, flowed away from her groin, reached out into her arms and her legs, convulsed her lips, sent her head tossing to and fro as sweat flowed out from the thick yellow hair. He was there, and without him nothing would have been possible, and yet, having launched her on this path, he was no longer a necessity. He seemed to know that his business was just to be there, holding her, while her body attempted to chase her spirit into the dreamland of a subconscious heaven.

155

She rolled him onto his back, and rose on her elbow above him; their bodies matched since he was only a couple of inches taller than she. Her hair flopped over his as her nipple rose against his and her toes flicked against his, as her fingers gently caressed his softness.

"I love you," he said.

She kissed his mouth, her leg thrown across his. It was a slow, long kiss, the deepest they had shared because of their earlier impatience, and as she kissed him she laughed at feeling him rise again into her hand.

"You *will* love me," she said. "Soon."

"I meant *love*."

"Is this not love?" she asked, and kissed him again. "Because I love you too. No man has ever touched me, as you."

His turn to push her flat, and sit beside her. "I don't want only to love your body," he said. "To feel you and smell you and want you. I want to love *you*."

She held his hand and placed it on her breast. "Love my body," she said. "My body has never been loved, like this. Love my body."

It was not possible to refuse Tatiana Nej, when she *wanted*. But in time even she was sated, at least temporarily, and appeared to sleep. Clive Bullen got out of the bed and stood by the window to watch the first suggestion of dawn.

"Why are you not here with me?" she asked.

"I suppose I have too much to think about," he confessed. "Tatiana—"

"Will you come back to Russia, with me?"

He frowned at her. "I can't."

"Because Ivan would put you in prison," she said.

"Well, I hadn't really thought of that. But I have my work, my—"

"Your family?"

He shook his head and sat beside her again. "I have no family that would matter, if I could be with you."

"But you cannot come to Russia with me."

"Tatiana . . ."

"So you see, you must not ask me to stay in England with you. Because I do have a family, my children, who matter very much to me. And I too have work to do, and a career to follow. And I too feel that if I left Russia and came here I would be put into prison."

"That is nonsense."

"You do not know my brother," she said, and sat up again to hold him in her arms. "But we will meet again, and again, while I remain in England. Will we not?"

"I would like that."

"And I. And then, when we are apart, we will dream of each other, and you will write to me."

"Will my letters be allowed to reach you?"

"Oh, yes." She laughed again. "After Ivan has read them, of course. But it will do him good to read them."

"I hate to think of you at the mercy of that monster."

"I am not at the mercy of anyone, Clive. I am Tatiana Nej. You will write to me, and I will write to you, and we shall meet again and again. To renew our love."

He kissed her on the nose. "You are an impossible romantic, Tatiana Nej. You cannot live your life like the heroine of a novel."

"You mean you will stop loving me if you cannot see me every day?"

"Of course I do not."

"Then you are just as romantic as I," she pointed out. "And why should we not be romantic? If we love each other, why should we not be romantic?"

"I suppose because life does not always work out exactly the way two lovers might wish."

"It is always possible to have life work out as you might wish, Clive," she said, "if you have enough love, enough determination . . . and enough patience. I have been waiting for you all my life. Without even knowing you existed, I have been waiting for you. I have been raped, did you know that?"

He shook his head.

"Does that matter to you?" she asked.

"Nothing matters to me, besides the fact of you. Besides, I knew . . . well, you could not be the woman you are had your life not been eventful."

"When I was raped, I wished to die. I have often wished to die. But then I have thought, If I die, there is nothing. And I will have known nothing. So I have chosen to live. Because there must be happiness somewhere. I always knew that. And now it has been proved to me."

"You are a very wise, and a very brave, young woman."

"Oh, no. I am mad. Quite mad. That is what they have always said of me. Quite mad. But you will be mad with me too, will you not, Clive Bullen?"

"Willingly," he said. "Happily."

"Then you will be happy, and I will be happy. Now you must send me home, in a taxi. I must rehearse at ten o'clock."

"I shall take you home, my darling girl. Myself."

She shook her head, got out of bed, and went into the bathroom. "There will be somebody watching this house."

He stood in the doorway as she brushed her hair. "Nikoyan?"

She shrugged. "Or one of his people." She found her handbag and applied makeup, nose close to the glass of the mirror. "And after they have followed us back to the hotel, they might attempt to interfere with you." She smiled. "And after last night, they might use weapons."

"I don't think—"

She laid her fingers on his lips. "I know you are not afraid of them. Dare I say that is one of the reasons I love you? But I still will not risk you being hurt."

"I *am* afraid of them, Tatiana, for what they might do to you."

She regarded herself, seemed satisfied, and started to dress.

"I am Tatiana Nej," she pointed out.

"Is it always like this?" Ilona shouted above the din.

Tatiana hugged her sister. "It always has been, before. I had not expected such a response in London."

People pushed them to and fro, surging through the backstage area of the Royal Opera House and overflowing onto the stage itself, trying to shake Tattie's hand, to obtain her autograph, to give her flowers. But the family party in the middle, speaking Russian, was able largely to isolate itself from the din.

"What did you think, George?" Tattie asked, accepting a kiss on the cheek.

"I . . . well, I don't really know what to say." He had seen her dance before, on that unforgettable day he had been taken to visit Rasputin's salon. He had been shocked then, when she was only eighteen. He supposed he would have to admit that he was even more shocked now.

She laughed, and kissed him on the mouth. "You don't approve. I want you to meet Clive Bullen." She pulled him forward. "My lover."

"Your . . ." George stared at the Englishman.

Clive shrugged even as he flushed. "Tattie's way, I'm afraid. But I do love her, very much."

"I think we all do," George agreed. "Johnnie. Come on. Wriggle in here."

John Hayman was thrust to the forefront of the crowd. "I bet you don't remember Auntie Tattie."

"Ivan," she screamed, and held him close, then held him at arm's length. "But you are—"

"Seventeen," he admitted, face crimson.

"Seventeen. How marvelous to be seventeen. Are George and Felicity with you?"

"At the hotel," Ilona said.

Tattie pouted. "You thought they would be shocked?"

"I thought they were a little young for an evening out. You are coming to supper with us, Tattie?"

"Of course I am. The five of us. It is going to be absolutely splendid."

"It is forbidden," Nikoyan said, as ever at her elbow.

"Go and drink some vodka, comrade," Tattie said. "I am going to have supper with my sister and her husband, and no one is going to stop me." She kissed Ilona again. "You go on ahead, and I will join you when I have changed. The Claridge's, is it?"

"No 'the,'" Ilona said. "But you have the right idea. All right, we'll go on ahead. Mr. Bullen . . ."

"Oh, take Clive with you," Tattie agreed. "I will see you there."

"She keeps being afraid these watchdogs of hers are going to hit me on the head," Clive said.

"Nikoyan's brain works in a mysterious way," Tattie laughed, and threw her arm round the policeman's shoulder, to his obvious discomfort. "When it works. Off you go. I shall not be long."

"May I see your dressing room, Aunt Tattie?" John Hayman asked.

She stared at him, as did his mother and father.

"Why, Johnnie, what a suggestion," George said.

"I think it's a lovely suggestion, Ivan Sergeievich," Tattie said. "Of course you will see my dressing room. You will stay with me while I dress, and we shall go to this Claridge's together." She smiled at Ilona. "Or are you afraid I will corrupt him?"

"Oh, Tattie," Ilona complained, blushing.

"I shall not be able to," Tattie pointed out. "Olga is there, and Nikoyan. Nikoyan is always there. We shall see you at Claridge's. Come along, Ivan Sergeievich." She took his hand and pulled him through the throng, a way being made for her by the stage manager and another of the Russian detectives. "What a big fellow you have become," she said. "Soon you will be as tall as your father."

"Was Papa a very tall man?" John Hayman asked.

"He was tall. Not as tall as the Borodins, of course. So you are certain to be very tall yourself."

"I think I've stopped growing," John said.

"Oh, nonsense. You will be over six feet tall. All Borodin men are more than six feet tall. Shall I tell you why? Because we always marry tall men ourselves, or tall women, as the case may be." She pouted. "Except for me. *My* husband is a midget. Isn't that so, Comrade Nikoyan? Commissar Nej is an absolute midget." She squeezed John's hand. "In every way."

Nikoyan held the dressing-room door for her. "One day, Comrade Nej," he said, "your husband is going to get angry with you, and then . . ."

She blew him a kiss. "And then he will hand me over to you, comrade?"

"And then not even your fame will save you from discipline," he said, his cheeks pink.

"He dreams," Tattie said, and gave a tinkle of laughter, "of me. This is Olga, my dresser. Olga, this is my nephew, Ivan Sergeievich. Do you know who his father was? Prince Roditchev."

Olga stared at the boy, her mouth a huge O, and Tattie gave another peal of laughter. "But he is not the least bit like his father. I give you my word."

"Papa was a faithful servant of the tsar," John Hayman said, standing at attention.

It was Tattie's turn to stare for a moment. Then she smiled, more gently than was her habit, held his face between her hands, and kissed him on the mouth. "Of course. Now they are both dead. Sit down in that chair by the window. I will change behind this screen, you see, and you will not even have to be shocked."

John Hayman sat down and watched his aunt and Olga go behind the shoulder-high screen. He glanced at the door to the dressing room, but Nikoyan had withdrawn, closing it behind him. "Doesn't he wish to stay in here as well?"

"Him?" Tattie removed the still sweat-damp silk blouse and trousers, and draped them over the top of the screen. "I have no doubt he would like to. But I draw the line somewhere. He stands out there with his arms folded, looking like a thug. Well, he is a thug. Ivan employs only thugs. That is his name too, you know. Ivan. My husband."

"Do you hate him very much?" John asked.

"Hate Ivan?" Tattie's hair was piled on top of her head and concealed beneath a rubber cap, and she stepped into the shower. "He is my husband."

"But—"

"I feel sorry for him, most of the time," Tattie said, while Olga soaped her with a loofah. "He is just a very little man trying to be great. Nothing is a more pitiful sight."

"Napoleon was a little man," John Hayman said, examining the catch on the window.

"I meant little, mentally," Tattie said, leaving the shower to be wrapped in an enormous bathrobe. She came round the screen to sit down while Olga laid out her clothes. "Anyway, it has never been proved that Napoleon was a great man, in my opinion. He invaded Russia, didn't he? And got beaten."

"Is that your criterion of greatness?" John asked. "The ability to beat Russia?"

"You are a very argumentative young man," Tattie said. "What are you doing with that window?"

"I was trying to open it," John said.

"Oh, Comrade Nikoyan wouldn't like that. He insists on all my dressing-room windows being locked. I think he feels I am going to escape if I can. Silly little man."

"But don't you find it rather warm?"

"It's hot, if you ask me," Tattie said. "But then, it doesn't do to push him too far, or he *might* insist on being in here while I change. He has the right."

"He'd never know," John pointed out, at last slipping the catch.

Olga was ready, and Tattie got up. "Don't you *like* Comrade Nikoyan?" Tattie asked. She laughed, a delicious gurgle of sound. "Do you know, neither do I? Open the window and let in some air. But you must close it again before we leave." She stepped behind the screen, and inhaled the evening air as John gently pushed the window wide. "That is good. How long are you in England for?"

"I think for as long as you are," John said, walking across the room towards the door.

"Oh, that is splendid. I hope we are going to see lots of each other. I hope . . ." Tattie stared across the top of the screen at her brother, just climbing in through the window. "What in the name of God—" She turned to look at John, who was locking the door.

"Don't make a noise, Aunt Tattie," John said. "It's all arranged."

"Arranged?" Tattie demanded, stepping round the screen, wearing only her slip, and looking very much indeed like an avenging Slav goddess. "You, Peter? Are you out of your mind?"

"Now, Tattie," he said. "Don't start being silly. I am the head of our family, and I have decided that you cannot be allowed to remain in Russia. You are coming back to America with me."

"You . . . you *silly* man," Tattie shouted, and swung her hand.

Peter ducked the blow, but caught the arm, bringing her against him. "The sack!" he shouted.

The man who had climbed in the window behind him promptly produced a sack, which, as Tattie pulled away and turned, gasping for breath, he dropped over her head. Olga screamed.

"Oh, shut her up," Peter snapped at John.

"Please," John said. "Don't make a noise. We don't mean to hurt you."

Tattie was screaming, inflating the sack as she tried to shout and fight at the same time.

Bang, bang, bang, came the thumps on the door. "What is happening in there?" Nikoyan bawled. "Are you all right, Comrade Nej?"

"Hurry," Peter snapped, and the third man climbed out of the window again and dropped to the ground. Peter inserted his wriggling, kicking sister's legs into the opening, and the man seized her ankles.

"You stop that," Olga shouted, and ran forward. John Hayman seized her round the waist and sat her down in the armchair, holding her there. Tattie was already through the window now, into the arms of the man below, and Peter was dropping down beside her. Behind them the door to the dressing room began to splinter. John hurried to the window.

Olga started to get up again. "You will suffer for this," she shrieked. "You, Roditchev's son, you will suffer for this."

John gave her an apologetic smile as he straddled the window sill. "It is for her own good, comrade," he said. "You will understand one day. For her own good." He dropped into the alleyway behind his uncle.

"Oh, my God," Ilona said. "Oh, my God, my God, my God."

"Quite," said Chief Inspector Dorrington.

"Are you seriously trying to tell us that Johnnie is involved?" George demanded.

"That is what I understand to be the case," the chief inspector said. "But I'm afraid I don't speak Russian all that well. Your son was definitely in the dressing room when the kidnapping was carried out. If it was a kidnapping."

"I'm not with you," George said.

"Well, sir, as I understand it, the man being accused by these people is Madam Nej's own brother. Would that be correct?"

"I wasn't there," George said.

"But Madam Nej does have a brother?" the chief inspector asked patiently. "Who is also your brother?"

"Yes," Ilona said.

"And he is presently in Europe?"

"I believe so," Ilona said. "George?"

"Yes," George said. "As far as I know." When he had forbidden Johnnie ever to attend any more of his uncle's meetings, the boy had just stared at him in that remarkable manner he had. And there hadn't been any obvious way to take the situation any further. He did not doubt that Johnnie *had* continued to visit the Borodins. Yet when he had suggested this visit to England to meet up with Auntie Tattie, Johnnie had been delighted. Apparently. And George had also been delighted—being, he now angrily realized, an utter fool.

"Well, Mrs. Hayman," Chief Inspector Dorrington was saying. "Brothers do not as a rule go around kidnapping their sisters, do they?"

Ilona bit her lip and looked at George.

"I don't think Tatiana—Madam Nej would have left through a window in such a manner of her own accord," Clive Bullen said.

The chief inspector regarded him stonily.

"I'm afraid she *was* kidnapped," George said.

"Are you serious, sir?" Dorrington asked.

"Quite serious, Inspector. My brother-in-law is a Russian prince. Or was a prince. Not only does he regard himself as the head of the family, with the right to do whatever he thinks necessary to protect the members of the family and its name, but he is also a rabid anti-Bolshevik who has long held the opinion that Madam Nej was being detained in Russia against her will."

"Oh, my God," Dorrington said in turn. "This will be a Foreign Office affair."

"It may well be."

"An international incident," the chief inspector said, and sat down.

"Have a glass of brandy," Ilona suggested.

The chief inspector drank deeply. "Do you agree with your husband, Mrs. Hayman?"

"I'm afraid he's probably right. Peter virtually kidnapped Tattie once before because she had been misbehaving herself is St. Petersburg."

"He was also fairly heavy-handed regarding you," George pointed out.

"You don't think he'll harm her?" Clive asked.

"She's far more likely to harm him, if she gets the chance," George said.

"And do you suppose Mr. Borodin kidnapped your son also?" Dorrington asked.

"No," George said.

"George," Ilona protested.

"Well, my love..."

"Isn't it possible young John was trying to protect his aunt?" Clive asked.

George shook his head. "I'm afraid not. Johnnie is completely under his uncle's influence. He is also a rabid anti-Communist, and it would be quite easy for Peter to convince him he was doing the right thing. My God, what fools we were! When he asked to see Tattie's dressing room it must all have been part of a plan."

"The possible repercussions are quite frightful," the chief inspector said. "Madam Nej—well, she is an internationally famous *artiste*. What the amabassador is going to say... And there are Americans involved, too."

"Don't remind me," George said.

"You must have some idea what happened to her," Clive said, "where she's been taken."

"My dear sir," Dorrington said, "we don't even know what sort of a vehicle she was taken away in. The hall was just emptying its audience. There were cars, taxis, buses, everywhere. One of them must have been driven down that alleyway, and I have no doubt at all that in the course of time we shall find a witness who will be able to describe what kind of a car it was. But that *will* take time. And she could be well out of London by now."

"Roadblocks?" Ilona suggested.

"My dear Mrs. Hayman, this is not the Soviet Union, or even Chicago. It would be quite impossible to block every road leading out of London without calling out the army and bringing the country to a standstill. That Nikoyan fellow was talking about putting the country under martial law. My God."

"Seaports?" George asked.

"Ah, well, sir, we have been able to do that, certainly. The police in every seaport have been alerted, and a search will be made of every vessel lying in the Port of London. But there is a lot of England that is seacoast, Mr. Hayman. And of course the whole thing is complicated by... Well, sir, despite your help, we don't *know* the lady was kidnapped. What I mean is, sir—well, if we really pull out all the stops, and then we find them and then this Madam Nej says that she left the Royal Opera House of her own free will—well, sir, we could be in for damages and charges of false arrest and destruction of private property and heaven knows what else."

"Oh, quite," George said. "It could be a nasty business."

"Indeed it could, sir. So you'll understand that we must proceed with due caution. Now, sir, what I had in mind, if you and Mrs. Hayman would be willing to cooperate, would be an advertisement—an appeal, if you like sir—from you to Mr. Borodin and young Mr. Hayman, pointing out that they have broken the law—"

"Don't you suppose they know that?" Clive asked.

Dorrington decided to ignore him. "And would be doing the wise thing to return Madam Nej as soon as possible, and also, perhaps, pointing out to Madam Nej the distress and indeed dangers to peace that her disappearance is causing. Just in case she did go of her own free will."

"Do you seriously suppose that will accomplish anything?" George asked. "I doubt they'll even read a newspaper."

"Criminals—I beg your pardon, sir—those fleeing from the police often do. And besides, we could put it out on the radio service."

"Oh, really, inspector, you can't suppose Peter is going to hunt for a house with a radio aerial just to listen to a broadcast?" George sighed. "There is just one way that we might appeal to Johnnie that would make a difference." He looked at Ilona.

"No," she said. "No, no, no. We don't know it would work. And the effect on Johnnie—"

"Ah . . ." Dorrington looked from one to the other. "May I inquire—"

"No," George said. "You may not."

"May I remind you, sir, that this could develop into a most serious international incident?"

"You may remind me," George said. "But my wife's decision in that matter is final."

"I see." Dorrington looked at Ilona rather, she thought, as Ivan Nej had done on her last visit to Moscow. She smiled at him. "But you are prepared to help us in every other way," he finished.

"I intend to do more than that," George said. "It is my family that is involved. I intend to find Madam Nej, if she can be found."

"And I intend to help you," Clive Bullen said.

The taxi squealed to a halt. "There's the car," Lupin, the driver said.

"Is the street empty?" Peter Borodin sat in the back seat next to Tattie, who had temporarily run out of breath and had ceased wriggling and fighting. But he still held her wrists, which she had managed to get out from under the sack.

"Looks empty," said the driver.

"We'll tie these, anyway. Come along, Ivan."

John Hayman took the length of thick cord from his pocket, but hesitated. Suddenly he was not at all sure what he was doing here, and wished he weren't here at all. When Uncle Peter had read of the coming tour of Europe by Tatiana Nej and her dance troupe, and had said, "Good for her. She's coming out. We must be there to help her," it had all seemed tremendously exciting and daring. And for Aunt Tattie, too. He had last seen her at Christmas 1917, just before he and Mother and little George and Felicity had started that unforgettable long journey across Siberia, and all those months in Ekaterinburg, when he had met the tsar. He was only nine then, but he could remember almost every moment of those six months.

Just as he could remember Aunt Tattie. Life on Starogan had been pretty dull for a nine-year-old, surrounded by women as old as his mother and grandmother, with only the two smaller children as playmates. But there had also been Aunt Tattie. She had been somewhat moody, had spent a lot of the time in her own room playing on her piano, or dancing to herself. But often enough she had come down to play with him, to take him for walks or just to sit on the front porch in the swing and rock the pair of them to and fro. He had found her enchanting.

And she had talked to him. She had talked to him of Rasputin—with amazing frankness, he now realized, even though then he had understood very little of what she had been telling him.

But he understood now. And so much more. Whispered conversations between Mother and George, more open conversation between Uncle Peter and Aunt Rachel. He had tried to pump Aunt Judith about it, when she had stayed with them three years before. But then he had only just been beginning to understand, and Aunt Judith had refused to discuss Russia at all, which was surprising since she attended Uncle Peter's meetings.

But even without any help from Aunt Judith, his imagination had run riot. Aunt Tattie had danced for Rasputin with hardly anything on. No wonder Uncle Peter had been so angry with her. And then, soon after *he* had left Starogan, she had been raped by the Reds. No one knew for sure how many men or how many times. But she had been raped. He wasn't at all sure just what would have been involved.

And then tonight, he had seen her dance. He had gone back to the dressing room with her. But by then the pulsing excitement as *the* moment had approached had been clouding his ability to see, and to absorb. Not once during those anxious seconds had he for a moment considered not going through with it. Even now he had no doubt at all that Uncle Peter was right. Her resisting them was merely an instinctive reaction. No one could possibly wish to go on living in Soviet Russia when she had the opportunity to escape to the West, to America. As Uncle Peter had said, she was confused because recently the Soviets had been treating her very well, and she was not intelligent enough to know that they were only doing it for the propaganda value. He had always accepted that Aunt Tattie was not very bright; indeed, it was possible to say she had been born a little weak in the head, Uncle Peter had said, and therefore needed to be looked after, needed to be told what was right and wrong, and what was best.

So there could be no question but that they were doing the right thing in taking her away from the Russians. But now, to be told to tie her wrists together . . . He wondered if the Bolsheviks had tied her wrists together before raping her?

"For God's sake," Uncle Peter snapped. "Hurry up."

Johnnie drew a deep breath, looped the cord twice round his aunt's wrists, pulled it tight, and tied the knot. Her fingers opened and closed, jerked ineffectively as the wrists pulled to and fro.

"Now let's change cars," Peter said, and opened the door. "Come along, Tattie. Don't be foolish, now."

She aimed a kick at his leg, but since she could not see through the sacking she merely missed and half fell out of the car. He caught her easily enough and stood her on the pavement. Her bare feet stamped up and down as the chill struck them.

"Come *on*," Peter said.

John got out of the back of the taxi. Lupin was already behind the wheel of the small English Austin Uncle Peter had bought for this adventure, because it would be inconspicuous on English roads. But it looked even smaller tonight, like a matchbox standing on end. They pushed Tattie up to the back door, Peter glancing up and down the deserted street.

"You get in first," he commanded.

John got in, saw Tattie being thrust towards him.

"Catch her," Peter said.

She had tripped and was falling. Johnnie caught her shoulders but her weight still pushed him against the far side of the seat. Peter gathered her legs and thrust them in, then slammed the door.

"But—" John protested. Tattie was half lying across him, head on his shoulder; he could hear her panting through the sack.

"There's only room for two," Peter said, getting into the front beside the driver. "Besides, I can keep a better eye on her from here. For God's sake, Lupin, let's *go*."

A gear grated. Even Lupin was nervous tonight. Then the engine roared and they drove up the street. "The Great North Road?" Lupin asked.

"Of course not. That's where they'll look. Stick to the side roads and country lanes. There's no hurry."

John was wrestling Tattie round to sit her properly on the seat beside him. To get her straight, it was necessary to hold her legs and pull them out in front, and she tried another kick, which caught him on the shoulder and once again pushed him against the side of the car.

"If you don't behave, Tattie, I am going to hit you," Peter warned.

"I think it's because she can't see, Uncle Peter," John said. "Can't I take off the sack?"

"She'll see where we're taking her, stupid boy," Peter said.

"Does it matter? We're taking her into the country anyway."

Peter hesitated, then shrugged. "I suppose not."

John unfastened the cord that held the sack in at Tattie's waist, and cautiously lifted it over her head. Her face was a mass of golden hair, scattered every way, which a fierce toss failed to return to order. She put up her bound hands to uncover her eyes, and blinked into the darkness of the car.

"You wretch," she said. "You abominable little wretch . . ."

"Now, Tattie," Peter said. "Ivan was only carrying out my orders."

Tattie glared at the front. "As for you," she said, "when I get my hands free . . ."

"You aren't going to have your hands free," Peter pointed out, "until you promise to behave."

"Promise *you*?" She seemed to bristle, like an angry lioness. "I'm going to have my hands free one day," she said, "and then I'm going to twist your balls right off." She turned her head to look at John Hayman. "And then I'm going to fix you, too."

With a speed and a violence Johnnie had never suspected his uncle to possess, Peter leaned over the front seat and seized his sister by the front of her slip, jerking her forward with such force she fell off the seat and onto her hands and knees, on the floor.

"You listen to me," Peter said. "This is not a game. As far as I'm concerned you're diseased. That is what Communism is, a disease. And diseased, you are a disgrace to the family, to the memory of the tsar, to the grand duke and to everything we are fighting for. You are a traitor, Tatiana Dimitrievna— a foul, loathsome traitor. It is my curse that you also happen to be my sister. But I swear to you that sooner than let you go back to Soviet Russia, I'll kill you myself."

"They used a taxicab." Chief Inspector Dorrington sat at his desk and looked quite pleased. "We found it abandoned down a side street in Harrow. That's north London."

"And you're sure it was Peter and Tattie?" George had slept and shaved and felt better, physically, but mentally he was still trembling with the utter absurdity of what Peter had done. The dangerous absurdity.

Clive Bullen did not appear to have slept at all.

"Yes indeed, Mr. Hayman." Dorrington said. "There is no

question of it. There are even traces of Madam Nej's, ah, scent."

"So where are they now?" Clive asked.

"Ah, well, they changed cars. We even have a wheel mark to go on. A small car, I'd say, an Austin Seven or some such thing. Unfortunately, as you will understand, there are an awfully large number of Austin Sevens in this country."

"Can't you positively identify the car?" George asked. "Get a number plate or something? After all, it must have been stolen, or hired."

"Or bought, Mr. Hayman. I rather think a man like the prince would have bought the car."

"Well, then . . ."

"Under an assumed name, almost certainly. And quite a few of these cars are sold every day. We shall find out, of course. I have men looking into it now. But it will take time. Perhaps two or three days."

"Days?" George shouted. "For heaven's sake, man, can't you put more people on to it?"

"Doing what, sir, would you suggest?"

"Well, they changed cars in North London. That means they're heading north."

"Does it, sir?"

"It seems fairly obvious to me, Inspector. Now we know Peter can't get Tattie out of the country, and he knows that too. Not if she doesn't want to go. So it stands to reason that he's taking her to some secluded spot where he can talk, or bully, her into going with him of her own free will. That means north Wales, or the Lake District, or Scotland. But first of all he must get there. It's a two- or three-day drive, isn't it? So if you'd get your provincial police on to checking all Austin Sevens heading north—"

"My dear Mr. Hayman," Dorrington said, "I thought I had explained that. My men, and our provincial police, have more important things to do than gallivant about the country on wild-goose chases. My dear sir, Madam Nej is with her brother, and therefore is hardly in physical danger. Now, sir, if, as you suggest, he manages to talk her into accompanying him of her own free will, then there is absolutely nothing either you or I can do about it. If, on the other hand, she continues to refuse to cooperate with him, then you may rest assured that we will certainly find them in due course. Then, should she wish to prefer charges, we will of course take the matter further."

Clive sighed. "I suppose that about sums it up."

"Like hell it does." George turned on his heel and strode out of the office, slamming the door behind him.

Clive hurried to catch up. "Well, as the man says, Prince Borodin *is* her brother."

"You don't know the half of it, Bullen. He is also Prince Borodin of Starogan, and he hates the Bolsheviks the way you or I would hate the people who had murdered our parents, because they *did* murder his parents. As far as he is concerned, Tattie is a traitor to everything he or his family have ever held dear. He has dreamed of getting her out of Russia for five years. I'm damned sure he has no intention of ever letting her go back."

"But . . . what exactly do you mean?"

"I'm getting my own people onto this, and we're heading north. I think Tattie may be in considerable danger."

"You should eat something," Peter said. "We have turkey sandwiches, and ham sandwiches, and there is a bottle of champagne." He popped the cork as he spoke, and filled one of the cups.

"I am not hungry," Tattie said, looking out the window at the dawn. They were parked at the side of the road, by a wooded copse, just the three of them for the moment. Lupin had departed with the now-empty five-gallon can to refill it from the gasoline pump they had passed in the village a couple of miles back, as he had been doing at regular intervals since leaving London.

"You will become hungry," Peter said. "You are a silly little girl. Ivan?"

John took a sandwich and a cup of champagne, chewed slowly, and watched his aunt. Had she been frightened by Uncle Peter's threat? Since he was her brother, she had to have known it was only a threat. Yet she had not spoke again throughout the night's drive. Perhaps she had slept. Certainly she had leaned against him, her head on his shoulder. And now in the daylight her scantily clad beauty was highly disturbing, for all that he had taken off his jacket and put it around her shoulders.

"I wish we could find her some clothes," he said.

"Trust Tattie to be virtually naked when the time came to leave," Peter said, refilling his cup. "Well, she'll have to stay that way for a while."

"I have no feelings in my hands," Tattie said.

"If you give me your word that you will not try to escape . . ."

"Of course I will give you my word," she agreed.

He looked at her for some seconds, eyes slightly narrowed, then he shook his head. "You must take me for a fool."

"Well," she said. "I wish to pee. If you do not let me out to pee, I shall do it right here on the floor."

"For God's sake," Peter complained. "You are quite disgusting. You always were disgusting, Tattie, but since you've been living with the Bolsheviks—"

"All right," Tattie said, and spread her legs.

"Oh, take her behind a bush, Ivan," Peter said. "One of those over there. But don't let her out of your sight."

"Me?" John cried in alarm.

"There is nobody else," Tattie said, smiling at him. "Be a good boy and help me out."

John sighed, got out of his own door, and went round the car to open hers. She stood on the road and looked at the grass between her and the trees.

"If there are thorns," she said, "you will have to carry me."

"I very much doubt he could lift you," Peter said, watching them.

"Why don't you choke on a wishbone?" Tattie suggested, and gingerly stepped onto the grass.

John walked at her side as she tiptoed towards the copse. "You'll like America," he said hopefully.

"I am not going anywhere near America," Tattie said. "I might like *it*, but I don't like Peter. I loathe every bone in his body. I wish to God Ivan *had* captured him during the war, and had him hanged."

"But he's your brother," John protested.

"He's a pain in—Ow," she yelped, and stood on one leg. Hastily he caught her elbow to stop her overbalancing. "There's a thorn in my foot."

"Well, when we get back to the car—"

"I can't move, unless it comes out," she said. "Unless you want to carry me."

"Well . . ."

"Take it out." She said, and seemed to slide down him until she was sitting, legs thrust in front of her. Cautiously he knelt and lifted the offending foot, found the thorn, looked past it up the long stretch of magnificent white flesh towards a silk-clad wonderland, and hastily closed his eyes.

"Is it bad?" she inquired.

"No." He easily took it out with the nails of thumb and forefinger.

Tattie gave a sigh of relief. "That's better. Do you think I'm beautiful, Johnnie?"

"Well..."

"Of course you do. I can tell it from the way you look at me. Besides, all men think I'm beautiful. Would you like to touch me?"

"Aunt Tattie!"

She shrugged. "Listen. I'll let you touch me if you take off this rope. I'll let you lie on top of me if you'll help me to escape."

John scrambled to his feet, aware that his face was burning. "You're my aunt. You're Mother's sister!"

"Pharaoh's always married their aunts, or their sisters, or something," she pointed out. "Help me up."

He pulled her to her feet, and she looked back at the car. "Ugh, creepy Lupin is coming back. Over there will do." She went behind the bush and smiled at him. "You'll have to pull down my panties for me."

"Please, Aunt Tattie, don't be absurd. You can do it yourself. I know you can."

She shrugged, lifted her slip, removed her panties, and squatted, watching him all the while. He looked away, down at the car.

"You're supposed to look at me," she said. "What is Peter paying you for committing this crime?"

"Paying me?" He turned back without meaning to. But she was standing up again, carefully inserting her feet into the crumpled panties. "He's not paying me anything. And it isn't a crime. We're trying to help you."

"Kidnapping is a crime," she pointed out. "When you are caught you are going to go to jail for a very long time. Do you know, I think in some countries they hang you for kidnapping? Or is it the electric chair?" She settled her slip. "Ivan is always going on about criminal codes in other countries. He takes it quite seriously. But they don't hang you for kidnapping in England," she said regretfully. "You'll just go to jail for life."

"Aunt Tattie . . ."

"Isn't that silly, when you could be free? I mean, *why* are you doing it, if you're not getting paid?"

"We must get back to the car," he said, watching Lupin putting the gasoline can into the trunk.

"Tell me why," she said.

"Well . . . For heaven's sake, Aunt Tattie, the Bolsheviks are our enemies. I work for Uncle Peter."

"Without pay?"

"Of course without pay. I've taken an oath to spend my life fighting for the downfall of Bolshevism, for the overthrow of Soviet Russia."

"That doesn't sound very patriotic to me."

"Don't you understand?" he shouted. "The Bolsheviks murdered the tsar. The murdered your mother and all our family. They—" He stared at her.

"You were going to say that they raped me," she said. "Do you suppose being raped by Ivan was any worse than your mother being raped by your father?"

"Oh, really, Aunt Tattie."

"Because that's what it was. Your father beat your mother almost every night of their marriage."

"Don't be ridiculous."

"You ask her," Tattie suggested. "Almost every night. He thought it was good for her, just to remind her who was the head of the family. Ivan has never raised his hand to me in his life. At least, not recently. If he did I'd break it. So the Bolsheviks murdered the tsar, and a few others besides. Don't you suppose the tsars murdered a lot of people? More people than Lenin ever did."

"Now you *are* being absurd. And telling lies."

"Am I? I suggest you ask your parents' friend Judith about that one. Ask her what happened to her when she was sent to Siberia by the tsar, when she was being interrogated by *your* father, Ivan Sergeievich. And then ask her, and your mother, what happened to them when they were captured by the Bolsheviks. Compare the two."

He stared at her. "Are *you* a Bolshevik?"

"Of course not. I'm Tatiana Nej."

"Well, then—"

"But I know there isn't much difference between the way the Bolsheviks are governing Russia and the way the tsars used to."

"I . . ." He had to take refuge in simple facts. "If you hated my father that much, then you must hate me too."

"Why should I do that?"

"Well, because I must be very like him."

"You're not, thank God. Except in obeying Peter in this stupid fashion. You're a Borodin. And besides, you've been brought up by George Hayman. It shows. If I were you I'd model myself on him, rather than on your silly uncle."

"George doesn't go much for Bolshevism."

"Well, of course he doesn't. He's an American capitalist. But he's not stupid enough to take an oath to bring it down."

"Uncle Peter says—"

"Oh, damn uncle Peter," she shouted. "There's no hope for him, anyway. But if you go on this way, you're going to ruin your life. And you're not going to get anywhere. Take it from me, because I know. The Bolsheviks may not survive, true enough. But nobody is *ever* going to put the tsars back on the throne, and nobody is ever going to give Starogan back to Peter. Think about it."

"Are you coming back?" Peter shouted from the road. "Or do I have to come and fetch you?"

"I may have something for you, Mr. Hayman," Crowther said, standing in the doorway of the sitting room of the hotel suite and twisting his hat in his hands. He was a little man who looked like a ferret, which was appropriate for a private detective.

"What?" George put down his coffee cup, and Ilona emerged from the bedroom wearing a dressing gown, the dark shadows under her eyes indicating a sleepless night.

"Well, sir, I would estimate that Prince Borodin is driving north along the A6, and that he passed through the village of Padley, for example, about dusk last night."

"Sit down," George invited, "and tell us how you figure that."

Ilona poured coffee.

"Well, sir, madam," Crowther said, flushing. "I put the known and assumed facts together." He ticked off his fingers. "Small car, therefore he would need to fuel fairly regularly. Heading north with a reluctant lady, therefore he couldn't risk just driving into a station and asking for petrol. Gasoline, sir. So I had my lads sit down with every telephone book covering the midlands and north, and had them call every filling station and garage, saying we would like to hear if any station filled a petrol can for a man on foot during yesterday. Well, sir, the filling station in Padley not only filled a five-gallon can for a man at dusk last night, but the man spoke with a heavy accent of some kind."

"Prince Borodin?"

"Well, sir, the man doesn't fit Prince Borodin's description. But surely there will be some other people involved."

"Agreed," George said. "You feel this is reliable information, Crowther?"

"Oh, yes, sir." Crowther cleared his throat. "I did offer a reward of a hundred pounds for any information."

"That's fine. That's very good, Crowther. Now I want you to get me a big fast car, and I want you to keep your men on the job. Have the car here in half an hour. Now, remember, I'll be telephoning your office for a progress report every few hours, so keep in touch there."

"Yes, sir." Crowther finished his coffee and hurried from the room.

"If you'd like to get dressed, my love," George said.

"Five minutes," Ilona agreed. "Do you think—"

"It's our best chance."

"What about Clive?"

George picked up the telephone. "I'm going to get him now."

They drove all day, Peter and Lupin taking turns behind the wheel, stopping only outside of small villages to let Lupin walk in with the gasoline can. Apparently the trunk was stuffed full of sandwiches and bottles of champagne, as well as a couple of gallon-size cans of water. John loosened Tatiana's wrists to allow her blood to circulate, and for the rest tried not to look at her, because she was most certainly looking at him. Every time he turned his head he was conscious of those deep blue eyes seeming to penetrate him.

She knows I am her best hope, he reasoned. The weakest link. And was she not absolutely right? It was true that he was committing a crime, if she absolutely refused to agree to go with them. Of course she was wrong in her thinking, and in what she had said about his father and about the tsars. So what if Father had been the head of the tsar's secret police? He had had to deal with murderers and criminals and subversives of every kind. And he had earned his reputation when putting down the Moscow revolution of December 1905; he had used artillery on the rebels who had seized the center of the city. John was not at all sure whether *he* would ever have had the determination to blow people to bits, some of whom must have been innocent, just as he was quite sure he would never be able to browbeat anyone into confessing to a crime, but he had to respect his father for possessing such qualities.

But Aunt Tattie, having been forced to live with the Bolsheviks for seven years, would naturally have been exposed to their points of view all that time, and being weak in the head, as Uncle Peter had always said, she would in time believe what she was told, even to the extent of believing that Father had tortured his prisoners, which everyone knew was pure Bolshevik propaganda. Uncle Peter had been absolutely right from the beginning to try and get her out. She was the very last remaining member of his family to be caught up in the Communist web.

But if she definitely didn't want to come with them...

"We'll stop here for the night," Peter said. "We could all do with a good sleep." He pulled off the road, drove down a bumpy lane, and stopped in the opening to a field. "No one will think of looking down here at night." He opened the door, got out, and inhaled the evening air. "Not too cold. Now then, we three will sleep outside the car, and you can stay inside, Tattie, since you don't have any clothes. You'll have to curl up a bit, but I'm sure you're tired."

"Go to hell," Tattie said.

They ate sandwiches, and drank some more champagne. There were blankets in the trunk as well, and they were each given one of those, while there was newspaper for the men to lie on to protect them from the damp in the ground.

"We're moving again at first light," Peter said. "So get some sleep. By tomorrow evening we'll be at Fort William."

"Where are we now?" John asked.

"Somewhere in the Lake District. Stop worrying. No one has any idea where *we* are."

He closed his eyes, and a moment later was asleep. John was slowly realizing that his uncle was playing a game, re-capturing all the adventure of a few years before, when he had been Denikin's chief of staff, in the civil war against the Reds, sleeping in the open, making decisions, freed from the neces-sity of obeying laws or even observing manners. As for Lupin, he just did what Peter told him.

He watched the car move as Tattie thumped around trying to get comfortable; he did not suppose she would, as it was not a very big car. But she was better off in there than out here. Even wrapped in his blanket he was already feeling chilled. He closed his eyes, and slept. And awoke again some time later, when the night had now grown very dark. What had awakened him?

He sat up and stared at the car, just a glimmer of reflected metal in the gloom. But one of the doors was open. It had made the sound that had awakened him.

He threw off the blanket, scrambled to his feet and ran to the car. He looked inside, then left and right, and saw her, a long sliver of white flesh and tangled golden hair, hurrying down the cart track.

He gave a quick glance at the still sleeping men, then ran behind her. She heard his footsteps, ran herself, tripped, and fell to her hands and knees. He followed quietly.

"Aunt *Tattie*!" He kept his voice to a whisper as he stood above her.

"I've cut my toe," she complained.

He took her arm to help her up, and looked at her hands.

She blew him a kiss. "I sawed through that cord. On the gear stick."

"Oh, Aunt Tattie. Uncle Peter is going to be very angry."

"Damn Uncle Peter. We'll be miles away before he wakes up."

"We?"

"You're going to help me, John. Of course you are. Or you wouldn't be speaking in a whisper."

"Oh, no," he said. "I can't. I swore an oath..."

Tattie took his hand and rested it on her left breast. "Of course you're going to help me, Johnnie."

"Aunt Tattie..."

"Mr. Borodin!" Lupin shouted. "Wake up!"

John glanced right and left. "Quick," he said, dragging her by the hand through a gap in the hedge on their left.

"Ow," she said again. "My toe."

"We must hurry." He half-dragged her, half-carried her across the field, his arm round her waist.

"There!" they heard Peter shout. "Come back, you silly fools. Ivan, you are breaking your oath of allegiance. Come back, or I'll shoot."

Johnnie held Tattie's hand, panting as they stumbled over the uneven ground.

"All right, Lupin," Peter shouted. "Bring them down. Aim at the legs."

They heard the sound of the shot. Where the bullet went it was impossible to say, but Tattie stopped running. "Shooting at me," she said. "My own brother. When I get my hands on him—"

"Aunt Tattie, please," Johnnie begged. "Look, there's a stile. Once we're over that..." He dragged her forward, listening now to Peter's voice cursing at Lupin as they ran forward.

"You couldn't hit the side of a barn," Peter panted. "Oh, don't bother to shoot again, we'll catch them."

"You'll never guess what I just stepped in," Tattie complained. "Obviously they keep cows in this field."

"Oh, come on, do." John begged, getting one foot across the stile, and for the first time looking back. His uncle and Lupin were very close, running across the field. "Oh, Christ, we won't make it."

"Then don't let's bother," Tattie said. "You take Peter."

"But..." Still sitting astride the wall, he watched his aunt delve into the earthen wall beneath her for a moment, straighten carrying a large clod of earth, and as Lupin reached her, she hurled the earth-covered stone straight into his face. He gave a tremendous gasp and fell backwards, and Tattie jumped into the air and landed on his stomach with both feet close together and all her weight behind them.

"For God's sake," Peter said, and made a grab for her. She fell off Lupin and sat down with a thump, equally winded.

"Johnnie!" she screamed.

John leapt down from the stile and reached for his Uncle's shoulder. Peter Borodin turned in mingled surprise and irritation, and John hit him on the chin with all the strength he could muster. Peter seemed stunned by the blow, at least for the moment.

"Well," Tattie said, getting up and dusting herself. "He put the keys in his pocket. I think, considering the circumstances, that we are entitled to take the car."

The room was crowded with policemen, with newspaper reporters, with officials from the foreign office, with officials from the Russian embassy. Ilona stood on one side of Tattie's chair; she had wrapped her own mink around her sister's shoulder. Clive Bullen stood on the other side, holding her hand. George Hayman stood behind the other chair, in which his stepson was seated. Chief Inspector Dorrington, in front of them, was trying to keep Nikoyan at bay while he talked to them. The two policemen had driven north together, and had each been distinctly put out to discover the Haymans and Clive already on the scene. By driving all night, stopping only to call Crowther's office, George had actually been at the Carlisle police station when Tattie and Johnnie had arrived.

"It does not matter whether Comrade Nej wishes to prefer charges or not," Nikoyan insisted, speaking English. "It was kidnapping. These men . . . that man—" He pointed at John Hayman. "—must be imprisoned. And the others must be charged. Especially must the man Borodin be caught."

Dorrington looked at George. "Perhaps you'd explain it to him, Mr. Hayman?"

"You see, comrade," George said. "There is no proof of any kidnapping, of any crime having been committed, unless Madam Nej is prepared to supply it."

"She will supply it," Nikoyan insisted. "When she has slept on it, and thought about it—"

"When you've had some time alone with her, you mean," Ilona said.

"It is my duty to look after Comrade Nej," Nikoyan said, "to show her what is right and what is wrong."

"Go to hell," Tattie said.

Nikoyan stared at her for a moment in impotent anger, then his face brightened. "Anyway," he said, "we have proof. The dresser, Olga Mikhailova. She was there. She knows what happened. That man held her down."

"Johnnie, you didn't hurt her, did you?" Tattie said.

"Well . . ."

"Oh, I am sorry," Tattie said. "You shouldn't have taken things so far. It was all a game, comrade. All a game. I am sorry Olga got hurt. I hope she is all right."

Nikoyan's mouth opened and shut like that of a stranded fish.

"You are willing to give me a sworn statement to that effect, Madam Nej?" Dorrington asked. "That it was all a game between you and your brother and your nephew?"

Tattie gazed at Johnnie. But it was her decision; no matter if he *had* tried to kill her, she couldn't send her brother to jail, possibly for a very long time.

"Of course I am. I will write it out now."

"Well—" Dorrington looked around the room. "—that seems to close the matter. I shall call off the search for Mr. Borodin and the man Lupin."

"You will let them go?" Nikoyan shouted.

"I have no reason to hold them," Dorrington said. "My only possible course of action is to bring charges against all four of them, including Madam Nej, for creating a public nuisance."

"You see?" Nikoyan said. "You see what you have done?"

"But considering the circumstances," Dorrington went on, "and in view of the financial loss the touring company will be suffering through the cancellation of the rest of its visit to Britain, I feel—"

"Cancellation?" Tattie stood up. "My tour has been canceled?"

"Orders from Moscow, comrade," Nikoyan said happily. "We are to return the moment you have been found. And since you *have* been found, I already have the tickets."

It was Tattie's turn to stare angrily.

"When I get hold of that brother of yours—" George muttered. "And as for you . . ." He looked at John.

"Oh, don't be angry with Johnnie," Tattie insisted. "I can quite understand how Peter persuaded him. As for Peter, well, Johnnie hit him. That's punishment enough." She shrugged. "I am sorry about the tour. And having to leave you so soon."

"But you're going back?" Ilona said.

Tattie frowned at her. "Well, of course I am going back."

"You don't have to, you know," George pointed out. "You are completely surrounded by friends. There's not a damned thing Nikoyan can do if you announce that you wish to stay."

"To come back to America with us," Ilona said.

"Why should I wish to do that?" Tattie said.

"Well . . ." George glanced at Ilona.

"You're starting to sound just like Peter," Tattie pointed out. "Moscow is my home. It is where my school is, and all my girls. It is where my children are." She smiled at them. "It is even where my husband is. I have no intention of leaving Moscow."

The room was silent, as she looked about her.

"So I must say good-bye," she said. "I will come to see you all again, or you will come to see me." She kissed Ilona on each cheek, then George, gave Johnnie a great hug and two more kisses. "To see you, in particular." She smiled at them, then at the chief inspector. "And now, policeman, I would like five minutes alone with Mr. Bullen."

"With—" Dorrington stared at Clive with raised eyebrows.

"It is absolutely forbidden," Nikoyan said. "I absolutely forbid it."

"*You* absolutely forbid it?" Tattie demanded.

Nikoyan waved a sheet of paper. "I have been given full authority, from Moscow, to return you as rapidly as possible, and to use whatever means I see fit to ensure your correct behavior. I have carte blanche, Comrade Nej."

"Let me see that," Tattie said, striding across the room and taking the paper from his hand. She scanned it for a moment, then tore it in two.

"Comrade Nej—" Nikoyan's voice rose to a squeak.

"You listen to me, Comrade Nikoyan," she said. "When I leave this police station, I will bow to your silly carte blanche. I give you my word. But until I do leave this police station,

I am surrounded by my friends. And I intend to say good-bye to Mr. Bullen." She turned back to Dorrington. "So, policeman, tell me where I can go."

Dorrington looked at the local inspector.

"I suppose the charge room, Mr. Dorrington. It's just along here."

"Thank you," Tattie said, following him into the corridor. Clive Bullen gave the room at large an apologetic glance, and then hurried behind her.

"You'll be all right here," the inspector said. "You won't be interrupted."

"Thank you," Tattie said again. "Please to close the door." She faced Clive. "I am sorry," she said in Russian, "that this should have happened. My brother is a mad fool. And I was so looking forward to having some more beautiful nights with you."

"Tatiana . . ." He held her hands. "You *could* stay."

She shook her head. "That is not my destiny. And you would not really expect me to desert my children."

"Surely it could be arranged for them to leave Russia?"

"Ivan would never agree. But there is more than that. I *am* Russian. It is in my blood. I can only behave like a Russian. Ilona is different. She is Ilona. She moves in a world of her own. She can exist, she can prosper, and she can be happy, anywhere. Because she needs nothing, beside the fact of her existence. But I am like a fish that needs water, Clive. I cannot exist outside of Russia."

He sighed. "I understand what you are saying. Then I suppose this *is* good-bye. Forever."

She kissed him on the mouth, a long, slow, deep kiss. "Not forever, Clive. Never forever. Either I will come to you, or you will come to me. I know that. If we both wish it. And in the meanwhile, we have the memory of that night. I shall never forget that night."

"And you? When you get back to Russia? To your husband? Will you be all right? This fellow Nikoyan—My God, the thought of him getting his hands on you—"

Tattie kissed him again. "Nobody is going to get his hands on me, Clive. Nobody is going to punish me. I am Tatiana Nej. Vladimir Ilich's friend."

Chapter 8

AS THE TRAIN PULLED TO A STOP. THE BAND STRUCK UP. MOS-cow Central was filled with booming sound, and the vast crowd started to applaud even before the door swung open.

Comrade Nikoyan was first out, smiling, having his hand seized and shaken by Commissar Ivan Nej, for if the entire Presidium was on the platform to greet their returning heroine, Ivan was the husband, and this day in the position of honor.

Olga Mikhailova came next, also smiling and waving, also to be seized and kissed on each cheek by Ivan. Then the entire troupe disembarked, each one to be given an ovation by the crowd as well as the dignitaries patiently waiting.

Tattie was last off the train. She stood on the step for a moment, and smiled at the throng, then gave them a wave. The noise became quite deafening, drowning out the throbbing of the drums. Ivan was holding open his arms, and she stepped down and into them, briefly, before shrugging him aside and embracing each of her children, who were in their nurse's charge. Then it was the turn of the Presidium, at last.

"Tatiana Nej," Commissar Stalin said. "To have you back—It is a great day."

Tattie kissed him on the cheek. "You should never have doubted, Joseph Vissarionovich," she said. "And was not my tour a success?"

"Your tour is already immortal."

"As much for its end as for its artistic value," Michael said, holding her close for a moment. "All the publicity has been good."

"My dear child." Krupskaya squeezed her hands. "You are a Heroine of the Soviet Union. I have told them that they must make you one."

"And commissar for culture, of course," Bukharin said. "There can be nobody else. You were elected by a unanimous vote of the Politburo."

"I don't see Lev Davidovich," Tattie said. "Why is he not here to greet me?"

"Ah . . ." Bukharin glanced at Stalin.

"Comrade Trotsky is still very busy," Stalin said. "In the Caucasus. And now we must let you go home to rest, and be with your children," Stalin said. "There is to be a state banquet tonight in your honor. You must be at your best. There will be photographs. But first, you will wish to rest."

Her arms were filled with bouquets, presented by two little girls, and as she emerged from the rear of the station she faced the crowds, cheering and chanting her name, clapping and even weeping. She wondered if, had she gone to America with Peter, she would have been greeted like this.

An official car waited for her, the chauffeur already opening the door. She got in, and Ivan got in beside her. She faced the door, and saw Nikoyan also getting in.

"Where are the children?" she asked. "I wish the children to ride with us."

Ivan leaned across her and pulled the door shut. "The children will be coming in another car," he said. "Now I wish to hear Comrade Nikoyan's report."

Tattie looked out the window of the car, at the houses of Moscow whizzing by, at the river on her left, at the rising walls of the Kremlin beyond. She loved Moscow. She had always loved Moscow, from the first day she had come here, with Ivan, back in 1919. She could not understand how Ilona had always claimed to have been bored in Moscow. Of course, Ilona had been tied to Sergei Roditchev, quite the most unpleasant man she had ever met. Except possibly Ivan Nej. To whom *she* was tied.

She glanced at him, perusing the closely written sheets, brows slowly drawing together, as he raised his head. "Is this true?"

"Every word of it, comrade commissar," Nikoyan said. "My people will testify. Olga Mikhailova will testify."

Ivan turned to look at his wife. "Is this true?"

"I am quite sure it is, according to Comrad Nikoyan's point of view," Tattie said.

"Did you or did you not prefer charges against your brother?"

"Of course I did not."

"He kidnapped you."

"He thought he was helping me," Tattie pointed out.

"He is an enemy of the state," Ivan said. "An enemy of Russia."

"According to you," Tattie said. "According to him, *you* are an enemy of Russia."

Ivan gazed at her for a moment. "And this John Hayman, whose real name is Ivan Sergeievich Roditchev?"

"Oh, I like him," Tattie said. "He is young, and handsome, and charming, and everything he should be."

"He is a tsarist swine."

Tattie met his gaze. "As you are a Communist swine."

Nikoyan appeared to be choking. Ivan gave him an impatient glance. "One day you will go too far, Tatiana Dimitrievna. Tell me about this man Bullen."

"Home," Tattie said, as the car drove under the arch to the inner courtyard of the apartment building. "It is always so good to be home." It was her turn to glance, at her husband. "Even when the home is a two-room apartment. It is still home."

"Tell me about Bullen," Ivan said.

"Clive?" The car had stopped, and a guard was opening the door for her. "He is my lover," she said, and got out. Another guard was waiting, holding the elevator door open for her. She looked through the archway, but the car with her children was not yet in sight. She stepped into the elevator, and was joined by Ivan and Nikoyan.

"Your lover?" Ivan asked. "Your lover?" he shouted. "You can stand there and admit adultery, to me?"

"He has taught me what love is all about," Tattie said dreamily. "I never knew it could be so wonderful." The elevator whirred softly as it climbed. "After all," she explained, "the only man I have ever known was you. I thought *all* men were just like you."

Comrade Nikoyan seemed to be having trouble with his breathing again.

"Because Father Gregory didn't really count," Tattie went on. "I mean, he liked putting his finger into me, and that was very nice, but he didn't really *do* anything. Just like you," she explained, smiling at Ivan.

"You—you dare to speak to me," he shouted, "of this man Bullen?"

"You asked me."

"Of this Rasputin?"

"I was very fond of Father Gregory," Tattie said. "I have never forgiven Peter for taking me away from Petrograd. That is the real reason I didn't go to America with him, you know. Because he took me away from Petrograd, and Father Gregory."

"Leningrad," Comrade Nikoyan suggested, urgently. "Leningrad."

The elevator was stopping, the doors opening.

"As for having him murdered," Tattie said, "that is another reason I didn't go to America. Judith Stein is there. You remember Judith Stein? She killed Rasputin. Well, she helped. And Peter is married to her sister. I could never forgive them for that."

She walked across the lobby, and into the open door of her apartment, Ivan at her heels, Nikoyan scurrying behind, anxiously and eagerly.

"I am going to beat you," Ivan said. "I am going to flog you within an inch of your life."

Tattie, already at the door to the bedroom, stopped and turned, and Ivan took a step backwards.

"Comrade Nikoyan is going to help me," Ivan said.

"Me?" asked Comrade Nikoyan, hesitating in the doorway.

"Close the door," Ivan commanded.

Nikoyan closed the door.

"Now you," Ivan said, hopefully pointing at Tattie, "go in there and undress, and lie across the bed."

Tattie began to breathe sharply.

"Take her in there, Nikoyan," Ivan commanded. "Strip her and stretch her across the bed. I am going to teach her a lesson she will never forget."

"It is a husband's prerogative to beat his wife," Nikoyan agreed. "But it should be a matter between man and wife."

"I am commanding you," Ivan said, "as your commissar."

"Of course, comrade commissar." Nikoyan licked his lips and slowly advanced across the room. "You have heard the command, Comrade Nej. Go into the bedroom and take off your clothes."

He was within range. Tattie swung her right arm. Nikoyan saw the blow coming, and got his left hand up to catch it. But her hand met his face, the face was swept sideways, and the body followed it. Nikoyan toppled over and came to land on the settee, which immediately toppled over and came to rest against the wall.

"You . . . you . . ." Ivan had got his belt free of his trousers, and stood there, watching her advance on him. "I shall beat you!" he shouted.

Tattie reached for him, and he swung the belt. The thong curled round her hand, and she grunted with pain, but her fingers had closed on it and now she jerked it and Ivan forward. He found himself crushed against her chest as she seized him under the armpits, lifted him from the floor, and set him down again with a crash. Ivan's spectacles flew off his nose and landed in the corner.

The door of the apartment opened, and two OGPU guards stepped inside, revolvers at the ready. Tattie had released Ivan, and he slid down her front to the floor. He began scrabbling for his spectacles, shouting as he did so. "Arrest that woman," he bawled, oblivious of the fact that his face was caught up in her skirt. "Arrest her. Take her to headquarters. Chain her up. I will be there shortly."

The guards stared at Tattie, who carefully stepped on Ivan's glasses with a dreadful crunching sound and then stepped on his hand as well, for good measure.

"Ow," Ivan screamed. "My God—"

Tattie stepped past him. "I am Tatiana Nej," she said. "I

am a Heroine of the Soviet Union, and I am also the new commissar for culture. If you do not leave this flat this instant, I shall report you to Comrade Stalin."

The two men gazed at Ivan, now sitting on his heels as he blinked at them. Behind them in the lobby, quite a crowd was gathering, headed by the nurse with the two children.

Ivan reached his knees. "You—" he shouted. "You—"

"I will give you two minutes to go," Tattie said. "And take that rat with you."

Ivan reached his feet. "You'd better go, Nikoyan," he said. "As you say, this is a domestic matter."

Nikoyan pushed himself up.

"And take the guards with you," Ivan said.

The guards hastily stepped outside. Nikoyan followed. They closed the door. Tattie stepped behind them and opened it again.

"What do you think you are doing?" Ivan demanded.

"I am preparing to leave," Tattie said.

"Leave?"

"With Gregory and Svetlana."

"You—"

"I do not think we have any reason to live together any longer," Tattie said, smiling at the group gathered outside the door. "You can no longer, apparently, give me babies. You do not approve of my dancing. The whole world approves of my dancing, but you do not. I can see nothing but quarrels ahead of us, and I would hate to have to beat you every night."

"You—you—you cannot leave me," Ivan shouted. "I am Commissar Nej, deputy commissar of the OGPU."

Tattie smiled at him. "But I am Commissar Nej, too, Ivan," she pointed out. "I am commissar for culture." She spied Michael and Catherine at the back of the lobby, peering through the crowd, and gave them a wave. "I shall be across the hall if you need any socks washed."

"A sad business." Joseph Vissarionovich Stalin leaned back in his chair, both hands resting on the desk in front of him, and smiled benevolently at Ivan Nej. "Domestic strife is always sad. Believe me, my dear friend, I know just how you feel. Were my dear Nadezhda to leave me I do not know what I would do."

"She has no right," Ivan grumbled. "None at all. She is the one at fault. She is an adulteress. And she has been consorting with tsarists and subversives and dissidents. That whole tour was a disaster, Comrade. I knew it. I said so beforehand, but no one would listen to me."

"I am quite sure you are right, Ivan Nikolaievich," Stalin agreed. "In cold terms, and perhaps even in terms of Tatiana's character. But events fall out strangely, and the successful man is he who can take advantage of whatever strange events may occur. Your wife's dancing may be obscene, she may have grievously dishonored your marriage, and she may well have been involved with tsarist agents, but her tour was an un-qualified triumph for the Soviet Union. We could never have dreamed of so much favorable publicity. The kidnapping was just the crown of the whole affair. It does not matter whether she went of her own free will or not. She was regained, and said the right things to the newspaper people. It has represented us to the world in an entirely new way. And world opinion, Comrade Nej, is important. It may not be a perfect world, but it is a world in which we are forced to make our way, and survive, until we can mold it to our advantage."

"I understand all that," Ivan said. "And I appreciate it. I have no longer any determination to arrest her. But I wish her back as my wife. I would like to take her, if she will not come. It is my right." He paused to peer hopefully at Stalin through his new glasses. But the expression behind the huge mustache never changed. "But it is difficult, because, as commissar for culture, she is technically senior to myself."

"As you say, she is commissar for culture," Stalin agreed.

"Cannot she be removed? Commissar for culture! Don't you realize what her ideas of culture are? She is interested only in dancing, *her* sort of dancing; in that wild, barbaric music that people like that young scoundrel Shostakovich writes; in trans-lating English novels into Russian. Do you call that culture?"

"Possibly not. Perhaps in the course of time we will have to lay down some guidelines as to what is acceptable Soviet culture and what is not. I know that Vladimir Ilich had some such program in mind. But that is for the future. For the moment, Tatiana Dimitrievna is giving us the right publicity. I don't think you *do* appreciate that, Ivan Nikolaievich. It was not the content of her tour that was the success. My understanding is that it shocked quite as many people as it attracted. No, no. It was the personality of Tatiana herself. It was the realization, on the part of the European press—and even the American press, for she was fully reported there as well, thanks to your friend Hayman—that the leaders of Soviet Russia are not all bandit thugs. For that is how they think of us, you know. But here they had a beautiful and talented and above all exuberant and happy young woman, developing a new form of culture, being *allowed* to develop a new form of culture, and presenting to the world a picture of a happy, forward-looking Soviet Union. My dear Ivan, that is the picture that Vladimir Ilich always wished to project. He was unsuccessful. But Tatiana has been a tremendous success. Her success has even gone some way towards resolving that unfortunate quarrel with the British. She really was the best ambassador we could have found. And for the moment, she is the best commissar for culture we could possibly have. Therefore she must remain there. And therefore she must not be seen to be coerced or restricted in any way. Even by her husband."

"You mean I must just let her go?"

"For the time being, Ivan Nikolaievich. For the time being. Things will change. They always do. One has merely to be patient and work for one's goals, of course. And you have a far more important goal, at this moment, than merely regaining your wife."

"Have I?" Ivan sounded doubtful.

"You and *I* have a goal, Ivan Nikolaievich, have we not? A goal of a greater and more powerful and therefore more prosperous Russia. A goal of a Russia that will stand in no need of world opinion, of ambassadresses like Tatiana Dimitrievna. Is that not so?"

"Well, of course," Ivan said.

"Exactly." Stalin pushed back his chair and got up. He walked to the window and stood there with his hands clasped behind his back, looking out at Moscow. "I think the time may have come to take another step nearer to that goal, Ivan Nikolaievich."

"In what way?"

Stalin continued to look out of the window. "Whatever feeling of uncertainty there may have been over the removal of Trotsky from the Politburo and command of the army, it has now died down. It is a *fait accompli*. I think the time may be ripe for him to be removed altogether."

"You mean . . ."

"I do not mean assassination. That would be a mistake. No one could have any doubt who was responsible. But I think it may now be possible for us to prove to the Soviet, to the country, and to the world, that Comrade Trotsky is in fact a dangerous deviationist, who is bent on the destruction of the Soviet state, or at least on its remolding to his own specification."

Ivan scratched his head. "I don't think that is quite the case, Joseph Vissarionovich. All the evidence in my possession suggests that Comrade Trotsky, perhaps more than any other one of us, is determined to preserve the unity of the Soviet. He showed that in the matter of Lenin's testament. Would it not have been to his advantage to have that testament made public? It virtually named him as Vladimir Ilich's successor. But he actually suggested its suppression, in the name of party unity."

At last Stalin turned back from the window. Still his expression remained benevolent, revealing not even a suggestion of impatience. "I am not interested in what Comrade Trotsky may or may not believe, may or may not *wish* for Soviet Russia. I am interested in what you, my old friend and my most trusted ally, can *prove* he wishes."

"But—"

"Listen to me." The voice suddenly became brisk. "Can you doubt that, whatever his intentions regarding Russia, Lev Davidovich bears a grudge? Certainly towards me. But equally towards all those he counts as my supporters. Your name will be prominent on that list."

"He is harmless, down in the Caucasus."

"It will not be possible to keep him in the Caucasus, harmless, forever. He is still Comrade Trotsky. Still the best known of us all, the most respected of us all, in some quarters. No, no, Ivan Nikolaievich. We cannot take the chance that he may reappear, here in Moscow, riding a wave of popularity. He must be discredited, utterly, while he is temporarily, as you say, harmless. I wish you to make that your first priority, as of this moment."

"It will take time."

"Not that much time. I wish it done within a year."

"But . . . finding people who will testify—"

"Will not be so difficult for you, Ivan Nikolaievich."

"You mean—"

"I do not wish to know your methods. I must not be involved. But I have no doubt at all that you do have the proper methods, Ivan Nikolaievich. I have no doubt at all that you could persuade the Archangel Gabriel to accuse God of being a secret Satanist, if you could have the poor fellow for long enough in your cells."

Ivan licked his lips.

"But keep your eventual witnesses to the lower ranks," Stalin said. "They must be important in their own ways, but not in the higher echelons of the Party."

"Yes," Ivan said absently. "Michael will not like it, you know."

"Michael Nikolaievich will be unable to do anything about it, in the face of the evidence you will produce." Stalin stood behind his chair. "I see a great future for all those men who will help me to mold our Russia."

Ivan's eyes gleamed. "I should like to be Commander of the OGPU. Not just here in Moscow, but over the whole country."

"Comrade Dzerzhinsky is not yet due for retirement," Stalin said. "And I am surprised that you should wish to succeed him, right this minute."

Ivan peered at him.

"How old are you?" Stalin said.

"Thirty-seven."

"There you are. Still a young man. There is ample time for you to receive the outward marks of success. I would prefer it if you remained just below the top, Ivan Nikolaievich, for the next few years. That would be a far better arrangement. The man at the top becomes a very public figure. I would prefer you to remain in the shadows, keeping an eye on the man at the top, on my behalf, eh? And doing other things as well on my behalf. You will get your reward, I promise you."

Ivan sighed. "I will need a capable and trustworthy assistant."

"Of course."

"Ashcherin."

Stalin frowned. "He was sent to Irkutsk because of that fiasco with the Haymans, three years ago."

Ivan nodded. "Nevertheless, he is a good and reliable man. I can trust him."

"Then by all means recall him from exile. I leave the whole thing in your hands, confident that it will be a success. But remember, time is important."

"Yes," Ivan said, and got up.

Stalin studied him for a moment, realizing that he was still not completely happy. He threw his arm round the little man's shoulders and gave him a hug. "And I have an idea," he said. "For the moment Tatiana is beyond your reach. But perhaps she was never the right woman for you. After all . . . well, who can say? Why do you not find yourself another woman?"

Ivan's head turned. "I am married to Tatiana Dimitrievna."

"I did not mean as a wife. I should have thought one wife was sufficient for any man. No, no. I was thinking more of a . . . a secretary. A very personal, very private secretary. Find yourself a young girl. She must be persuaded, however, not kidnapped. But if you can persuade some handsome child to come to work for you, why, you can mold her as you see fit. You can discover the perfect woman, Ivan Nikolaievich. It is all a matter of molding." He smiled. "Think about it."

"There's a letter from Tattie," Ilona said. She sat by the fireplace, watched the flames leaping, and only half turned her head to consider her husband as he took the drinks from Harrison's tray. "She's perfectly happy living at the Academy . . . it became too crowded at Michael Nej's apartment, once Catherine's baby was born. She must be nearly six months old now. Tattie says they've named her Nona, after Michael's sister, who was killed.

"Do you know, George," Ilona looked up, "I've never really understood about Catherine. Do you suppose Michael knew her before we met her?"

"Possibly." George gave her a glass, stooped to kiss her forehead, then sat opposite her with a sigh. "But I'm glad things are working out well for Tattie. What news of the detestable Ivan?"

"Well . . ." Ilona scanned the sheets of notepaper, the

scrawled handwriting. "He doesn't seem to be troubling her
at all, although I suppose she's still legally married to him.
She keeps going on about Clive Bullen. They correspond
apparently, and Clive's firm is making a bid for some hydroelectric project to do with the Volga. I do hope she knows
what she's doing."

"I wouldn't bother too much about Tattie, if I were you."
He finished his drink and leaned back. "Johnnie home?"

"It's a chess-club evening," Ilona said. "By the way, darling, some of Johnnie's friends are coming for a party on Friday,
the twenty-second. I know he'd be pleased if you were here,
if only to meet everyone."

"Friday the twenty-second," he mused, and opened his diary. "I think I have something on. Anyway, it'll be a young
people's affair, won't it? I imagine they'll want us to clear
out."

"Ah."

George Hayman, she thought. The sweetest and kindest and
most gentle man on earth. As well as the most honest. Lying
to his wife.

She wasn't angry with him. She did not suppose she could
ever be angry with George; he was too essentially a part of the
adventure that was her life. That had *been* her life, up to a few
years ago. Rather did she feel a great sense of sadness. The
afternoon, only a few months ago now, that she had telephoned
the Hayman Newspaper building to be told that Mr. Hayman
had just left, only to be told by *him*, when he had finally got
home at half past eight, that he had worked late at the office,
she had not even felt a sense of shock. Concern, certainly. But
it had rather been like knowing there is something wrong with
you, and finally having it confirmed by a doctor. In some
inexplicable fashion her marriage had lost its way since the
end of the war. At least, down to last year, he had slept with
her as often and as enthusiastically as ever before; only the
intimate conversation, the instant rapport had been absent. Now
even his visits to her bed were infrequent, which she could
understand; George was forty-nine, and for all his fitness he
could not really be expected to keep two women completely
satisfied.

So, she wondered, what is she like, George, this mistress
of yours? Is she a fluffy blonde from some chorus line? That

eemed incredible. But she had to admit to herself that the very idea that George could prefer anyone to her was incredible. It simply could not be a purely physical attraction. Therefore it had to be some intellectual, possibly a writer, with whom he could share his hopes and his fears. The latter were becoming predominant, and this she also could not understand—therefore there was no hope of his wishing to share with her.

She felt so utterly helpless. She could do nothing about Johnnie, either. No one could do anything about Johnnie. Johnnie was eighteen, soon to be an adult. He attended college because it was the thing to do, not because he seriously wished to do anything with his life. He appeared only to wish to play chess, and he played well; but George had consulted experts like Frank Marshall and had been told that while Johnnie was a very good player, he would never be master material. He lacked the essential chessplayer's imagination, that could look at a full board and transform it into an almost musical score of ideas and concepts, and then produce the mental energy to translate those ideas into positions and combinations. He was a plodder. She knew that unlike some plodders, however, he had a terrible sense of failure. The fiasco over Tattie's kidnapping last spring had been almost more than he could bear, as she, his mother, could well appreciate. However wrongheaded Peter was, and had always been, he had been like a flagbearer to his nephew, a constant reminder of what had been, and what should be again, of a world in which Sergei Roditchev's son would have been sure of himself, and of his advancement to a proper responsibility. To have been led astray by such an idol, to have quarreled with him, to have actually struck him . . .

Of course George also understood the trauma through which his stepson was passing and transparently worried about him, all the time, without ever being able to penetrate the cocoon of reserve in which the boy had wrapped himself. Could this ever-present, ever-growing crisis in their lives be responsible for the estrangement between George and her? She supposed it could. But not entirely. There were other things pounding at George's consciousness. He worried about the growth of organized crime, a direct result, he claimed, of the absurd Prohibition law. He worried too about the unending, frenetic boom that had overtaken the country. Worries she could not understand at all. There had always been crime, there woul[d] always be crime. And if there had not always been boom time[s] well, surely no one could complain when there was one. Calv[in] Coolidge didn't seem to have any doubts about the streng[th] of the economy, the continuance of the boom, and neither di[d] Herbert Hoover. They were men George liked and respecte[d] but preferred to disagree with—because he was a pessimist b[y] nature? Or because he was wiser than they?

So what did this mistress of his *say* to him, to reassure hi[m] when he was in one of his doubting moods?

He sat up so suddenly he took her by surprise. They flushe[d] together, and then smiled together. When they could smile [at] each other like that, she thought, she could not even hate hi[s] mistress, who might be fulfilling nothing more than a te[m]porary need.

"You look tired," she said. "Would you like another ma[r]tini?"

"If you're going to have one."

She got up and brought the shaker to their glasses. He caug[ht] her hand. "Ilona . . ."

She waited. She had not expected anything so sudden.

George sighed. "The State Department is withdrawing a[ll] financial support from Peter."

Ilona sat down. "Because of Tattie?"

"Oh, undoubtedly. They've been brooding on it ever since[.] The fact is, if it ever came out that they were supporting th[e] organization, and therefore were involved, even indirectl[y] with the kidnapping—well, it would be very embarrassing."

"But what will they do? Peter and Rachel, I mean?"

"It's a problem. They lost a lot of émigré money, too, afte[r] that business. People began to feel that Peter was in this thin[g] just for the benefit of his own family. But I must admit tha[t] in my opinion, it would be the best thing in the world if th[e] organization did fold. It's a crazy way to waste his life."

"But they can't just starve. George—"

"Of course I'd help, if I thought he'd accept it. He won'[t] you know. Only perhaps if you paid them a visit—"

"Yes," Ilona said. "Yes, I'll go and see them."

On the third landing Rachel Borodin paused to breathe—no, to gasp for air. How odd it would be, she thought, if were to drop down dead right here.

But would anyone care?

From the third landing, she could look down at the lobby, three floors below, or she could look up, at the stairs, criss-crossing from landing to landing, for another three. And her new apartment, if it could be called an apartment, was at the very top. At least ten minutes of chest-paining belly-gasping endeavor away.

Rachel Borodin, she thought bitterly. Princess of Starogan. The highest-ranking lady in the Russian world, except for roy-alty itself, panting her life away in a walk-up.

She had only been to Starogan once, when it had really been Starogan. That had been for those unforgettable two days in July 1914, when she had been a sort of chaperone for Judith, when she had watched the Borodins at play, and experienced some of their cruel humor into the bargain, when she had bathed in the river with Tattie, the first time she had ever taken off all her clothes in the company of another human being. When she had been bewitched with the splendor of it all, as well as the decadence and the basic immorality of having too much money, too much time, and too little purpose. The de-lights of being a princess.

When she had returned, four years later, it was *as* a princess, all but. And Starogan was a haunted ruin. All her life, from that moment, had been a haunted ruin, she thought. All her life.

She reached the top floor, wheezing, right hand clutching her left breast through the shabby coat as if by holding it she could drive away the pain, drive away the future, because the future did not exist.

She opened the door, lurched inside, and gazed at Ilona Hayman. Instinctively she straightened, tossing lank black hair from her forehead as she pulled off her woollen hat, and gazing around the room suspiciously.

Ilona stood up. She had taken off her mink but her dress had hardly come from anywhere closer than Paris. Her golden hair was up in a snood but was clearly as long and as carefully groomed as ever, although even Ilona Hayman was prepared to make some concessions to modern fashion—her hem ended an inch beneath her knee. Rachel realized with a start that it was the very first time she had ever seen Ilona's legs. And they were as beautiful as the rest of her.

"I didn't mean to surprise you," Ilona said. "Your Mrs. Couchman let me in, and I offered to sit for her."

"Where's Ruth?" Rachel asked.

"Here I am, Momma." Ruth Borodin, at seven years old looking amazingly like her aunt Judith, appeared from behind the threadbare settee, where she had been undressing a doll. "Aunt Ilona brought me doll. Isn't she a lovely doll?"

Rachel stared at the doll, mentally estimated what it must have cost. She sat down, hands dangling. "That was kind of you," she said. "She isn't *my* Mrs. Couchman, you know. She just lives the next floor down. She comes in when I have to go out."

"That's very kind of her," Ilona said, also sitting, one knee immediately and elegantly draped across the other. "Isn't the weather awful?"

There was no heat in the apartment, and Ilona immediately flushed. Rachel got up again. "There's some coffee." She waited.

"I don't think I will, thank you." Ilona said. "Ruth is growing into a fine girl."

"Yes," Rachel said, sitting down again. "I suppose she should go to school."

"I suppose she should," Ilona agreed.

"Yes," Rachel said.

Ilona bit her lip. "If there is anything . . . well . . . Is Peter working?"

"He's out," Rachel said.

"Yes, but . . ."

"He is the Prince of Starogan," Rachel pointed out.

"Yes," Ilona said. "I thought we might have a word. George . . . well . . . he and I . . . George would be perfectly willing to have Peter back on the newspaper, you know."

Rachel got up, took Ruth's hand. "Into the bedroom, sweetheart," she said. "Aunt Ilona and Mommy have things to talk about."

The bedroom door closed behind the girl.

"Of course," Ilona said, "he'd have to . . . well . . . promise to behave. George simply could not have him attempting to undermine the Russian government while working for Hayman Newspapers."

"The Russian government," Rachel said contemptuously.

"Well, it is there," Ilona said. "George says a newspaper's business is informing the people of what is happening, not causing it to happen in the first place."

"I'm dying," Rachel remarked.

Ilona gazed at her for some seconds with her mouth open.

"It's my heart," Rachel explained. "I saw the doctor today. God knows how we'll pay for it. But he says that the pain I've got is my heart. I collapsed last week, you know. Just keeled over. It's not very nice."

"Oh," Ilona said. "Oh, you poor darling."

"He says," Rachel went on as if she had not spoken, "that I need rest and care. That I must move from this apartment, for a start. He says these stairs are going to kill me. Would you believe it? I'm thirty-two years old, and I'm dying."

"Of course you aren't dying," Ilona said. "For heaven's sake, nobody dies of a heart attack at thirty-two. Anyway, all you have to do is take it easy, move from here . . . I'll find you an apartment, on the first floor."

"And who'll pay for it?"

"Why, I will."

Rachel shook her head. "Peter would never agree."

"He'll simply have to," Ilona said. "For heaven's sake, if you're ill, he'll have to let me help you."

"I don't think he will," Rachel said. "He doesn't really want me to go on living."

Once again Ilona discovered that her mouth was open.

"He doesn't love me," Rachel explained. "He never has. He took me out of Petrograd in 1918 and we had to live together for a long time, and so we made love, because I loved him and he needed to make love to somebody. But he's never loved me the way he loves Judith. If I were to die, he could marry Judith. Don't you see?"

"That is absurd," Ilona said. "Of course he loves you," she insisted, as if the evidence of her own eyes did not prove the lie. "He's . . ."

"A perfect gentleman," Rachel said. "But he *would* like me to die. And what do I have to live for? Only Ruth. But you'd look after Ruth, wouldn't you?"

"Well, I—of course I would. But you're not going to die, Rachel. For heaven's sake—"

"I think I may as well," Rachel said. "There's not a lot for me to live for, is there?"

"Tell me about Rachel," George said.

Judith sat up, hung her legs over the side of the bed, and reached for a cigarette. She struck a match and blew a thin stream of smoke at the wall. His finger was tracing the ridges made by her vertebrae down the curve of her back, giving her little shivers. "It's stress, or something," she said, "according to Dr. Kelly." She shrugged. "I think it's just frustration, really. Rachel has always *dreamed* too hard."

"How ill *is* she?"

Judith lay down again and looked at his face. Dear George. He genuinely wanted to help. George always wanted to help, had never been able to understand that sometimes it just wasn't possible.

"I don't know. She has chest pains and runs out of breath on the stairs. Things like that. But Dr. Kelly did say she should take it easy, maybe move from that apartment."

"And what is Peter doing about it?"

"Not a lot. I don't think he feels she *is* terribly ill. And maybe he's right."

George raised himself on his elbow, the better to look at her. "Do you see a lot of him?"

"I go there once a week."

"That isn't what I meant."

"It's what I said."

He gazed at her for some seconds, mouth twisted, then kissed her. She wondered why he put up with it. He was George Hayman. Presumably there was hardly a woman in New York who would not be happy to be here instead of her, and he had to know that. Having loved her for more than two years, he surely could no longer find her either mysterious or terribly exciting, and undoubtedly he found her more acid moods trying.

"I wish . . ." he said.

She smiled. "I'm sorry. I didn't mean to be sharp. Peter does make advances, from time to time. He doesn't do it with much conviction, which makes it easier for me to say no."

"I was going to say," George said, "that I wish it could be possible for you and me to spend some time together. I mean, really together. A week or so. I'd like to see you at six in the morning, one day, rather than at six at night."

"You'd get a fright. And you have seen me at six in the morning. In Russia."

"That was different. That was before . . . well, before *us*."

"Is *us* important, George? Really and truly?"

"To me it is."

She stared at him. Oh my God, she thought, this is getting out of hand. She forced a smile. "I wish you'd tell me why."

"I wish I could, too. No," he reflected, "I'm glad that I can't. If you could put into words what you felt about someone, then it wouldn't be a feeling any more, would it? It'd be reasoning, deduction. You should never be able to reason out love. At least the principals shouldn't."

"It's six o'clock," she said.

Once again his mouth twisted. Then he got out of bed. "They shouldn't be afraid of it, either," he said, and went into the bathroom.

She could've ended it there and then, she thought. She could've told him he was sharing her with Peter, even though it wasn't true. For the two years of their affair he had been wonderful. He'd let her write articles about Zionism as well as about Russia. He'd let her use the paper for appeals, for funds as well as support. He'd been even more useful, in fact, than she'd ever hoped. And besides that, he'd made her happy, had given her this gorgeous apartment, and now he was preparing to give her, or at least offer her, even more. Something she couldn't possibly accept, because it would mean hurting Ilona irrevocably. She *had* to end it, here and now.

But she loved him.

And as for hurting Ilona, could Ilona possibly be hurt more than she was being hurt right now, even if she didn't know it yet?

He knotted his tie. "Spending the evening in bed?"

Now, she thought. Now there is no need to lie. Now you can tell him the truth, and bring it to an end.

"I suppose so," she lied. "It's a bleak night."

"You can say that again," he agreed. He bent over her and kissed her lightly on the lips. "You'll let me have a copy of that article tomorrow?"

"First thing. There's not much to it, you know. There's not

much happening over there at the moment. Merely this con
tinuing debate about the profit factor. And even that is dying
down. Do you suppose the entire Bolshevik revolution wil
just dwindle away, now that Lenin is dead and Trotsky seem
to have retired?"

"I think it'll be around for a while," George said. "They've
just made a rather commonplace discovery, that's all; even ii
a Communist state, a man must have some incentive for work
if you want him to work hard and well. Anyway, I don't think
Trotsky has retired. I think he's just waiting for Bukharin and
Stalin and Nej and that bunch to make a mess of things, before
really taking over. He's the only man who can possibly do it
But don't suggest that in the article. Our business—"

"Is to report the news, not make it happen," she said. "Right
chief." She squeezed his hand. "Drive carefully."

He blew her a kiss and closed the door behind him. Judith
relaxed, lit another cigarette, and gazed at the ceiling. In five
minutes she would have to get up, shower, wash away the
evidences of having made love, make herself up and dress
herself, and prepare to entertain Boris. A purely business re
lationship. They talked about Russia, and she obtained infor
mation. As simple as that. And he would hold her hand and
eventually kiss her good night. In between he would devour
her with his eyes. But he would never suggest they sleep to
gether. Boris was far too much of a gentleman.

And George would also regard it as purely a business meet
ing, even if she had told him it was going to happen. George
Hayman was never going to be jealous of Boris Petrov.

Not even if she tried another lie, and claimed that she slep
with him, every time he called? She would have to do some
thing like that, eventually, if George was to be prevented from
making a terrible mistake.

But she loved him.

"Come in, comrade, come in," Ivan Nej said, turning a
beaming face towards the door.

The man hesitated, still in the doorway, glancing from lef
to right, almost attempting to look over his shoulder, and ther
changing his mind. He knew what, or who, was behind him
Ashcherin and another guard.

"Come along," Ivan said. "You must be tired, standing there."

The man moved, slowly and uncertainly. Even his clothes had an uncertain look. The suit had looked quite smart yesterday, the tie knot neat and well centered, the shirt collar crisp, the trousers recently pressed. This morning the entire outfit bagged, just as his stubbled chin bagged. There were bags under his eyes too, and his lank black hair seemed to bag on either side of his scalp. He came into the room and stood before the desk, arms hanging limply at his side.

"Sit down," Ivan invited. "Ashcherin, Comrade Karpov would like a cup of coffee. I would like a cup of coffee." He leaned across the table confidentially. "We shall *all* have a cup of coffee, eh, Comrade Karpov?"

The man stared at him as a rabbit might stare at a snake; Ashcherin gave the necessary orders to the guard. And Ivan smiled. This he enjoyed. There was no feeling quite like it, knowing that he possessed *power* over this man. The power to raise hope and crush hope. The power to dominate. The power to destroy, as and when he chose. Savoring the power was better than performing the deed.

The deed was always disappointing. Never had it measured up to his dreams. He had been dreaming ever since he could remember. Mainly, of course, of the Borodin girls, whose blossoming womanhood had fired the dreams of his adolescence. But then those dreams had come true, leaving him breathless with his own audacity. To possess Tatiana Borodina, to take her by force, had to be the greatest thing that could happen to any man. But he had been disappointed. She had submitted because there had been nothing else for her to do but die. Her submission had always been a part of the dream. But it had been almost an unconscious submission, not a collapse into quivering terror. She had not moaned, she had not moved, she had not gasped, she had not even wept. She had asked him, in a very reasonable tone of voice, not to hurt her. Which had made him want to hurt her the more. But he had known it would be pointless. He had supposed, then, that there had been some deep psychological barrier to his enjoyment; despite all, she was the mistress and he the serf. The barrier would be overcome by possession, he had supposed.

Instead the barrier had grown into a mammoth, impenetrable mountain range. In the beginning he had attempted to ill-treat her, had forced her to drink large quantities of vodka, had cursed at her and even on occasion struck her. She had been confused and unsure of herself, uncertain even of her survival. But he had found no pleasure in it. The pleasure in beating someone arises from their response, their activation of your own impulses. Tattie had merely looked at him, and the expression in her eyes had sent a shiver down his spine.

Until the day she suddenly woke up and hit him back. He had been so surprised he did not know what to do. He had never really discovered what to do. He had never discovered what Tattie feared, and what Tattie desired, what caused her pain and and what caused her pleasure. Lacking those essential pieces of information, he had always been groping in the dark.

Had Clive Bullen found out those things about her?

But the fact was that he did not only grope in the dark after Tattie. Working with Dora Ulyanova, he had been given the job of interrogating the White prisoners taken during the civil war. He had been desperately excited when the first man had been brought in. Some of the excitement had communicated itself from Dora herself, but more was generated by the feeling of power, and by the knowledge that he was about to cause another human being exquisite pain, was about to be allowed to realize any or all of his most lurid midnight fantasies. And that man had *felt*, in a way he had never been able to make Tattie feel. He had screamed and he had writhed as Dora had burned him, and Dora's excitement had grown and grown, while Ivan had felt . . . nothing. He had looked for an overwhelming sexual experience, such as certainly was overtaking Dora. But how could he, when the man had been ugly and battered, filthy and sweat-stained. What pleasure could there ever be in destroying anyone ugly?

There was his curse. None of the people who were brought in here to face him had ever been handsome or even pretty, much less beautiful. Perhaps the mere fact of having been arrested by the secret police robbed humanity of beauty, turned them immediately into sweating slabs of lard. There had been only two exceptions, and both of those had slipped from his grasp before he had been properly aware that he possessed them. It had seemed like another dream come true, to be able to arrest Ilona, to bring her down here, to make her submit. And Ilona was not the least like Tattie. Ilona had been capable of fear; he had felt it stirring.

And then his nerve had failed. He could have ridden it out. He had no doubt at all now, considering the matter with hindsight. He could have destroyed her, at least partially. And what would have happened? A diplomatic incident with the United States? A dressing-down from Lenin, already failing? Stalin would have protected him. As for Catherine Lissitsina, she had been just a name; he had not supposed she would be worth looking at, and so he had not bothered to go and look. What a fool he had been. And now she had also remained, to haunt him, while he stumbled on, obeying Stalin because there was nothing else he could do, increasing his reputation for ferocious brutality while he was unutterably bored by every moment of it, waiting, endlessly, for beauty to stumble through that door, one day.

But not today. Comrade Karpov was a more than usually repulsive slab of lard. He should be disposed of as quickly as possible. But he couldn't be disposed of. He had to be remolded to Comrade Stalin's requirements.

The coffee was placed on the desk. Ivan nodded, and Karpov grabbed his cup, hand shaking so much the liquid slopped into the saucer. He gulped at the heat.

"You have had time to study the letter," Ivan said.

The cup rattled against the saucer as Karpov put it down. But he had regained some of his strength. He attempted to straighten his tie.

"Now all you have to do is sign it," Ivan said.

Karpov licked his lips.

"I have a pen," Ivan said, taking it from his pocket.

"Comrade Trotsky is a friend of mine," Karpov said. "That letter suggests it is in reply to one from him. It suggests that we are engaged in a conspiracy."

"I have read the letter," Ivan said, and smiled. "In fact, I wrote it, Comrade Karpov. I know what it suggests. All you have to do is sign it."

"I couldn't," Karpov said, glancing at the coffee cup as if wondering if he dared drink some more. "I couldn't. It would harm Comrade Trotsky. It would harm me."

Ivan shook his head. "It will not harm you, comrade. If you

cooperate with us, if you sign that letter, we will make sure that no harm comes to you, because you will have helped us. But if you do not . . . Tell me, have you been harmed as yet?"

Karpov stared at him.

"Oh," Ivan said, "you have spent the night in a cell, and you have not slept. People seldom do, in cells."

"I was kept awake," Karpov said. "They shone lights on my face, and they came into the cell every fifteen minutes. Him." He pointed at Ashcherin.

"To make sure you were not attempting to harm yourself." Ivan's voice was reasonable. "Some people do try to harm themselves. But you would not have slept anyway. Now, you are very tired. But all you have to do is sign this letter, and we will let you sleep. We will give you a good breakfast and a bottle of vodka and a soft bed. Doesn't that sound nice?"

"I couldn't sign that letter." Karpov said.

"If you don't," Ivan said, "we are going to hurt you."

He stared at Karpov, and Karpov licked his lips again.

"We are going to take down your trousers and beat you like a child," Ivan said, still speaking quietly. "And then we are going to put you into a cold bath and hold your head under the water until you think you are going to drown. And if you don't sign then," Ivan said, smiling at him, "we are going to hold you down and put broken glass up your ass until you are cut to ribbons. You will never shit again, Comrade Karpov, without screaming in pain." He held out the pen.

Karpov stared at it for some seconds, while he slowly sucked his lower lip between his teeth. Then he took it, and scribbled his name.

"Thank you, comrade," Ivan said. "Captain Ashcherin will now take you to your bed, and your breakfast, and your bottle of vodka."

"And then you will let me go home," Karpov said.

"Eventually, Comrade Karpov. Eventually."

"But . . ."

Ivan waved his hand, and the guards pulled Karpov to his feet and hurried him from the room.

"That was well done, comrade commissar," Ashcherin said.

"Yes," Ivan said, and sighed. "Give him his vodka." He got up and walked to the window. Thank God the fool had signed. There was no pleasure in stamping on a slab of lard.

Why couldn't Karpov have been . . . he looked down from the window at the street beneath, at the snaking line of schoolgirls, ranging from very young to fifteen and sixteen years old, winding its way along beneath him.

"Sit down, comrade commissar. Sit down." Comrade Tereshkova beamed, an expression she seldom assumed, Ivan guessed. Her face was neither hard nor cruel, but rather severe. She was a woman with a great deal of responsibility resting on her shoulders, because all the girls in the orphanage had lost their parents during the great civil war, and most of the parents had been fighting on the White side. He had in fact opposed the foundation of the orphanage. White children should follow their White mothers and fathers, into the black earth of the Don basin, in his opinion. Any attempt to remake them into good Bolsheviks was sure to be a failure, especially where the older ones were concerned.

Now he was glad he had been overruled. Who could ask for anything better? Several hundred girls, among whom there had to be at least one or two of real beauty, just sitting here, under his very nose, waiting to be destroyed. Why hadn't he thought of it before? Because it simply had never occurred to him that he could arrest anyone who had not actually committed a crime. It had taken a man with the breadth of vision of Joseph Vissarionovich to make him realize that he really could do what he liked, providing he was prepared to prove that his reasons were sound.

How could anyone doubt that Comrade Stalin was the best man to govern Russia?

"I am assuming that you have no cause for investigating *us*, comrade," Comrade Tereschkova said jocularly, tight worry lines streaming away from her eyes and her mouth. "My girls live a very secluded life, really. We have no politics other than those taught by the professor."

"Of course you do not," Ivan said, equally jovial. "No, no, Comrade Tereshkova, I am here on a personal matter."

"Indeed, comrade commissar?" Comrade Tereshkova waited, some of the brilliance of her beam disappearing as she realized it might not be necessary.

"I . . . ah . . ." Ivan realized that his cheeks were burning. "I am looking for a personal assistant."

Comrade Tereshkova placed her elbows on her desk and made a tent of her fingers. Now the beam had definitely disappeared.

"It will have to be someone of rather special qualities," Ivan said. "My work requires rather special qualities."

Comrade Tereshkova gazed fixedly at him.

"So it occurs to me," Ivan said, "that the ideal would be to find a young woman straight out of school, and train her in the . . . ah, special qualities that will be required."

Comrade Tereshkova still did not speak.

"I was thinking of someone about fifteen or sixteen years of age," Ivan said. "She will have to be bright and intelligent, with a good academic record. Do you have any girls who might qualify?"

"I have a great number of bright and intelligent girls," Comrade Tereshkova said. "I have high hopes for them academically."

"This is a good position, comrade," Ivan pointed out. "The girl I select will do well."

"I have no doubt of it," Comrade Tereshkova said, and got up. She went to a filing cabinet in the corner, pulled out half a dozen files, and placed them on the desk. "Perhaps you would like to look through these."

"Perhaps later," Ivan said. "I would prefer to look at the girls first."

Comrade Tereshkova's lip started to curl, and then corrected itself. "There is no question of this girl being requisitioned?"

"Requisitioned?"

"I mean, if the girl you choose does not wish to work for you, she has that right," Comrade Tereshkova said.

"Of course," Ivan agreed, getting up.

Comrade Tereshkova regarded him for some seconds, and then opened the door. "If you will follow me," she said.

Ivan followed her into the corridor, entered a world of subdued noise, a hush of whispers and faint scrapings, whether of pen or chair. His heart began to pound. It really did not matter what Comrade Tereshkova thought, or even said. She would have to be careful what she thought, or said, about the deputy commissar of the OGPU.

He felt like a small boy about to open a present.

Comrade Tereshkova opened a door and stepped inside,

then waited for him. The immediate whisper became submerged in the scrapings of the chairs as they were pushed back. Ivan caught his breath. The girls were all about sixteen years old, he supposed, and there were about twenty of them. Never had he faced such an accumulation of attractive young women.

"You may sit down, comrades," Comrade Tereshkova said, and the girls obeyed.

"It would have made more sense to read the files first," Comrade Tereshkova said to Ivan. "Then you would have known exactly which girl I was referring to."

"I have chosen," Ivan said and pointed. "I will take that one."

Now Comrade Tereshkova's lip did curl; he was pointing at the prettiest girl in the room.

"This is Commissar Ivan Nikolaievich Nej, Anna," Comrade Tereshkova said.

Had she heard the name before? Her expression was only slightly watchful. Her face was really quite remarkably calm. In her wealth of midnight hair, which she wore loose and well past her shoulders, restrained from clouding her face by a barette over each temple; in her steady black eyes; in her features, large but perfectly chiseled; and above all in her complexion, which was as utterly white as her hair was utterly black, she made him think of a madonna, if such thoughts were possible in Lenin's Russia. He supposed that she had some Tartar blood; unlike Michael's Catherine, it had not affected her figure, which was tall and slender and long-legged. More than that was not readily discernible beneath the somewhat shapeless school uniform; and he reminded himself that she was only sixteen. But that she was beautiful, and on the verge of becoming even more so, was undoubted. His heart was pounding so hard he was sure she could hear it.

And of course she would have heard of him. Everyone in Russia had heard of Ivan Nej.

"Comrade Nej." She stood at attention to speak his name. Her voice was quiet, in keeping with the rest of her.

"Comrade Nej would like you to—" Comrade Tereshkova's mouth hardened. "—work for him."

"Comrade Tereshkova?" Now the girl spoke sharply, and her head turned.

"If what he has in mind interests you," Comrade Tereshkova said.

The girl looked at Ivan.

"I would prefer the interview to be private," Ivan said.

Comrade Tereshkova considered the matter, and then shrugged and got up. "I think I should have a word with you first, in private, comrade commissar. Wait outside, Anna."

"Yes, Comrade Tereshkova." The girl left the room and closed the door behind herself. Comrade Tereshkova sat down again.

"You will know, of course, Comrade Nej, that each month I make a full report on my senior girls to the commissar for the interior. Should Anna wish to leave school, it will have to be approved by the ministry. Her reasons for wishing to leave, as well as the exact work to which she is going, will have to be submitted."

"I do know that, comrade," Ivan said.

"I would also have to report that you took the girl against my advice, should you persuade her to go with you," Comrade Tereshkova said.

"You are advising me in this matter?" Ivan found himself starting to get annoyed.

"Yes, comrade commissar," Comrade Tereshkova said. "This girl is not what you are looking for. You will not find her file among those on the desk."

"How can you say what I am looking for?"

Comrade Tereshkova almost smiled. "I think I can. And Anna is not the one. You may think she is, and she may give the impression that she is, but comrade commissar, I have watched this girl from the age of ten, and I can say that if you take her you will be making a grave mistake. A very grave mistake."

"You will have to be more explicit than that."

Comrade Tereshkova shook her head. "I have said enough."

"Then be good enough to let me make my own mistakes."

"As you wish." Comrade Tereshkova opened the door and beckoned the girl. "It is your decision, Anna, whether you wish to work for Commissar Nej or not. You should remember that once you leave here, you will not be able to return."

"Yes, Comrade Tereshkova," the girl said.

The door closed. Ivan moved to sit behind the desk. The

irl allowed her gaze to drift, for an instant, to the chair Ivan
ad just vacated. But he preferred not to invite her to sit.
standing, he could see more of her. And besides, he was not
ooking for friendship, only obedience.

"Tell me your name," he said.

"Anna Petrovna Ragosina," she said.

"Your parents are both dead?"

"Yes, comrade commissar."

"And you have no other relatives?"

"I have two brothers, comrade commissar."

"And where are they?"

"They are younger than I, comrade commissar."

"So they are in the boys' orphanage. I see. Tell me, Anna,
lo you know what I do?"

"You are deputy commissar for the Unified State Political
Administration," she said.

"You are well informed. Do you know what my work en-
ails?"

The girl's expression became slightly more guarded.

"You may say whatever you wish, Anna," Ivan said. "One
hing I demand of those who work for me is complete honesty.
What do you think I do?"

"You are responsible for the internal security of the state,
Comrade Nej," she said.

"Would you like to take part in that work?"

The girl's lips moved against each other; she did not speak.

"You would find it rewarding. Working for the OGPU,
working for me, you would be able to help almost anyone you
chose, in Russia. Questions of loyalty, of deviation, even of
he deviation of one's parents, would no longer affect you, or
hose you chose to help, because you would be working for
me. Do you understand me, Anna?"

The girl nodded.

"And you would be in a more privileged position than anyone else," Ivan pointed out, "because you would be working
or me. The position I have in mind is that of personal assis-
ant." He drew a long breath. "You would spend all your time
with me. You will never leave my side for an instant, even
when we are both asleep." He paused, watching her. Her gaze
never dropped from his face. He smiled. "Of course, I am
afraid you would have to go back to school for a while. There

are things you would have to learn, things I would teach you
Would you like that, Anna?"

The reply was a long time coming. She gazed at him, ob
viously thinking carefully. Certainly she was intelligent. It wa
clear she had understood every threat, every suggestion, ever
promise. Now she was prepared to weigh all those against wha
he would want from her, against what might become of her
if she refused, and against whatever loyalty she might fee
toward her brothers. His heartbeat even managed to increase
To own such an *aware* personality, especially when it wa
housed in such a perfect frame, was going to be the experience
of his life. She had to accept.

But on his terms. Since she had not yet answered, he leaned
forward again. "I will teach you to be my second self," he
said. "I will teach you to think with my brain, feel with my
body. But you must understand that I—we—are responsible
for the security of the state. Sometimes we have to do sad
tragic, terrible things. But these things must be done for the
good of Soviet Russia. There must never be any doubt in you
mind, or my mind, that they must be done. No hesitation. No
misplaced kindness. No softness. You will have only one friend
in the world. Me. You will have only one master in the world
Me." He drew another long breath. "You will have only one
lover in the world. Me."

Once again she made that peculiar movement with her lips
working them against each other. She does not like me, he
thought. She fears me, and she might even hate me. But does
that matter? Will it not, in fact, be even more splendid, to
know that she hates and fears me, and yet obeys me? The
perfect slave. Because for all her dislike, her hate and her fear,
she knows she has no alternative. No alternative for herself,
and even less for her brothers. To make an enemy of Ivan Ne
is to book a one-way ticket to Siberia, at the very best. So
hating, and fearing, and loathing, she will submit and submit
and submit, and obey, and obey, and obey.

The perfect slave.

"Well, Anna Ragosina," he said. "Do you think you would
like to work for me?"

The girl's head moved, another surprising gesture as it tilted
back so that her chin pointed at him. The bodice of her gown

swelled as she inhaled. "Yes, comrade commissar," she said. "I think I would like to work for you."

There was so much to be done with her that he didn't know where to begin. First of all there were her clothes and personal belongings to be collected, a pitifully small bundle, which only reinforced his growing awareness of possession. That she was pleased to be leaving the orphanage could not be doubted for a moment. Was it also pleasure at having accepted his offer? If so, she was a fool, because Comrade Tereshkova—to protect them all, as she explained with a grim smile—had her sign a statement that she was voluntarily accepting the position as personal assistant to Commissar Ivan Nikolaievich Nej. As he looked down on that glossy black head bending over the table as she wrote her name, Ivan felt almost about to burst. She was actually, deliberately, and before a witness placing herself entirely in his power.

He was in a hurry to study her reactions, to start breaking down her reserve. She was only a girl; she could have no mental stamina on which to call. He had them driven first of all to the OGPU headquarters. "This is where I work," he said, showing her his office.

She looked at the desk, walked to the window to look down at the street.

"It is where you will work as well," he explained. "I will have a desk put over there for you."

"I will like that, comrade commissar," she said.

"Here we control what is going on inside Russia," he explained. "We keep our fingers on the pulse. And when it either slows or beats too fast, we take action."

Anna Ragosina nodded.

"But basically, our business is with people. It is people who cause trouble. People who attempt to subvert the state. You must have no pity, Anna Ragosina. I have no pity. Any man, or any woman, who is an enemy of the state is an enemy of me, too. You understand that?"

"I understand that, comrade commissar."

He looked at her for a moment, and she returned his gaze, her face expressionless. Well, then, he thought, let us put some expression into that face.

"Come," he said, and led her down the stairs. Orderlies and junior officers came to attention, as did the female clerks. But Ivan was in a genial mood; he smiled at them as he returned their salutes, pleased that the girl should have this early glimpse of his prestige and power.

Doors clanged behind them, and they were in the cellars. The damp chilled their flesh, and in the distance someone screamed, aimlessly and endlessly.

"Who is making that noise?" Ivan asked the jailer.

He consulted his list. "Number thirty-nine, I suspect, comrade commissar."

"Well, shut him up," Ivan said. "This is the male section," he told the girl. "But we will start with the females."

Another door clanged, and they were in the presence of women, standing rigidly at attention, but eying Anna Ragosina with interest.

"Let me see your list." Ivan said.

He studied it, also surreptitiously watching the girl. She returned the gazes of the harpies standing around her, also with interest, but quite without either fear or revulsion. Either she was totally lacking in fear, or totally lacking in imagination. Or both. She would have to be shown.

"Number eighteen," he said.

"She has proved difficult, comrade commissar," said the head wardress. She was the woman who had searched Ilona Hayman. But now was not the time to think of Ilona Hayman. "The doctor has said she must be left to rest for at least forty-eight hours, or she may not survive."

"I wish to see her," Ivan said, "not interrogate her."

The woman nodded and led them along the corridor, their nostrils stung with the stench of disinfectant.

"What is this woman guilty of, comrade commissar?" Anna asked.

Ivan turned his head in surprise; it was the first time she had taken the initiative in speaking.

"She was arrested while circulating subversive literature in Kharkov," he said. "We would like to know from where and whom she obtained this literature. We suspect that she may be a part of an anti-Bolshevik organization led by a tsarist terrorist, a certain Peter Borodin. We would like to find out about this also."

The wardress was unlocking the door marked 18, pulling it towards them. The woman inside the cell was not huddled, as were so many of the inmates here. She was beyond feeling cold, for the moment. She lay on her back, arms and legs flung wide, no doubt exactly where she had been thrown by her interrogators. She was naked, and there were bruises on her thighs and ribs where she had been kicked. Her eyes were open, and staring at them. For a moment she did not seem to see them, then her eyelids flickered and her mouth moved, while her right leg gave a twitch, as if she would have moved it, if she could.

"They held her in the water too long," the wardress said. "They were very careless. They have been disciplined."

"How would you deal with this one?" Ivan asked the girl. "With someone who would rather die than confess her accomplices?" He studied her. Her nostrils had distended and then closed again. But it might have been the disinfectant.

"Bear in mind, of course," he pointed out, "that she may have to appear in court, unmarked."

Anna Ragosina considered, gazing at the woman. "I would use pepper," she said at last.

"Pepper?"

"Strong pepper. It is very painful, in the right place." Her mouth moved in what might have been the semblance of a smile. "I spilled some on myself once. I screamed with pain."

Ivan stared at her. He was suddenly realizing that he could simply not imagine this girl screaming with pain. Yet it was his dearest ambition, to make her do so.

"Well, well," he said. "Did you hear, Natalia Ivanova?"

"The doctor says—"

"Of course," Ivan said soothingly. "When the doctor says she has recovered sufficiently. I will be interested in your report."

He showed her the men's cells, but without interest now. He wanted to get her home as soon as he could. His entire body was seething with emotion such as he had not felt since the day he had led the Starogan mob to sack the Borodin estate.

"I suppose you would put pepper on them too," he remarked.

Anna Ragosina gazed at the man with more interest than she had looked at the woman. "I do not know," she said. "I do not know how a man feels. But if he feels like a woman, *there*, then pepper will work on him also."

"I can assure you that he does," he said, and had them driven to the apartment building.

He let her climb the stairs in front of him, so that he could watch her ankles and her calves, the movement of her thighs beneath her heavy skirt, the slow sway of her black hair, like a midnight sea in its serene rhythm. They reached the landing, and she paused, waiting for him to direct her to the right door.

"My brother lives here," he said, "with his wife and their child."

She waited, uninterested.

"My wife lived with them for a time, with our two children," Ivan said. "Now she lives at her dance academy. My wife is commissar for culture."

"Your wife does not live with you, comrade commissar?" she asked.

He smiled at her. "Not any more, Anna Petrovna. That is why you are here."

He waited for a reaction, and got none. She merely acquiesced with the slightest inclination of her head. But she knew about feeling and about pain, and in a moment he would find out how much she knew. He opened the door and admitted her. She looked around her.

"It is a nice apartment, comrade commissar," she said.

"It is yours to keep clean," he said.

"I have done this at the orphanage." She turned to face him. "I have dreamed of an apartment of my own."

"It is my apartment," he said.

"Of course, comrade commissar," she said. "But I am your woman, am I not?"

"Yes," he said. "Undress."

She looked from left to right, placed the bundle—her clothing, with the two photographs of her brothers and a very faded photograph of her parents—on a chair, and unbuttoned her blouse. Now it was necessary for him to pretend indifference, and hope that she would not be able to hear the pounding of his heart. He picked up the faded photographs. "How did they die?"

The blouse was laid on the chair, and she sat down to take off her shoes. Her surprisingly heavy breasts seemed to be falling out of the brassiere; she wore no petticoat. "They were shot."

"By the Whites?"

"By the Reds, comrade commissar."

He frowned. "Then you hate the Bolsheviks."

Anna Ragosina stood up, released her waistband, and allowed her skirt to fall to the floor. "The Bolsheviks saved my life, comrade commissar. They took my brothers and me and put us in the orphanages." She shrugged, an absorbing sight as, at the same moment, she released her brassiere. "I was only nine. Michael was five and Vasili three. They told us our parents were criminals, fighting for Kolchak."

"And you believe them?"

Anna Ragosina hesitated, then slid the last of her undergarments to the floor behind her skirt. "I must believe them, comrade commissar." She stood straight. "Do I please you?"

Ivan had to swallow. The body was thin, almost undernourished, and he did not wonder at that, when he thought of Comrade Tereshkova. And yet the breasts were heavy, and full, and the bush of black pubic hair seemed to glow at him; he had never seen anything so luxuriant. But he was here to hurt, not admire. This girl was here to expiate all the hate and all the fear he had felt during his years with Tattie, and all the lust that he had been unable to inflict upon her because of that hate and that fear.

He seized the breasts, one in each hand, squeezed them, and then threw them, and her, away from him. She lost her balance even as she gasped in pain, and fell over onto the settee. He slapped her twice on the face, sending her head and her hair flailing to and fro, then seized her wrists and dragged her, half on her knees, across the floor and into the bedroom, and threw her across the bed.

She fell on her face, but rolled onto her back to watch him. Now he should beat her, as he had always wanted to beat Tattie. But instead he found himself undressing. He could not wait another moment. He leapt onto her, forced himself inside her, even as she moaned in pain, and came a few seconds later. It had been more tumultuous for him even than the rape of Tattie. It was a feeling he had never known before.

He pushed himself up to look down at her. "Now you hate me, Anna Petrovna," he said.

A tear of pain had escaped one eye, and she was still gasping for breath. He could not remember having kissed her, but her lip was cut, and she cautiously licked it before replying.

"It does not matter what I feel, comrade commissar," she said. "I am your woman. You have made me so. That is all that matters." She put her arms around his neck to bring him down to her again.

Chapter 9

JUDITH READ THE REPORT IN A FLAT VOICE. "'AS A RESULT OF the documentary and other evidence supplied by Comrade Stalin, the Congress unanimously recommended the accceptance of his proposed that Comrade Trotsky be expelled from the Communist Party." She raised her head.

George leaned back in his chair. "Good God."

Judith looked down at the report once more. "'Comrade Stalin was then reelected to the post of Party secretary by acclamation, and Comrade Bukharin proposed a vote of thanks to the secretary for his unending vigilance and unsparing efforts on behalf of the Party and the Motherland. Replying, Comrade Stalin reminded the Assembly that he had but done his duty, and that his ability to do his duty depended entirely on the support given him by all true Party members, and in particular by the members of the Unified State Political Administration. To these devoted men and women, he said, his own thanks, the thanks of the Party, and the thanks of the Motherland must be accorded. This too was greeted with acclamation.'"

"Ivan Nej," George said.

"Which tells us just about everything." Judith sat down uninvited before the desk, something she rarely did; in the office she was determined to keep their relationship strictly professional.

"About *how* it happened, to be sure," George agreed. "Just give me your own rundown of what it all means."

"What has happened," Judith said slowly, "is that on the one hand Trotsky has virtually been declared an outlaw, and on the other Stalin has virtually been made dictator of Russia."

George frowned. "He's still only Party secretary. Sure, he's managed to get rid of his chief rival, but he still has to tread carefully. People like Bukharin and Zinoviev, and even more, Michael Nej, aren't exactly one hundred percent behind him."

"They were one hundred percent behind him at this All-Party Congress," Judith pointed out. "They were all there, and the vote was unanimous."

George's frown deepened. "I had always thought Michael was a friend of Trotsky's. I do remember that during the civil war he almost worshipped the man."

"I remember that too," Judith said.

"And . . . ?"

She shrugged. "Michael has this capacity for running with the hares and hunting with the hounds. He is the most pragmatic man I have ever met."

"He must have some ideal, some sense of honor. For heaven's sake, he proved that when he released Ilona and the children from Ekaterinburg."

"That was nine years ago," she said, her mouth twisted. "And it was an exchange, wasn't it? Ilona for me. Men always seem to be doing that, I can't imagine why."

George leaned across the desk. "Judith . . ."

She shook her head. "No. I'm sorry, George. I broke my own rules then. It just slipped out. Not another word. As for Michael—well, I think he does have an ideal. I think he dreams of a Russia as great as it ever was under the tsars, but governed for the people rather than for a handful of aristocrats. If you'll excuse my saying so."

"I agree with you."

She got up. "So it will stand to reason that he'd go for the man most likely, in his opinion, to bring about that state of affairs, no matter what it costs. Is the cost of backing Joseph Stalin going to prove prohibitive? That's something he'll have to wait and find out. As we all will."

"But you'd say categorically that Stalin is now in charge, Politburo or no Politburo?"

"I'd say he's put himself out front," Judith said. "And I'd say he means to stay there. As to whether he *can*, that's up to Bukharin and Zinoviev and Michael, as you say. But I'll tell you this, George, if they don't pull him down very quickly, they're not going to do it at all."

So what do you think of it all, Judith Stein? she wondered. She sat at her desk and chewed the stem of her pen. As she'd once told Boris Petrov, her being born in Russia was an accident of history. A fairly grim accident of history, as it had been for five million others. But she was out. Momma and Poppa had been put against a wall and shot, and Joseph had turned his back, but she and Rachel were out. As if that was going to do Rachel a lot of good.

Nearly five million remained, however. Five million she had hoped to help, through Trotsky, when the time came. So much for that. But had it ever been anything more than a dream? A nice, self-deluding daydream. The impetus to go to Palestine and join with others in creating a Zionist state had long dwindled. She was in New York and she was going to stay in New York—because she loved George Hayman, because she was sure of seeing him every weekday and at least two evenings a week as well. Because to be somebody's mistress was as much as she could ever aspire to, as much as she had ever been able to aspire to. Where was the eighteen-year-old girl who had refused Prince Peter Borodin of Starogan, riding in a carriage beside the Moscow River? Remembering that day was like watching a movie about someone else.

The telephone rang, and Lucy picked it up and looked at her over the receiver. "Monsieur Petrov."

Well, it had to be. "Good morning, Boris," she said.

"You've seen the news from Russia?"

"Came in this morning. Comrade Stalin seems to have fallen on his feet."

"Yes," Boris agreed. "Judith, will you lunch with me?"

"Today? I was going to see my sister. She's not very well, you know."

"This is quite important."

Russia's unofficial envoy to the United States, on the day of Stalin's triumph—that had to be business rather than pleasure. "Well," she said, "if it is important, I'll meet you at a quarter to one."

But she was distinctly nervous, and found herself lighting her fifth cigarette in fifteen minutes before he came into the small restaurant they both liked, handing his hat and coat to the waiter even as he sat beside her.

"When I see you the day grows a little brighter."

"You've been at the vodka again."

"I wish I had. This is a terrible business."

"I never knew you were a Trotsky supporter."

"I'm not. I never was, although I have never doubted that he is an able man. A far abler man than Stalin. But it is Stalin's coup that disturbs me more than Trotsky's eclipse."

"Ah," she said. "Then you'd agree with me that it is a coup."

"Oh, certainly. Shall we order?" He waited until the waiter had taken the order before he resumed. "Stalin is utterly ruthless. Ruthless in a way Lenin never was, and Michael Nej never could be. Getting rid of Trotsky is just a first step. You watch."

"You don't think Trotsky is in danger?"

"Of his life? Oh, no. Not even Stalin would go that far. But of more and more disgrace. Then there will be others. Stalin means to be sole ruler of Russia, and within a very short time."

Judith nodded thoughtfully. Here was powerful ammunition to present to George to back up her own opinions.

"So the question is, what is to be done about it?" Boris said.

"What do you mean?"

"Well, we cannot just accept it."

"But . . . it's just been endorsed by the entire Congress."

"Then it is the duty of all true Russians to see that it is reversed at the next All-Party Congress. He must be resisted, Judith."

"I see your point," she said. "But I think you'd be sticking your neck out. If you really don't like the way things are going over there, why don't you ask for political asylum here? I'm sure I could persuade Hayman Newspapers to help you. Even give you a job."

He frowned at her. "Wouldn't that be running away?"

"Why . . . I suppose it would. But there's not much sense in battering your head against a brick wall, is there? And I imagine that's what Russia is like at the moment."

"It will be difficult," he admitted. "It will take a great deal of time, and it may put my career at risk. Yet it is very necessary, and very worthwhile, if one has the mental stamina, the necessary support. I have no doubt of the support, politically. I am in correspondence with several people, high in the Party, who are as sure as I am that something must be done. But it is the sustaining of the necessary determination when one is away from crowds and rostrums that is the more difficult. That is when one needs . . . Judith—" He leaned across the table and took her hand. "Will you marry me?"

Judith drank some wine to wash down the mouthful of veal she had swallowed without chewing.

"You know I love you," Boris said. "I have loved you almost from the moment we met."

"You fell in love with a reputation," she said. "A legend. They never measure up to reality." Think, God damn you, she told herself. Think.

"Your legend interested me, to be sure," he said. "But it was the woman I fell in love with."

"And now you wish me to go back to Russia with you."

"Why not? You have more friends there than over here, I am sure. And you are something of a heroine over there. Or at least you would be if you went home again. They are inclined to play down your role in the revolution now, because it is bad publicity for a woman like you, a woman who fought on the barricades with Lenin in 1905, who wrote a book on revolutionary tactics, who was sentenced to life exile for her part in the Stolypin plot—" He held up his finger as she would have protested. "That is what the book says. It is bad publicity to admit that she has fled Russia for another country. But if you went back, things would be different."

Judith shook her head. "I hate Russia. I only started to

breathe when I finally left it."

"Well," he said. "It was a dream, perhaps. You and me, going back to Russia together—working together, fighting together, if need be—to achieve what we know is right."

She smiled sadly. "You are still a revolutionary. I'm retired, Boris."

"Then I retire too, here and now. I do not know what that makes me, in choosing a woman over my country. But I do know that I love you, that I cannot live without you, that there is only one choice I *can* make. All right, Judith. Marry me, and I will work for your Mr. Hayman."

Oh, my God, she thought, staring at him.

"Just one word, Judith my love," he said. "Just one word."

"Oh, my God," she·said aloud. Had she ever met a kinder, more gentle, more loving man? Well, she had, which was one reason she had to say no. And the other was that if she accepted, she would be wrecking this man's life as she had wrecked so many other lives.

"Judith?" he asked.

"I can't," she said. "Boris, I can't marry you."

"But... because I am a Communist?"

She shook her head. "No. Nothing like that. It's just that—"She drew a very long breath. "I'm in love with somebody else."

It was his turn to stare.

"People do fall in love," she pointed out. "And this man— Well, I knew him before I ever knew you."

"He is your lover?"

"Yes. Yes, he is."

"But... you have been going out with me for three years now."

"I know. I'm sorry. I... well, I have to live a normal life as well. And I do like you, Boris. So very much."

He was frowning. "You mean this man cannot marry you. Because he is married himself."

"Something like that."

"You know that is futile? You know that some day he will throw you over for the sake of his wife and family?"

"I imagine you're right."

"And you still persist in the relationship?"

She shrugged. "I love the man."

"As I love you. And as he, perhaps, does not love you."

She bit her lip. She had never really considered the matter, mainly because she had never dared consider the matter. George certainly loved her body, and more than that. But as to whether he was in love with Judith Stein, as she was today, or whether he was in love with a memory, she could never be sure.

"You see," Boris said, "I am at least offering you love. And perhaps, in time, you will grow to love me. I will work at it."

She squeezed his fingers. "I know you would, Boris. But I cannot."

"Because you love this married man."

She hesitated.

"That is the only reason?"

Judith sighed. It seemed to her that she had been lying all her life. "Yes," she said. "That is the only reason."

Joseph Vissarionovich Stalin rubbed his hands together as he came into the office. It occurred to Ivan Nej that his master had a greater capacity for looking pleased than any man he had ever known.

"Sit down, Ivan Nikolaievich," Stalin invited. "Sit down."

Ivan obeyed him. "Was there no protest at all?"

"Almost unanimous approval. Trotsky is condemned as a deviationist. We cannot really ask for anything more, at this moment."

"Then I can bring evidence against him, directly?"

Stalin shook his head. "We will continue to hurry slowly, Ivan Nikolaievich. As of this moment he is as harmless as if he were blind and deaf. You will continue to apply pressure, of course. Make life difficult for him, and for everyone who associates with him. But no overt violence against him. Not now."

Ivan shrugged. "Were there no dissenting votes?"

Stalin smiled. "Your brother."

"I wonder you put up with it."

Stalin looked shocked. "My dear Ivan Nikolaievich, Michael Nikolaievich is one of the most senior members of the

Politburo. He is entitled to his opinion. Everyone is entitled to his opinion," he said expansively. "We govern Russia by committee, not by the will of one man. Besides—" His eyes twinkled. "Michael Nikolaievich is an *honest* man. His honesty shines like a beacon, and is appreciated not only by the masses, but by the world press. Fortunately he is also something of a fanatical patriot. Convince him that his dissent is against the best interests of the Motherland, and he will always change his mind."

"Um," Ivan said skeptically.

"But you, Ivan Nikolaievich, you have done magnificently. You know that I cannot show my appreciation publicly, at this moment, but you may be sure it is there. And will be there, forever. I give you my word on this, Ivan. For the rest of my days, you will walk at my shoulder."

"And in your shadow," Ivan said, and flushed.

Stalin gazed at him for a moment, almost threatening a frown. "Why, that is where I wish you to be, of course. Where you can at once protect me and be disguised from my enemies, who will never be sure whether you are there or not. And now, my friend, I have an important task for you, much more important than the elimination of Leon Trotsky."

Ivan raised his head.

"The Politburo will soon approve my idea for a five-year plan, Ivan. Our recovery has been too slow, and has been bedeviled by all these financial crises, entirely a result of allowing profit-making, in my opinion. Don't misunderstand me. I am not criticizing Comrade Lenin, or any of his decisions. The New Economic Policy was very necessary, in 1921. Without it we might never have recovered at all. But it has served its purpose. It is now time for us to resume our proper way, the way of socialism, of the collective state. I wish to see this nation once again a great military power, a great industrial power, and above all I wish to see this nation self-sufficient in food. We must socialize our farming, Ivan Nikolaievich. Our production must be on a state basis, with each region divided into collective farms, all of which will pull together for the good of the state. Initially I am putting this in your charge."

"Me?" Ivan sat up straight. "I know nothing of farming, Joseph Vissarionovich."

Stalin smiled. "You will have experts to aid you. Ivan Nikolaievich, I do not expect you to know about farming. But I expect you to know about the art of persuading people, because that is your business. These farmers, these men who have made themselves fat at the expense of the State, these kulaks, Ivan Nikolaievich, will have to be persuaded to hand over their land and their cattle and their crops into a collective pool."

"The kulaks," Ivan said softly.

"You know them well," Stalin reminded him.

Ivan nodded. "They may resist."

"I have that in mind. Which is why I am appointing you to the post of persuading them."

Ivan gazed at him. "I must have authority."

"You will have it. Authority to use whatever methods you consider necessary." He leaned across the desk. "These kulaks are weeds, Ivan Nikolaievich, which would clutter up our Soviet garden. Now, it may be possible, with certain weeds, to treat them so that they never grow again, so that they remain forever, doing useful work, perhaps, in binding the soil together, but never take vital nutrients from the healthier plants around them. In certain cases, it may even be possible to turn a weed into a useful plant. I do not know that this has ever been successfully done, but it may be possible. But for the vast majority of weeds, there can be only one answer. They must be rooted out of the soil, and thrown on the compost heap. When burned there, their dissipating energy may provide fuel for some more valuable, more worthwhile endeavor. And if, of course, in pulling up a weed, it hurts your hand, Ivan Nikolaievich, why then you would crush it out of existence as you would a worm. Would you not?"

Ivan nodded slowly.

"Well, then. I give you the Ukraine, and I give you the Donbas, as your garden, Ivan Nikolaievich. I leave all decisions to you. I will support your judgment. I give you my word on that. But within two years at the most, I wish that garden to be free of weeds. Do you understand me?"

"I understand you, Joseph Vissarionovich. When do I begin?"

"Now. The very moment you have assembled the force you consider necessary."

Ivan nodded again. "I thank you, Joseph Vissarionovich, for giving me this assignment."

"I give it to you because I know that you will carry it out," Stalin said, smiling genially. "Now tell me, how is this pretty little assistant of yours working out?"

"Very well," Ivan said.

"I wonder you do not divorce Tatiana Dimitrievna and marry this Ragosina," Stalin suggested.

Ivan frowned at him. "Tatiana is my wife," he said. "I will never divorce her, never." He did not add, however, that he had replaced her, completely and totally. If he wanted Tattie back, one day, it would be to torment her and destroy her, at his leisure. He no longer wished to worship at that shrine.

He closed the door behind him and walked down the corridor, oblivious of the people around him. At last, the kulaks. He wondered if Ashcherin would be pleased. Ascherin had a streak of softness, almost of humanity, which sometimes led him astray. And there would be no place for softness in this assignment.

Judith left the office early and took a taxi to Greenwich Village. She had meant to visit Rachel during her lunch hour, but her day had turned chaotic with the latest news of Trotsky. Now she would be arriving at an hour that Rachel would undoubtedly find inconvenient; Judith's sister spent a great deal of time nowadays under sedation, and only really woke up at mealtimes. By now she'd probably be asleep again.

The taxi pulled up to the brownstone and Judith paid the driver. She had found the first floor apartment herself, and even if Peter had at first refused to move on the grounds of an increase in rent, she had finally persuaded Rachel to put her foot down, and had made up the additional rent herself. This Peter had been able to accept, although he would never agree to any support from the Haymans; that Ilona was subsidizing ten-year-old Ruth's schooling had to be kept a secret, just as Ilona's visits had to be kept as much of a secret as possible. She was there now, in fact. As she got down from the taxi Judith could see the Cadillac parked down a side street; where George drove a Rolls-Royce simply because he regarded it as the best, Ilona was too determinedly American to consider a foreign car.

She knocked and entered the apartment.

Rachel was sitting in an easy chair. Since she took almost no exercise, she had put on a considerable amount of weight in the past several years; her thin, haunted face had sagged into puffy jowls, and her hair, as always, needed washing. She sat on the sofa with her legs up and covered by a blanket, although it was warm enough inside the apartment. Her humor had dwindled along with her health and today she did not smile at her sister. "Don't tell me you've been fired," she said.

"I decided to take the rest of the afternoon off. Ilona, how are you?"

Ilona looked as elegant as ever, her hair caught in a chignon, one knee draped over the other, a diamond and emerald bracelet dropping from her right wrist to match the diamond-studded watch on her left.

"Well enough. George tells me there's exciting news coming out of Russia."

"Depressing, you mean," Judith said, and sat down in the remaining easy chair. "Trotsky has been banished to Turkey. His expulsion from the party was incredible enough, but this . . . it's an amazing piece of work, even for Stalin."

"I don't see that there's much difference between Stalin and Trotsky," Ilona said. "I really can't see why Michael Nej doesn't step in and do something about it. He'd have made a perfect replacement for Lenin."

"He hasn't got the intellectual background for it," Judith said.

"I can't believe that."

"And he's a murdering bastard just like the rest of them," Rachel said. "That's what Peter thinks, anyway."

They stared at her, surprised by her interruption.

"Does Peter talk about it a lot?" Judith asked.

"Peter doesn't talk about anything a lot," Rachel said. "He's hardly ever here. God knows what he does with himself, all day. I know he doesn't like to be at home. He says I depress him. But for heaven's sake, he could tell me where he goes. Don't you know where he goes, Judith?"

Judith shook her head.

Rachel looked at Ilona, who also shook her head and hastily attempted to change the subject. "You were going to tell me about Ruth."

"She has a cold," Rachel said. "She always has a cold."

"Perhaps you should have kept her home," Ilona suggested.

"Then she'd never go to school at all," Rachel pointed out. "I told you. She *always* has a cold."

"Maybe she should see a doctor," Ilona said, looking at Judith in an appeal for help.

"So arrange it," Rachel said.

"I'll arrange it," Judith said.

"Yes, well..." Ilona got up. "You've got more company now, Rachel, so I think I'd better be getting home. Johnnie's back from college this evening. He's on his semester break."

"Do ask him to give me a call," Judith said. "Is it true he's coming into the paper?"

"Well, he keeps badgering George to give him the chess column after he graduates in May. And George keeps saying he should start as a cub first, and learn something about reporting if he's ever going to get on, and he says he's not *going* to get on, and George says why not, and he says because the paper by rights belongs to young George, and so it goes. Like a record which has gotten stuck. I suppose they'll iron it out eventually."

"Well," Rachel said, "the paper *should* go to George junior, shouldn't it?"

They gazed at her.

"Well," Rachel said, "it's not as if George was Johnnie's father, is it? And after that business in England—"

"That was several years ago," Judith protested.

"It shows something. You haven't forgiven Peter for that, and he's your own brother, Ilona. And he was only trying to help Tattie. Why should George forgive Johnnie?"

"Because George doesn't bear grudges," Judith said.

"He'd be perfectly willing to give Peter a job, if Peter would be at all reasonable," Ilona said. "And you know that."

Without warning Rachel started to weep. "That's right, gang up on me. Anyone would think you two were the sisters, and I was only the in-law."

"Now Rachel..." Judith attempted to sit beside her on the sofa and was almost pushed off.

"And it's such a laugh," Rachel said, her tone bitter. "You two, old friends, all lovey-dovey. It's such a laugh."

"What do you mean?" Ilona asked, her tone cold.

"If you only *knew*," Rachel said.

Judith stood up, her heart seeming to slow just as her stomach seemed to do a complete roll.

"Knew what?" Ilona asked, looking from one sister to the other. "Do you know what she's talking about, Judith?"

"I have no idea," Judith said, surprised that she could speak at all.

"Ha," Rachel said. "Peter knows all about it. He's known for months. That's why he doesn't want to see either you or George."

"Peter?" Ilona asked. "For heaven's sake, will someone tell me what this is all about?"

"Rachel," Judith said. "For God's sake, shut up."

"Why should I shut up?" Rachel shouted angrily. "Why should I lie here dying while you two are so happy? Why should you have George? Why should either of you have George, much less both of you?"

"Both of—" Ilona stared at Judith, her mouth open.

Judith felt her cheeks burning, and knew she had been overtaken by catastrophe.

Even Rachel seemed to have realized that now, for she looked from one to the other, and her own cheeks were glowing.

"Both of us?" Ilona asked quietly.

"Well, ask her," Rachel said.

Ilona looked at Judith. "Is this true?"

"I . . ."

"Please don't lie to me," Ilona said.

Judith's shoulders slumped, and she sat down.

"And Peter knows," Ilona said. "How does Peter know?"

Judith looked at Rachel.

"Well," Rachel said. "He went over to see Judith one night, and George was there. That's all."

That's all, Judith thought. That's all the proof. If only the wretched girl had come out with it right away, there need have been no fuss. But now she had as good as confessed.

"Yes," Ilona said, moving to the door, "that's all. As I said, I have to go home. Johnnie is coming in on the late train." She closed the door behind herself.

"I'm sorry, Judith," Rachel said. "It—it just slipped out. Sometimes I get so *angry*, just lying here, doing nothing, having nothing. If you only knew..."

"I know a great many things," Judith said. "And one of them is that you have just done a hateful thing. Hateful to me, and even more hateful to Ilona. I hope you're happy." She followed Ilona down the stairs, but the Cadillac had already pulled away.

The wail of a police siren broke into Ilona's thoughts. Her head jerked, and she looked in the rear-view mirror. Then she sighed, and braked, and pulled in to the side of the road.

Thoughts? There had been no coherent thoughts, just a chaos of conflicting emotions. What was she so upset about? Hadn't she known for a long time that George had a mistress? And wasn't it obvious, if she had ever allowed herself to stop and think about it, that it would be Judith? But *Judith*? Judith Stein? One of her oldest friends, in fact, her very oldest *living* friend. Oh, she had been such a fool, imagining George to be involved with some manicured young beauty. Because if it was Judith...

The motorcycle pulled to a stop beside her. "So where's the fire, lady?"

"I'm sorry, officer," Ilona said, giving him a smile. "I'm afraid I was thinking."

"Not about driving," the policeman said.

"No," Ilona said. "Not about driving."

"You'd better let me see your driver's license, lady."

Ilona nodded, opened her handbag, and gave it to him. He peered at it, notebook in hand, then at her. "Mrs. George Hayman?"

"That's right."

"You the wife of that newspaper fellow?"

"That's right."

"Well, now. Say, does he write those editorials himself?"

Oh, Lord, a policeman who wanted to start a political argument. "I'm afraid he does."

"Then you must be the lady from Russia."

Ilona sighed. "Right again."

"Well, what do you know," the policeman said. "I read your husband's articles every day, Mrs. Hayman. I bet he knows more about foreign affairs than anyone else in this country. And you know what, Mrs. Hayman? I think he's right. I think there is a lot happening that this country should be thinking about." He handed her the licence and put his notebook back into his breast pocket. "You tell him Patrolman Larry Smedley said so."

"I will," Ilona said. "Aren't you going to book me?"

"Now why should I do that, Mrs. Hayman? Like you said, you were thinking. About the international situation, I guess. Just don't kill anybody on the way home." He saluted and got back on to his bike.

"I'll tell him," Ilona said weakly. "I'll tell him what you said."

She drove more slowly then, both hands tight on the wheel. She was Mrs. George Hayman. A far more important fact, in a world of dramatically changing values, than having been born the eldest daughter of the future Prince of Starogan. It occurred to her that she had never fully realized that before. She had always thought of what she had given up to run away with George, all compensated for by her love for him, and by his for her. She had never regarded the marriage as a climb, because it had not seemed a climb, in 1911. But looking back she, as well as everyone else, could now see that the seeds of the destruction of Romanov Russia had already been bursting into bud in 1911. She had been the lucky one. So was she going to divorce George for having an affair? Would she ever have dreamed of divorcing Sergei Roditchev for having an affair? She had welcomed his affairs.

But she had not loved Sergei. There was the vital difference. She had not cared whether he lived or died. Oh, yes, she had cared. After their very first night together she had cared. But her wish had been too dreadful even to think about.

She did love George. And she was sure, whatever was lacking in their relationship, that he still loved her. He needed something outside their marriage, and she couldn't decide what it was. Up to this moment she had not cared very much; she had been sure that it had to be temporary. Now that she knew what it was, or who it was, she could fight it. That made a great deal more sense than flying off in a rage and seeking a divorce from the only man she had ever loved.

But if only it hadn't been Judith Stein.

She turned into the driveway, pulled to a halt, and left the keys in the ignition so Rowntree could put up the car; she wouldn't be going out again. She smiled at Harrison, patted the dogs, went upstairs and told Linda, her maid, to prepare a hot tub. She sat and soaked, hair piled on top of her head. The first thing to decide was whether or not to have it out with him. Trouble was, she had never personally confronted George with anything. Others had, and had regretted it, from Sergei Roditchev all the way down to Ivan Nej. But it was still essential, she thought, to let him know that she knew. To let him know that she intended to fight. And to win.

The telephone rang. Linda, waiting in the bedroom, answered, and knocked on the bathroom door a moment later. "It's Prince Peter, madam."

"Peter?" Ilona leapt out of the bath, scattering water. Linda held up the robe, but Ilona ignored her, and crossed the carpeted floor in long strides. What on earth could Peter want? But she was aware of feeling breathless, of *knowing* that something was wrong. "Peter?" He had not telephoned her in several years.

"Ilona." His voice was flat. "Can you come down here, right away?"

"Down where? Your apartment?"

"That's right."

"But . . ." She bit her lip, decided against telling him she had only left the apartment just over an hour ago.

"Please Ilona," Peter begged, "it's terribly urgent. Rachel has killed herself."

They walked slowly away from the graveside, a surprisingly large assembly. Every Russian émigré of note in New York had attended the funeral of the Princess of Starogan on this bleak February day. The last Princess of Starogan. Perhaps, in the futility of cutting her own wrists, she had managed to encapsulate the futility they felt all the time.

More likely, Judith thought, as she picked her way carefully along the icy ground, they just wished the opportunity to get together, even on such a mournful occasion. She walked beside Menachem Yanowski. He had come because he was her friend, not because of Rachel, for the Princess of Starogan had necessarily renounced her religion. Judith was sad about that. But there were so many things to be sad about, if sad was even the appropriate word. She had confessed them all to Menachem, and he had done his best to reassure her. Rachel had not killed herself out of despair at having alienated the only two real friends she had in the world, at having possibly ruined her sister's life just as she had possibly ruined her sister-in-law's life. She had killed herself because for years she had been waiting, unsuccessfully, to die.

All true. And all irrelevant.

She walked immediately behind Peter and Ruth. Peter held his daughter's hand; even from behind, Ruth's shoulders could be seen trembling as she wept. Ruth had loved her mother desperately, mainly because, Judith supposed, Peter had so seldom been there to be loved. She wondered what *he* thought of it all. Certainly during the last few years he had given the impression that he regarded Rachel as a colossal nuisance, and he had never troubled to deny that he had married her only because he had thought Judith was dead. Yet he had apparently been as shattered as anyone by her death.

And she walked immediately in front of George and Ilona. She and Ilona had looked at each other once, during the service, and then looked away again. But Ilona had not yet done anything about the situation. Judith knew that, because she would have seen it in George, and George had been his usual self. Oh, she thought, if only there were some way to prevent Ilona ever doing anything about the situation. I have caused enough misery in this world, she told herself. Therefore I must go to her, very simply, and say, I promise, I swear, that I will never see George again. But that was an absurdity; they worked in the same building, and she was required to take in the Russian news to the president every morning, as Ilona well knew. Therefore she must give up her job as well. And if she was going to do that, there was nothing left for her in New York at all. In America at all. Even Menachem must realize that.

She would go to Palestine then. Go to heat, and poverty— and bloodshed, from the latest reports of Arab-Jewish clashes at the Wailing Wall. Go to forget all her dreams of helping millions of Jewish refugees, and become one of them herself, a microcosm who needed help as badly as anyone else. What arrogance, to suppose that she was better than anyone else, could ever have been better. But having been raised above the common herd, to slip back into their midst was not going to be easy. No doubt Menachem knew that as well.

They reached the gate, and she turned to face him. "I think I'd like to come with you, Menachem, and have a talk. If I may."

"Of course, Judith. I—"

"Judith." Peter's voice was harsh. Ruth was already getting into the hired limousine.

"Yes, Peter?"

"I'd like you to come with me. There are things to discuss."

She frowned at him. But there *were* things to discuss, and Rachel had been her sister. "Oh," she said. "Well, I suppose . . ."

"I think you should go with Prince Borodin," Menachem agreed. "You can always come to see me later."

"Oh. Yes." She turned to find George and Ilona immediately behind her. "Well," she said. "Good-bye." She stared at Ilona as she spoke, willing her to understand.

"Good-bye, Judith," Ilona said.

"Take tomorrow off, if you wish," George said.

"I . . . yes. Thank you." Once again she looked at Ilona. Then she turned and got into the car.

Ruth was in the front beside the chauffeur. Peter sat beside Judith in the back. "She left a note, you know," he said.

"Oh?" She gazed at him.

"She wrote, 'I've messed everything up.' Just that."

"Yes," Judith said.

"Do you know what she meant? If she meant anything at all."

"We'll talk about it later," Judith said.

He nodded, and looked out of the window. What *does* he feel about it all, she wondered?

They reached the apartment building, and the car stopped to let them off before driving away. "You'll come in for lunch," Peter said, and gave a half-smile. "You'll have to cook it, though."

She followed Ruth up the stairs, took off her coat, and went into the kitchen. The only food was a couple of cans of baked beans. But there was some bread.

"It won't take a lot of cooking," she said. "Maybe we should go out."

"No," Peter said. "Not today."

He was as elegantly dressed as ever, and she was sure his suit was not more than a few months old. It contrasted strongly with Rachel's best dress, in which they had buried her—a relic of 1923, with every seam let out.

"I'm not hungry," Ruth said. "I'd like to lie down."

"I think that would be a good idea," Peter said. He went with her into the bedroom, gave her a kiss, and carefully closed the door. Judith served baked beans.

"What are you going to do?" she asked.

"About what?"

"Well . . . Ruth, for a start."

"She needs a mother," Peter said. "She's never really had one. Just as I need a wife. I've never really had one either."

"*Peter.*"

"It's perfectly true. We've each had a little girl playing at being princess. God alone knows what would have happened if she had had to *be* princess."

"That's very cruel."

"It's a cruel world. Will you marry me, Judith?"

"Marry you?"

"I've always loved you, Judith," Peter said. "I fell in love with you the first time I ever saw you, in Sergei Roditchev's house. Remember, in 1907? My God, more than twenty years ago. I was married then too." He reflected. "And you turned me down. Oh, if only you hadn't turned me down, Judith."

"You . . . your wife was *buried* this morning." Judith cried.

"We never loved each other," Peter said. "She was a pretty girl, and the world was falling apart. We each possessed something the other wanted, and neither of us supposed we were going to survive long enough to regret it. That's not love."

"You are quite the most outrageous man I have ever known," she said. But he was behaving as the Princes of Starogan had always behaved. What was done was done. Now the next step, the next position, must be considered.

"Listen." He leaned across the table. "You think the way

I do. You hate Communism as much as I do. The Bolsheviks murdered your mother and father, just as they murdered my family. Rachel never felt anything about that. Rachel never felt anything about anything, except Rachel. But you *feel*. I can see that. All right, so you told me all about Siberia. You told me how Roditchev deflowered you with a stick. You told me how you had a child by some criminal. I know all about you, Judith, and I still want you. I want us to be together. We've wasted twenty years. Don't let's waste another single moment."

"You're mistaken," she said. "You don't know anything about me at all. Have you forgotten I lived with Michael Nej for two years, as his mistress?"

"Well, of course I haven't forgotten. Everyone knows that."

"I lived with your valet. Your *valet*, Peter."

"As I said, it was a collapsing world. I—" He changed his mind, but she knew that he had almost said, "After all, I married the daughter of a Jewish lawyer." Presumably the gulf between a Prince of Starogan and the daughter of a Jewish lawyer was even greater than the gulf between the daughter of a Jewish lawyer and the Prince of Starogan's valet.

But what he was proposing was quite impossible. "And Rachel's death," she said. "Do you know why she killed herself?"

He frowned at her. "Do *you* know?"

"Yes. Oh, she'd been ill for years, and maybe she felt life wasn't worth living. But I know what triggered it. It was because she told Ilona about George and me."

He frowned. "George and you?"

Judith leaned across the table. "For the past five years, Peter, George Hayman and I have been lovers. But you knew that. You told her."

"Of course I knew. I can't see why she would wish to tell Ilona. That was a dreadful thing to do."

Judith stared at him. "You mean, you don't *care* that I have been sleeping with George?"

Peter ate the last of his baked beans, chewing slowly. "I am going to leave New York," he said at last. "Ruth and I will go to England. I do not understand the Americans, and I will tell you that quite frankly. They will not recognize the Bolshevik regime, which is perfectly correct of them, but they will not support me in my efforts to bring down that regime. Besides, the grand duke himself is in Paris, and he has invited me to take command of the counterrevolutionary forces in Europe. It was probably my decision to accept his invitation that upset Rachel just as much as any quarrel with you did. She always wanted to enjoy the perquisites of her title without accepting any of the responsibilities. I only came to American at all, Judith, because George was apparently prepared to give me his support. Now that has been withdrawn, I cannot see any reason to stay. There are great things happening in Russia. People are dissatisfied with the way things are going. Even the Bolsheviks are dissatisfied with the way Stalin has treated Trotsky. But the people in the south—my people, Judith—they are at last prepared to do something about the situation. The Ukraine and the Donbas are the granary of Russia, and they are getting fed up with being dictated to by doctrinaire Socialists in Moscow. I have it on best authority that the kulaks would respond to a positive lead. I must be there to give them that lead, at the right moment."

"And what about money?" Judith asked.

Peter shrugged. "There is money. I have money invested, and the stock exchange has been booming these past few months."

"But—could you not have spent some of it on Rachel?"

"How would you suggest? On buying her clothes? That would have been a waste."

"On making things easier," Judith shouted.

"In many ways," he said sadly, "you are as emotional as she. That money was donated to our cause, to the cause of bringing down the Bolsheviks. I had no right to spend it on my wife."

"But you will spend it on moving to England, or France, or somewhere."

"If it is all a part of defeating Stalin and Nej and their crew, it is well spent. And you are also a part of that ultimate victory, Judith. With you at my side I know we will succeed. You are a woman who succeeds in everything you determine to undertake. Come with me to Europe, Judith."

To Europe. Back to Europe. But more important, away

from America. Away from the lives she was wrecking. Away from her dreams and her hopes. But not necessarily away from her dedication to the cause of Zionism. There were millions of Jews in Europe to set beside the millions of Jews in Russia. Since she had wrecked her own emotional life, as she had wrecked so many others' emotional lives, what did she have left to offer?

But with Peter?

"You want me to go with you?" she asked. "Despite all? Despite George?"

"We belong together, Judith. We have always belonged together."

She gazed at him. Much of what he had said was perfectly true. She did hate the Bolsheviks; they had murdered her parents. But she could never hate with his fervor, or devote her entire life to such a destructive cause. For a man such as Peter Borodin to become so consumed with such a single, horrible purpose was tragic. And yet, she had loved him once, and he had saved her life once, at great personal cost. And he was a dedicated man, even though his dedication often led him into strange or cruel paths. But these were all a part of his dedication. If such dedication could ever be harnessed in the cause of Zionism... It was at least worth a try.

Besides, she wanted to get away. Away and away and away. And, she reminded herself, she owed it to Rachel to look after Ruth to the best of her ability.

"I'll come with you, Peter, if you want me to. I'll come with you, and I'll look after you and Ruth. But I won't marry you. And," she added, "I won't sleep with you either. All that is over."

Peter Borodin smiled briefly. "I suppose one must be thankful for small mercies. Just come with me, Judith. Just come with me."

"Now let me get this straight," George said, resting his elbows on his desk. "You are resigning the Russian desk?"

"Yes," Judith said breathlessly.

"And you're going back to Europe. With Peter?"

"Well... Ruth needs a mother."

"And what does Peter need?"

"I don't think you have any right to ask me that," Judith said. She had braced herself for this ordeal and was quite prepared to see it through.

"But I *have* asked," George said quietly. She remembered that he was, if anything, more determined a person than herself.

"Do you know when it was Peter first asked me to live with him?" she asked. "Twenty years ago. Before I even knew you existed, George Hayman."

"And you refused him."

"I was still young enough, and stupid enough, to think that life consisted of right and wrong, then."

"What do you suppose it consists of now?" he asked.

"Well..." But it was necessary to be cruel, to be kind. Perhaps that was what Peter practiced, in his own way. "I have to go, George. If you can't see that you're a fool. We're getting serious. You're getting serious."

"You don't think love is a serious business?"

"It had better not be, if you can't marry. George..." She sucked air through her nostrils until her lungs were full. "Ilona knows."

"What are you talking about? How can she possibly know?"

"She knows because Rachel told her. Rachel told her in my presence. She told her, and then she cut her wrists and got into a hot bath."

George stared at her. "You expect me to believe that?"

"It happens to be true."

"And Ilona has said nothing, done nothing?"

"She hasn't. Because before she could even make up her mind, I should think, she heard about Rachel's death. But she will say something, soon. What are you going to do then, George? Tell her you'll leave her for me?"

George leaned back in his chair, thoughtfully pulled at his chin.

"Because if you do that, George Hayman," Judith said urgently, "then you *are* a fool. Ilona loves you. And she is everything you want. God knows what has gone wrong between you, but if I were you, I'd try to straighten it out. She's too good to lose, George."

He leaned forward again. "And you?" His voice was very soft.

She shrugged.

"Do you imagine you can spend the rest of your life doing the self-sacrificing bit?"

"It's better than just sitting around," she said, and forced a smile. "Or lying around." It was her turn to lean forward. "Please let me go, George. Let me go and forget about me. These last few years have been the best of my life. I shall never forget them, or you. I shall never want to. But we both knew it couldn't last forever, didn't we?"

He gazed at her, but she knew the crisis was over. She pushed back her chair and got up.

She didn't really know what to say, or do. She'd never ended an affair before. Her abortive early relationship with Peter had collapsed in a welter of dramatics as the Princess Irina had stormed into the house, and she had simply run away from Michael Nej.

"But George . . ." She held out her hand. There was really nothing more to say. "Good-bye."

He squeezed her fingers, and, still holding them, got up. "You'll take six months' severance pay. I insist."

She shook her head.

"Now, Judith . . ."

"I owe *you*, George, since I'm leaving without adequate notice. And what would it make me, if I accepted all that money?"

"How do you propose to live?"

"Peter has more than we thought, apparently."

He nodded, as if this satisfied any doubts he might have had as to her relationship with Peter. "I did promise you my help once."

"And you've helped me too often since then."

"I doubt I've helped you at all," he said. "But you'll remember, Judith, that if you ever do need help, *ever*, I'm still here."

A last squeeze of his fingers, and then she freed her hand and went to the door. "I'll remember, George."

George Hayman left the Rolls for Rowntree to park and went inside to the noise of barking dogs.

"Mr. Hayman?" Harrison raised his eyebrows. It was the

first time his employer had been home at three in the afternoon on a weekday that he could remember.

"No ghost, Harrison. Where can I find Mrs. Hayman?"

"On the grounds, sir. She's inspecting the damage the deer have made."

George nodded, made his way through the obstacle course presented by the leaping Labradors, and went on to the patio, where he stopped to watch his wife. She wore slacks and rubber boots, a heavy jacket, and a floppy hat, as she made her way around the hedges and the flower beds, which would show their first color in a few weeks. Her hair was out of sight, obviously in a bun beneath the hat. Anything less like the cool, elegant creature who presided at their parties could hardly have been imagined.

The excitement of the dogs, which had now reached the three Dachshunds that were busily surrounding her, alerted her, and she turned her head and frowned at him. "George?"

"You sound as disapproving as Harrison."

"Well . . ." Instinctively she put up her hand to do something about her hair. "Nothing's wrong?"

He went closer. "Nothing that I can't put right, I hope."

Her gaze searched his face.

"And since I'm home," he said, "why don't you take the afternoon off, as well?"

She looked around the grounds almost as if she'd never seen them before. Then she started toward him. "I'm always happy to do that."

He held her hand, and they went inside together. The servants had all tactfully disappeared. The dogs gazed at them in a disappointed group as they climbed the stairs.

"Did you know that Peter is leaving New York?" George asked.

She stopped, and turned to face him.

"He's going back to Europe—to England, I think, with Ruth." He drew a long breath. "Judith is going with them."

"Judith?"

"As his housekeeper. I don't know whether she eventually means to marry him or not, but of course it's far too soon after Rachel's death for them to consider it yet anyway. But Peter has always been in love with her, as you must have known."

"I'm sorry, George."

"About Peter?"

She resumed the climb, one step in front of him now. "Won't you miss her?"

"I'll find another Russian editor."

"I'm sure you will." She opened the bedroom door. "I really should take a shower."

"I'll join you. If I may."

She hesitated, then went in front of him into the bedroom, and dropped her clothes on the floor. She was still the loveliest woman he had ever seen. And how he wanted her. Because love was an act of will, and the will had suddenly returned to him, to love his wife? Or because he was, deep down, relieved that the Judith episode was over? Which would make him a real bastard. Or maybe, merely a typical, ambivalent male. Judith had been a want, a surging desire, of his ever since their return together from Russia. But because he was by nature an honest man, he had not been able to take her without convincing himself that he no longer loved his wife. Absurd, and yet now perfectly clear.

They stood beneath the shower together, bodies pressed against each other, while the water bounded off her rubber shower cap, scattered across their shoulders, ran down their arms and legs. He looked down into her face; her eyes were closed, and those flawless features looked as if they were carved from stone, onto which rain was dripping. She had won a bloodless victory, because her opponent had surrendered without firing a shot. Was she pleased about that, or contemptuous? But Ilona had never been a contemptuous person.

He kissed her on the mouth. "I love you," he said.

Her eyes opened, closed again to avoid the water, and she stepped away from him, through the curtain in search of her towel.

He followed her. "And I would like to apologize. If it's possible to apologize for four years."

Her head turned. Perhaps she had not realized it had gone on for as long as that.

"It would be nice," he suggested, "if you would say something."

Ilona dried herself, slowly and thoughtfully. "I was thinking," she said, "how splendid it was when it was just you and me against the whole world, George. We must try to be just you and me again, from time to time."

"I'd like that." She was again in his arms.

It was where she wanted to be, no matter what had happened. And what *had* happened? He had had an affair. Well, she had once had an affair, with Michael Nej, and her affair had been far more serious, since it had made her a mother. So then... but it wasn't the same thing at all. She had fled to Michael's arms because she had been married to an absolutely hateful man, whereas George... and to Judith. Of all people, Judith.

She wondered if she feared her, not merely for her looks or her strength, but for her past, the many bits of it she had shared with George, the memories which *only* they could share.

But it *had* to be forgotten, or forgiven, or she must end the marriage now. And she was not going to do that. She loved this man. Thus she must think as he might think, and as a Princess of Starogan might think, too.

"And don't apologize," she said. "Not ever. I came to you via Sergei and Michael Nej, and you took me back to see Michael again. Don't apologize." She reached up to kiss him on the chin. "But I'm glad she's going. George, do you suppose we could take a trip together? A nice long, slow trip, like that one to Russia in '22, only with none of the traumas?"

"I'd like that too, sweetheart. But I can't, not this year. It's just too soon after the election." He saw the disappointment in her face. "I can't, my darling, not after leading Herbert's campaign. But as soon as he's been in the White House a while, we'll be off. Just you and me, my darling. Just—" He raised his head as the bedroom door burst open. "What the devil?"

Ilona turned in his arms, hastily reached for her robe, and pulled it on. "For heaven's sake, Johnnie, I do wish you'd knock."

John Hayman stood in the center of the room, eyes blazing. "You're sending Uncle Peter away," he said.

George wrapped a towel round his waist. "I have no idea what you're talking about."

"You're making Uncle Peter leave New York," John accused. "You're making him go to Europe."

"He told you that?" Ilona asked.

"He's going, isn't he?"

"I had no idea you were still seeing Peter," George said. "I thought you and he had fallen out."

"You hoped that," Johnnie said. "Oh, you hoped that. But it didn't work out, did it? Not without Aunt Tattie there to seduce me."

"Oh, really, Johnnie," Ilona said. "Don't be ridiculous."

"She did," Johnnie declared. "Uncle Peter watched her do it, and he knows. He says she can seduce anyone, if she wants to."

"Yes," George said. "Well, old man, whatever happened then, you've got it wrong this time. I'm not sending your uncle anywhere. I'm not the government."

"You have enough friends in the government to do it," Johnnie said. "The press is always saying what a powerful man you are. You can do what you like."

"Peter is going because he doesn't want to stay here anymore," Ilona said. "It's as simple as that. You really must not get so worked up about things. But look, darling, since you and George are both here, we could have a chat about your graduation party. I know it's months away, but you probably won't be home again before May."

"I don't want any party," Johnnie said. "Not from you. Not from either of you."

"Now just a moment," George said. "You can rant and rave all you like, Johnnie, but I'm not having any rudeness to your mother. I think you should just trot off and cool down. We'll talk about the party this evening."

"I'll trot off," Johnnie said. "I'll trot off for good. If Uncle Peter goes to Europe, then I'm going to follow him, just as soon as I graduate. I'd rather work for him against Communism than for a newspaper, anyway."

"Now, Johnnie," Ilona said.

"I'm going," Johnnie said. "And you can't stop me. After all, I'll be twenty-one."

Chapter 10

"HERE ARE SOME LETTERS," GEORGE HAYMAN SAID, PLACING them on the table. "One to the manager of our London office. He'll give you a job if the going gets tough. One to Barings, my London banks. I've opened a credit with them, in your name, of up to two hundred pounds a month."

John Hayman picked up the envelopes, looked at them, and put them back again. "I can't take these."

"Don't be more of a fool than you're already being," George said. "And it doesn't matter whether you take them or not. Copies have already gone to the other end, and they'll be expecting you."

"You think I'm going to fall flat on my face, don't you?" John said. "And come crawling back here for help."

"I very much doubt that you will do that," George said. "But you're Ilona's son, and therefore my responsibility, whether you like it or not." He smiled. "Whether I like it or not, either. I happen to think you're being asinine. I also happen to think you deserve to be punched on the nose for so distressing your mother. But I also have some idea of how you feel. Maybe going off on your own will do you a lot of good." He held out his hand. "Good luck."

John Hayman looked surprised, then squeezed the proffered hand. "Well, thanks, George. I don't have anything against you, really. It's just that—"

"Forget it," George said. "But you'll take those letters."

John hesitated, then nodded, picked up the envelopes, and placed them in his inside breast pocket.

"And a word of advice?"

John waited.

"Admire your uncle as much as you wish, Johnnie. But for God's sake, don't get involved in his harebrained schemes." He watched the face in front of him seem to close, and sighed. "The others are waiting to say good-bye."

In the foyer, John shook hands with George junior. "I'll be back," he promised, "to see how you're running the paper." He kissed Felicity, at sixteen already his height, on the nose. "And to make sure you marry the right guy. No tears now."

Felicity sniffed. "Soon, Johnnie. Soon."

"Soon," he promised, and went out the front door, to where his mother was waiting on the veranda.

"All ready?" she asked.

"All ready, Mother."

She bit her lip, looked at the two bags, then the floor, then back at him. "I'd like to come see the boat off."

He shook his head. "I'd rather you didn't." He smiled at her. "Then I might change my mind."

"And you don't want to change your mind."

He held her shoulders. "I've got to go, Mother. I've got to. You know that. I'm not a Hayman. I can never be a Hayman. If I stay, George is going to take me into the newspaper, and make me a vice-president, and turn me into something I'm not. That's George junior's business, not mine."

"And what do you suppose *is* your business? Not being a Russian prince, Johnnie. That's over and done with, and you know that."

"Being myself, Mother," he said. "I have to find myself." He flushed, because she would know that he had read that in a book.

"Yes," she said. "Well, take care, my own sweet darling. Oh, take care."

He held her close for a moment, kissed her on the forehead, and went down the steps to the waiting Rolls.

George came through from the inner room to hold her hand. "Maybe you should have told him the truth," he said.

"Then he would have been even more confused," Ilona said. "Don't you think?"

"I guess." He sighed. "He's going to be seeing a lot of Peter."

She nodded. "But there'll be Judith too. Maybe she'll have a calming influence." She glanced at him. "Do you think of her a lot?"

"No," George said, and flushed. "I mean, yes. That was automatic husband talk. But not the way you mean. That's over and done with."

She gazed at him. While she believed him, she knew that they had not yet regained whatever it was they had lost. Was it just a matter of waiting for the next Judith?

The car started, and John Hayman leaned out of the window to wave. Ilona turned away. "Well," she said. "The first to leave the nest. I'm going to lie down and cry a little, I think."

Peter Borodin opened the door of the London flat and frowned at his visitor. "Good God," he said. "What are *you* doing here?"

"I've come to see you, Uncle Peter," John Hayman said.

Peter peered past his nephew at the corridor, suspiciously, saw nothing to disturb him, and stepped back. "Well, you'd better come in. How did you know where to find me?"

"Aunt Judith wrote Mother."

"I might have known." Peter Borodin closed and locked the door, and dropped the safety chain in place. "One can't be too careful."

John put down his bags and looked around the tiny living room, dominated by the enormous desk in the far corner by the window. Not a great deal of light was coming through the window, since it was a typical London summer's day, with heavy clouds and intermittent showers. The place looked gloomy, and was the smallest apartment he had ever been in;

the kitchen was merely an alcove off the living room, and through the opened door he could see that the bedroom was hardly bigger. But then the area in which the apartment was situated, north of Hyde Park in the borough of Bayswater, was hardly where he would have expected to find the Prince of Starogan either.

"I hope you're not planning to stay with us," Peter said.

"Of course not," Johnnie lied. "I'll find myself a place somewhere. Aren't Ruth and Aunt Judith with you?"

"Ruth is at school," Peter explained. "And Judith is out." Once again he followed the direction of his nephew's gaze. "I'm afraid it is a bit crowded. I could afford somewhere bigger, of course, but I mustn't be conspicuous. I don't want the Reds to know I've left America at all, you see. Well, I suppose they must know that by now. That spy of theirs, Petrov, will have told them. But I don't want them to know where I am." He waved his arm. "Sit down."

Johnnie sat down. "Do you really have people going in and out of Russia all the time, Uncle Peter?"

"People? Going in and out of Russia? What's that to you?"

"I—I'd like to help."

"You?"

"I know I let you down over Auntie Tattie. But I was so young, then. And she did seduce me, just like you said she would. It wouldn't happen again. I promise. I want to help."

Peter Borodin gazed at his nephew for some moments. "Help," he repeated. "How could you help me?"

"Well . . ." John Hayman licked his lips. "I speak Russian fluently. I can pass for a Russian. I mean, I am one, really."

"So go to Russia."

Johnnie sighed. "I *can* help you, Uncle Peter. I know I can. Listen. I've been doing chess journalism back in the U.S. I'm quite good at it. And the Russians are crazy about chess. I'm sure I could go in as a chess correspondent and no one would be the wiser. That way I could see people for you, and then come back out and report. It'd be a perfect cover."

"You think it's all some sort of a game, don't you?"

"Of course not. I—"

"A game you can resign from whenever you choose. You want to go to Russia, and see people on my behalf. Do you know what would happen to them, if you let them down?"

"Well, I—"

"They'd be handed over to your uncle, Ivan Nej. And what he would do to them doesn't bear thinking about. And when he was finished, he'd have them put against a wall and shot. No game, Ivan Sergeievich. It could happen to you, too."

"I've said I wouldn't let you down again, Uncle Peter," Johnnie said. "And I'm not afraid. I hate the Bolsheviks as much as you do. I want to bring them down."

Once again the long stare.

"I . . . I can contribute to the cause, too," Johnnie said. "George has given me an allowance. Two hundred pounds sterling a month, if I want it. I'd contribute it all to you, Uncle Peter, if you'd let me work for you."

"Two hundred pounds a month? George has given you this?"

Johnnie nodded.

Peter Borodin stroked his chin. "From his bank account? His name?"

"Yes. But I'm sure he wouldn't like to know I was giving it to you. His name would have to be kept out of it."

Peter Borodin smiled. "He'd never know, Johnnie, not unless we tell him. The money would be transferred from his account to yours . . ."

"I haven't got an account."

"We will open one for you. And then you would transfer it from yours to my émigré account. Yes. That would work very well."

"And you'd let me work for you?"

Peter Borodin sat down beside his nephew and crossed his knees. "If you really are that desperate to do something for the Motherland."

"I am, Uncle Peter. I swear it."

"Hm. It can probably be arranged. You'd need a false identity, of course. The name Hayman isn't exactly unknown in Russia. A false passport . . . but that would be necessary anyway, since you couldn't go in and out of Russia on a U.S. passport, the way things are at the moment. I wouldn't dream of employing you, you know, except that things are moving towards a crisis. Do you have any idea what is happening in Russia, at this moment?"

"Not a lot."

"Well, I can tell you there is the most gigantic power struggle going on. This man Stalin, just about the worst of the lot, is trying to take over the entire Communist Party. He has already destroyed his chief rival, Trotsky. Soon he will start destroying his other potential rivals—Bukharin, and Zinoviev, and Michael Nej. I can tell you that the Bolsheviks are at last about to fall out among themselves, and that means the collapse of their entire filthy regime, and *that* means our opportunity. There are millions of Russians, *in* Russia, who think like you and me. Particularly in the south. Do you know what the word kulak means?"

"Well peasant, I suppose. Well-to-do peasant."

"Exactly."

"I had no idea there was such a thing under Bolshevism. I didn't know people *could* become wealthy in a socialist state."

"They're not supposed to," Peter Borodin agreed. "But men will always become wealthy if they can. Lenin encouraged it. That is, he was forced to. There was no food in Russia in 1921 and 1922, and the peasants were hiding their grain, what little they had, rather than handing it over to the state—they weren't allowed to sell it, you see. So Lenin realized there was nothing else to do. He allowed the peasants to keep a part of their grain, and sell it for whatever they could get, if they would hand over the rest to the state. And everybody was relatively happy for a while. But of course the successful ones got rich, and the unsuccessful ones went to the wall. Some of the kulaks even rented the poorer ones' land—that way they managed to extend their holdings despite the fact that they couldn't *buy* more land. That is the law of nature—the law of capitalism, as the Bolsheviks would call it. But it worked, and Russia got back on its feet at least as far as food production was concerned. But naturally, the kulaks accumulated a lot of ill feeling and jealousy, from the poorer peasants, and inside the Communist Party, where they can't stand to see anyone doing well. So now there is a movement afoot to make them hand over their land to vast collective farms, and abolish the profit incentive entirely."

"That seems unfair," Johnnie said.

"Of course it's unfair. And the kulaks don't like it at all.

This is our opportunity. If we can unite them under proper leadership, we could light a flame in the Ukraine and the Don basin that would sweep right across Russia, sweep the Bolsheviks off the face of the earth. But it will take some organizing. Are you prepared to play your part in that?"

"Of course."

"Hm. There's a man named Brusilov. He is the wealthiest kulak in the entire Donets area. Through his rentals, he controls a great deal of land. He is the natural leader of the movement on the ground. My people have reached him already, have told him which way the Politburo's mind is working, and he is certainly sympathetic to us. But he is reluctant to make a move. He is one of those men who will have to be pushed. And if we wait for events it will be too late. I have often thought that if I could go and see him, speak with him, he would remember me, and be prepared to follow my lead. But of course I cannot go back to Russia. Too many other people know me as well. I wouldn't even get past the frontier."

"But I can go, Uncle Peter," Johnnie said. "No one knows me."

"Yes," Peter said, "and if you could go to see this Brusilov, and identify yourself to him, reveal yourself as my nephew, and as Sergei Roditchev's son, tell him something of our plans, of the international support he will be sure of receiving, once he starts his counterrevolution—"

"*Will* there be international support, Uncle Peter?"

"Of course," Peter said irritably. "The English hate the Soviets. So do the French and the Germans. Oh, they are just waiting to have a legitimate opportunity to topple them. I know this."

"Then I'm your man," Johnnie said. "And it so happens, Uncle Peter, that a Russian chess championship is to be held at Kharkov this summer. Nothing could be better."

"At Kharkov? I didn't know that. Why, Ivan Sergeievich, as you say, nothing could be better."

"Peter." Judith Stein opened the apartment door, banged it behind her, and smiled at Peter Borodin. "You'll never guess."

Peter raised his head. "I probably won't. What?"

She blew him a kiss. Sometimes she even supposed she was

happy. Not in a sexual sense. Not even in a domestic sense. Peter Borodin had none of the charm, none of the pulsing manhood, none of the humor, and none of the gentleness of either George or Michael. He was a Russian prince, the senior Russian prince, and he was engaged in a life-and-death struggle, not to regain his titles and prerogatives, because she felt that even Peter knew that was impossible, but to avenge the dead. The rest of life was necessarily a perfunctory, unsatisfactory business. There could be no true happiness for an exiled Prince of Starogan. And therefore none, in that human sense, for the woman at his side. But suddenly she was where Fate must have intended her to be from the beginning. It was even possible to imagine, sometimes, that she was caring for her own daughter; she and Ruth looked alike, and they thought alike. The intervening years of her bargain with Michael, her guilty affair with George, might never have been. Certainly her new role made more sense than anything else that had happened in her tangled and uncertain life.

And that she was at last doing the right thing was suddenly being supported by outside events, again for the first time. She waved the letter at him. "It's from Joseph. You remember Joseph, my brother?"

Peter frowned at her. "I remember Joseph. An utter Bolshevik. He once tried to have me shot."

"Yes," Judith said. "Well, times have changed. He's realized his mistake. He's out."

"He's left Russia?"

"He's in Berlin." She threw her arms round Peter's neck and kissed him on the cheek. "God knows why Berlin. I suppose it was all he could get to. I'll write him and tell him to join us here."

"Here?" Peter disengaged himself. "What for?"

"Well . . ." Judith sat down, and fanned her flushed face. The summer day was warm. "He'll be safer here, and besides, I want to see him again, after all these years. And he may be of some help to you."

"He's probably a Bolshevik spy," Peter said.

"Oh. Well, I'd like him to come to England," she said, and got up again, eternally restless. "Johnnie coming in for supper?" It had been such a pleasure having the boy around, and with him there she could pretend she was expiating her sins by taking care of Ilona's eldest.

"No," Peter said. "He isn't."

"Oh. And I've brought home his favorite too, fish and chips. I'll just put them in the oven."

Peter got up in turn, and took a position in the center of the room. It was a stance she knew well. "Johnnie won't be coming in again, for a while."

Judith, kneeling before the little stove, raised her head. "He hasn't gone back to New York, has he? Without saying good-bye?"

Peter cleared his throat. "He's gone to Russia, as a matter of fact."

Slowly Judith pushed herself up, stood straight, and turned to face him. "To Russia?"

"It was a matter of waiting for his new passport to be ready, his new identity," Peter explained. "But they came through yesterday."

"To *Russia*?" Judith's voice rose an octave. "Nobody told me he was going to Russia."

"Well," Peter said, "I don't tell you everything that we mean to do. You would only have raised objections."

"You're damned right I would have raised objections," Judith shouted. "Johnnie? How can you possibly send Johnnie to Russia?"

"But there's no one better," Peter protested. "He is Russian."

"And when they find out who he really is?"

"How can they possibly do that? I've just told you that he has a false passport, false identity, everything. He'll be perfectly safe. And right now I need every agent I can lay my hands on. There are great things about to happen over there."

"Great things," Judith said contemptuously. "There'll be a great number of shootings, you mean. And among them Johnnie Hayman. Your own nephew. Peter, you must stop him."

"I can't stop him, Judith. Not now. He's on his way."

"You can! You have means of getting in touch with your people. I know that. You've told me that. You can at least get him back out of there. I know you can do it."

Peter stared at her, his face cold. "I cannot call him back,

Judith. And even if I could, I would not, now. He is fighting for Russia. For you and me, for all of us. For the overthrow of Bolshevism. I will not call him back."

"John Harding?" Feodor Brusilov spoke the words in Russian, haltingly, and peered at his guest. "That is not a Russian name."

"It is an English name," Johnnie explained, continuing to look around him. He could understand why Uncle Peter was so sure of this man's support against the Bolsheviks, where he had doubted. He had ridden across this farm for miles before coming to the main buildings, had admired the rolling fields of wheat, the cattle, the evidence of industrious success that had surrounded him. As now, inside the house, he saw the oak-paneled walls, the ikons, so suggestive of those hung on the walls at Starogan, and the carpets on the floor, clearly from Persia. He had even been shown into Feodor Brusilov's office by a butler.

Brusilov continued to frown. "You are English? How did you come here? By the train?"

"As a matter of fact, no," Johnnie said. "I hired a horse in Poltava. I went for a ride in the country. Nobody seemed to mind."

"Then you must be hungry, and thirsty. Boris Alexandrovich, we will have vodka. And there will be another place at supper. You will stay to supper. Come." He clapped Johnnie on the shoulder, and took him from the office across a hallway and into a delightfully pleasant drawing room, from which open windows led on to a veranda overlooking a sloping flower-filled garden bordered by the river, immense and sluggish, flowing past the farm. "Alexandra, I would have you meet an Englishman, Mr. John Harding."

"Madam." John bowed over her hand. She was slightly taller than her husband, and not so gray.

"Mr. Harding, welcome. My daughter, Natasha Feodorovna."

"Mr. Harding." The girl held out her hand, and John took it slowly. She was about eighteen, he estimated, and had her mother's height and flowing reddish-brown hair. Facially she resembled her father, with rather long features, and solemn green eyes. The impression he got was one of supreme grace rather than beauty. Her every movement was graceful; even the way she stood still had a natural flowing grace.

"Mademoiselle Brusilova." He shook the slender fingers. "It is my great pleasure."

"Sit down, Mr. Harding, sit down," Feodor Brusilov invited. The butler was placing the vodka jug and the glasses on the table, together with a plate of black bread and a bowl of caviar. "What is an Englishman doing, in south Russia?"

"I am a journalist," Johnnie explained. "A chess journalist. I'm here to cover the championships in Kharkov. But since I arrived early, I thought I would see something of the countryside."

"It is beautiful, here in the Donbas," Alexandra Brusilova agreed. "It is the most beautiful part of Russia."

"Oh, it is," Johnnie agreed.

Brusilov was frowning at him. "One would almost suppose you have been here before, Mr. Harding."

"Yes," Johnnie agreed. "I rode out here to see you, Mr. Brusilov. I wonder if we could possibly have a word in private, at some time?"

Brusilov's frown deepened. "To see me? You have heard of me?"

"Yes."

Alexandra Brusilova got up. "I must see what the cook has prepared for supper. Come along, Natasha Feodorovna. The men wish to talk."

"You'll excuse us, Mr. Harding," the girl said.

"For only a few minutes, I hope, mademoiselle," he said, standing to watch her leave the room. "How charmingly she moves, if you will pardon me, Monsieur."

"Well, it is natural, Mr. Harding," Brusilov explained. "She is a dancer."

"Indeed?"

"One day, we hope, a great dancer. She studies at the Tatiana Nej Academy, outside Moscow. Why, according to her reports, Madame Nej regards her very highly. She is her protégée, eh? You have heard of Madame Nej?"

Oh, my God, Johnnie thought. The one person in all Russia who must not know about John Harding was Aunt Tattie. Of

all the bad luck. "Yes," he said. "I have heard of Madame Nej.
I saw her dance once, on her tour of Europe a few years ago."

"Of course. It was a great success, I have been told. I have
never seen a performance. I have been to see Natasha practic-
ing..." He shrugged. "I am an old man. I do not understand
this modern dancing. Still, it is very popular. You wished to
speak with me, in private?"

Johnnie drew a long breath. "I am a messenger from Prince
Peter Borodin of Starogan."

Brusilov's head came up, and he stared at the young man
for a moment. Then he got up, walked across the room, and
shut the door. "Are you mad?"

"I was told you had heard of him," Johnnie said, wishing
his heart would stop pounding.

"Of course I have heard of Prince Peter Borodin of Starogan," Brusilov said. "He used to own much of this land. Starogan is but forty miles away. I can remember his grandfather.
And his father, before we went away to the wars."

"But more recently," Johnnie said, "Prince Peter has sent
you messages."

Brusilov sat down again. "Prince Peter is a proscribed man,
in Russia. How can he have sent me messages?"

"Because you have replied to them, Feodor Brusilov. I have
seen the replies. Thus he has sent me to you, to tell you that
the moment is at hand. Since you remember him, most of the
other people in the Donbas will remember him too, and be
eager to follow his leadership to overthrow the hated Bolsheviks. Will they not?"

Brusilov stroked his chin.

"He wishes to know—he has sent me to find out—what sort
of a force you could muster, when the time comes. He has
worked out a plan of campaign, a plan to seize Kharkov and
Poltava, but above all, Sevastopol and the Crimea. He has
international organizations standing by to ship in arms and
men, when the moment comes. But the intial step must be
taken here, by you and those who would support you. And it
must be soon."

Brusilov continued to gaze at him. "If Prince Peter is so
sure that the time is nigh," he said, "he should come here
himself."

"Now you know that is impossible," Johnnie said. "As you have just said, he is proscribed in Russia, and there is no hope that he could escape undetected. He has sent me in his stead."

"You?" Brusilov asked. "You are nothing but a boy."

"I am Ivan Sergeievich Roditchev," Johnnie said, and flushed.

Brusilov frowned. "Ivan Sergeievich . . ."

"Roditchev," Johnnie said again. "My father was Prince Roditchev. My mother is Princess Ilona Borodina."

Feodor Brusilov stared at him. "It could be," he said at last. "It could be. There is something familiar about your features."

"It is true," Johnnie said. "I have come back to act for my uncle, until you are ready to strike."

"Ready to strike," Brusilov muttered. He got up and moved about the room. "There is a lot to be done, Prince Ivan. A lot to be done." He glanced at the boy. "You are going to stay here?"

"Not this time. I am here as a chess correspondent, and I must cover the championship. Then I must return to England with your answer. But I will come again."

"But you will stay to supper with us," Brusilov said, at last seeming to realize just what had happened. "A prince, dining in my house. You will stay, Prince Roditchev?"

"Of course," Johnnie said. "It will be my pleasure. But Monsieur Brusilov, my identity must be a secret between you and me and no one else, not even your wife. You will give me your word on that."

"Not even my wife?" Brusilov looked heartbroken.

"I'm afraid not. And especially not your daughter. She is at my aunt's school."

"My God, yes," Brusilov said. "Tatiana Nej is your aunt. My God."

"And she is a confirmed Bolshevik, as you will know, Monsieur Brusilov."

"Yes, yes. She is married to Commissar Nej. My God, yes."

"So you will understand that if she were to find out that I am in Russia she would tell her husband, and our plans would be worthless."

"Yes, yes, of course. But to have a prince dining here, and

not be able to tell my wife—"

"She'll know, in the course of time. When I'm able to declare myself. When we have won."

The enormous auditorium was crowded, full of hushed conversation, of breathless anticipation. The sonorous tones of Comrade Bukharin, making the opening speech, rolled across the heads below the stage. The players were gathered in a group behind him, whispering to each other and smoking cigarettes, well-dressed and confident young men with only a smattering of veterans, like Levenfisch and Dus-Chotirmirski, who had been masters before the war. The rest were comparative newcomers, unknown in the West, products of the passionate Russian interest in this most interesting of indoor games.

Johnnie glanced down the list, idly. He had been so excited, so preoccupied by the real reason behind his mission, that he had done almost no homework regarding the chess players themselves. But of course his reports would have to be thorough and authoritative. Fortunately the official program had brief biographies of each of the contestants, and he could add to that a careful study of each of the games as it was played. Now was the moment to familiarize himself with their names. Botvinnik, from Leningrad, only seventeen years old; Iljin-Genevsky, a man who had covered himself in glory a few years ago by actually beating the former world champion, the immortal Capablanca, in tournament play; Nikolai Nej, aged only nineteen . . . Nikolai Nej?

Johnnie stared at the stage; he was surrounded by polite clapping as Comrade Bukharin came to the end of his peroration. The chess players, clapping as well, walked forward to take their places, each man sitting opposite his opponent, while Comrade Bukharin stood next to Grandmaster Levenfisch's board, as he was to make the first move. Nikolai Nej, born, according to the program, in the village of Starogan in the Basin of the Don. Which one was he? Certainly he had to be small and dark, but there were at least three who qualified under that heading.

But only one who was clearly still a teen-ager. A small young man, with straight black hair and an incipient mustache, horn-rimmed spectacles and an intense expression. Ivan Nej's son. It had to be. His own cousin, by marriage. His mother would have been the schoolmaster's daughter, Zoe Geller.

He frowned. Ivan had had two sons by Zoe Geller. And both of them had supposedly been killed in the massacre of the village by the White armies under Denikin and Uncle Peter. Now here was an interesting situation. Someone to be studied, at no risk to himself. There was no possibility of Nikolai Nej ever recognizing Ivan Roditchev; they had seen each other only once in their lives, when both were small children.

Comrade Bukharin had left the stage, and the tournament had begun. The room once again settled into a deep quiet, broken only by an occasional cough, the scraping of a match or a chair. Concentrate, Johnnie reminded himself, on the chess. He studied the huge demonstration boards behind the players. Levenfisch was playing a very sharp variation of the King's Gambit. What a way to begin a chess tournament, harking back to the days of Tchigorin, of the tsars and romantic notions. Hardly a totalitarian attitude. Nikolai Nej, on the other hand, was conducting a careful French Defense as black, playing with great concentration, and so far as Johnnie could remember, following the recommended line with commendable if unimaginative accuracy. That was definitely Ivan's son. Johnnie started to make notes, but was disturbed by a new sound, which seeped through the open windows of the hall, and filled the air with grinding motion.

Heads turned; even the chess players were disturbed. People moved to the windows to discover the cause of this sacrilege. Johnnie went with them, together with the other journalists, and peered out at the street, at the huge, cumbersome armored cars rolling through the center of the town, machine guns protruding from their ports, at the grim-faced men sitting in the little conning towers, and in particular at the open car leading the parade, carrying two passengers. One was a startlingly pretty young woman, hardly more than a girl, wearing the uniform of a Russian officer and staring straight ahead, her face expressionless. The other was a small, dark man, with a thick mustache and spectacles that seemed to fill the entire area between the brim of his peaked cap and his chin. He too stared straight ahead, apparently oblivious to the disturbance his force was causing, and indeed to the fact that he was passing through a city at all.

"Commissar Nej," someone whispered. "Commissar Nej."

Commissar Nej. Johnnie stared at him, at the tight lips and the thrusting chin. The bootblack become secret policeman. The most feared man in Russia, Uncle Peter had called him. On his way where? And to do what?

He glanced at Nikolai Nej, who had joined the other chess players at the upper window. The boy's face was flushed, and his teeth no less than his fists were tightly clenched. Certainly there was no affection, or even respect, in the way he looked at his father.

The column rolled down the dusty road, between the endless acres of waving wheat. Starogan had looked like this when he was a boy, Ivan Nej recalled. How long ago that seemed.

He glanced at the girl seated beside him. Was she at all interested? Was she interested in anything, except in being Ivan Nej's personal assistant? Would she wish to know that he had seen these fields before, often? Or would that be an essential weakening of the man she worshipped?

Because she certainly worshipped. In turning over stones, looking for one to cast into the sea, he had uncovered a nugget of the purest gold. If he could believe it. His innate pessimism, his inescapable sense of inferiority, told him that it could not be true. She had surrendered to him, had accepted his proposals, because she could see no alternative way of life; there was no doubting her extreme intelligence or the quickness of her wits. As the daughter of a man executed for supporting the Whites, she could have had no doubts about the uncertainty of her own future. That she should have turned out to be everything he had ever sought in a woman—in her obedience, her compliance, the way she responded to him—was surely just his good fortune. And since he had been unfortunate with women all of his life, why should he not deserve a little fortune now?

Except that the willingness, the eagerness, with which she had fitted into his world, was unreal, unbelievable. She was seventeen years old. He knew this because he had seen her birth certificate. She had spent the major part of her life up to now in an orphanage under the strict control of Comrade Tereshkova. Everything in life that mattered had to be there for her to learn. Yet she had shown neither fear nor disgust, from the very first day. Presumably she was possessed of utterly frigid emotions. But they were emotions she was prepared to surrender, as she surrendered her body, to her master whenever he chose.

Thus after that first day he had never lifted his hand to her, had done nothing more than enjoy her. He had fallen in love with a seventeen-year-old psycopath, because nothing else could explain her. Was that why he was frightened of her? Because he was. He could admit this to himself. He was more afraid of Anna Ragosina than he had ever been of Tatiana Borodina.

Or was it just his fate to be afraid of women, throughout his life?

It was something she could never be allowed to suspect. And today would really be the acid test. Today would be something big. He had no doubts about that. Brusilov was not going to surrender. Today would lack the privacy of a cell beneath the street, the freedom to stop when one chose. Today, once started, would have to be finished. It was a task to which he had looked forward for several years. What did she think of it all?

Her face remained as composed as ever; her hands rested lightly on her uniform skirt. She was aware that he was looking at her and turned her head. She did not smile—she seldom so indulged herself—but the expression in her eyes were inquiring.

"We shall soon be there," he said. "This land is all Brusilov's. Is it not a crime, that one man should control so much?"

"Of course, comrade commissar."

Would she ever call him Ivan? And when she did, what would happen then?

"Yet he has done well," Ivan mused. "When last I was here, in the autumn of 1921, this was empty desert. There had been a drought, and the land was ruined. Now, look at it. Part of our task must be to harness such expertise with socialist principles."

"But the socialist principles come first, comrade commissar," she said softly.

"Oh, indeed," he agreed. She had the remarkable ability to make him feel guilty.

The time for thinking was over. The column had topped a gentle rise, and in front of them there was the river, and the cluster of farm buildings. Many more buildings than he remembered from his previous visit.

A motorcycle roared, and an orderly pulled in beside his car.

"The column will remain here," Ivan ordered. "I will go down and see Comrade Brusilov."

"Yes, comrade commissar." The orderly saluted.

Captain Ashcherin, in the front seat beside the driver, turned his head. "Is that necessary, comrade commissar?"

"Why? You think he will fight this time, comrade colonel? I doubt that. I really doubt that. Comrade Brusilov is not a fighter. Drive on."

The car drove down the slope towards the gates, which were closed, and guarded by three men. The car rolled to a stop, and Ivan felt the heat beating on his neck and shoulders. The eight years might never have passed. And this time, despite his words to Ashcherin, he knew they would fight. But by their principles, not his.

He stood up. "Where is Comrade Brusilov?"

"I am here, comrade commissar." Brusilov stood beside the gate, where other men were gathered. And women. And guns. Even, he saw with a quickening pulse, several machine guns. They had accumulated an arsenal, behind these walls. Where had they obtained such weapons?

Brusilov stepped into the gateway. "My taxes are up to date, comrade commissar. What brings you here?"

"The day for taxes is over, Comrade Brusilov," Ivan said. "Now it is the decision of the Supreme Soviet that a complete socialization of our farming system must be carried out. It is the initial step in Comrade Stalin's five-year plan. Your farm will be collectivized with the others in this district to form one kholkoz. It is for the good of the state."

"I see," said Comrade Brusilov. "Is this not contrary to the laws of Comrade Lenin?"

Ivan smiled at him. "Comrade Lenin is dead, Comrade Brusilov. Have you not heard that?"

"I would ask for an hour, comrade commissar," Brusilov said.

"An hour? Would you seek to disobey a command of the Supreme Soviet?"

"By no means, comrade commissar. But my fellow kulaks have come here at the news of your approach. They do me the honor of considering me their leader. I cannot answer for them all without discussing the situation."

"Discussing the situation?" Ivan asked again. "Answering for them all? What is there to answer for, Comrade Brusilov? What is there to discuss? The Supreme Soviet has made a law, a law of the Motherland. It must be obeyed, and immediately. You will move yourself and your family from that house. I will appropriate it as my headquarters, for the time being, while the kholkoz is being established. Your neighbors will also move out of their houses, so that my men can be quartered."

"And where will we live?" Brusilov asked, his voice soft.

Ivan shrugged. "It is summer. But you will get to work, to build the kholkoz. You will build new houses for yourselves, comrades. That is not a difficult task." He smiled. "They need not be as large as that one. There is no necessity for a large house. But I will give you your hour to discuss, to confer. One hour, Comrade Brusilov. One hour."

He tapped the driver on the shoulder, and the car turned, reversed into the pasture which bordered the road, and then drove back up to where the column waited, on the brow of the shallow hill.

"Tell your men to attack, Colonel Ashcherin," he said. "They may move on a broad front, and may destroy the farm and the buildings."

"But comrade commissar, you gave them an hour."

"Yes, and they might well have surrendered without fighting. They are a spineless lot. It is necessary to make an example, though, comrade colonel. Comrade Brusilov will make a good example. I have authority from Comrade Stalin."

Ashcherin glanced at the girl, still sitting impassively beside her master, then he stepped from the car and walked over to the commander of the armored-car regiment.

"We can see best from over there," Ivan told the driver.

His heart was pounding pleasantly. He had never commanded an army into action before. In 1915 he had been a private in the midst of several million other privates, an utter nonentity, and when those millions had been scattered and destroyed by the Germans, he had been even more of a nonentity, a prisoner of war. In the civil war the command had been Michael's. He himself had always been behind the lines when the armies had clashed, waiting to interrogate prisoners. Besides, in the civil war, he had been deathly afraid. It had been a brutal conflict. But here . . . this was nothing more than a collection of peasants. That made victory all the more certain. He could enjoy the spectacle and the excitement without any fears for the outcome, or for his personal safety.

The armored cars started to move, spreading out along the brow of the hill, rolling down over the pasture, bumping and heaving, leaving plumes of dust behind them. As yet there was no shooting, but that there would be shooting could not be doubted by the people behind the walls. A great hubbub of dismayed excitement rose from down there, and the yard seemed to seethe. Through his binoculars he watched people running to and fro, humping machine guns, handing out rifles, but mostly just running. It looked like a farmyard suddenly disturbed by the presence of a fox.

The guns opened fire, a deadly chatter that spread across the plain. Pieces of masonry, chips of wood, flew into the afternoon air. Pieces of human bodies, too. Ivan watched a man spin round and crash to the ground, another throw up his arms and stagger back from the earthen wall and strike the ground heavily, his rifle thrown away. He glanced at the girl. Her nostrils dilated, but he could not see her eyes, since she too was watching through binoculars.

Now shots were being fired in retaliation, but these did no more than strike the steel plating of the armored cars and ricochet into the distance. And already the cars were at the walls, blasting away pointblank with their heavy machine guns. Now there were no men on the walls, only heaps of bodies scattered about the yard. And now too the buildings were on fire, ripped open by the searing bullets, starting to plume smoke into the summer air. Men were disembarking from the cars, rifles at the ready to complete the liquidation of the resistance.

"I think we can go down there now," Ivan said.

The car eased forward, down the slope. The firing of the machine guns had ceased, and there was only an occasional sharp report from a rifle. As they approached they could smell the heat and the scent of scorching wood, the sweat and the fear, the stench of death. The car stopped in the gateway, and Ivan got out, Anna Ragosina at his heels. Colonel Ashcherin saluted. "There are no casualties to report, comrade commissar." he said.

"Good," Ivan said. "Good. And among the kulaks?"

"Fifteen dead, and several wounded. There are twenty-seven prisoners."

Ivan walked towards the huddled group. Now the heat from the burning buildings was intense. He gazed at the family house. It had been a splendid house. Now the roof was falling in and through the collapsed door he could see a burning icon.

"Murderer!" Alexandra Brusilova ran forward, waving her fists. "Assassin!"

A soldier caught her arm and swung her round so violently she fell to her knees, panting, gray hair scattered, skirt torn, great tears rolling down her cheeks.

Ivan stood above her. "Where is your husband?"

"Comrade Brusilov is dead, comrade commissar," Ashcherin said. "He fell at the gate."

"Assassin," Alexandra Brusilova moaned again.

"And the daughter?" Ivan asked. "There was a daughter." A child who might well have become a beautiful woman, he remembered. There was a pleasant prospect.

The woman's face closed.

"Your daughter, woman," Ivan said. He drove his fingers into the gray hair, held her scalp tight, shook her head to and fro. Alexandra Brusilova gasped, and her false teeth flew out. "Pick them up," Ivan said. "And tell me about your daughter."

The woman scrabbled for her teeth, crammed them back into her mouth. "You'll never get her," she said. "You'll never get her."

"I will," Ivan said. "And if you do not tell me where she is, if you make me look for her, I will shoot you. I will shoot you and all these people. The women too. I will shoot them all."

Alexandra Brusilova gasped, and panted; her breast heaved. "You do not want her," she said. "She is a friend of yours, Comrade Commissar."

"Of mine?" Ivan smiled. "Yes. I would like her to be a friend of mine."

"Well, she is," Alexandra Brusilova said. "She is with your wife, at the academy. She dances for Comrade Nej."

"She . . ." Ivan stared at her. "Don't lie to me."

"It's true," Alexandra Brusilova shrieked. "She is at the academy. The summer term began only yesterday. She went up to Moscow the day before. It is true."

"Damnation." Ivan turned away.

"Did you wish this girl, comrade commissar?" Anna Ragosina's voice was hardly more than a whisper.

He glanced at her. "I wished to stamp out the entire family, yes."

"Well, then, can we not take her out of Comrade Nej's academy?"

"Take her out of the academy? You do not know my wife, Anna. Take her out of the academy? Moscow would tremble. She is commissar for culture. Anyone she has chosen is inviolable."

"Of course, comrade commissar," the girl agreed. Was her lip threatening to curl?

Ivan turned away from her angrily. "Shoot them," he told Ashcherin. "All of them. Every last one of them. I do not wish there to be any survivors. Shoot them all." He stamped towards the car.

Rumor had spread, and all of Kharkov had turned out to watch the returning column. The troops had been gone a week. Seven days, seven farms belonging to the wealthier kulaks, destroyed or appropriated. By order of the state.

Who in this city could feel sympathy with a kulak? But did the word apply also to those townspeople, those entrepreneurs who had taken advantage of the New Economic Policy to grow rich? Where did they stand now that Commissar Nej's blood-stained column was returning to base?

And even if they hated the kulaks, even if they were the best Communists in the world, they could hate Ivan Nej and his methods. The chess tournament was by now well advanced, with several positions reaching the critical stage, but all boards were abandoned, by players as well as spectators, to watch the armored cars roll into town behind their commander and his aides. The end of a dream, Johnnie thought. For us, no less than the Brusilovs. Theirs had been the first farm to be destroyed. But the girl—would she already have left? If so, would she now be hunted down, and killed, as the daughter of a kulak? She might as well have been a leper.

He made his way through the throng and stood by the window beside Nikolai Nej. Over the past week he had made the boy's acquaintance, had shown great interest in his technique and his opening repertoire—the easy way to a chess player's heart.

"They tell me that is the famous Ivan Nej," he said. "The same name as yours."

Nikolai glanced at him. "He is my father."

"Your father, a deputy commissar?" Johnnie asked. "You must be very proud of him."

Nikolai Nej glanced at him. "Proud?" he asked. "Of that?"

"But . . . he is your father."

"He deserted my mother and my brother, left them to die." Nikolai said. "Me too. He did not care about us. He took the yellow-haired Borodin girl and made her his wife, without caring about us. And when he heard that my mother was still alive, he divorced her, just like that. That is Comrade Commissar Nej, my friend."

"Oh," Johnnie said. "I hadn't realized. I can see that you might not be too fond of him, at that."

"One day," Nikolai Nej said, "he will be dead, and I will be alive. It is as simple as that. Otherwise, what would be the point in living?"

Chapter 11

ILONA HAYMAN SAT AT HER DESK AND CHEWED THE STEM OF her pen. Her office at home was on the first floor, and looked out over the beach at Long Island Sound, one of her favorite views—because it led to the Atlantic.

Did she have any real desire to cross the ocean again? She doubted that. But she could think, if only...

Letters from Tattie always upset her. Tattie possessed too great a gift of happiness, could make anyone else, even her own sister, wonder what on earth *she* was doing with her life. There was no arrogance in what Tattie wrote and said and did, no intentional arrogance, anyway; Ilona was sure of that. She was just Tattie, and the whole world might have been created especially for her delectation. This could not help but be irritating to those less fortunate than herself. It was also a little frightening to those who might believe that life always evened itself out, over a period of time. If Tattie was so outrageously happy, so outrageously successful now, what would happen when that happiness and that success came to a sudden halt?

But in fact, for all her mixed feelings, Ilona thoroughly enjoyed hearing from her, and even more, writing to her. Tattie, at once a sister and a member of an alien society, residing at a distance of some seven thousand miles, made the perfect confidante. To Tattie she could pour out her heart.

"One can't help feeling," she wrote, "that the administration doesn't really understand what has hit it, and doesn't really have any idea what is going to happen or what can be done to prevent it. Americans have for so long been dedicated to the concept of utter freedom, of the right of every man either to go broke the way he wishes or to become a millionaire, that the idea that almost the entire nation has gone broke is just too apocalyptic to be believed. Of course there have been depressions and recessions and what have you before, so the natural inclination was to sit back and say well, in a couple of months we'll have seen the end of this one. But it's lasted so long this time, and just seems to get worse and worse and worse.

"And now it seems to be spreading to Europe as well. George tells me that there are politics involved over there. He seems sure that if the French had been prepared to help, that Austrian bank need never have crashed. But the French are afraid of making Germany too strong again, and they seem to be quarreling over the possibility of a unification of Austria and Germany, an *Anchluss*, they call it. It seems incredibly childish to spend the rest of eternity looking over our shoulders while millions are close to starving. I can only hope it doesn't reach Russia. You've had troubles enough.

"There's no need to worry about us. We lost a few thousand dollars, but George has never been a very keen player of the market, and people do seem to need to buy newspapers, if only to find out how bad the news is. We've had to cut back in some directions of course, mainly because we feel it's a little immoral to have big cocktail parties when so many men are on the breadline. And that world cruise we were going to go on has yet again been canceled for the time being. But this is because George doesn't really want to be away from New York for any length of time until there is some sort of a recovery. Since he spent the last ten years telling both Coolidge and Hoover that this was going to happen, he's become a financial pundit as well as a Russian pundit, but they still won't take any of his advice on how to put the nation back on its feet.

They are starting to call him a socialist, and as he says, it'll take a Democratic victory this year to shake them out of their complacency.

"But I suppose that's enough politics. I only wish I could send some good news on the domestic front. After three years, we've more or less resigned ourselves to the fact that Johnnie seems quite uninterested in coming home. He's got himself a job as chess correspondent for some newspaper I hadn't ever heard of before he started working for it, and has expenses-paid trips all over Europe. Who knows? He might even turn up inside Russia one day. I suppose the Soviets do allow chess.

"Anyway, he seems perfectly happy, but I can't pretend not to miss him, and not to worry about him too, especially if the Depression *is* going to spread to Europe. On the other hand, maybe that'll drive him home; his passage is waiting for him at George's London bankers whenever he wants to pick it up.

"George junior is the youngest editor ever of his college paper. He's very good, George tells me, and we are all eager to see him start on the *American People*. He's moving with a rather wild set, though—Greenwich Village people. Greenwich Village, in case you don't know, is a part of the town where people calling themselves artists and writers and what have you gather, doing as little as possible. How some of them live I have no idea. He's taken up with a girl called Elizabeth Dodge, who paints. Believe me, Tattie, my dear, I can only say how sorry I am that you have all of this still in front of you. If it weren't for Felicity I'd go mad. But I wish we could find something for her to do.

"I'm afraid I haven't heard from Peter since he left New York three years ago, or about him since he and Judith quarreled. I don't even know what they quarreled about, although as we both know Peter is the easiest man in all the world to quarrel with. I do worry about Ruth, who must also be a teen-ager by now. But I don't see that there's much I can do about it. Judith seems happy; she writes me occasionally from Berlin. She lives with her brother now, and they are both working for some Zionist organization, making arrangements for Jews who wish to emigrate to Palestine. I suppose they're doing the right thing, but there seems to be a lot of trouble there too.

"You'll be thinking me the world's greatest pessimist. Tattie, my love, I am so happy for you, that Clive has got that contract at last. Who would have imagined it could take so long? But do, do be careful. You know that Ivan will be informed if Clive comes to call..."

Ilona put down her pen and hurried from the room at the sound of a car. She discovered her heart was pounding. George junior was bringing Elizabeth Dodge to meet them, and the girl was apparently planning to present them with a painting. If only she could *like* this girl. If only...

It was George.

"Well," he said. "I felt I should be present for the great unveiling."

He kissed her mouth. It was a tender, loving kiss, but not a passionate one. She was as sure as any woman could be that he had had no other mistress since Judith. George was not a promiscuous man; his whole nature was to be faithful, and Judith had simply been a phenomenon that had dominated his life for too long to be resisted. They had discussed it, and she believed him, and now she was certain that it was over and done with. But that did not mean that their marriage had recovered. To the casual observer it might appear so. They entertained together and they holidayed together and they laughed together, and they slept together, with passion. But this was because, even in middle age, he remained an active, attractive man just as she remained a beautiful woman.

But they no longer *loved*, as they once had, ignoring family and tsar and even God in their tumbling mutual desire. To regain that careless rapture, Ilona would have given several years of her life, but she had no idea how to set about recapturing it. She was a Russian princess born and bred, and regarded as such even here in America. People, men, even her own husband, came to her. She did not go to them.

Worst of all was the feeling that they were both running out of time, that there was nothing she could do about it now, even if she knew how. That this quiet, unexciting relationship was the inevitable result of the quarter-century they had shared their love.

And the problems of their children. He released her. "They're right behind me."

"Oh." Hurriedly she entered the drawing room, made sure everything was just so—as if Harrison would ever let her down. She saw George watching her with a smile even as the butler hurried up the hall to open the front door. She sat down and smoothly crossed her ankles. "First impressions are most important."

"Entirely." He crossed the room to stand beside her. "But do remember that this girl is far more afraid of you than you can ever be of her."

She watched Harrison open the door, and saw her son, smiling proudly, and the girl—about twenty, she estimated—small and dark and animated with prettily petite features and straight black hair worn in a short pageboy that did not quite conceal her ears. Ilona supposed she was attractive, but anything less like a Borodin woman could not be imagined. The reflection that there was no earthly reason why George junior *should* choose someone who looked like his mother or his sister only made her suddenly angry.

"Elizabeth Dodge," George junior was saying proudly. "Beth, my mother and father."

The girl shook hands. "I've heard so much about you, Mrs. Hayman."

George kissed her cheek, to Ilona's disgust. "We've heard a lot about you, too, Beth. Are you really an artist?"

"A very good one," George junior said. "In fact, she's brought you one of her paintings."

Ilona realized for the first time that he was carrying a large, flat, brown-paper parcel.

"I hope you like it," Beth said. "It's of George. People are my passion. I mean, people are what I paint."

"A portrait of George?" George said. "Why, that sounds great. Especially done by you. Don't you agree, Ilona?"

"Yes," Ilona lied.

"Well, may we have a look at it?" George asked.

Elizabeth Dodge flushed. "It's a bit—well, avant garde. But George said he thought you'd like it."

George junior was busily unwrapping the picture. "Of course they will," he said, and held it up. "*Voilà.*"

Ilona stared at the nude in utter disbelief. There could be no doubt that it was George junior. In fact, the artist had managed to catch the flavor of his personality as well as every detail of his features, while, since he was half-turned away and looking across his shoulder, there was nothing obscene about the seated figure. But the *idea*.

"Good Lord," George said, and decided he couldn't stop there. "I had no idea you were so muscular, George."

George junior was watching his mother, as was Elizabeth. "I thought you might like to hang it in the sitting room off your bedroom," he said.

Ilona glanced at her husband and realized he was struggling not to laugh. She was suddenly furious.

"I have no intention of hanging a picture like that anywhere in this house," she said. "And I'd be obliged if you'd remove it immediately."

That night she added a postscript to her letter to Tattie. "I'm afraid I'm not the most popular person in the world, at the moment," she concluded. "But I really am quite disgusted. This girl apparently does things like that all the time. If she marries George junior it's going to be over my dead body."

Tatiana Nej sat at her desk and looked through an open window at the slopes of the recently named Lenin Hills, stretching to the north of Moscow. It was her favorite view, even in the winter, when the snow-covered slopes were used for skiing, a sport she had never tried. But in the summer it was a delight of green grass and sprouting yellow flowers, and to sit here and look at it, with a background of tinkling pianos and slithering feet seeping through the huge academy, was the pleasantest part of the day. Well, it wouldn't be the pleasantest part of this day, she hoped. But usually.

Carefully she folded her sister's letter and replaced it in its envelope. Poor old Ilona. She was really feeling her age. But then, Ilona had always been inclined to pessimism. She had what could be described as a typically gloomy Russian mentality. Clive had explained it to her in one of his letters. It came, he said, from being surrounded by such an immense amount of land, and being subject to such extremes of climate and temperature. She supposed Clive was right, as he was right about most things, although she did not quite see how it applied to Ilona, who had spent her adolescence in Port Arthur, with the sea a stone's throw from her bedroom window.

The real trouble with Ilona was that she just didn't know when she was well off. She never had. Married to George Hayman, living in a country where even if they seemed to have temporarily run out of money no one was actually starving to death, grumbling because she couldn't go on a cruise around the world . . . she should have to understand some of the real tragedies in life. Tattie brooded at the slopes in front of her. Even up here they were beginning to turn brown. What the south—the Donbas and the Crimea and old Starogan—were like didn't bear consideration. It hadn't rained for months and months and months, and according to Michael they were in a 1921 situation all over again, with millions soon to die.

Michael felt very bitter about it. He felt that if the kulaks had been left alone, the country would have been able to ride out another serious drought. She even thought Michael opposed the liquidation of the kulaks on plain humanitarian grounds, even though Joseph Vissarionovich had claimed that it had all been their own faults, that they had opposed collectivization, even with arms, and that in fact, according to Ivan, they had been plotting a counterrevolution. But then, Ivan always had stories like those ready to justify any of his atrocities. But Stalin and Ivan had certainly got themselves into trouble now, because Michael's point of view was shared by most of the Politburo, admittedly with hindsight; people like Bukharin and Zinoviev were saying that liquidating the kulaks had been a monumental blunder, and when Stalin pointed out that he couldn't have been expected to know there was going to be another drought, they had merely said that there had been no need to take the risk so early. Someday soon there was going to be a tremendous fight in the Politburo. And of course the situation wasn't helped by Stalin's preoccupation with Nadezhda Alliluyeva's illness. Ilona should try getting mixed up with that bunch of bickering nincompoops.

But the fact was that she also felt that the liquidation of the kulaks had been a ghastly mistake. Of course it was awful to cause so many people to die. And besides, some of her best girls had come from kulak families. She smiled grimly. At least she had been able to prevent Ivan from getting his hands on *them*. They had actually turned up here, Ivan and that zombielike creature who was always at his elbow—wishing to arrest Natasha Brusilova, because, he said, he had evidence that her father had been plotting against the state. When she had ordered the pair of them from her premises, the louse had gone to Stalin. And got nowhere. Stalin liked her, just as Vladimir Ilich had liked her. She was their favorite woman.

But it was very upsetting for the girls. Natasha Brusilova was the most serious case, because she was the most talented. She was going to be a great dancer, Tattie had no doubt at all. Perhaps as great as she herself had ever been, or even poor dear Isadora. And great dancers had to concentrate on their art, not brood on their mothers and fathers being shot. She had had to be quite strict with Natasha Brusilova, remind her that her own mother and father had both died violently, as well as her uncle and aunt and her cousins, and that she was still able to smile, and to dance, and to find life worth living.

After that, Natasha had pulled herself together, and now she danced better than ever. But she never smiled. And a dancer had to smile. It was an essential part of her equipment, would make a plain face pretty and a pretty face beautiful. Natasha was a long way from being ready for a public appearance yet, except in the corps.

A car engine growled in the courtyard, and in the same instant Tattie was on her feet, pushing back her chair and only then remembering to stand still, to wait for her heart to stop pounding. It was six years since that unforgettable night. And besides, it had been only one night. He had written her at least once a month throughout those six years, but she could not be sure he still felt the way he had then, or even if he would be the same man, after six years.

That was silly. She was thirty-eight now, but she was still exactly as she had been. She tossed her golden mane, looked at herself in the mirror on the wall opposite. Exactly as she had been. So what did she have to be nervous about? She was Tatiana Nej.

If only he hadn't changed either.

She opened the door, walked along the hallway, deliberately slowly, listening to the music arising on every side of her, smiling and nodding as she came across half a dozen girls hurrying from one practice room to the next, pausing at the top of the stairs to the lower hall, watching the door opening, watching him come in. He didn't look up, but spoke to the reception clerk, who frowned at him. As well she might. It wasn't possible just to walk into the academy and ask for the director. The girl shook her head severely, and turned away, looking up the stairs as she did so, her jaw dropping as she saw her employer standing there.

Clive followed the direction of her gaze, and then turned to face the stairs, moving forward as he did so. Tattie started down, and the girl left her desk and hurried forward, as if she would interpose herself.

"Comrade Nej, this person, this Englishman . . ."

"Is an old friend, Valentina Vasilievna," Tattie said.

They stopped at the foot of the stairs, looking at each other.

"*My* old friend Nikoyan is outside," Clive said. "He's been following me from the station."

"And it's such a hot day," Tattie said. She blew him a kiss, stepped round him, and went to the door, where she called out from the top of the steps: "Comrade Nikoyan, do come in. Comrade Valentina will give you some vodka."

There was a moment's hesitation, then the door of the black car swung open and Nikoyan got out. "This is most irregular, comrade commissar," he protested.

"Would you sit there and die of thirst, in this heat?" she asked. "Come in, man. Come in. You know Mr. Bullen? Of course you do, or you wouldn't be here. Valentina Vasilievna, you'll give Comrade Nikoyan a glass of vodka. And comrade, just so you won't be confused, I shall tell you what we are going to do. Mr. Bullen and I are going upstairs to have a little talk, then we are going to a restaurant to have some lunch, and then we are going back to my apartment and we are going to spend the rest of the afternoon and this evening and all tonight in bed, making love. We won't be going anywhere again until tomorrow morning, so if you just want to go home and write that up in a report you can be sure it will be accurate." She linked her arm through Clive's. "We are going to do all those things, aren't we, my darling Englishman?"

"Every single one of them," he promised, and kissed her on the mouth. Comrade Nikoyan sat down, and Valentina Vasilievna hastily looked the other way.

And Tattie sighed, with relief. He hadn't changed, either.

Joseph Stalin sat at his desk and surveyed the four men seated in front of him. They were his most trusted associates in the business of governing Russia to his own satisfaction. Strangely, he even included Michael Nej in that category, although he and Michael saw eye to eye on very few matters. But Michael was utterly faithful to Russia, and he had enough acumen to understand that only Stalin could possibly hold this still experimental society together. As for the others, Molotov and Beria and Ivan Nej, they were his people through and through.

If only he could concentrate. Nadezhda was dying. None of the platitudes offered by the doctors could change that fact. It was so unfair, he thought. His first marriage had been a disaster. His wife had understood nothing of his beliefs, had refused to attempt to understand his activities. When he had been sentenced to exile in Siberia for that bank robbery, she had refused to accompany him, had been happy to see him go, he thought. Abandoning her had been one of the most sensible things he had ever done. Nadezhda, on the other hand, had been everything he had ever wanted, ever dreamed of. She had been his Krupskaya, and even better than Krupskaya, bécause she had given him children. And Krupskaya had outlived Lenin, was still alive. He had always supposed Nadezhda would do the same, for him. But to lose her at such a moment of crisis, when Russia seemed to be back where it had been ten years before, when there was mounting criticism of his leadership, when people were starting to remember Trotsky, now lecturing in Copenhagen . . . that was more than a man could be expected to bear.

Molotov cleared his throat. Everyone present was used to their leader's lapses into deep preoccupation, but time was passing.

"Yes," Stalin said. "The situation is serious. Michael Nikolaievich?"

"We need help," Michael said. "If you would let me—"

"Appeal to the Americans?" Molotov sneered.

"They have no money, in any event," Beria pointed out.

"But they have a great deal of grain, which their own people cannot buy," Michael said.

"And we can?" Ivan asked.

"It should be possible to do some sort of a deal."

"Oh, indeed," Molotov said. "Some sort of a deal involving our acceptance of the tsarist debts."

"That would be better than having several million Russians starve to death," Michael said. "If I could be allowed to negotiate—"

"With George Hayman, I suppose," Ivan said.

"He is our best chance, yes," Michael said. "He knows me, and he knows our problems here. He would be the best man to express them to the American government. And I trust him."

"He is a capitalist swine," Beria said.

"He is a man who takes a wide view," Michael insisted. "And what is the alternative? Do you not remember that it was sheer hunger that brought down the tsarist government? No one would have listened to a word we had to say if their bellies had been full, and there had been no war. They still regard us as better than Prince Roditchev and his bullies—" He paused to give a scornful glance at the OGPU men, Beria and Ivan Nej. "—but they will not continue to do so if they are left to starve. We have a crisis, comrades, and ideological claptrap about dealing with capitalists is not going to solve it."

"I agree," Stalin said, to the surprise of them all. "I think that Michael Nikolaievich is entirely right. We *do* have a crisis, and we must take immediate steps, and if necessary radical steps, to improve it. I think Michael Nikolaievich should be allowed to open negotiations with the Americans, both for grain supplies and for a recognition of our regime. If it is necessary to acknowledge certain debts, certain international obligations, then we shall have to do it."

They stared at him.

"I also think," Stalin went on, "that we should apply for membership in the League of Nations."

"I have been advocating that for years," Michael said.

"And now I agree with you. So you will implement that decision immediately, Michael Nikolaievich," Stalin said. "Contact your friend Hayman." The mustache moved in the semblance of a smile. "Even contact his beautiful wife, if you choose. But do it quickly, and with the utmost secrecy. That is most important. Not a word of what you are doing must reach the press, *any* press, until you are successful. I make that your charge, Michael Nikolaievich. That will be all, comrades. You will stay, Ivan Nikolaievich."

The other three, already starting to rise from their chairs, paused in surprise, then continued on their way. Ivan, also rising from his chair, subsided back into it, and waited for the door to close.

"You do not agree with me, Ivan Nikolaievich," Stalin said softly.

"I am sure you know best, Joseph Vissarionovich," Ivan said. "But I cannot see that American help is going to come soon enough to assist us, assuming it comes at all."

"You are absolutely right," Stalin said.

Ivan stared at him. "Well, then . . ."

"But still, it is the correct thing tó do," Stalin said. "Our country is in trouble, through no fault of its own. Since we are responsible statesmen, we must take steps to remedy it, even if some of those steps are distasteful to us. Soviet Russia must be seen to be a responsible member of the international community, Ivan Nikolaievich, if we are to prosper. When we have prospered—why, that will be a different matter. Do you understand me?"

"Of course I do, Joseph Vissarionovich. But in the short term—"

"I have a solution for that, also, Ivan Nikolaievich. A solution that will at once distract our people's minds from their empty bellies, and incur international sympathy for us."

He paused, and Ivan waited, used to his chief's pregnant silences.

"We must discover a plot against the regime," Stalin said finally. "*You* must discover such a plot."

"I have already—"

"That was a Russian plot, Ivan Nikolaievich. A kulak plot. That has earned us no sympathy. That whole affair has earned us no sympathy. No, no. I want an international plot, financed and created by international capitalism, designed to bring down the Soviet regime for its own vicious ends. Tell me, was there not an explosion last week at one of the hydroelectric plants the British are building for us?"

"An accident," Ivan said.

"Was it an accident, Ivan Nikolaievich? I am sure you know better than that. I am sure that, like me, you understand, and are capable of proving, that it was but the first episode in a long planned series of terrorist acts against the Soviet Union." He held up a finger to keep Ivan from speaking. "I do not wish to know how, or why, or by whom, Ivan Nikolaievich. I wish only to know that it has been done. It is facts we need. People on trial. The world must understand how we are patiently trying to build a country, and a socialist regime, despite being constantly beset by these capitalist thugs. That is what I wish, Ivan Nikolaievich. That is what I want from you."

Michael Nej threw open the door of his apartment with unusual vigor, causing both his wife and daughter to look up in surprise. At six Nona Mikhailovna was very like her mother, with the high cheekbones and the clipped features of the Tartar, as well as the crisp black hair. Now, seeing her father's smile, she abandoned her doll and ran forward, to be swept from the floor and hugged.

Catherine watched them with deep black eyes. She always looked just a little suspicious, even of him, Michael thought. Or perhaps of him most of all. It was years since her traumatic experience at the hands of the secret police, and he did not think she had ever truly recovered, perhaps because she had never been able to understand why it had happened. That wasn't surprising; he did not really understand that business himself. He was only sure that it had been part of some devious scheme of Ivan's, but it was difficult to decide what had been accomplished if anything.

But, like her daughter, she could be reassured by her husband's smile—he didn't smile very often. She put down her darning and stood up. "There is good news?"

"Very good news." He set Nona back on the floor to put his arm round Catherine's shoulders. "At last we are to move forward. Russia, I mean. I have been given the go-ahead to negotiate with the Americans, and for a seat in the League of Nations. Isn't that splendid news?"

"Splendid," she agreed, although he doubted she truly understood why.

"So I will be leaving Russia for a while," he said. "I have not left Russia since 1917."

She watched him anxiously. She had never left Russia at all. He shook his head. "I must go alone. It is a very secret matter. Besides, I am to meet with George Hayman."

Little lines gathered between her eyes, as he had supposed they might. He had never asked her what had happened between her and Hayman during the week she had acted as his interpreter-guide in 1922, but he had no doubt that something had happened; that was why she was here, the mother of his daughter, as Hayman's other woman was the mother of his son. Their lives, and the lives of their women, had been inextricably intermingled ever since the American had so strangely ridden into his life, that Manchurian spring day in 1904.

Was the fact that she had been George Hayman's woman—*might* have been George's woman, however briefly—the *only* reason he had married her? Certainly she had made him a good wife and housekeeper. She had settled into domesticity with all the ease, and indeed the enthusiasm, of her Tartar background. But for a man who had held both Ilona Borodina and Judith Stein in his arms, she had never been anything more than comfortable in bed.

Had she been no more than comfortable for George, as well? Or did George possess a certain quality that could get more out of a woman, and which *he* lacked? Or was it simply that he had never tried hard enough with Catherine, had never really regarded her as a lover, only as a conquest seized from George? Had never even perhaps properly assessed her as a woman? And she *was* an attractive woman. Her breasts were heavy without sagging, her legs, if not as long as he might have liked, were well shaped, her entire body was hard-muscled and firm-textured. She had the sweet scent of complete health, and she could *feel*. But for him?

"Does that interest you?" he asked.

"Mr. Hayman? I hardly remember what he looks like. I cannot understand why he is so important. He is not in the government."

"In America men who own newspapers *are* more important than men in government. Besides, he is a friend of Hoover's. And of mine, I suppose. And of yours?"

Catherine shrugged. "I do not think he liked me very much."

A lie? Would he ever know the truth? But suddenly he wanted her, as he had not wanted for too many years. It must be because he was happy, because Joseph Vissarionovich was at last revealing qualities of leadership rather than merely seeking personal aggrandizement. He found himself propelling her towards the bedroom, his arm still around her shoulder. She realized this too, and turned to look at Nona in alarm.

"Play with your doll, Nona Mikhailovna." Michael said. "Mother and I have matters to discuss."

The bedroom door closed behind him, and he released her. She turned to face him, her cheeks flushed, her fingers playing with the top button of her blouse. Gently he moved her hands and unbuttoned the blouse; she wore no brassiere, and he stooped to kiss her. She remained absolutely still, utterly surprised.

Michael straightened. "Do you love me, Catherine Pavlovna?"

She stared at him. He had never asked her that before.

He brought her against him. "Well, then, would you *like* to love me, Catherine Pavlovna?"

Her hair brushed his chin as she tilted her head back to look at him. "I should like to love you very much, Michael Nikolaievich, if you would let me."

It occurred to Michael Nej that no woman had ever said that to him before, either.

Ivan Nej placed Nikoyan's report on his desk, leaned back, and stared across the room at the girl. Anna Ragosina could feel his gaze, and raised her head, faint color creeping across her throat and up into her cheeks. Ivan enjoyed seeing it, because that quick flush happened every time he made love to her, and he had been making love to her now for nearly six years. He never tired of it, because he had come to realize, during those years, that she hated every moment of it. Thus, by extension, he supposed she must hate him in equal proportion. But she submitted, and even responded, because that was what he wished her to do, because she could see no other way of survival and advancement in this world in which she had found herself, and because she was determined to survive, and if possible prosper.

He could understand reasoning like that. The knowledge that *she* understood her advancement could only come through pleasing him was a joy. Possession.

Only her attitude to her work was at all confusing, because he was beginning to suspect that she hated that, too. Yet she carried it out to *his* satisfaction, determined never to give him the slightest cause for criticism. He supposed he was really conducting an interesting exercise in psychology. Would she, eventually, surrender entirely, and become the cold-blooded psycopath she appeared to be, and many thought her to be already? Or would she one day kneel down and vomit at the prospect of another day of visiting the cells, of twisting the minds and the bodies of often innocent men and women just to make them say what Ivan Nej wanted them to say, knowing that every such day would be finished by getting into Ivan Nej's bed, and submitting to whatever Ivan Nej wanted her to do, and be, and feel?

"We have been given a task," he said.

She waited. One of her more attractive habits was silence.

"There is a plot against the state in existence," Ivan said. "An international plot, financed by international capitalism, and being implemented by the many foreigners who have come to Russia in the last couple of years."

Anna Ragosina frowned. She knew of all the information that passed through the office, and she could remember nothing like this.

"I have been told to unearth it," Ivan explained. "And I know already where to look. The man Bullen, for example. He is clearly a capitalist agent."

Anna's frown cleared. She was beginning to understand. But as a good private secretary she must point out the pitfalls. "The experts say that the hydroelectric scheme, when completed, will prevent the possibility of another drought like this one, comrade commissar."

"Nothing can prevent drought," Ivan declared. "Only rain. And Clive Bullen does not have the ability to make rain. No, no. He is undoubtedly one of our principal adversaries. But it will not be easy to break down such a man, and as you have observed, he has powerful friends. When he is arrested, I wish to possess incontrovertible proof of his guilt. There must be a courier system for carrying messages and instructions to and from the various agents they have planted in Russia. Carrying messages to and from Peter Borodin, the self-styled Prince of Starogan. He is involved. I know that he is involved. What we must do is lay our hands upon one of those agents, and extract a confession."

Anna Ragosina waited.

"So tell me, Anna Petrovna," Ivan said, leaning back in his chair. "Which foreigners travel to and fro, in and out of Russia?"

Anna considered. "Newspaper correspondents," she said at last.

Ivan snapped his fingers. "The very thing. But we must be careful. These newspapers are powerful concerns, and it is good publicity we are seeking, not bad. What would I give to arrest the correspondent of the *American People*. We *shall* arrest him, Anna. But not until we have the proof I seek. It must be someone from a lesser-known newspaper, an unknown newspaper . . . Let me have a look at that list of all the accredited newspaper correspondents who have come to Russia over the past four years."

"Of course, comrade commissar," Anna got up, took the list from the filing cabinet, and placed it on his desk. She remained standing beside him, bending so that she also could see; her midnight hair brushed his shoulders, and he could inhale her faint scent.

Ivan ran his finger down the list.

"Chess," Anna said. "Chess correspondents. They are in and out every year."

"Sometimes twice in a year," Ivan said. "Chess correspondents. Intense young men who have nothing between their ears except pieces of carved wood. We could not ask for anything better. When is the next big chess tournament, Anna?"

"The all-Russian championships begin in two weeks, comrade commissar."

"Those will do. And I see that there will be a dozen or so foreign correspondents coming to cover them." He counted. "Five of whom were here the last time, and the time before. I think you should attend this chess championship, Anna, in an unofficial capacity. Go home and learn something about the game, and then attend as a spectator. And choose me a suitable spy, by the end of the tournament."

John Hayman had been to Russia so many times in the past few years that he sometimes felt he had never left it at all. Often he wished he did not have to. In Russia he felt at home, and in Russia chess players, and those who reported their games, were not treated as irrelevant nuisances; chess was the Russians' national pastime.

Thus he was an old friend of most of the competitors now, could greet them familiarly, exchange a quip, and a joke, and information about the outside world. Never politics. No Russian was going to talk politics to a foreign correspondent. Nor did he wish to talk politics with them. He was, in fact, beginning to wonder if Uncle Peter's dreams could ever possibly come to fruition. Certainly his uncle's concept of a kulak-led uprising in the south, to which he would lend his name and his prestige and his military ability once it got going, had come crashing down. Uncle Peter argued that that had been pure bad luck, that the Soviets had not known of the existence of any plot, had just decided to move against the kulaks only a few months before the kulaks had been ready to move themselves. That night well be true, but the results had been tragic. When he thought of the Brusilovs, and more especially that pretty, quiet girl, then he truly wished to bring down the whole bloodstained crew in the Kremlin, truly hated with all of Uncle Peter's hate.

But how was it to be done? Only by patient spadework, Uncle Peter said, although over this last year, as he had watched the climatic figures and estimated the grain returns, he had become excited all over again. Russia would starve, once more, as it had done in 1921. People were becoming discontented with the regime. Soon, he had said, soon . . . but for the moment it was necessary just to be patient, and continue as they had done before, taking information in, and bringing information out. As now. It was all very simple.

John sat at his desk, overlooking the auditorium where the play was already in progress, and took copious notes, while Tigran Borsentski sat beside him, also making copious notes. Tigran worked for a Moscow newspaper, and every so often they exchanged their notes. No one guessed that every other sheet of notes had nothing at all to do with chess, that Tigran's contained details of Soviet troop dispositions, of grain deliveries, and of the increasing shortfalls of the five-year-plan, and that John Hayman's contained instructions of future information to be gathered, and told Tigran something of what the émigrés were doing and planning. There was nothing suspicious about it; the two men were known to be friends. Even the slight element of risk that once gave a certain spice to what he was doing had faded. He was accepted into this world within a world that was master chess, and within that world he was as free as air.

When the day's exchange was completed, he could sit back and enjoy the chess, and look forward to talking with Nikolai Nej after the day's session, a conversation he always enjoyed, not only because he liked the young man, but because of the immense secret of which Nikolai was quite unaware—the fact that they were cousins, at least by marriage.

Besides, Nikolai was one of the great reassuring factors in believing that Uncle Peter was right, and that eventually there had to be an explosion, an upheaval that would sweep the Bolsheviks from power and allow Russia to resume its old way of life. Nikolai was utterly patriotic, would stand for no outside interference in Russian affairs, and yet he hated his father and all he stood for—and therefore, by inference, those who had made him what he was—with a burning anger that equalled Uncle Peter's. Or Ivan Sergeievich Roditchev's?

His trouble was, he found it difficult to hate anyone, even Ivan Nej.

The exchange of information completed, he got up, thrust his hands into his pockets, and walked slowly up and down the row of seated players, pausing to look at the boards, to study expressions, to note the amount of time each player had taken on his clock. And occasionally to glance over the spectators, for the hall was, as always in a Russian tournament, crowded. He was struck by the sight of a quietly dressed young woman sitting in the front row, watching the players, but obviously also watching him, for when she found him looking at her a faint flush spread upwards from her neck into her cheeks, a dramatic contrast to the almost dead white of her complexion. In fact, he realized that he was looking at a remarkably handsome girl—for she was hardly more than twenty—whose shroud of raven hair surrounded features that were both beautifully tranquil and at the same time disturbing, because of the intensity of the black eyes which gazed at him. There was something familiar about her, but for the life of him he could not think where he had seen her before.

He turned away from her with an effort, but the feeling of satisfaction that he had been enjoying before had disappeared. Suddenly the huge room was hot and stuffy, and filled with unbearable rustlings; he needed fresh air. He opened the door and went outside into the building's entry hall, where the doors stood open and a welcome breeze seeped in, where the sunlight

filled the street outside, and the hum of the Moscow traffic
sounded reassuringly close. Spectators were still coming in
even if at this late stage there would be standing room only,
and among them were several young women, fashionably
dressed and obviously students, laughing and talking as they
came up the steps. And in the midst of them was Natasha
Brusilova.

They saw each other in the same instant, and that she had
recognized him could not be doubted; the smile on her lips
died at once. Alarm at having been discovered mingled with
relief that she should have survived the massacre of her family,
and then was replaced by alarm again as he suddenly remembered where he had seen the white-faced girl before; it was the
absence of her uniform that had confused him earlier. And
Natasha was about to enter the auditorium—to be seen by Anna
Ragosina.

He stopped at the top of the steps, as the girls reached him,
and watched them pass. Natasha Brusilova's head turned, so
that she looked at him again, her expression now under control.
But she was trying to convey a message, as was he. And now
she slowed, and dropped out of the group as it approached the
ticket collector. One of the other girls spoke to her, and she
replied with a shrug. The other girl looked as if she would
have waited for her friend, but Natasha sent her on, watched
the group go through the doorway, and then turned to face
John once again.

He drew a long breath and stepped forward, but she shook
her head, then walked away from him, back onto the porch
outside, and down the steps to the lawns surrounding the hall,
where there were park benches. She chose an empty bench and
sat down, and Johnnie sat beside her.

"You mustn't go inside," he said. "There is a woman there.
I saw her in Kharkov the day your mother and father were
—" He hesitated, and then shrugged. "—murdered by the
OGPU. She was with the OGPU."

"Anna Ragosina," she said.

"You know her?"

"Everyone knows Anna Ragosina. She is Commissar Nej's
personal assistant. They say she is far worse than he."

"Then you must get away from here."

Natasha shook her head. "She cannot harm me."

"But—your mother and father—"

"Were murdered by the OGPU, as you say. And they wished to execute me too, I think. But I am protected by Comrade Nej."

"Comrade . . . ?"

"The famous dancer. Tatiana Nej. I study at her academy. She wishes me to become a famous dancer too, I think. And Commissar Ivan Nej, in case you didn't know, is her husband. They are separated. But she is commissar for culture, and Ivan Nej can do nothing against her decision. When he came to arrest me, she gave him a tongue-lashing. Comrade Ragosina was with him."

"Don't you hate her?"

Natasha Brusilova shrugged. "She is OGPU. Everyone hates the OGPU. But you . . . if she were to find out that you had visited my father . . ."

"She never can. Unless you tell her."

Natasha Brusilova almost smiled. "I am not likely to do that, Mr. Harding."

"You mean you even remember my name?"

"But of course."

"And you hate me too."

"Why should I do that, Mr. Harding?"

"Because the death of your father and mother, the destruction of your farm, may have been connected with my visit."

She gazed at him for some seconds. "If it was, Mr. Harding, then I have no doubt they died in a good cause."

"Do you believe in that cause, Natasha Feodorovna?"

Her face was again sadly serious. "I have nothing to do with causes, Mr. Harding. I cannot, and I dare not. Comrade Nej would not have it."

Comrade Nej. Aunt Tattie, whom he had last seen in an English police station, and whom he had helped to escape from Uncle Peter, after having kidnapped her in the first place. Of all the people in Russia he must not meet, Aunt Tattie stood at the top of the list. She had saved this girl's life, but only because she wanted her to dance. To Aunt Tattie, only dancing mattered.

But what a shame that he should meet this girl again, have so much he wished to say to her—because in all Russia she was the first woman he had met with whom he could be himself, even share his secrets—and know she was beyond his reach.

She got up. "I must go in, or my friends will come and look for me. I told them I felt dizzy and would sit in the fresh air for a while."

Was she beyond his reach? Was anything beyond their reach, if they *both* wanted it badly enough?

"I should like to see you again," he said.

"To involve me in your plans, Mr. Harding?" she asked. "I suppose I am a coward, but I have no desire to be shot." She gave a little shiver. "Or to be given to Comrade Ragosina for interrogation."

"Just to talk with you," Johnnie said.

"Then come to the school," she suggested. "Comrade Nej welcomes visitors."

He shook his head. "I cannot."

Her eyebrows raised. "The school is quite safe."

"Not for me." He drew a long breath. This was unforgivable of him, he knew, but suddenly, seeing this girl again, talking with her and getting to know her, was the most important thing in the world to him. "Did your father not tell you who I am?"

She sat down again. "He said you were very important."

"I am Prince Ivan Sergeievich Roditchev."

Her mouth sagged open slightly, then her head turned left and right to make sure no one had overheard.

"So your Comrade Nej is my aunt, and she knows what I look like. If she were to see me, it would be all over for me."

"But . . . excellency—"

He shook his head. "Mr. Harding. Or John. I would like John. May I see you again?"

She gazed at him. But all her life she had been taught to respect and obey the aristocracy. "If you wish it, Mr. Harding."

"Can you leave the academy at night?"

"Some girls do. When they are caught they are severely punished."

"Would you risk it for me?"

"If that is what you wish, Mr. Harding."

My God, John Hayman, he thought: what a cad you are being. But suddenly the sheer fact of knowing this girl, of being with her, of sharing with her was making him realize how lonely he had always been. Besides, why should she be caught?"

"Tonight?"

"It can be tonight."

"The Timiryazev Park? It is close to the academy. I will be by the railway line."

She hesitated, and then nodded. "I can be there by about midnight."

"I'll be waiting for you."

She nodded, and stood up again. "May I ask, Mr. Harding, why this meeting is so imperative?"

"Until tonight," he said. "I will tell you then."

"Well, Lydia Alexandrovna," Tattie said, busily writing. "What is it you wish?"

Lydia Polientsa was a large, stout woman, matron to the senior girls at the academy. She took her duties very seriously. "I have a report."

"Well?" Tattie continued to write. She really was in no mood to listen to Lydia's unending complaints. She just wanted to sit at her desk, and remember last night and the night before that, and the night before that as well. And anticipate.

"It concerns the Brusilova."

Tattie raised her head, the pen motionless, her pleasant thoughts distracted. She regarded the girl almost as a daughter.

"She has been leaving the dormitory at night, Comrade Nej," Lydia Polientsa said.

Tattie put down her pen. "Natasha Brusilova has been doing this? Are you sure?"

"I am perfectly sure, Comrade Nej."

"When?"

"Every night for the past three."

"How do you know this?"

"It has been reported to me, Comrade Nej. And I am reporting it to you."

Tattie sighed. Telling tales was so ingrained in the modern Russian character. It was not a habit of which she approved.

"Obviously she is meeting a man," Lydia pointed out.

"Obviously," Tattie agreed.

"She must be punished," Lydia said.

"Why?"

"Well, she is breaking a rule of the academy, in leaving at night. And the man must be unsuitable."

"Why do you say that?" Tattie asked.

"Because if he were not," Lydia said triumphantly, "why should she have to meet him in the middle of the night? Why could she not have him come here, as so many of the girls do? Or why should she not meet him openly, on holiday afternoons? No, no, Comrade Nej, you may mark my words, this fellow is already married, or is unsuitable in some other way. Natasha Feodorovna must be confronted with the facts, and when she has admitted her crime, she must be punished. I would forbid her to leave the academy for a month, on pain of a thrashing. That is what I would do."

"I am sure that is what you would do, Lydia Alexandrovna," Tattie said. "But do you know, I saw Natasha smile, yesterday morning? I have not seen her smile since her parents died. I thought I must be mistaken. But now I know I am not mistaken. I would like you to forget that you have been informed that she is leaving the academy at night, Lydia."

"But . . . a married man—"

"If he makes my Natasha smile," Tattie said, "then I do not care if he has a hundred wives."

"It is very irregular. I could never approve," Lydia Polientsa said.

"I am a very irregular person," Tattie said. "And you do not have to approve, Comrade Polientsa. *My* approval is all that matters. You will forget all about Natasha Brusilova's midnight escapades."

Lydia Polientsa snorted, and withdrew. And Tattie picked up her pen again, to chew the stem. Dear Natasha Feodorovna, snatching at happiness once again, after so very long. She discovered she was extremely curious to know who the man might be.

Anna Ragosina sat in the front row of the spectators, as she had throughout the tournament. She had enjoyed herself these past two weeks. Not because of the chess—she was not interested in the game—but because of the opportunities it had given her to study people, and because of the immense feeling of power she enjoyed in knowing that eventually she would pick one of these eager young men in the journalists' gallery to be her victim. And now that they had arrived at the last day of the tournament, her time was up. He must be chosen today.

She had already narrowed the field down to five. All the older men had been discarded immediately; she did not like older men, had all too much of an older man in her life. Besides, on purely scientific and psychological grounds, a young man was far more likely to cooperate, once he found himself in the loneliness of Lubianka. So it was just a matter of choosing between a German, a Hungarian, an Italian, and Englishman, or an American writing for an English paper and traveling on an English passport. Which, she supposed, must mean that he was a naturalized Englishman—or that he was traveling on a forged passport. She hadn't thought of that before, but it was an interesting, and damning, possibility. Add to that the fact that he was seeing Natasha Brusilova almost every night—since she had narrowed her choice she had had each of the five under constant surveillance—and he became very interesting indeed.

That John Harding was seeing Natasha Brusilova had to be a coincidence, but it raised another interesting possibility; if she chose to have John Harding arrested on grounds of anti-Soviet activities, could she not then have Natasha Brusilova arrested on the same grounds, since they were meeting every night? That would certainly please Commissar Nej, if she could get away with it. But it would not please Commissar Nej if his wife were to get annoyed and go complaining to Stalin, and undoubtedly that was what would happen. So it would be best to leave Natasha Brusilova alone. And, regretfully, this probably meant it would be best to leave John Harding alone, which *was* a pity; he was by far the best looking of the five young men, and he possessed a quality of subtle arrogance that suggested he would not break easily. He would break eventually, of course. Anna Ragosina did not suppose there was a man in the world who could resist her forever. But it would have been most enjoyable.

When she thought like that, Anna could induce within herself a tingling, shivering feeling that left her quite breathless, a mixture of anticipation and sexual ecstasy and sheer self-disgust. It was a relief to know that even after four years the self-disgust was still present. She was not yet a monster. But in the course of time she would become a monster.

That was because Anna Ragosina could remember. She could remember men in uniform, and she could remember her mother holding her against her breast. She could remember one of the men in uniform pulling her away, and she could remember her mother being ordered outside, where Father already was. They had left the door open, and through the door she had watched Mother and Father being made to kneel, and in her innocence she had supposed that they were being made to pray. Now she knew that they had certainly been praying. And one of the men in uniform had stepped up to Mother and put his pistol barrel to her ear and blown her head clean away, left nothing but splattering red blood and trailing gray tendons. Even then she had not properly understood what was happening. Father had. His head had jerked, and turned, his eyes opening again, and he had screamed his outrage and his fury and his misery, and tried to get up. But before he had even been able to leave his knees the man in uniform had placed the gun muzzle against his ear as well, and again squeezed the trigger.

The uniform the men had been wearing was the same that she would put on when she returned to the office.

Then she had wanted to kick and spit and bite, and destroy the uniform. It had been the only thought in her tiny mind, and the men wearing the uniforms had laughed, and picked her up under their arms, as they had picked up Michael and Vasili, and dumped them in a waiting wagon.

She had dreamed of that day, every night for the next four years. Even now she occasionally dreamed of it. In the beginning she had wanted only to die, had attempted not to eat, had been force-fed by Comrade Tereshkova and her aides. And gradually she had come to realize that to die would be the most senseless of all her options. Dead, what could she do, except perhaps be with Mother in heaven? But there seemed to be a good deal of doubt as to whether there was a heaven. Besides, there were her brothers to be thought of. She was the only family they still had in the world, and they remembered nothing of the past. Alive, she could educate them, whenever they all escaped the orphanages. And alive, there was the possibility that one day she might again meet the men in uniform who had put the revolver barrel to Mother's head—when she was grown up, and would know what to do about men like that.

With such an ambition, such a determination, life had become purposeful, almost enjoyable. Work had been a blessing, and a pleasure; the better the results she achieved on her examinations, the better the position she would be given on leaving school, the better she would be placed for dealing with the men in uniform when the time came. But then she had encountered two considerable shocks, in her middle teens. She had for the first time realized just how many men in uniform there were; and also, just how powerful they were. She was proposing to take on a state within a state, it seemed, headed by the most feared men in all Russia. And while she had still been digesting that information, Alexandra Markovna, who was always up to tricks and constantly being punished, had indulged in her greatest escapade; she had broken into Comrade Tereshkova's office, pried open the filing cabinet, and been able to read the private files that were kept on each of the senior girls. She had made notes, and the dormitory had sat up all one night comparing them, and deciding that of them all, Anna Ragosina was the one least likely to succeed.

Not that they truly understood the report. Not even she truly understood the report.

"This girl," Comrade Tereshkova had written in her small, precise hand, "has been my most difficult charge. On the surface she is the best-behaved girl in the school, quiet, respectful, a hard worker, and conscientious at her studies. But she is utterly without feeling, a shell of a human being. She does not laugh, she does not even smile, she takes part in no games and in none of the school activities, prefers to be by herself. I am convinced that there is some deep psychological problem here. Undoubtedly her difficult background is partly responsible, but I have to report my opinion that I cannot recommend her for higher education, since it would be a waste of time. In fact, she could be taken from the school tomorrow and placed in some menial position without any waste of talent."

"What difficult background?" the other girls had wanted to know. And she had told them to shut up, and turned her face to the wall. But not to sleep. How could she, surrounded by thousands of the men in uniform, ever hope to combat them from her knees beside a mop and pail?

And then, amazingly, alarmingly, only a few weeks later Ivan Nej had appeared, and out of all the senior school, apparently, had invited her to be his assistant, in commanding the men in uniforms. He had actually invited her into their midst, offered to surround her with their protection, put her in that hated uniform. And grant her the opportunity to find the men she sought.

He had wanted a great deal more than that, as she had known from the moment of his invitation. He had wanted her for his woman. She had never known a man before Ivan Nej, and she would hardly have chosen him for her first. But since she had made survival the keynote of her life, she could hardly have discovered a better lover, from the point of view of protection and prestige. What he actually wanted to do with her body was nearly always painful and very often disgusting, and was rendered the more confusing for a girl as inexperienced as she by his frequent spasms of impotence. But without it she did not suppose she would have survived. His attentions made her angry enough, vicious enough, and at the same time aware enough of herself to satisfy him in her other role, because, as he had made clear on that first day, he wanted her to partner him in more than bed.

Ivan Nej, she had very soon realized, for all the men and women he commanded, and for all his power, was the loneliest man in all Russia. He lived entirely in his dreams, and since reality could never for an instant approximate what he dreamed about, if only because he could not be both tormentor and victim at the same moment, and thus *feel* both the ecstasy and the agony together, as he could imagine in his dreams, he lived his life in a continued state of frustrated disappointment. Which could be, apparently, slightly alleviated either by tormenting her or by having her torment other people in his presence. He was, she supposed, a genuine monster, in the age-old Russian tradition of monsters, which encompassed men like Ivan the Terrible and Peter the Great, and Ivan's predecessor as a secret policeman, Sergei Roditchev.

She had understood all this only very slowly. In the beginning she had been anxious only to please, to establish herself at the center of the spider's web, that would in time bring her to her parents' assassin. She had always supposed pepper rather harmless, had thrown out the suggestion only because once in cooking class one of the girls had put some down the front of her dress and she had screamed in mingled pain and humiliation. But from that careless suggestion had come unnumbered ghastly hours for unnumbered ghastly people in the cells below the office. Pepper, properly used, could destroy, drive men and women mad, even kill them. Ivan counted her fertile imagination a treasure.

And she had had to learn to live with it. More, she had had to learn to enjoy it—a lesson, she supposed, in corruption, because she *had* learned to enjoy it. She had trod in the footsteps of her master, and absorbed some of his sadism, reminding herself always that nothing mattered, no one counted, beside the opportunity she possessed for going through the personnel files, for making up her list, for gradually whittling it down to the men who were in the right vicinity at the time of her mother's death. It was still a very lengthy list, and there had been only five men. There was still a tremendous amount of work to be done. But it would be done, and in the meantime she must continue to harden herself, to eradicate the last trace of feminine weakness, to be ready both to kill, when the time came, and to be killed. Because she did not doubt that would also happen. Nor would she have had it any other way. Over the past five years she had become a monster, and prospered. There could be no possible reason for her to stay alive once she had completed her mission in life.

But there was no reason why, from time to time, she should not endeavor to enjoy herself, as she had during these last few days. Nikolai Nej. A carbon copy of his father in appearance, except that he did not wear a mustache. And quite a good chess player, even if she suspected he would never be a Botvinnik. A young man her own age, and Ivan's son. But Ivan's estranged son, obviously, since Ivan had never mentioned him. A young man it might be amusing to torment with all the weapons she had at her disposal, and all the hate for his father, for his very name, that she had at her fingertips. She had discovered that she was very nearly indispensable to Ivan; he would never punish *her*. But what would he do to his son, and indirectly to himself, were he to discover a liaison between him and his mistress?

The thought, the delightful possibilities, had been roaming through her mind with increasing intensity for the past few days. And now was the time to implement the plan, if she was ever going to. Nikolai had just finished his game, his last game in the tournament, a draw which would leave him comfortably eleventh in a field of twenty. Now he was shaking hands with his opponent and preparing to leave the stage.

Anna got up and waited at the foot of the steps. "Good afternoon, Nikolai Ivanovich."

He checked, glanced at her, and flushed. "Good afternoon, Comrade Ragosina."

"Ah," she said. "You know my name."

"Everyone knows your name, Comrade Ragosina."

"I am complimented. Well, then, as you know my name, you know who and what I am. Therefore would you not like to take me for a cup of tea?"

He stared at her. "You are—"

"I am almost your stepmother," she pointed out. "It would be courteous."

"I . . . I am already meeting someone for tea," he said.

"Are you? Who?" She turned to follow the direction of his gaze. "The American correspondent?"

"He is English. John Harding."

"Of course. How stupid of me. But it would be a pleasure for me to meet Mr. Harding." She linked her arm through his. "You will take me to tea, Nikolai Ivanovich, and I shall meet this Englishman of yours." She realized that she had, after all, made her choice.

Chapter 12

TATIANA NEJ AWOKE TO A VIOLENT BANGING ON HER BED-
room door, the noise accompanied by the sound of other doors
opened in protest at the midnight disturbance.

Tattie and Clive sat up together, while she reached for the
light switch, at the same time shouting, "What is it? Oh, come
in, do."

The door burst open, to admit Natasha Brusilova and Lydia
Polientsa.

"This wretched girl," Comrade Polientsa bawled, "breaking
rules, waking the entire school—"

"Comrade Nej," Natasha cried. "Oh, Comrade Nej—"

Tattie got out of bed, reaching for her dressing gown.
"Whatever is the trouble? Calm down, child, for God's sake.
Comrade Polientsa, what is happening?"

Comrade Polientsa cast a scornfully inquisitive glance in
the direction of Clive, who had lain down again and drawn up
the covers. "Not content with breaking out of school, Comrade
Nej, this wretched girl must come breaking back in, making
a noise like a herd of elephants. She must be punished, comrade. I insist upon it."

"*You* insist upon it?" Tattie demanded.

"Comrade Nej—"

"Oh, be quiet," Tattie said, advancing to the door and glaring down the corridor at the students and instructors who had gathered outside. "Go back to bed," she shouted, "all of you. Go back to bed." She closed the door, and faced Natasha, who was sobbing her heart out. "But you are a very wicked girl, Natasha Feodorovna. In leaving the academy at night at all, and certainly in making all this noise. I'm afraid that Comrade Polientsa is quite right, and you will have to be punished."

"Oh, Comrade Nej," Natasha wailed. "I do not care what happens to me. But the most terrible thing has happened to someone else. If I could speak with you—"

"You *are* speaking with me, silly girl," Tattie pointed out.

Natasha glanced at Comrade Polientsa. "In private, Comrade Nej."

"Ha," Lydia Polientsa snorted.

"Well," Tattie decided. "Perhaps you had better leave us, Lydia Alexandrovna."

"She means to beg for mercy," Comrade Polientsa said. "I should stay."

"And I have decided that you should go."

Lydia Polientsa hesitated, then left the room, banging the door behind her.

"Now then, my child," Tattie said. "Tell me all about this terrible thing that has happened."

Natasha looked at Clive Bullen.

"I have no secrets from Mr. Bullen," Tattie said.

Natasha licked her lips, and Tattie gave her a handkerchief.

"Blow your nose," she recommended. "And come and sit on the bed, and tell me what has happened." She seated Natasha on the bed, and Clive hastily moved his feet.

"Now then," Tattie said. "You went out tonight, as you have been doing regularly this last week, to meet your boy friend."

Natasha stared at her with her mouth open.

"Of course I know all about it," Tattie said. "I know all about everything that happens in the school. You silly, naughty girl. Comrade Polientsa warned me that the man had to be no good. And now I suppose she is proved right, and he has assaulted you. Do you wish to bring a charge of rape? I can telephone the doctor and have you examined."

Natasha slowly shook her head.

"Well, then?" Tattie said.

"He didn't assault me," Natasha said. "He'd never do that. He's a perfect gentleman. Well, he'd have to be. He's..."

"Tell me his name." Tattie said.

Natasha drew a long breath. "He calls himself John Harding."

"That's not Russian."

"No, Comrade Nej. He travels under an English passport, although he is an American. But he was born in Russia."

"He sounds a very cosmopolitan type," Tattie said. "What does he do?"

"He's a chess correspondent," Natasha said. "He came to Russia to cover the championship."

"Ah," Tattie said. "Then you met him the day you and the other girls went to watch." She frowned. "That was only just over a week ago. It does not take you long to make up your mind, Natasha Feodorovna."

"I had met him before, Comrade Nej."

"Indeed? Where?"

Natasha sighed. "At my parents' home. Before... before it was burned."

It was Tattie's turn to stare. "But that must have been—"

"Three years ago," Natasha agreed. "He came to see Papa. That is why..."

"I see," Tattie said. "This romance has been going on for three years, without my knowledge. You are his mistress."

"No," Natasha insisted. "I swear it."

"You have known this man for three years," Tattie said severely. "You have left the academy every night this past week in order to meet him, and you expect me to believe he does nothing more than kiss you on the cheek?"

"Well..." Natasha flushed, and gave Clive an uneasy glance. "We kiss on the mouth. And we talk. And—"

"A true romance," Tattie said, her severity disappearing behind a happy smile. "I am so glad. But tonight he wished more."

"No, no." Natasha said. "Tonight we were to say good-bye. He is to leave today, for Berlin. He *was* to leave today. But Comrade Nej..." Once again the tears welled out of her eyes.

"He has been arrested, by the OGPU."

"My God," Clive Bullen sat up, forgetting the covers
"What has he done?"

"I don't know," Natasha Brusilova cried. "I don't know
They didn't say."

"Well, obviously he has done *something*," Tattie said. "No
even Ivan goes around arresting people for nothing. Tell u
what happened, exactly."

"Well." Natasha drew a deep breath and blew her nose
"We were sitting on a park bench, and talking..."

"What about?" Tattie asked.

"He was telling me about America," Natasha said, flushing
"He would like me to go there."

"Indeed?" Tattie started to look severe again. "And wha
were you *doing*?"

"We were holding hands. Nothing more than that, Comrad
Nej, I swear it!"

"I believe you," Tattie said. "Go on."

"Well, suddenly these men appeared. I think they had bee
hiding in the bushes. And the woman Ragosina was there a
well."

"My God," Tattie said. "Then Ivan *is* involved. Then i
must be something serious."

"Oh, yes, Comrade Nej. I am sure of it. They seized Mr
Harding, and handcuffed him before he could stop them, an
hurried him towards the car. I tried to protest, and they jus
pushed me aside. But he called out to me to tell you, Comrad
Nej."

"Me?" Tattie cried.

"Because his name isn't really John Harding, comrade,
Natasha explained. "He is really Prince Ivan Sergeievich Rod
itchev."

"Who?" Clive Bullen inquired.

"*What* did you say?" Tattie shouted.

"It is true, Comrade Nej. He is Prince Roditchev."

"Prince Roditchev," Clive Bullen said, thoughtfully. "
seem to have heard that name."

"You are thinking of his father," Tattie said. "Natasha i
talking about Johnnie. Johnnie Hayman. You remember John
nie Hayman, Clive. But...Johnnie, here in Russia, under a
assumed name? And you say you first met him three year

ago, Natasha? My God. He must still be working for Peter."

"John Hayman?" Clive asked. "But if he is working for your brother . . . my God."

"Yes," Tattie said. "The silly young fool." She got up.

"Will you help him, Comrade Nej?" Natasha begged.

"Oh, I will help him." Tattie threw her dressing gown on the floor and dropped her slip over her shoulders. "Not that he deserves it, the young idiot, coming to Russia under a false name, seducing one of my girls, not even coming to see his aunt . . ."

"He explained that he couldn't, that it would be too dangerous."

"But he wants my help when he is found out." Tattie snorted. "He shall have it, but I will have a few words to say to him, you can be sure of that." She buttoned her blouse. "Off you go to bed, Natasha Feodorovna. Your prince will be with you for breakfast." She escorted the girl to the door and closed it behind her.

"You're going out *now*?" Clive asked.

"Well," Tattie said, "I can't leave him in the hands of Ivan's people. You have no idea what they do to people. It is quite horrible. Ivan has told me about it. I must get him out of there right away."

"I'd better come with you." Clive got out of bed.

"No, no," Tattie said. "That would be a mistake. You are also an alien, and I have an idea that Ivan does not like you very much. He knows all about us." She pulled on her summer coat and fluffed out her hair. "I shan't be long. You go back to sleep."

"Now how can I do that, my darling?" He caught her hand.

"Well, then . . ." She kissed him on the nose. "Lie awake and think of me." She went downstairs and summoned her chauffeur. As she sat in the back of the car for the drive into the city, she thought, that stupid, stupid boy. Of course he was guilty. Working for Peter, he had to be. Ivan was going to be difficult, no question about that. On the other hand, she had never doubted her ability to handle Ivan, one way or another.

The car stopped before the apartment building.

"I will not be long, Alexei Igorovich," she said, and went upstairs, to bang on the door of her old apartment.

"Are you mad?" Ivan blinked the sleep from his eyes.

"Waking me up at three in the morning?" He seemed to realize for the first time that he was looking at his wife. "*You*?"

Tattie pushed him to one side and swept through the living room, curious to see what *she* looked like in bed. "Where is your little friend?"

Ivan stood in the bedroom doorway. "Working."

"At this hour? You should keep an eye on her, Ivan Nikolaievich. I see you haven't managed to give her any babies, either."

"She is not here to have babies," Ivan said. "She is here to work. What have you come for?"

Tattie returned to the living room and sat down. She opened her coat. "I have come to ask a favor of you, Ivan."

"You? Have come to ask a favor of me?" Ivan sat beside her. "At three o'clock in the morning?"

"Yes," Tattie said. "Your people made an arrest tonight."

"My people make arrests every night. The OGPU never sleeps."

"No doubt," Tattie agreed. "But you will find this one simple to identify; your little friend was there. He is a chess journalist named John Harding, who was arrested not two hours ago. Now Ivan, I know you are going to be angry, but the fact is, his name isn't really John Harding at all. It's John Hayman. Ilona's son." She paused, hopefully, while Ivan stared at her.

"Ilona's son? Roditchev's son?"

"Well, of course he is Roditchev's son. He probably thinks of himself as the new Prince Roditchev. But Ivan . . ."

"Roditchev's son." Ivan got up and slapped his hands together. "Here in Russia. Well, well. What a coup!"

"Now Ivan—"

"You won't deny that he has to be guilty of *something*," Ivan said. "Why else would he have come to Russia under a false name."

"He is a chess journalist," Tattie said. "He loves chess. He follows it all over the world. Well, he knew that he would never get a visa to enter Russia under his own name, so he changed it."

"Nonsense," Ivan said. "Why, he must be working for your brother. Of course he is."

"Possibly he is," Tattie agreed. "But he is just a boy. And he is your nephew, Ivan Nikolaievich, at least by marriage.

You simply must let him go. Oh, tell him he can never return to Russia, but you must let him go."

"Let him go?" Ivan was incredulous. "One of Peter Borodin's agents?"

"You don't *know* he is working for Peter," Tattie reminded him. "After all, he helped me to escape from him, back in '25. They must have quarreled then. Why, Johnnie hit him."

"Well, they seem to have made it up," Ivan said, and this time rubbed his hands together. "Roditchev's son, Borodin's agent, here in Russia. And under arrest. That girl is a treasure. An absolute treasure."

"Ivan," Tattie said. "I want you to let him go."

"Are you mad? Let him go? He will stand trial. It will be the trial of the century. And the people he will implicate, when we interrogate him . . . my imagination is hardly equal to it," he said smiling at her.

"Ivan," Tattie said again. "I am asking you to let him go."

"You? This has nothing to do with culture, Tatiana Dimitrievna. This is an affair of state, and family matters cannot be allowed to interfere with an affair of state."

"Nevertheless," she said, "I would like you to let him go, Ivan." She sighed. "I am prepared to be very nice to you."

Ivan looked at her.

Tattie sighed again. "Very nice," she promised.

Ivan smiled at her. "You will let me play with you? You will let me come in from behind? You will love me as you love that Englishman?"

Tattie shrugged. "If that is what you wish, Ivan. But you don't know how I love Clive."

"I want you to love *me*," he said. "While it is happening."

Tattie sighed once more, got up, and took off her coat.

"That was very nice," Ivan said, getting out of bed. "You really are quite an adorable creature, Tattie. I can think of only one woman in the world who could possibly equal the *feel* of you."

Tattie nestled herself deeper into the bedclothes. She actually felt contented. Probably, she reflected, because it was the second time that night. Ivan was really a hopeless lover. He had huffed and puffed, and she had let him do everything that he seemed to like doing, a lot of which was pretty dis-

gusting, in her opinion, and she really had accomplished noth
ing for herself. And yet she felt contented. She wondered i
Anna Ragosina ever felt contented. "Not that silly little girl,"
she remarked, lazily.

"Good God, no." Ivan started to dress; he did not even wash
himself. She supposed, no matter what happened to him, he
would always remain a simple muzhik from the steppe. "I was
thinking of Ilona."

Tattie sat up in surprise. "Ilona? You?"

"Why not? I am not ashamed of it. I think your sister is the
most beautiful woman in the world. Why do you suppose I like
you? It is because you look a little like Ilona."

Tattie lay down again. "Well, well, well," she said. "Al
these years, dreaming and drooling. You *poor* little man. Hav
ing to put up with a substitute."

Ivan put on his jacket and buttoned it. "I have not always
had to put up with a substitute."

Tattie frowned at him. "You and Ilona? When?"

"You are forgetting I had her in my custody, for a night."

"And you—" Tattie laughed. "I don't believe a word of it
You wouldn't have dared."

Ivan drew himself up. "I am Commissar Nej," he pointed
out.

"And you'd be afraid of your own shadow, unless it was
tied down by your thugs. Anyway, Ilona would have told me."

"There are some things women prefer not to talk about,"
Ivan said.

"I don't believe you, and I shall never believe you, unless
she tells me so herself," Tattie said. "So there. Where are you
going?"

"To Lubianka."

"Well, wait a moment and I will dress and come with you
I want to give that young man a piece of my mind."

Ivan shook his head. "You cannot see him. He is a prisoner."

"I'll wait until he is released." Tattie threw back the covers
and got out of bed.

Ivan hastily moved to the door. "He is not going to be
released."

"Not going . . . what are you talking about?"

"Did you really suppose you could come here and wave
your bottom at me and get me to release Ivan Roditchev?" Ivan

held the door handle. "Why, he is probably the most important agent my department has ever arrested."

Tattie glared at him. "You . . . you unutterable bastard," she shouted. "You miserable little worm. You—" She charged at him, but he had anticipated it, slammed the bedroom door in her face, and ran for the outer door. Tattie wrenched the bedroom door open and raced behind him, but he was already halfway down the stairs. "You wait until I get my hands on you," she bawled. "You wait . . ." She heard the outer door bang, turned and went back into the bedroom. She picked up a glass vase and dropped it on the floor, and then kicked the remains against the wall. Then she got dressed. Silly little man, trying to outwit her. It really was hardly worth getting excited about, except that he had had her into the bargain. But she'd get even with him for that.

Johnnie's freedom came first. She went across the hall, and banged on the door. After repeated thumps it was opened by a sleepy Catherine Nej.

"Tattie? What on earth?"

"I wish to speak to Michael."

"But—" Catherine thrust her fingers into her close-cropped black hair. "You'd better come in. Michael isn't here."

"For God's sake," Tattie shouted. "Doesn't anyone sleep in Moscow any more? What is he doing?"

"He's in Geneva." Catherine closed the door.

"Geneva?" Tattie cried.

"Sssssh," Catherine begged. "It's a deadly secret. He wasn't even supposed to tell *me*. He's on a mission to meet up with the Americans, some Americans, I think even with Mr. Hayman. It is all part of some diplomatic thing. I don't know anything more than that."

"Geneva," Tattie breathed. Meeting with Americans, indeed. With George. But George could not possibly know anything about what Johnnie was up to. And time was going to be the problem. "Oh, well," she said. "I will have to go to Joseph Vissarionovich. All right, Catherine. Go back to bed. I'm sorry I disturbed you. And I won't mention Geneva to a soul."

"Is there something the matter?" Catherine asked, anxiously.

"Good heavens, no," Tattie said. "What could be the matter?

There was just something I wanted Michael to do for me."

"At five in the morning?" Catherine asked.

"Why not?" Tattie pointed out. "Nobody else seems to b asleep. Go back to bed, Catherine Pavlovna. Go back to bed.

She went down the stairs, summoned her chauffeur, wh was half asleep behind the wheel of her car, and commande him to drive to the Kremlin.

"Comrade Stalin cannot be awakened," said the secretary

"Don't tell me he is actually asleep?" Tattie inquired. "An you will awaken him. Tell him it is Comrade Tatiana Nej o a very urgent matter. Besides, it is nearly six o'clock. Comrad Stalin is always awake at six o'clock in the morning."

"He was up very late last night, Comrade Nej," the secretar said. "I do not think he will be rising at six o'clock this morr ing."

"Wake him," Tattie said, in a tone that brooked no argu ment. And ten minutes later she was confronting a very sleep Joseph Vissarionovich, wrapped in an enormous dressin gown.

"Tatiana Dimitrievna?" he inquired. "What can be the mat ter?"

"Ivan," she said.

Stalin's eyes suddenly became opaque.

"He is up to his tricks again," Tattie said. "He has arreste my nephew."

Stalin sat down behind his desk. "You do not have a nephe in Russia, comrade Tatiana."

"But I have one in America," Tattie said triumphantl "John Hayman. My sister Ilona's son by Sergei Roditchev."

Stalin scratched his head. "You are telling me that Ivan ha sent to America to arrest Roditchev's son?"

"Oh, good Lord no," Tattie said. "Johnnie is here in Russi And Ivan has arrested him. He didn't even know who he wa but he has been arrested. I want an order for his release. Depo him, if you like, but he can't stay down at the OGPU headqua ters. You know what they are like."

Stalin leaned back in his chair. "I do not know what the are like, Tatiana Dimitrievna. I do know that I have ever confidence in Ivan Nikolaievich."

"Then you need your head examined," Tattie said withe ingly.

Stalin's eyes woke up at last. "You come in here," he said, "throwing your weight around—"

"Joseph Vissarionovich," she protested. "I didn't mean to hurt you."

"Well, you have. There you are, spending your time worrying over some foreign agent whose father was a tsarist thug, when you should be worrying about deviationists in our midst. This boy Shostakovich, for example. I have heard some of his music. It is bourgeois claptrap. There is nothing revolutionary about it at all. He will have to change his style. Mark my words, Tatiana Dimitrievna. There is too much deviationism creeping into our society. As commissar for culture it is your business to weed it out, not encourage tsarist agents."

"I know you're right," Tattie said humbly. "I will set to work immediately. But Joseph Vissarionovich, this boy is my nephew. My favorite nephew. I can't have him remaining in the hands of Ivan's thugs. Sign me an order for his release, and I will look seriously into the matter of Dimitri Dimitrievich's music."

"That boy is a tsarist spy," Stalin said. "You come here, waking me up, plaguing my life with irrelevancies, when Nadezhda lies dying? Dying, I tell you. I was up with her half the night. She is dying. My Nadezhda." He got up, great tears rolling down his cheek. "Leave me alone, Tatiana Dimitrievna. Concern yourself with your own affairs, and let Ivan get on with his. And leave me alone."

John Hayman was bundled into the back seat of a car, his hands secured behind him, an OGPU officer on each side. Anna Ragosina, seated in the front seat beside the driver, turned round to look at the young man in the back.

The officers immediately began to search their victim. Rough fingers poked into pockets, pulled out the linings, accumulated whatever they found in a cloth bag. The interior light was on—the blinds were drawn in the back—and as far as she could see, it did not look like a very interesting collection. The officers apparently agreed. When they were finished, one grasped the front of John Hayman's trousers and gave it a squeeze. "Only that left, eh, comrade?" he asked. "But Comrade Ragosina will soon get rid of that for you."

John Hayman stared at the woman. He was not lacking in

courage. And how good-looking she was. She thought sh
would have guessed he had a Russian background, even ha
Nikolai Nej not told her. And she had a feeling that it wasn'
any muzhik who had been his father, either. She began to fee
quite excited.

"May I ask what this is all about?" he asked, in a quie
voice. "If you have hurt that girl . . ."

One of the officers hit him in the ribs and made him gasp
"Shut up," he said. "Your job is to answer whatever question
Comrade Ragosina wishes to ask. Then you can talk, comrade
Not until then."

They were already turning into the gateway to the OGPl
headquarters; the car had been driven very fast. Johnnie wa
thrust out, into the custody of two more officers. "You'll searc
his hotel room," Anna told the two men who had accompanie
her to the arrest. "I want anything and everything."

"Of course, Comrade Ragosina. We shall bring you his las
bead of sweat."

It excited them to think of her interrogating prisoners. Well
she thought, it excited her as well. "Search him again," sh
told the guards. "Everything. Tell me when you are finished.

She went upstairs to her office and sat down. She had n
desire to watch or take part in the search. Searches were un
pleasant, dirty things. And actually, now she should go hom
to bed. It was standard procedure, laid down by Comrade Ne
himself, that prisoners were to be left entirely to themselve
for twenty-four hours, in an empty room, with no clothes an
no food and nothing to drink, only their thoughts and thei
fears to keep them company, and their looming apprehensions
Very often nothing more was needed. After twenty-four hour
of anticipating hell and enduring misery, a surprisingly larg
number of people were ready to confess to anything, sign an
documents.

But they were Russians, born and bred in the fear of th
secret police. She did not really think John Harding woul
succumb as easily as that. Besides, she was impatient to se
him again, to discover what he was really like.

There was a knock on the door, and one of the guards thrus
in his head. Under his arm he carried a bundle of shredde
clothing. "There was nothing, Comrade Ragosina." Well c
course there would be nothing; he had nothing to hide.

"We did not remove the handcuffs," said the guard. "You gave us no instructions about the handcuffs."

Anna nodded. "Give me the keys."

The guard handed over the keys, saluted, and left. Anna got up, slowly and thoughtfully. She was a monster. But on people like John Harding she could exercise her hate. And he was such a good-looking boy.

She went down the stairs, and then down the other flight of stairs, into the basement. Guards saluted, and unshaded electric bulbs glared at her. This was her world, the world where she was queen. She thought of Persephone; Comrade Tereshkova had been a classical enthusiast.

And Ivan Nej made a suitable Hades.

She went down the last corridor, unlocked the door, and looked at the young man. He had seated himself in the far corner. Now he got to his feet, with difficulty. His initial reaction was concern at receiving her in his condition, then he seemed to recollect that if a slight embarrassment was his worst experience he had very little to worry about; already his ribs were red where he had been punched.

He shrugged. "Your men took away my clothes, Comrade . . . Ragosina, is it?"

"That is my name." She closed the door. Now she could inspect him more closely. What a splendid man he was, broad-shouldered and narrow-hipped, and hardly older than herself, she thought. "It is necessary for you to be searched," she explained. "Many enemy agents conceal cyanide tablets on their persons, and if left alone for a moment they will bite them. Some of their hiding places are quite remarkable."

"I take your point," John Hayman said. "I don't think I have a whole tooth left in my head. But Comrade Ragosina, I am not an enemy agent. I am a chess correspondent who happened to have a date with a Russian girl. Is that a crime? If so, I promise you I won't ever attempt to see her again. Just tell me that she is all right."

His tone was reasonable, and modulated. There was only the slightest trace of strain. He was keeping his fear well under control.

"You are an enemy agent," she said. "At least, you are going to confess to being an enemy agent, Mr. Harding. It is my business to see that you confess. I will draw up a statement, a confession, and I will also draw up a list of people who are in the plot with you. This you will also sign. Then all you have to do is behave yourself, confirm the confessions when the case comes to trial, and undoubtedly you will receive a light sentence, perhaps five years in a labor camp. Then you will be free to go. Free even to see this girl again, if you wish to. I have nothing against your dating Russian girls. Of course, even if you retract the confession, you will be found guilty anyway, and then your sentence will be much heavier. But you are not so stupid, are you, Mr. Harding?"

He had been slowly shaking his head as she spoke. "You . . . you can stand there," he said, "and outline to me, so casually, such a travesty of justice? Do you know, if you were a little more sensible, Comrade Ragosina, you might have succeeded? I might have agreed to sign a confession implicating myself, just to save being beaten up. I don't suppose I'm very brave. But if you really think I'm going to implicate a lot of other people—"

"I can destroy you, Mr. Harding," she said. "I might even enjoy doing that, while it was happening. I am good at my job. On the other hand, I would regret it after I was finished, because you seem an attractive man, because I think you are quite brave, and because, most of all, I would not have my confession, if you lasted to the end. It would not matter, you know, because I would then arrest someone else, and sooner or later I would find someone who would sign my confession, and implicate those I wish to be implicated. Your stubbornness would only have caused someone else to be imprisoned." She went closer, stroked her finger down the line of his jaw, watched the muscles bunch, and watched too the muscles bunching in his shoulder—but he was helpless with his wrists still handcuffed behind his back. She wondered if he would try to kick her. Then she would have an excuse to use her hands. Since she knew the warder was watching through the observation window, she had to have an excuse; she dared not consider what Ivan might say were she ever to reveal any feminine interest in her victim. "But do you know, Mr. Harding, I do not think you would be able to resist what I would do to you, if you refused to cooperate. I think you would break down."

He stared at her, then raised his head as the door opened.

"I am not to be interrupted when interrogating a prisoner," she snapped. "How many times do I have to tell you that?"

"I consider this important, and relevant to the interrogation, Comrade Ragosina."

Anna glanced at John Hayman, then went outside and closed the door. "Well?"

"We found papers in the man Harding's room, comrade. Well concealed. We think they may be important."

"Papers?" Anna frowned. "Where are these papers?"

"In your office, Comrade Ragosina."

She hurried ahead of him, refusing to consider what these papers might be until she actually saw them. She sat at her desk and flipped through the notebook.

"It was concealed in the lavatory, comrade," the officer explained.

Most of the writing was in English, which she did not understand. But there were one or two Russian phrases and odd words that set her heart to pounding. Could she really have stumbled onto something?

"I want this translated, immediately," she said. "Wake up one of the English-speaking secretaries, and put her to work."

"Immediately, Comrade Ragosina." He took the notebook, saluted, and withdrew.

Anna leaned back in her chair. He really was a spy. And she had been completely taken in by his air of injured innocence, had almost regretted what she would have to do to him. She felt quite upset at her own gullibility, and at the same time quite exhilarated. Because what she would do to him now . . . The door opened, and Ivan Nej came in. Hastily she stood up. He insisted upon proper respect even from her.

"Anna," he said. "You are a treasure."

"Comrade commissar?"

He held her face to kiss her on the lips. "You have struck pure gold, in this arrest of yours. Did you know that?"

"The man Harding?" she frowned. "I only chose him because he seemed the most likely prospect. But comrade commissar, in a search of his room, my men found a notebook filled with what I think is information about Russia, military information as well as economic. I have been lucky."

"Lucky. Ha!" Ivan sat behind his desk, and leaned forward. "You are the luckiest girl on the face of this earth, which is why I treasure you. So you have found a notebook! Why, that is just splendid. But not terribly relevant now. Do you not know who this John Harding is?"

Anna sat down again. "Is he somebody important?"

"His real name is John Hayman. Which means that he is my nephew, the son of Tatiana's sister Ilona by Sergei Roditchev. You have heard the name?"

"The tsar's police chief?"

"The very same. Which means that this young man is actually Prince Ivan Roditchev. What a coup, eh? Prince Roditchev on trial for espionage inside the Soviet Union. Espionage and sabotage. Supported by evidence. And a confession. What a coup."

"Yes," Anna breathed. A prince. A real live prince. Young and handsome and unafraid. And all hers. "Since I have been so fortunate thus far, comrade commissar, may I ask to be allowed to continue the interrogation?"

"Ha ha, you little monster, you. You wish to hear a prince scream, eh? But that will not be necessary. Nor even, I think, politic."

"But comrade commissar—" She leaned forward.

"You let the girl Brusilova go," he said.

"Well, comrade commissar, after what happened when we tried to arrest her three years ago—"

"Oh, quite, quite. But this time it will be possible to arrest her, at least for a while, because Tatiana Dimitrievna will not be there. She is rushing around the Kremlin trying to get an order for Roditchev's release. Besides, we have a justifiable reason. The girl has been consorting with tsarist agents. Even my wife will have to admit there is cause for suspicion. I have sent a squad to get the girl. Now listen to me. When she is brought in, she will be taken to interrogation cell one. By then, I wish you to have Roditchev in interrogation cell two. You will leave the door of that cell open, so that he will be able to hear the girl scream. That is all that will be necessary. He is a prince. He has ideas about chivalry. And this girl is his mistress. To save her from further torture he will do anything we ask. I know this."

"It is possible," Anna argued. "But left to me for a week, he will do anything we ask as well. I know *this*."

"Anna, Anna," Ivan said. "There will be other handsome

young men. Many of them, I promise you." He smiled at her.
"Even a prince, perhaps. But none as important as Roditchev.
Don't you see? He was arrested at half past midnight this
morning. I wish him to write down the time, in his own hand,
on the confession he shall sign. So he will have confessed
within eight hours of being arrested. And then, later on this
morning, I shall summon the Moscow Press Corps and show
them the young man, completely unhurt and healthy, not even
lacking sleep, but having already signed a confession. He will
be proven to have feet of clay. More important, it will prove
to all these would-be deviationists that they can put no trust
in princes, neither this one, nor that arch-prince, Peter Borodin,
in London. So off you go to prepare him."

Anna sighed, and got up. "So you have the girl, and I have
nothing," she said.

"I have promised you, you will have many," Ivan said.
"But not Ivan Roditchev. He is too high for such as you, Anna
Petrovna. When he is convicted, and sent to a labor camp for
life, perhaps then, briefly. But not before."

"In there," Anna Ragosina commanded, and John Hayman
obeyed. She watched the muscles rippling in his shoulders, the
buttocks moving against each other as he walked. She had
never actually wanted anything in her life before, until now.
But surely he was made of sterner stuff than Commissar Nej
supposed.

Now he stopped, looking at the bars, the clamps for wrists
and ankles set against the walls, the adjustable lights. She heard
him inhale.

But he was determined to be brave. "Don't you think this
is all rather old-hat?" he asked.

"It works," she said, and sat down in the chair, behind the
desk, placing her papers in front of her. There was one other
chair in the room, bolted to the floor, and facing her at a
distance of several feet. "Why don't you sit down?"

John Hayman glanced at the door, still standing half open,
and at the warden who waited just outside. Then he sat down.

"Is there anything you would like to do, or have, before we
commence talking?" Anna asked.

"Yes. I would like to go to the toilet."

"Afterwards," she said. "I will take you myself."

"If I do not go now, and you start to beat me," he said, "I may do it on the floor."

She smiled. "Why should I beat you, Mr. Harding? We are going to talk. You know that my people found a notebook concealed in your hotel bedroom?" She studied his face. Certainly it had changed. "It is being translated now. But you must see that it will hopelessly incriminate you."

He shrugged. "Then I will have to confess."

She raised her eyebrows. "And sign the papers I have prepared?"

"My own confession, Comrade Ragosina. Nothing else."

"That is very silly of you," she said. "Do you really wish to be forced to crawl on that floor at my feet? Is that sensible? Is not dignity the most important thing any human being possesses? Once it is lost, you know, Mr. Harding, it can never be regained."

"It can be expiated," he suggested, "in hatred."

"Which is self-destructive," she pointed out, and listened to footsteps in the corridor outside. John Hayman turned his head to look through the half-opened door, at the men marching along the corridor, the terrified girl they were pushing in front of them. He leapt to his feet as if scalded.

"Natasha!"

The girl glanced at him, her mouth sagging in horror, then was whisked past.

"You bastards." John Hayman went towards the door, and the guard stepped inside, his truncheon hanging at the end of his fingers. John's shoulders sagged, and he looked at Anna Ragosina. "Do you really suppose she is involved?"

"It is certainly our business to find out, Mr. Harding," Anna said. "Just as it will be in her best interest for you to sign my papers."

He gazed at her. "You are unutterably filthy," he said. "Unutterably despicable."

"They will be undressing her now," Anna said, with patient tolerance. "That room is exactly like this, you know. Once she is undressed they will clamp her to the wall, in that contraption over there. You will observe that her legs will be spread, and her weight suspended from her wrists. This is uncomfortable."

"One day," John Hayman said, "I am going to kill you. So

elp me God, I am going to wrap my hands around that white
hroat of yours and choke you to death."

"Once she is in that frame," Anna said, "they will put pepper
on her. You know, between her legs. The pain is quite excru-
iating. Too much, and the area can swell to such an extent
hat death follows."

He stared at her, and then slowly lowered himself back into
he other chair. But he was reacting to what she had been
aying; breathing very hard.

"Do you really wish that to happen to her?" Anna asked.
She picked up the sheets of paper and showed them to him.
'I do not think you actually *know* any of these people, Mr.
Harding. What happens to them can hardly be important to
ou." She smiled at him. "Not as important as what happens
o Natasha Brusilova, surely."

John Hayman sucked air into his lungs, and then suddenly
eleased it again as a scream drifted down the corridor. His
head jerked as he stared at her. Then another scream, louder
nd more desperate than the first, wailed towards them.

"Stop it," he snapped. "Stop them. They must be stopped."

"Of course," Anna agreed. "And you must do it."

He licked his lips. "All right," he said. "Tell them to leave
her alone and I will sign your paper."

Anna shook her head. "Sign first."

Another scream broke into the morning.

"All right," John Hayman cried. "All right."

Anna got up, gestured him to his feet. She took the keys
rom her pocket and released the handcuffs.

John Hayman slowly clenched and unclenched his fists. The
guard watched him from the doorway.

"Sit at the desk," Anna said, and gave him her pen. "If I
were you I would not waste time in reading the papers. Listen."

Another scream, but this one muted, as if the girl in the
next cell were already exhausted.

John Hayman sat at the desk, picked up the pen, scribbled
his name, and again, and again on the third sheet. Anna stood
at his shoulder, her thigh brushing his arm. "Very good," she
aid, and snapped her fingers. "You may take him back to his
ell," she said.

John Hayman left the room, and she sat down in the chair

he had just vacated. So Ivan was once again proved right, and she was left with nothing, save the triumph of having arrested the prince in the first place. And some vague promise. Suddenly she was very tired.

The door opened, and Ivan came in. "Well?"

Anna gave him the signed papers.

"Splendid," he said. "Absolutely splendid. The best day's work you have ever done."

"What did you do to the girl Brusilova?" she asked.

"I have sent her back to the academy."

"To . . ." She stared at him.

"Well, if I had harmed her, Tatiana Dimitrievna would have caused a great deal of trouble. She is very angry with me in any event. I explained that it was all a mistake, and sent her home again. I'm afraid I had to say the order for her arrest was given by you, mistakenly, my dear Anna Petrovna, and that I rescinded it the moment I discovered who she was."

"But—" Anna thrust her fingers into her hair. "Those screams—"

"Were made by a secretary. I just wanted Roditchev to see the girl here, in our custody. But now, now we have everything we need. You are a treasure, Anna. I have told you so before. Take the rest of the day off. Go home to bed, and leave it all to me."

Anna got up. "You will not be coming home?"

"There is work to be done. Work."

He patted her bottom. Never had she known him to be so pleased. And never had she hated herself and her situation so deeply. "Then I will go," she said. She kissed him on the cheek, and went up the stairs into the real world, where the sun was shining and there were even people smiling. And she had to smile too, or she would go mad, she realized. She had to smile with someone young like herself, and possibly good-looking. Someone with whom she could make up in some way for being Ivan Nej's woman.

She caught a bus to the apartment building where Nikolai Nej lived.

Ilona Hayman sat in bed and read her newspaper, casually. She was bored. George had given her the choice of any capital in Europe to wait in while he went off on his secret mission, and she had chosen London. She did not really know why she had chosen London, except that it was the only city in Europe, apart from Moscow, in which she still had a living relative. And yet, since her arrival she had spent very little time with Peter, and felt no desire to see him again.

And London itself, in the absence of George, was unutterably boring. She had been to three plays, the opera, and the ballet, to the Zoo, and to Madame Tussaud's, and that seemed to have about exhausted it. London, England—all of Europe, for that matter—was in the grip of a financial crisis every bit as severe as that afflicting America. People were depressed and unhappy, and that made their entire country depressed and unhappy.

She did not even know where George was, or what he was doing, except that he was meeting with Michael and would not take her along. It was some terribly secret diplomatic mission on which he was embarked, with the support and indeed the recommendation of Hoover. And in fact she had no great desire to know what was going on, or even to meet Michael again. Had the conference been taking place in Russia, now . . . but she had asked George if he were going to Russia, and he had said no, and then had asked her not to question him any further. But if only he would come back. Or if only she had decided not to come, but had remained in New York. But she had wanted to get away from the depression that was afflicting New York, from the depression that had been afflicting her own life. Try as she might, she could not approve of this Elizabeth Dodge. The girl lived a life totally alien to any Ilona had any concept of. That she should paint men and women in the nude, that she should drink and smoke, that she seemed to wake up only at noon on most days, and never went to bed much before two in the morning, was all so totally not Borodin, and not even Hayman, that the thought of her as a daughter-in-law was positively frightening. And yet George junior seemed utterly and irrevocably in love. And then there was Johnnie, lost somewhere over here. She had contacted the newspaper for which he worked, since he had not been at his London flat, and had been informed that he was away covering the Russian chess championships. She hadn't been able to let him know in advance that she was coming—everything had been arranged in such a rush. With Johnnie completely out of touch, and George junior about to marry someone she knew she would never like, she was left with just Felicity as an intimate, and Felicity was a reserved girl, confusing to her mother.

Idly she turned the pages of the paper, not really reading it, half wondering what she would do with the day, and suddenly felt her entire chest and neck seem to constrict so that she could hardly breathe.

RUSSIANS CRACK TSARIST SPY RING

said the small headline on page three.

"With the arrest of Prince Ivan Roditchev," the article said, "the Soviet secret police, the OGPU, claim to have cracked a tsarist spy ring that has been operating within Russia for the past three years, and which, it is claimed, has been responsible for many acts of sabotage and terrorism in that time.

"At a conference at Lubianka prison this morning, the deputy commissar of the OGPU, Ivan Nej, presented the arrested prince to the press. Prince Roditchev is a young man in his early twenties, every inch a tsarist prince. His father, by an odd coincidence, was the head of the tsarist secret police, and had a fearsome reputation during the last days of the Romanovs. He was executed by the Bolsheviks during the civil war.

"Prince Roditchev appeared to be unharmed and in good physical condition, but he refused to answer any questions. However, Deputy Commissar Nej assured the press that he has signed a confession without hesitation, although his arrest had taken place only the previous night. 'He is being very cooperative,' the commissar said, and went on to promise that there would be widespread arrests as a result of what the prince had told him.

"The Soviet authorities are elated at having at last cracked this apparently very dangerous anti-Bolshevik conspiracy, which, they claim, is intended to return millions of helpless Russians beneath the iron rule of the tsars and their supporters, men like the infamous Roditchev senior."

It went on for some lines longer, but Ilona was just beginning to breathe again. The article was dated yesterday. Therefore Johnnie had only been in Ivan's hands for thirty-six hours. But what would they have done to him in that time?

Johnnie, in Ivan's hands. Johnnie, a spy for a tsarist organization. My God, she thought. My God. She reached for the telephone, gave the number to the operator, and found herself screwing the newspaper into a ball as she waited.

"Yes?"

"Peter."

"Ilona? Are you still in London? I hadn't heard from you this week, so I thought you had gone home."

"Listen. Have you read today's newspapers?"

"One of them."

"Have you read about Johnnie?"

"You think this fellow calling himself Prince Roditchev is really Johnnie?"

"Of course it must be Johnnie," she shouted. "And you sent him there!"

"Me? I have nothing to do with Johnnie, Ilona."

"Don't lie to me, Peter."

"Nothing at all," Peter repeated. "If it is he, then he is a fool to have let himself be arrested, and a traitor to have confessed so easily, if that part is true."

"True?" she shrieked into the telephone. "What do you suppose they *did* to him?"

"That I couldn't say. He is still letting down a great number of people. But then, he has done that before."

"Letting down?" Ilona cried. "You can talk of letting down, while you sit here safely in London, and Johnnie is in some prison cell . . ."

"You are being hysterical. I have told you that I have nothing to do with it. And even if I did, I would not be able to help him now. I suggest you call me back when you are in a more reasonable frame of mind."

The phone went dead. Ilona stared at it for some seconds, then replaced it on the hook. No brother of hers, anymore. No brother, ever again. But merely hating Peter was senseless. And unproductive.

She threw back the covers and got out of bed. George and Michael. Of course. They would read the report, and they would immediately do something about it. They both knew the truth about Johnnie. They'd never let anything happen to him.

But suppose they didn't read the papers? If their meeting was so very secret they might not even be given newspapers.

And there was no telling how much longer they'd be at it. While every day Johnnie remained in Ivan Nej's hands . . . Never had she felt so alone.

She turned back from the window, hands rolled into fists. She was being stupid. Ivan no doubt genuinely supposed that Johnnie was Roditchev's son. Once he was told that Michael was Johnnie's father, everything would be all right. No question about that.

But who was to tell him, since Michael wasn't even in Russia, and Johnnie didn't know?

Except her. Ivan would believe her. When last they had met, ten years ago, he had been reasonable enough, after that initial mistake, caused entirely by his people. Everyone in the Kremlin had been reasonable. If Viktor had actually been shot, well, he had almost certainly been involved in Peter's absurd scheme for espionage and sabotage. So, according to the newspaper, Johnnie had been involved, but he was Michael's son and *had* to be treated differently once they became aware of that fact. And if Michael was secretly meeting George for the sake of Russia, well then. . . .

Besides, there was no way she could just sit here in London and wait, while Johnnie was in the hands of the OGPU. She picked up the telephone again. "I wish to send a telegram," she said. "Then I wish you to book me on the first available train for Moscow."

Judith Stein thumped the telephone hook several times, and listened to the clicks running down the line.

"I am trying to connect you," the operator said with studied patience.

"Yes?" said a voice, finally, on the end of the line.

"I have a call for you from Berlin," the operator said. "Go ahead, please, Berlin."

"Berlin?" Peter Borodin asked.

"Peter," Judith shouted. "What are you doing about Johnnie?"

"For heaven's sake," he said. "You have telephoned me half way across Europe to ask me that?"

"Haven't you read yesterday's newspapers? I've been trying for hours to reach you."

"Of course I have read the papers. The fool has got himself

caught and is shrieking his head off in the hopes of saving his skin. I'm afraid I can feel no sympathy for someone like that."

"No sympathy?" she shouted. "You are responsible for him."

"I am responsible for no one," Peter snapped. "Get that through your head. No one. Good-bye." The phone went dead.

Judith slowly replaced the receiver on the hook. Had she really expected anything better? To Peter all people, even the members of his own family, were just pawns in the great game he was conducting against the Soviets. And when a pawn was taken, it was merely removed from the chessboard.

But Johnnie. What would Ilona say when she heard the news?

She got up, stood at the window to look down on the street. There was nothing she could do. Absolutely nothing. In the last two years in Berlin she had gradually felt that all her control over her life, much less the lives of anyone around her, was slowly slipping away. She suspected a great many people in Berlin, in all Germany, were feeling that. They had simply had too many years of defeat and depression. The shock of 1918 had been succeeded by the shock of the collapse of the mark in 1923. Then had followed half a dozen years of painful recovery, of an almost traumatic indulgence in the good life after ten years of misery, only to have the whole thing start all over again. People, especially the young, were no longer willing to wait patiently for the next good time, even assuming there was ever going to be one. They were opting more and more for one or another of those groups that promised a more immediate salvation, however vague their proposals. The problem was that the opposing groups hated each other to the point of vicious physical antagonism. Since Joseph was a Communist leader, as well as a leader of the Jewish community, she supposed they were in a more privileged position than most; whenever she wished to go shopping or even attend the theater, she was accompanied by a guard of brawny young men, eager to protect her.

But by the same token, whenever she had not previously announced her intention of going out, she was trapped in the apartment until Joseph returned home to rescue her. Just as Johnnie Hayman was trapped in his Lubianka cell.

And that things were moving towards a crisis could no

longer be doubted. She had come here in such a spirit of determination, much of it sparked by her anger at Peter, by her realization that she had been merely frittering her life away, merely pretending to help. In Germany there had been something to do. Joseph had said so, and she had believed him. Even two years ago he had seen the Nazi menace as a cloud shadowing all of Germany's future. The Nazis had to be opposed; and as Jews, condemned to subhumanity by the Nazi creed, they were the ones who most imperatively must do the opposing. Joseph had not changed his Communist ideals, no matter how disillusioned he had become with the Kremlin, but that had not mattered very much to her in an idealogical sense, and it had been important in a purely political sense; the Communists were the only party even remotely ogranized enough to oppose the Nazis with any hope of success. She had been *doing* something with her life, at last, for Zionism, and if Germany gained into the bargain, well, she had nothing against the Germans. Indeed, if one went back far enough, the Steins were a German family, however many generations ago they emigrated to Russia.

But she hadn't really intended to take part in a slide towards civil war. She had been involved in a civil war before, and she knew just how terrible it could be. And she couldn't run away from this one. Having exhausted in turn Michael Nej and George Hayman and Peter Borodin, her own brother was the very last refuge she possessed in all the world.

Michael Nej! Of course Johnnie was in no danger. Michael would know that Sergei Roditchev had never had a son, that Ivan had to be holding his own Johnnie. She could not imagine why Michael had allowed things to reach such a stage as a press conference to announce the arrest. But whatever the reason, he would never let anything happen to Johnnie. Of that she was sure.

Relief came over her in great waves, and she sat down again, and picked up the sheet of paper on which she was composing a speech for Joseph. It was time to get back to work, time to . . . Footsteps, on the stairs. Joseph, home early?

She got up again, heart pounding. Joseph had warned her that he was a marked man to the Nazis, and that they might well attempt to beat him up or even murder him, as had happened to other Jewish or Communist leaders. And they were also aware that he had a sister.

Knuckles on the door. Cautiously she moved towards it, leaned against it. "Who is it?" she asked in a low voice.

"It is I, Judith. Boris Petrov."

Judith tore open the door, spirits bubbling in joyous relief. Boris Petrov. After all these years, Boris Petrov. She was in his arms before she could stop herself.

"Boris! Oh, how good to see you. How good—" She kissed him on the mouth before holding him at arms' length. "But here, in Berlin?"

He took off his hat and kissed her again. "I just happened to be in Europe—"

"In Germany?"

"Not exactly. It's all very hush-hush. A secret diplomatic meeting in Geneva—between your two old boyfriends."

She sat down. "George? And Michael?"

"I shouldn't really tell you this, but it's nearly over anyway. There are State Department people there too, and the whole thing could lead to recognition of the Soviet government by the Americans. I think it will. It will be a great triumph for Michael. And for George, too. He's been advocating normal relations between our two countries for years." He sat beside her. "But I have the weekend free, so I thought I'd dash up to see you, since I can't find out about you any other way. And it *is* good to see you, Judith. Why didn't you ever answer any of my letters?"

"Well it didn't seem fair after everything..." But she couldn't concentrate, not even on dear Boris. Something was lapping at her mind, some disturbing thought.

"Fair? I should be apologizing to you. Of course you're entitled to live your life as you choose." He picked up her hand. "But since George is no longer your lover, and since you're no longer living with Peter Borodin...Judith, I am about to leave my post in Washington. Moscow thinks I've been there long enough, and if this business is satisfactorily concluded, I am to get a reward: a first secretaryship in Paris. What do you think of that? Judith, I would still like to marry you. I would love for you to come to Paris with me." He shrugged. "I am no longer so anti-Stalin. Things seem to be working out. And if we can gain American recognition—Judith, it is possible for Russia to become an important, and a civilized, member of the world community. Judith—"

"Boris," she said, "how long have these secret talks been going on?"

He frowned at her. "For two weeks. Why?"

"Don't you read the newspapers?"

He frowned. "The newspapers? Not really. All information of any importance is given to us every day. Anything that might affect the outcome of the talks. Why?"

She handed him the newspaper, and pointed to the item.

"I'm afraid I don't read German very well," he said. "Is it about Russia?"

She read it to him.

"Yes," he said. "But why is it so upsetting to you?"

"That boy is Ilona Hayman's son. And Michael Nej is his father," she said. "Not Sergei Roditchev."

He looked completely mystified.

"It would take too long to explain," she said. "But you can take my word for it. I don't think Ivan Nej, or anyone in Russia except for Michael himself, knows that fact. But Michael must be told that John is in danger. Can you reach him, Boris?"

"There is a private line. But it is only to be used in moments of great emergency."

"Wouldn't you suppose this is a great emergency? My God, don't you know what Ivan Nej *does* to people?"

"There are rumors—"

"Rumors?" she shouted. "Those aren't rumors. Boris, you have to tell Michael. And George must be told too. Now."

He gazed at her for a moment, and then picked up the telephone. "Hello operator? Geneva, Switzerland." He gave the number, then put down the phone. "It will take a few minutes," he said.

"I'll make some coffee."

"And tell me the whole story."

"It's a bit complicated," she said, when she brought the coffee.

"My God," he remarked when she was finished. "I had no idea the relationship was so tangled. But Commissar Nej will then know that this boy is Ilona's son."

"Of course he knows that. But he thinks Roditchev was the

father. Everyone hated Roditchev. Everyone will hate his son, as well."

"Hm," Boris agreed. "But, if he's working for Peter Bordin, he is most certainly guilty of at least anti-Soviet activities."

"Does that *matter*," she cried, "if he is Michael's son? Can Michael's son really be tortured by the OGPU, put on a show trial, and then sent to a labor camp for life? That is what will happen to him, you know."

"Hm." Boris said again, and the phone jangled. He picked it up. "Hello. I want to speak to Commissar Nej," he said. The voice at the other end sounded excited. "It is very important," Boris said when he could get a word in. "It is Comrade Petrov on the line." He put his hand over the mouthpiece. "He is coming now."

"Let me speak to him."

"He will be very angry," he said. "No one is supposed to know where he is."

"Let me speak with him," she said, and took the phone.

Michael Nej opened the door of George Hayman's bedroom and pushed a protecting secretary to one side. "I have just had a telephone call from Judith Stein," he said.

George sat at his desk, writing. Now he raised his head to frown at his friend. "Judith? But—"

"From Berlin. Petrov went to visit her. He is in love with her, you know. It is all very irregular. I shall have words with him, you may be sure. But thank God he did go. Ivan is under arrest in Moscow."

"Ivan? Your brother?"

"No, George. Johnnie. My brother has him in Lubianka. Apparently it's been in the papers."

"My God." George got up. "The young fool."

"Yes." Michael said. "It seems he has already confessed to working for Peter. God knows what they have done to him. George, I must leave today, get back to Moscow and see what can be done. I am sorry about the talks—"

"The talks can wait," George said. "I'm coming with you."

"I thought you might say that. Well, throw some things in a bag. I've already ordered a car to take us to the station."

"Right away," George said, and stopped suddenly. "Ilona."

"Ilona?"

"She's in London. If the story was in yesterday's news-papers, she'll have seen it. She'll be going wild with worry. Give me ten minutes to phone her."

Michael nodded.

"Top priority," George told the girl on the switchboard. "London, the Dorchester. I'd like to speak with Mrs. George Hayman, please."

He listened, another frown slowly gathering. "Left the hotel? Where has she gone? The boat train for Holland? My God." He put down the receiver, and stared at Michael. "She's on her way to Russia."

"Ilona?" Michael shouted. "On her own? She must be stopped!"

"How the hell do we do that? She left yesterday morning. She'll be through Berlin in a couple of hours. Anyway, you can't blame her for rushing off. Johnnie is her favorite. And there was no way she could get hold of us."

"You don't understand," Michael said. "She's Johnnie's mother, and Peter Borodin's sister, so Ivan will have a legit-imate excuse for arresting her. Can you imagine?"

George frowned. "Would he dare? I thought he learned better ten years ago."

"I never quite got to the bottom of that," Michael said. "But I'm damned sure we don't want her in one of Ivan's cells, ever again. Berlin!" He snapped his fingers. "I'll telephone Judith and Petrov. They can get her off the train. Whatever happens, George, she mustn't get to Russia, not until we get there, at least."

Chapter 13

IVAN NEJ SPREAD THE TELEGRAM BEFORE HIM ON HIS DESK, the better to stare at the words.

"But what does it mean, Comrade Commissar?" asked Anna Ragosina. She was not the only person in the office who supposed the telegram was in some sort of a code.

"It means what it says," Ivan said, a great glowing exultation seeming to surge through his body.

'TERRIBLE MISTAKE,' read the paper. 'IVAN SERGEIEVICH NOT REPEAT NOT RODITCHEV STOP MICHAEL WILL KNOW STOP LEAVING IMMEDIATELY WILL EXPLAIN ON ARRIVAL STOP PLEASE ARRANGE ENTRY STOP ILONA HAYMAN.'

"I do not understand," Anna confessed.

"Neither do I, entirely," Ivan agreed. "But I understand that it means that Ilona Hayman has left London today." Once again he studied the telegram. *Michael will know.* Had she sent Michael a telegram also? If Michael was truly meeting with George Hayman, then the odds were she knew where they were, how to contact them. Michael would certainly wish to interfere.

To interfere with his dream, at last come true. But all his
dreams had suddenly come true, at last. Tattie had returned
to his bed, on his terms. And now Ilona was coming to surrender herself to him. He felt quite sick with anticipation.

But not if Michael were allowed to interfere.

"When will she get to Berlin?" he asked.

Anna did some mental calculations. "If she did leave this
morning, then she would have got to Paris by noon, and have
caught the express there. She would be in Berlin by about noon
tomorrow, I think."

"I have a mission for you, Anna Petrovna," Ivan said.

Anna came to attention.

"Requisition a light aircraft, a four-seater, and take one man
with you, and fly to Berlin. Be there when the Moscow express
arrives, and take Ilona Hayman from it."

"Take her?" Anna asked.

"Explain that you have come from me, and that you are to
facilitate her journey. Get her onto that plane, Anna, and fly
her back here."

"Yes, comrade commissar," Anna said doubtfully. "It may
be necessary—"

"Use whatever means you have to, but I do not wish her
harmed more than is absolutely necessary. Do you understand
me, Anna Petrovna?"

"Yes, comrade commissar," Anna said, although she clearly
did not understand. But why should she? She knew nothing
of his dreams.

"Then make haste," he said. "Bring that woman here to
me—in secret, Anna Petrovna. This is the most important
assignment I have ever given you. Bring her here to me."

The Tiergarten Station was crowded. "It is always like this,"
Nikoyan explained, "for the arrival of the Moscow express."

Anna Ragosina nodded. She was sure he was right. Never
had she felt quite so nervous; it was the first time she had ever
left Russia, just as it was the first time she had ever flown,
and it was her most important assignment. Ivan had said so,
even if she still could not quite understand why. And she was
not in uniform; she had never realized before how important
her uniform was to her confidence, how insignificant she felt
in a summer dress, high heels, and a patent-leather handbag

And now to be surrounded by all these people . . .

"The train," Nikoyan said, pointing down the track.

The express eased slowly into the station; it had shrunk somewhat since its departure from the Hook of Holland, the Prague and Vienna coaches having been detached. Here in Berlin it would become even smaller, since the German coaches would be removed—causing a very useful delay. Only the Warsaw and Moscow coaches would be left. And these occupied the front of the train.

"First class," Nikoyan said, unnecessarily. "She will be traveling first class."

Anna nodded and marched towards the first-class car, Nikoyan at her elbow. The Russian guard barred their way at the door. "You are not passengers," he said. "This car is fully booked."

Anna opened her handbag and showed him her OGPU identity card. His jaw fell open, and he hastily stepped back. Anna climbed the step, Nikoyan immediately behind her. "You have a passenger called Mrs. George Hayman," she said.

The guard went into his little office, consulted his list. "She is in number seven."

"Thank you, comrade," Anna said, and turned, as two other people got onto the train. The first was a tall dark woman with handsome features and curiously intense black eyes; she wore her hair short and was dressed well but somewhat carelessly. Accompanying her was a slightly shorter man, heavily built and with close-cropped dark hair, but attractive, open features.

"It is not permitted to board the train," the guard said, getting up.

"It is very urgent," the woman said, speaking perfect Russian. "You have a passenger on board called Mrs. George Hayman?"

The guard looked at Anna.

"I must speak with her," the woman went on. "My name is Judith Stein. If you will tell her my name, she will wish to speak with me also."

"Do as Madam Stein wishes," said the man. "I am Deputy Commissar Petrov, of the Commissariat of foreign affairs."

The train gave a growling jerk as the first of the cars was uncoupled. Boris lost his balance and his head half turned; Nikoyan promptly drew his pistol from the holster under his left arm, and with the butt struck Boris a savage blow on the back of his head. Boris fell to his knees and then to the floor without a sound other than the crash of his falling body.

Judith had also turned. "You—" she shouted, but Anna then seized her from behind, throwing one arm round her waist and the other hand over her mouth.

"Mmmmm," Judith shrilled, and kicked her on the ankle.

The guard stared at them with enormous eyes.

"Quickly, comrade," Anna gasped. "Use the needle from my bag."

Nikoyan hesitated, then picked up the dropped handbag, opened it, took out the hypodermic needle, seized Judith's right wrist, just in time to stop her from clawing at Anna's eyes, threw up the sleeve and thrust the needle into the vein just below the elbow. Judith kicked again, and this time struck Anna on the ankle. "Ow," she muttered, and stepped backwards, losing her grip. Judith swung her hand to catch Nikoyan such a blow across the head that he staggered and dropped the needle.

Judith turned, mouth opened for a scream, and Anna seized her shoulders and jerked her backwards with all the force she could manage. Judith's scream was stifled as she fell into the guard, who promptly sat down, Judith on his lap. But her eyes were already drooping shut, and a moment later her head also drooped.

The door of the next compartment opened. "What's the matter?" inquired a voice.

Anna jerked her head, and the guard scrambled to his feet, allowing Judith to fall to the floor, and hurried out of the tiny office. "Nothing is the matter," he said. "Nothing. It is the uncoupling of the carriage, you understand."

Nikoyan straightened his tie and looked down on the unconscious woman. "Judith Stein," he said. "I have heard of her."

"So have I, comrade," Anna said. "And of Comrade Petrov. That was quick thinking. You had better tie them up."

Nikoyan knelt beside Judith, pushed her skirt to her thighs, and began taking off her stockings.

"What is to happen?" the guard asked, returning.

"You will keep the woman and the man here," Anna told him, "while I go and speak with Mrs. Hayman. When I have

taken Mrs. Hayman from the train, Comrade Nikoyan will help
you to put the pair of them in Mrs. Hayman's compartment.
I do not wish them harmed, but I wish them taken to Moscow.
You will draw the blinds and permit no one to enter that
compartment, and twice in every day you will give them an
injection from this bottle. Do you understand me?"

"I . . . I—" The guard licked his lips. "I know nothing of
these affairs, Comrade Ragosina. I . . ."

Anna smiled at him and rested her hand on his shoulder.
"But you will carry out my instructions because you are a good
Russian, comrade. And because if you do not I shall be very
angry with you. More important, Commissar Nej will be very
angry with you. You would not like that, comrade." She looked
down at Judith; Nikoyan had bound her wrists and ankles with
her stockings, was now unfastening her dress to remove her
brassiere for use as a gag. He worked with ruthless precision
and an utter asexuality born of years of training and experience.

The guard gaped at the unconscious woman. "But comrade," he said, "there is the matter of food and drink. It is four
days to Moscow. They cannot be kept without food and drink
for four days. I cannot manage on my own. I—"

Anna sighed, but she continued to smile at him. "You will
not have to manage on your own," she said. "I will arrange
for two of my people to join the train in Smolensk and take care
of these people for you. They can survive without food or water
until then, especially if you keep them unconscious. Do not fail
me in this, comrade. And make haste, Comrade Nikoyan," she
commanded. "I am going now."

"Do you need me?" he asked, at last satisfied with Judith
and turning his attention to Boris, to whom he gave an injection
before removing his belt and tie.

Anna shook her head. "Wait here until after Mrs. Hayman
and I have left the train. Then join me at the car as quickly
as possible." She closed her handbag, went into the corridor,
and knocked on number seven. Her heart had settled down,
and she was quite calm again. Undoubtedly Ivan would be
equally pleased to get hold of Judith Stein, if he was busily
accumulating the entire Borodin ménage, and undoubtedly he
would be able to find out just what she was doing in Berlin,
and why she was trying to contact Mrs. Hayman. Certainly it
was all to do with the espionage system set up by Peter Borodin.

It occurred to Anna that when one started being lucky, one just became luckier and luckier.

As for the technicality that Judith Stein, unlike Ilona Hayman, had not intended to go to Russia in the first place, and was thus being kidnapped, well, she did not think that was going to bother Ivan very much.

She knocked on the door of number seven.

"Come in." Again, perfect Russian. And this was a Russian princess she would be addressing. Her heart began to pound again, but in pleasant anticipation. Ivan had always said that Ilona was far more elegant than her sister, and besides, it was impossible to regard Comrade Tatiana Nej as a princess.

Nor was she the least disappointed. Ilona Hayman, wearing a silk dress and expensive shoes, a huge solitaire diamond ring beside her thick gold wedding band, and a diamond-studded watch on her wrist, looked like a being from another world.

"Yes?" she asked, since Anna was temporarily tongue-tied.

"Forgive me, Mrs. Hayman," she said. "My name is Anna Ragosina. I am Commissar Nej's secretary."

"Michael's secretary?"

Anna smiled, and shook her head. "Commissar Ivan Nej."

"Ivan? And he has sent you to meet me here? But the train doesn't get to Smolensk until the day after tomorrow."

"That is the point, Mrs. Hayman. You are still several days from Moscow. And once you reach Russia there will be inevitable delays because you do not have a visa. Even with me to assist you, all we need is some thick-skulled immigration officer who will insist upon telephoning here there and everywhere . . ." She smiled and shrugged. "Besides, this is a most important matter, as Commissar Nej realized the moment he received your telegram. So I have been sent to take you to Moscow today."

"Today?" Ilona frowned at her. "How can you possibly do that?"

"By airplane, Mrs. Hayman."

"Airplane?"

"I have one waiting for me at Tempelhof. It is not far. There is a car waiting as well, which will take us there. And then you will be in Moscow by tonight."

"Good Lord," Ilona said. "I have never flown before. Is it safe?"

"It is perfectly safe," Anna assured her. "And much more comfortable than this slow old train."

"Well—" Ilona hesitated.

"There will be room for your bags and everything," Anna promised her. "I will carry them for you. And Commissar Nej knows how anxious you are to see your son. I must tell you, Mrs. Hayman, that there is great pressure inside Russia for him to be put on trial immediately. After all, he has confessed. Commissar Nej does not know how he can possibly resist these pressures. Certainly he cannot do so for several days. But if you *do* have information that might change the situation, and it could be presented tomorrow . . ."

"Yes," Ilona said, getting up. "Yes of course. It was silly of me even to think of refusing. The sooner I am in Moscow the better." She stepped into the corridor and looked over her shoulder. "Did you say you would bring the bags? They aren't heavy."

"Of course, Mrs. Hayman," Anna said, and smiled.

Flying was not half so terrifying as Ilona had thought it would be. The little airplane did not rise above six thousand feet, and they passed through some patches of heavy cloud that made it bump alarmingly and had her heart and stomach leaping up and down, but for the most part she was able to look down on the unfolding German, and then Polish, and then Russian landscape.

She had been a little disturbed when they had been joined at the airport by Nikoyan, but as Anna Ragosina had explained, Ivan had sent Comrade Nikoyan along just because he alone of the entire OGPU staff would be able to recognize Mrs. George Hayman, had the guard been uncertain who she was. And in any event, Comrade Nikoyan was obviously entirely at the command of this amazingly pretty, amazingly self-possessed, amazingly charming girl. Ivan's secretary. Russia was changing.

She was reminded irresistibly of coming here in 1922, just ten years before, and being met by Catherine Lissitsina, wearing that absurd heavy green uniform. It was very difficult to consider Anna Ragosina, in her summer dress, as belonging to the secret police at all. Now she smiled as she leaned over to point out the various places of interest, or offered Ilona sandwiches and tea from the enormous picnic basket with which she was equipped. If she was more to Ivan than just a secretary, then he was a very lucky man, Ilona thought; and after all, Tattie had treated him very badly over the past few years.

It was dusk when finally they landed at the new airfield just outside Moscow, and by then her very last apprehensions had been allayed. According to Anna Ragosina, Johnnie's release would be really just a formality, after she arrived there. And once again she was being given VIP treatment. The aircraft taxied to the far end of the airfield, where a large black car waited. They disembarked and got immediately into the car, and were hurried into the city.

"Can't we raise the blinds?" Ilona asked. "I'd love to see Moscow again after all this time."

"I'm sorry," Anna said, "but people love to stare into our cars. Besides, it is nearly dark. Tomorrow, why, I have no doubt that Commissar Nej himself will take you on a tour of the city."

"Since I'm here, I'd like to see my sister, of course," Ilona said.

"Of course," Anna agreed.

"Where am I staying?" Ilona asked.

"Ah . . . where you stayed before, Mrs. Hayman. But I am taking you directly to Lubianka. Commissar Nej is waiting for you there, and he knows you are anxious to see your son, as soon as possible."

"Oh, I am," Ilona agreed. "He *is* all right?"

"Of course he is, Mrs. Hayman. But you understand, being in prison at all is a bit depressing. Here we are."

The car turned through the dreaded gates, pulled to a stop in the courtyard, and Ilona felt a sudden apprehension. Again, so like ten years ago. Except that ten years ago, she had been shivering with fear and her thigh had been a mass of pain where she had been hit by the guard. And tonight was different in another way, she realized, as Anna held the door for her; there were no floodlights beating down on them. The courtyard was almost dark. Nor were there any guards waiting to receive her.

"Thank you, Comrade Nikoyan," Anna said, shaking hands. "Your assistance has been greatly appreciated. Come this way,

Mrs. Hayman." She smiled. "Your suitcases can stay here until you are ready to go to your hotel."

Ilona was led along a succession of empty corridors, heels clattering on the wooden floors, until the girl suddenly opened a door for her. She entered a small room, containing a cot with a rough blanket, a square wooden table, two straight chairs, a washstand with a china pitcher and basin, and Ivan Nej.

The car ground to a halt before the enormous mass of people, swaying and chanting, shouting and hurling stones and empty bottles.

"What in the name of God—?" George Hayman leaned forward to peer through the windshield.

"It is a demonstration," explained the driver.

"Looks more like a riot to me," Michael Nej said. He frowned at the young men blocking the road. "Are those policemen?"

"No, no, comrade commissar," said the driver. "They are brownshirts. Nazis, you know. Undoubtedly they are wrecking the shop of some Jew or other. This happens all the time, in Germany today." He turned down a side street and left the noise behind.

"My God!" George leaned back in his seat. "I had no idea things were as bad as this. But I can't believe there is any possibility of Hitler being invited to form a government."

"There is every possibility, my friend," Michael said. "That is what I have been telling you these last few days. The West needs Russia every bit as badly as Russia needs the West. There is something very nasty sprouting here in Central Europe, and it is a growth that will spread like a creeping fungus unless it is soon destroyed."

"Outsiders have no right to destroy something a nation actually wants," George mused, "assuming the nation does actually want it. And assuming, too, that it doesn't get internationally aggressive about it."

"Have you ever known a German who wasn't aggressive?" Michael smiled. "They are Saxons, just like your people, George. They are the most aggressive people that have ever existed, and I am not forgetting the Assyrians. Do you know what is probably the greatest stroke of fortune that the rest of

the world ever got. That Germany and Great Britain decided
to fight each other in 1914 rather than join together to take
over the rest of us."

"It's a point of view," George admitted. "But at least it's
not possible again. I mean, they can shout and scream all they
want, they can throw stones and they can hate the Jews, but
they don't have an army, or a navy, or an air force, and France
is just sitting there, waiting for them to make a wrong move,
in which case they'll choke them out of existence. The Naxis
may be a nasty bunch, but they're a pretty helpless bunch, I'd
say. But I hope to God Judith has the sense to get out before
she gets hurt."

"Why should she?" Michael asked. "All right, so maybe
Germany is not actually her home. It is certainly the home of
several million Jews, and they have been here a very long time.
Why should they move on just because Hitler tells them that
he doesn't like them? All they need to do is organize—"

"And start a jolly little civil war," George pointed out.

"That would surely be preferable to waiting around to be
beaten up," Michael argued.

The car drew to a halt before an apartment building. "This
is the address, comrade commissar," the driver said, and stifled
a yawn. He had driven at maximum speed all the way from
Geneva, and the two men in the back seat, obviously old
friends, had argued and wrangled all the way from Geneva as
well.

"Thank God for that," George said, looking to left and right
as he got out. But this street was quiet, the noise of tumult far
away.

"Wait here, comrade," Michael said, and followed George
into the house. They took the stairs two at a time, reached the
third floor, pressed the bell, and waited. Then George knocked.
"Judith?" he called. "Open up, it's me, George. I have Michael
with me."

"Who is it?" asked a voice, hardly more than a whisper.
"Who is there?"

George frowned at the door. "Herr Stein? Is that you? Joseph? This is George Hayman. Do you remember me?"

"You are alone?"

"I have Michael Nej with me. But don't worry, he's not

trying to take you back to Russia. We've come for Judith and my wife."

Bolts scraped, and the chain was taken off. Joseph Stein peered at them. He had always been a pinch-faced youth, George remembered, from when he had visited the Stein family on Petrograd Island during the war. Now he was a pinch-faced man, with gray skin and trembling hands. "Judith?" he asked. "And Mrs. Hayman? They are not here."

George frowned at him, then pushed him aside and went in.

"Comrade Stein," Michael said, following, "where is Deputy Commissar Petrov?"

"Petrov?" Joseph Stein repeated, staring down the stairwell. "You weren't followed?"

"Of course we weren't followed," George said. "Where—"

"They're after me, you know," Joseph said. "All the time. They follow me, and they watch this building. They're out to get me."

"Who is out to get you?" Michael asked.

"The Nazis," Joseph said. "My God, they are out to get me. They want my blood. Just as they had Mr. Zrinsky's blood. My God, it was terrible."

"Listen to me," George said. "Where is Judith? My wife should be with her, here, and Boris Petrov. Where are they?"

"How should I know?" Joseph asked. "There is a note . . ." He gestured at the table.

George leapt at it, and picked up the note. "Have gone to the station with Boris," Judith had written. "Back in an hour."

"But . . ." George stared at Michael. "What time does the Moscow express pass through Tiergarten?"

"Eleven-fifteen."

"My God, nearly twelve hours ago. My God. Where can they be?"

"The Nazis . . ." Joseph said.

"Do you suppose—" George began.

Michael shook his head. "No, no. Boris Petrov would have far more sense than to get involved with a demonstration. No." His face was unusually serious. "George . . . I think Ivan has proved too smart for us. I think he must have had his people on that train."

"Why? Why, on earth? He couldn't have had any idea Ilona was on her way."

"Well, she's not here now," Michael pointed out. "Neither is Judith and neither is Petrov."

"We must check the hospitals," George said.

"I think they are all on that train, on their way to Russia." George hesitated, chewing his lip in indecision.

"And there is nothing we can do," Michael said, "except follow by tomorrow's train."

"Like hell there isn't," George said. "When will the train get to Warsaw?"

"It's through there already."

"Um. No good. Its next stop is Smolensk, at the border, isn't it? Then that's where we'll go. We'll meet it at Smolensk. But I hope to God you're right, Michael, and they *are* on it."

"Smolensk?" Michael asked. "How on earth can we get there before that train?"

"We're going to drive out to Tempelhof, first thing tomorrow morning, and charter an airplane." George said. "This is 1932, Michael. The modern age. We'll be waiting on the platform when that train comes in."

"Mrs. Hayman," Ivan said. He took her hands and kissed them each in turn. "Ilona. You do not mind if I call you Ilona?"

"Of course I do not," she said. He was clearly in the grip of some very powerful emotion; his cheeks were pink and he could not look her in the eye. "I am very grateful to you for bringing me here so quickly. Is Johnnie—"

"Your son is fine," Ivan said. "Fine. You may serve supper, Anna Petrovna."

"I would like a word with you first, comrade commissar," Anna said.

Ivan frowned at her.

"It is urgent," Anna said.

"You'll excuse me," Ivan said, and left the room with the girl, closing the door behind behind him. Ilona took a turn about the room, then removed her hat, sat down at the table, and crossed her legs. She supposed she would just have to be patient. She did not in the least feel like eating, but if he had arranged some sort of a supper, then he would have to be humored. He really was an *odd* little man, totally confused, she thought, by the position of power into which he had been pitchforked.

The door opened again, and he came in, followed by a female orderly bearing a tray on which there was a bottle of champagne as well as a dish of caviar.

"Not bad news, I hope?" Ilona asked.

Ivan rubbed his hands together. "On the contrary, dear Ilona. Good news. Very good news indeed. Oh, yes. I do apologize for this room, but it seemed the most convenient." He smiled at her. "Other than these rooms, there are only the cells proper, eh? It is a badly designed building." He waved his hand, and the orderly withdrew. Ivan filled two glasses and gave her one. He drank some champagne, and stared at her, except that she realized he was not really staring at her, but at the bodice of her dress.

"I . . ." She searched her brain for something to say. "You have the most charming secretary. And most efficient."

"You are beautiful," Ivan said. "Every time I see you, you grow more beautiful. You are more beautiful now than you were in 1922."

"That's very kind of you," Ilona said, flushing, and suddenly feeling nervous. She hoped he wasn't going to become maudlin and embarrassing. "I'm afraid I've been around a long time."

"For me, you have been around forever," Ivan said, sipping champagne and resting his chin on his hand as he stared at her. "I saw you first in . . . oh, it must have been about 1902. You were sixteen, and Tattie left your bedroom door open one night when I was passing. You were magnificent."

"Saw me?" Ilona felt her flush deepen. "You don't mean . . ."

"And then I had to wait twenty years," Ivan said. "Twenty *years*, to see you again. Here in this prison."

Ilona put down her champagne glass, and pushed back the chair. For the moment she was aware only of anger.

"I watched you being searched," Ivan said. "There is a panel, you know, one-way glass. All the cells have them."

Ilona stood up. "I think I would like to see my son now, Commissar Nej," she said. "Will you arrange it, please."

"Your son," Ivan said, leaning back. "Roditchev's son. God, when I think of that lout pushing into you . . . Undress for me, Ilona. Quickly. Everything. I wish to see you again."

"You're mad," she said. "You have to be mad." She pulled open the door, and gazed at the guard who waited outside. "You . . ."

"He won't harm you," Ivan said. "Unless I instruct him to. Come along in here and undress for me."

Ilona slowly turned, pushing the door shut behind her. "You said I could see Johnnie."

"I have not actually said that," Ivan pointed out. "I did not invite you to Russia. You announced that you were coming. And do you know, there is not a soul in the world who knows you are in Russia? Except my people, of course. You could disappear tonight, or whenever I am ready, and no one would ever know."

Ilona's knees suddenly gave way, and she sat on the bed. He was mad. Mad. And she had placed herself in his power. But screaming was not going to help. She had to keep her head, reason with him, humor him, if possible. By undressing? She repressed an involuntary shudder.

But once she had undressed for Rasputin, as she had had to undress for Roditchev.

"If you don't do as I ask," Ivan said, "I will have you stripped."

Ilona sucked air into her lungs. "If . . . if I do, will you let me see Johnnie?"

He smiled at her. "Of course." He got up and took off his uniform jacket. "I wish to make love to you. If you are good to me, and make love to me, then perhaps it will be possible to let Johnnie go."

She stared at him. "Make love to you? No. My God, no!"

"Because you hate me?"

"No," she lied. Hate? He was the most loathsome creature who ever walked this earth. "Because you are Tattie's husband," she said, attempting to sound logical. "I could not possibly make love to my own sister's husband."

"Bah," he said. "Tattie and I have been estranged for years. She no longer matters. You will make love to me, Ilona Borodina. All my life, I have dreamed of having you. All my life. You will make love to me, or I will have your son shot this night. We will say he was trying to escape. It is all very simple."

Ilona wished her heart would settle down. And her stomach; she felt sick. She found it difficult to believe she was actually here, sharing a cell with a madman.

But she *was* here, and Johnnie was downstairs.

"If . . . if I do . . . everything you ask," she said, "will you let him go?"

"Of course," Ivan said.

He was lying. She was sure of it. But she had no choice. And it could be quick. My God, it had to be quick. She took off her clothes hastily, got into the bed, and closed her eyes as he came towards her. With her eyes closed, he could be anyone, she told herself. Except for his size—he was a short man—and his anxiety. He slobbered over her mouth, held and squeezed her breasts, massaged her bottom, squirmed and gasped while she tried to make herself relax. Suddenly he burst away from her.

She sat up without thinking, eyes open now, stared at him, then down at herself. But he certainly had not come, had not even entered her. Nor, she realized as she looked at him, had she even been in the slightest danger.

"Damn you," he shouted. "Damn you!" he shrieked, and to her horror she saw a tear rolling down his cheek. "Damn you!" He swung his hand, but she rolled away from the blow. "I am going to make you *scream*," he shouted, getting up. He pulled on his clothes, ran to the door, and flung it open. Ilona clutched the blanket to her neck, head spinning, heart pounding, stomach rolling, gazed at the men who hurried in, and at the girl, Anna Ragosina.

Ivan pointed at her. "Take her downstairs," he shouted. "Take her down and throw her in a cell. Leave her there, until I am ready for her. Leave her there." He glared at Ilona. "I am going to make you scream," he yelled. "I am going to make you scream."

There were three guards in the room now, apart from Anna Ragosina. One man seized Ilona's wrists and dragged her from the bed; the blanket clung to her waist for a moment then fell around her ankles. She stared at the girl, then looked down at the blanket. She would not beg them. Not now. But surely Anna Ragosina, who had been so kind . . .

"Take her down," Anna Ragosina said.

Ilona found herself in the corridor, and when she attempted to resist, the barrel of a pistol was thrust into her back with such force she thought it might have broken the skin. She gasped with pain, kept her feet with an effort. And fought against the rising panic in her mind, the churning of her stomach. She had been in the hands of these people before, although she had never before been dragged naked along a corridor by three men. But the essentials were the same. No matter what happened she must keep her nerve, must attempt to get a message out, to Michael, or failing that, to Tattie. My God, yes, Tattie, she thought. If Tattie were to discover she was in here . . .

Now there were women in green uniforms, surrounding her as if she were a wounded butterfly and they a horde of soldier ants. The male guards released her, reluctantly. The women seized her, and were halted by a word from Anna Ragosina.

"She is not to be beaten."

"She must be searched," said the head wardress.

"That has been done," Anna said. "Take her to a cell."

Ilona turned her head in gratitude. Anna had not entirely abandoned her.

A door was opened, and she was thrust into one of the bare rooms she remembered so well. She fell to her knees, turned her head, and gazed at Anna Ragosina.

"Thank you," she said.

"Do not," Anna said. "Those were Commissar Nej's instructions. He wishes to beat you himself."

"But *why*?" Ilona asked, struggling to keep her voice calm. "I have never harmed him. That he worked for my father was an accident of history."

"Everything is an accident of history, Comrade Borodina," Anna said. "You have never understood Commissar Nej, because you have never had to. He is a man who dreams—unattainable dreams. You are one of those. He has dreamed of possessing you, ever since he can remember. And now he has failed to possess you. So there is nothing left for him but to destroy you. And he enjoys destroying people."

Ilona slowly stood up. "Destroying people? You can't be serious. He's mad. Don't you know that? He's absolutely mad. He can't be put in charge of people. He can't be allowed to go around destroying them." She held out her hand. "You must stop him."

Anna smiled. "They say I am as he, Comrade Borodina."

"But . . ." Ilona stared at her. "You can't be. You're young, and kind."

Anna continued to smile. "When Commissar Nej comes in here to beat you, and hurt you, I will be with him. Perhaps he will wish me to hurt you. He likes to watch me hurting people."

"I don't believe you," Ilona said. "I can't. Listen to me. Take a message for me. If Commissar Michael Nej isn't here, go to his wife, Catherine. Or go to my sister, Tatiana. Either of them, Miss Ragosina. Go to them and tell them where I am and what is happening. Please. I will see that you are well rewarded."

Anna had stopped smiling, and her lip might have curled. Because I have begged, Ilona thought. Because she only came in to hear me beg. She sighed, and squared her shoulders. "Very well," she said. "But if you will not do that, I have another favor to ask of you. A mother's favor. Will you grant me that, at least?"

Anna Ragosina gazed at her.

"Will you please *not* let my son know that I am in here?" Ilona said. "It can make no difference to your evidence, or his confession. He has already confessed. I am asking you as a mother, Anna Ragosina, as you will one day hope to be a mother."

"Motherhood," Anna Ragosina said, "is not for one such as I." She turned and left the cell, and the wardress turned the key. Anna walked along the corridor and went up the stairs. She supposed she had never seen such a beautiful woman in all her life, nor such an elegant one. Destroying Ilona Hayman was going to be one of the most horribly exciting things she had ever done. Her entire body tingled, and she was aware of a tightness at nipple and groin. But it was not to be assuaged either by going home to Ivan's tormented bed, which would be more difficult than ever tonight, or by visiting her son. Nikolai was too like his father, at least in bed.

She entered the men's section of the prison, and selected the right key from those offered her by the night guard. There was no need to descend once again into the bowels of the earth; Prince Roditchev was a privileged prisoner, and had one of the rooms on the upper floor. She unlocked the door, switched on the light, and gazed at him. He slept on his side, facing her, the blanket up to his waist. Since he *was* a privileged prisoner, he had been granted clothes as well as the bed, table, chairs, and washing facilities. But he undressed to sleep. And certainly he had to be Ilona Hayman's son.

His eyes opened. He blinked at her once, and then sat up. She stepped inside and closed the door behind her.

"Well," he said. "Is it about to begin?"

Anna sat down at the table and crossed her knees. "No one is going to harm you, your excellency," she said. "Don't you understand that? You have confessed. You have been shown to the press. When you appear in court you must be exactly as healthy and as alert as you are now."

"And Natasha Brusilova? Is she healthy and alert?"

"Of course she is," Anna said.

"After what you people did to her?"

"They did nothing to her, Prince Roditchev. That was a ruse. One of our secretaries did the screaming. Brusilova was brought here for you to see and then taken away again."

John Hayman stared at her. "I don't believe you."

Anna shrugged. "It does not matter whether you believe me or not, although you may like to ask yourself why I should tell you a lie about that. I have no interest in putting your mind at rest about her."

"And those confessions I signed? Are they also ruses?"

Anna shook her head. "No, we need those. There have been acts of sabotage at several of the hydroelectric plants. And besides, these people are all Englishmen. We need to put them on trial to show that the Soviet Union is beset by international terrorists."

"And that they are innocent makes no difference to you at all."

"I wouldn't say they are *all* innocent, your excellency. There have certainly been acts of sabotage. It is an unfortunate aspect of life that it is sometimes necessary to harm a few innocent people in order to catch the guilty one. But the guilty one must be caught."

"Not a western philosophy, I'm afraid," he said. "Well,

Comrade Ragosina, you have undoubtedly scored a great victory, at my expense. If you are not going to ill-treat me by leaving the light on, would you mind leaving? I'd like to get some sleep, if I can."

He lay down, the blanket pulled to his chin. Anna Ragosina got up to stand beside him. His eyes opened again, and he saw her watching him.

"And dream?" she asked. "Of Natasha Brusilova?"

"I hope so."

"It will do you no good," she said. "You will never see her again, you know. After five years in a labor camp you will never wish to see her again. They are very rough places, and there are no women. It may be that after five years in a labor camp you will never wish to see any woman again."

"Then I'd better dream while I still can," he said.

Anna sat beside him, pushed hair from his forehead. "It will be several months before you are tried and convicted," she said. "I could make those months very pleasant for you, Prince Roditchev. Very, very pleasant." Her hand drifted from his head to his neck and then on to his shoulder, moving the blanket as it did so, while her other hand played with the top button of her blouse.

"Go to hell, Anna Ragosina," he said. "I'd sooner nest with a black widow spider."

Michael Nej looked along the Smolensk platform at the three men who stood together, watching the approaching train. "Secret police," he said. "I think we may have got here just in time."

"I hope so," George Hayman said. "By Christ I hope so."

Michael glanced at him curiously. He had never known George so agitated. Indeed, he had never known George to be agitated at all, even when, as very young men, they had been under Japanese fire.

"You must love her very much," he observed. "Even after twenty years, you must still love her very much."

George flushed. "I guess I do. I suppose, from time to time, I've forgotten that." He gave a guilty smile. "Men do."

"Indeed," Michael agreed, gravely.

"But never again. I'm not even going to let her out of my sight, ever again. I'm . . . let's get aboard."

The train was pulling to a stop. They ran for the first-class carriage, got to the door at the same time as the three men.

"There is no admittance," said the guard, looking at Michael.

"I am Commissar Nej, you fool," Michael said. "Stand aside."

"Commissar Nej?" The guard looked at George, then at the three men.

"Commissar Nej?" asked one of the men.

"Yes," Michael said, and produced his passport. "You may look at that, and then you can tell me what you are doing here."

The men opened the passport, looked at it, and handed it back. Then he glanced at his companions. "We are carrying out our orders, comrade commissar."

"Repeat them to me."

"I cannot do that, comrade commissar. But they were given to us by Commissar Ivan Nej himself. Your brother."

"Indeed? Well, I am countermanding them. You—" He turned to the guard. "You have a Mrs. George Hayman on this train."

"Mrs. Hayman?" The guard turned pale. "No, no, comrade commissar. I have no Mrs. Hayman. There is no one by that name on this train."

"You are lying to me," Michael said. "I am going to look into every compartment, and when I find Mrs. Hayman, I am going to have you arrested, comrade. You three," he snapped, at the still-undecided OGPU men, "wait here in order to arrest this man when I tell you." He climbed the step, George at his heels.

The guard hurried at their heels. "It was orders, comrade commissar. Orders from Comrade Ragosina."

Michael stopped before the first door. "Comrade Ragosina has been on this train?"

The guard's head pumped up and down. "In Berlin, comrade commissar. She was in Berlin."

"My God. Which compartment? Hurry man, or you will go to Siberia."

The guard drew a long breath. "Compartment seven, comrade commissar."

They opened the door, switched on the light, and looked Judith Stein and Boris Petrov.

"Dear God," George cried. "Are they dead?"

Michael shook his head, placed his ear close to Judith's mouth. "Drugged."

"I inject them every six hours," the guard explained. "It as orders from Comrade Ragosina."

Michael threw up the blinds and pulled down the window. You," he shouted at the waiting OGPU men, oblivious to the rowd gathering on the platform, the heads beginning to emerge om other windows on the train. "Fetch an ambulance immediately. You," he said to the guard, "will hold the train here ntil these people have been taken to the hospital. And you ad better hope that they recover unharmed. Now tell me, what as happened to Mrs. Hayman?"

"She—she left the train in Berlin, comrade commissar. With Comrade Ragosina."

"Left?" George demanded. "Or was taken?"

"She went of her own free will, sir," the guard said. "I wear it."

"Easy enough to accomplish," Michael said. "Ilona would ave no reason for mistrusting that girl. And she was in a hurry o see Johnnie, remember?"

"In Berlin?" George asked.

"They must have been using an airplane as well."

"But . . ." George frowned at him. "Then Ilona has been in Moscow since yesterday afternoon."

"Yes," Michael said. "We must hurry." He ran outside and ound one of the OGPU men still waiting by the door. "I am utting those two people in your trust," he said. "One is a eputy commissar for foreign affairs, and the other is a heroine f the revolution. If a hair on their heads is harmed, I personally m going to send you to Siberia. Have them taken to a hospital, nd when they are conscious, and tell them that I am in charge f them and that I will return for them as soon as I can. Do ou understand me?"

"Yes, comrade commissar." The man snapped to attention.

"And where are your colleagues?"

"Comrade Malinsky has already gone for an ambulance, as ou commanded, comrade commissar."

"Good." Michael said. "And the other?"

"I do not know where he has gone, comrade commissar. the policeman said. But his gaze was drifting. Michael followe its direction, and saw the third OGPU man in a telephon booth, speaking hurriedly into the handset.

Ivan Nej sat at his desk and crumpled pieces of paper int little balls. It was a matter of arriving at the right momen How many hours had he been waiting to arrive at the righ moment? But now . . . *now* . . . now he almost felt he coul take her, as a man. If he still wanted to. But he did not wan to. He could not take the risk, and in any event it would b useless now. There would be no enjoyment in it. At the decisiv moment she had humiliated him. She had been the princes she had always been, and he had been the bootblack he ha always been. He supposed he would carry that scar to his grave

But he could reduce her from a princess. He could mak her into a shivering wreck of a woman, crawling to his fee to beg for some respite from pain and misery and humiliation He wanted her, but only as a princess. If he could not hav that, then he would make sure that no one would ever wan her again.

He threw the last piece of paper into the basket, and stoo up. Anna Ragosina stood with him. She had watched hir throughout the morning, throughout their frugal lunch. She ha known what was going on inside his mind, what torments h was going through. Anna Ragosina knew altogether too mucl about him, that was the trouble.

And now she wished to know even more. But this was on thing he did not want her to know.

"You will stay here," he said.

"Here, comrade commissar? But—"

"You will stay here. She is a princess. She is not for you Stay here." He went to the door. "Tell them to put her i interrogation room number one. I am going down now."

He closed the door behind him and went down the stairs His heart was pounding, and he could feel his entire bod swelling. He *could* take her now. He was sure of it . . . Excep that he was sure of nothing where Ilona Borodina was con cerned. She had only to look at him and he would be afrai to touch her.

He hesitated at the door, then opened it and went in. She waited, in the center of the room, between two guards; her wrists were handcuffed in front of her. Her hair was untidy, but had lost nothing of its golden splendor; it draped over her shoulders and down her back, seemed almost protective in the way it attempted to shroud her face. But when she saw him she tossed her head, in a girlish, almost Tattie-ish gesture, the better to see him.

"That one," he said.

There were iron shackles set in the wall at various heights. The one he had chosen was on a level with her waist, and was now passed through the chain of the handcuffs before being closed again. Secured here, with her back to him, she was helpless; she couldn't even kick without banging her knees against the wall.

"Outside," Ivan said.

The guards left the room, and closed the door.

Ilona turned her head to look at him. Once again she had to toss away the hair clouding her face. "Why?" she asked. "Why do you hate me so, Ivan Nikolaievich?"

Ivan went to the other wall, where the whips were kept. He selected a thin steel rod, which bent and sang even as he took it from the wall. One stroke of this would reduce her to gibbering incoherence. He knew this from experience.

"Because you are Ilona Borodina," he said.

She licked her lips, gazed at the whip. But she could know nothing of what it could do. She was more apprehensive of the humiliation than of the pain.

"I don't understand," she said. "You are married to my sister."

"And one day, perhaps, princess, I am going to have her down here as well," he said.

She shook her head. "You *are* mad," she said. "Quite mad. For God's sake, Ivan . . ."

"Shut up," he said. "Shut up. The only sound I want to her from you is a scream." He grinned at her. "You may scream now, if you choose."

Ilona gazed at him. Her face was expressionless, but there was pity in her eyes. She felt pity for him. She, who was about to be destroyed by him, felt pity for *him*.

"Bitch," he shouted, and swished the whip. Her entire body

rippled, from shoulder to ankle, as her muscles contracted. But she kept her eyes open, gazing at him. She had *known* he was not about to hit her. She had *known*. No one could await a blow from such a whip with her eyes open.

He panted. It was a simple matter of transmitting strength from his brain into his shoulder into his wrists and then into his hand. A simple matter of watching the steel bite into the white flesh, of watching the blood come welling from the thin line that would be cut across her body. A simple matter of watching that haughty face dissolve, that firm mouth sag open, those eyes dilate, and that head toss back in agony. A simple matter of listening to the scream that would issue from those lips. A simple matter...

The door opened. "Outside," he shrieked, the whip cutting the air. Anna Ragosina had to jump backwards to avoid being slashed across the face.

"It is urgent," she shouted. "Comrade commissar, it is urgent. A telephone call from Smolensk. Urgent, comrade."

Ivan got himself under control with an effort. "Smolensk?" he muttered. "What from Smolensk?"

"Comrade Habalov, from Smolensk, comrade commissar. It is your brother. He was on the train."

Ivan stared at her.

"With Mr. Hayman. They are on their way to Moscow now, by plane."

Ivan turned to look at the woman. In the hours remaining to him he could destroy her. But she had heard the names. She returned his gaze, and now there was no longer pity in her eyes. Whatever he did to her, if he touched her at all, he was lost. As he knew. Not even Stalin would protect him after an act of personal revenge, personal brutality. Especially if the Americans were to become involved.

He threw the whip to the floor, and Anna Ragosina stared in amazement at the tear trickling down his cheek.

"*And* he has arrested Clive," Tattie accused, arm outflung, finger pointing at the far side of the office. "Just took him from his hotel the moment he got home from the academy. Talk about a personal vendetta. If you have harmed a hair on Clive's head, Ivan, I am going to twist your balls right off."

Ivan seemed to settle lower into his chair. He did not want

to look at any of their faces, at this moment. Least of all did he want to look at Joseph Vissarionovich's face, because Joseph Vissarionovich had his fate in his hand.

But as usual, Stalin wore an expression of extreme benevolence, as he sifted through the papers on his desk. "As I understand it," he said, "this man Bullen is among those listed by Prince Roditchev as being members of the conspiracy. He is in fact listed as one of the principals."

"It is absolute nonsense," Tattie declared. "If one hair on his body has been harmed . . ."

"Now you know that cannot be true, Joseph," Michael Nej protested. "You know that John's confession was obtained under duress—"

"Duress?" Stalin inquired mildly. "The young man has not been harmed, so far as I know."

"Of course it was under duress," Tattie said. "The harpy that Ivan keeps tied up somewhere in his lavatory came and arrested my Brusilova, and took her down to the Lubianka. She wasn't even questioned, she was just shown to Johnnie, and then taken away again. But he thought she was being tortured. He's a gentleman, and he's in love with her."

"I'm afraid the whole thing has got out of hand, Comrade Stalin," George said, speaking quietly. "When this story breaks to the world's press, any idea of American recognition of a regime that could permit such things to happen is quite out of the question. As for the League of Nations—"

"They wouldn't touch us with a barge pole," Michael said.

"Yes," Stalin said, thoughtfully. "Therefore, gentlemen, we must endeavor to make sure that the story never does break to the press, as you put it, Mr. Hayman—at least in its present unacceptable form. I shall need your assistance."

"*My* assistance?" George inquired. "You're a considerable optimist, comrade."

"I am trying to be a realist. Now tell me this, Mr. Hayman: Is Mrs. Hayman well?"

"As well as can be expected."

"She is unharmed? Then, is her mind affected by what she was forced to undergo?"

"Ilona isn't a schoolgirl," George said. "But she's under sedation. And I doubt she'll ever wish to return to Russia again."

Stalin nodded, as if to suggest that would be a good idea. "And your little Brusilova is unharmed," he said to Tattie. "And your Mr. Bullen—and your prince, Michael . . . a strange business that, eh?" He allowed his sleepy eyes to rest on George for a moment before continuing. "Indeed, none of the English technicians arrested has been harmed. Now, they will have to stand trial—"

"Now wait a moment," George said.

"Please allow me to finish, Mr. Hayman. Their arrest has been made the subject of a great deal of publicity. Simply to let them go would involve a great deal of explaining, and this we have just agreed is not practical. Besides, let me remind you that Prince Roditchev is most undoubtedly guilty, at least of espionage. The contents of his notebook prove that beyond a shadow of doubt. So, gentlemen, I propose that they be tried, which will happen as soon as possible, and be convicted and sentenced, and then deported, all of them. I give you my word in the interim—" He smiled at Tattie. "—not a hair on their heads shall be harmed."

"But—they will know they are innocent," Michael protested. "Bullen and his people. They will say so to the world."

"No doubt," Stalin agreed. "But guilty men often claim that they are innocent."

"It will be a stigma for them to carry for the rest of their lives."

Stalin shrugged. "What stigma? Of having tried to bring down our regime? That will make them heroes to a great number of people. That is my proposal, gentlemen. Please remember that you may be able to force me to let the British go, but you cannot force me to let Ivan Roditchev go, in view of the evidence. As a Russian he could well face the death penalty. Instead of which he, along with the Englishman, will be safely home within six months. I give you my word. Of course, none of them will ever be allowed inside Russia again."

"What did you say?" Tattie shouted.

Stalin continued to smile. "But I am sure our commissar for culture, as well as our commissar for foreign affairs, will find it necessary to travel abroad from time to time."

Ivan made a strangled sound from the corner.

"But all of this is conditional on our recognition by your

government, Mr. Hayman," Stalin went on. "And Russian acceptance by the League of Nations as a member."

"Hm," George said. "I have no doubt that your extreme clemency in the matter of the convicted British saboteurs will be greatly admired in the West, Comrade."

Stalin continued to smile, deciding to ignore the sarcasm.

"But," George continued, "I'm afraid I can't altogether go along with the idea that the people responsible for this travesty of justice, responsible for the attempt to humiliate and break my wife, should get away scot free."

"Indeed, I entirely agree with you," Stalin said.

Ivan Nej sat bolt upright, and for the first time looked directly at his master.

"I have been reading these reports very carefully," Stalin said, "and it does seem to me that this assistant of yours has proved herself somewhat over-zealous, Ivan Nikolaievich. It was she who carried out the arrest of this John Harding—correctly, no doubt, but after that she seems to have gone quite mad. It was her order that commanded the arrest of Natasha Brusilova, and all the other people involved by Roditchev; it was she personally who went to Berlin and not only kidnapped Mrs. Hayman from the train, but kidnapped Judith Stein and Comrade Petrov. I am afraid, Ivan Nikolaievich, that there can be no room in your department for people as misguidedly zealous as that."

"She will be punished, Joseph Vissarionovich," Ivan gabbled. "My God, she will be punished. Five years—"

"In a labor camp," Stalin said. "Justice must be *seen* to be done."

"In . . . in a labor camp?" Ivan asked.

"That is what I said."

Ivan gulped. "Yes, Comrade Stalin. It will be done."

"Good," Stalin said. "Good. Well, gentlemen, well Tatiana Dimitrievna . . ."

"It was not Anna Ragosina who tried to rape my wife and then threatened her with a steel whip," George said.

"Ah," Stalin said. "Yes, that was regrettable. But Mr. Hayman, think of it. There was Comrade Nej, in the midst of investigating what he had been told by this Ragosina was an enormous anti-Soviet plot, at the center of which was your

wife's son, proved guilty by the contents of his notebooks, and
then Comrade Ragosina produces the man's mother, whom she
claims is equally guilty. Now, is it not to Comrade Nej's credit
that, knowing who she was, he did not hand her over to the
tender mercies of this female Dracula, but interrogated her
himself?"

"Interrogated?" George shouted.

"Interrogated," Stalin said firmly. "There are many different
ways of interrogation. And you should note, Mr. Hayman, that
Commissar Nej never actually touched your wife. He endeavored to frighten her into admitting her guilt. But I am sure
he never had any intention of harming her in any way. Did
you, Ivan Nikolaievich?"

Ivan appeared to awaken from a deep sleep. "Never, Comrade Stalin."

"One day," George said. "I am going to find myself alone
with you, Ivan Nikolaievich, all over again. And then I am
going—"

"To twist your balls right off," Tattie said. "I am going to
help you."

"Well, gentlemen." Stalin stood up. "Will you excuse me
now? I must go to my wife. She is not well..." He sighed
and turned for the door before they could see his face.

"A labor camp?" Anna Ragosina asked. "A labor camp?"
Her voice dropped to a whisper. "Five *years*? You cannot,
comrade commissar. You cannot."

"Five years," Ivan said. "It is not so long, Anna Petrovna.
And you are young. Why, in five years you will be but twenty-
seven."

"And for five years I will have been starved and beaten,
and had my fingers torn to shreds," she said. "They will cut
off my hair." She touched the glossy black locks. "My God,
comrade commissar, what will I *be*, in five years?"

"That is up to you."

She gazed at him. "I had thought you were fond of me."

"I am, very fond of you. But you have exceeded your
authority, and you must be punished."

"I, I have exceeded my authority? I—"

"You have exceeded your authority, Comrade Ragosina.
There is no doubt about that, and no one is going to believe

anything different. As to what one makes of a labor camp, even if one determines to *survive* a labor camp, that is a personal decision. I would think about it very carefully, if I were you. You have one hour, then you will be arrested."

"Am I not even to be tried?" she asked.

He shook his head. "I have written out a confession for you. You have only to sign it."

"And if I refuse?"

Ivan shrugged. "Then you will be certified as insane, and sent to a psychiatric hospital. You may well find that less pleasant than a labor camp. I am told that a psychiatric ward, especially for those whose madness takes the form of opposing the state, can be even less pleasant than our Lubianka."

Anna hesitated, biting her lip, then she picked up the pen and signed the paper.

"Good girl," Ivan said. "Now go away and think about your future. As I said, you have one hour. Then you will be arrested." He smiled at her. "I will send Nikoyan to arrest you, and search you. He will enjoy that."

She stared at him, hardly breathing.

"And take off your holster now," he said. "Carefully."

Anna unbuckled her belt and laid the holster on her desk. Then she turned and left the room.

He wishes me to commit suicide, she thought, walking slowly down the corridor. It would be best for him, best for everyone if I were just to throw myself out of the window.

Best for me, too. She realized she was shivering.

But death was final. It was possible, even for young women on their own—even for a young woman who might possibly encounter someone she had sent there ahead of her—to survive a labor camp. It was *possible*. And when she came back, she would still have her hate.

She found herself before the cell door, unlocked it, and stepped inside. John Hayman sat at the table, reading a novel by Gorky; it was part of the reading material she herself had supplied to this most favored of prisoners.

"Well, comrade," she said. "Has your father been to see you yet?"

He frowned at her. "Have you gone mad, Comrade Ragosina?"

"Mad?" She gave a brief laugh. "Oh, yes, I am mad. I am

so mad I am being sent to a labor camp. There," she said. "Does that thought not fill you with joy?"

He stared at her.

"So," she said, "is there anything you wish of me, before I leave you?" She licked her lips. "Is there nothing you wish of this body? It will not be the same when next you see it, if ever you see it again."

"A labor camp?" he asked. "You? But why?"

She shrugged, and smiled. "I have made too many mistakes, comrade." She went closer, stood against him. "You were promised to me, in the course of time, but now you will be set free, soon. You will be able to walk with your Natasha again, and hold her hand, and kiss her mouth." She listened to feet in the corridor outside. "Like this," she said, and kissed him on the mouth. He stood absolutely still, and she stepped away. "Or maybe," she said, "not like that. But he *is* your father, Ivan Mikhailovich Nej. He *is* your father. Since you are so fortunate, enjoy it."

She turned away, stepped aside to allow Michael into the room, gave him a brief bow, and left.

"That harpy," Michael said. "What did she want?"

"To . . . to say good-bye," Johnnie said. "She is to be sent to a labor camp. I'm afraid I don't understand."

"You will. It is all part of a deal we made with Comrade Stalin. Or rather the one your stepfather made."

"And you—" Johnnie stared at him. "She said . . ."

"Did you believe her?"

"My mother—"

"Will confirm what I say here today. She committed a great crime, a great social crime, for those days, Ivan Mikhailovich. From the consequences of which she was rescued by George Hayman. We were enemies then. Now we are friends." He shrugged. "I am your father. I am also a Communist, and you have been brought up to hate the very word. I cannot expect you to change, and I would never ask you to leave your mother. In fact, I would ask you to go back to America with her, and live there, and be happy. You cannot return here, but perhaps I will be able to come and see you, from time to time. I should like to do that. But Ivan, I would ask you to stop hating."

"You can support a regime that employs people like your

brother?" Johnnie asked. "And allows them to do as they please, to murder thousands of people whose only crime is that they are not Communists?"

Michael sighed. "We are still in a state of revolution, Ivan, and revolutions not only require bloodshed, and occasionally brutality, but they also have a habit of throwing up the men and women who are prepared to carry out such deeds. I hope, before I die, to see Russia a more acceptable, a more civilized community."

"You hope," Johnnie said.

He shrugged again. "It can hardly be more than that, at the moment. But without hope, what is a man?"

Johnnie hesitated. "And Natasha Brusilova?" he asked at last.

"You will be allowed to say good-bye to her."

"Good-bye?"

"She cannot possibly be allowed to accompany you at this time. Ivan, to the world at large you are being expelled from the Soviet Union for acts of sabotage and espionage. For God's sake, be thankful for your blessings. In a year or two, who knows—"

"A year or two," Johnnie muttered.

"It is not so long a time. Now tell me, have you no embrace for your father? You may believe that I have watched over your progress with the greatest interest, that I have always loved you, and that I *shall* always love you."

"Even if I hate?"

"Even if you hate, Ivan Mikhailovich."

Johnnie hesitated, and then stepped forward, into his father's arms.

There were thirteen to dinner.

"An unlucky number," Michael Nej smiled, "if we believe in luck. But we, my friends, have triumphed over luck."

He looked around the table. He had never supposed it would be possible to witness such a gathering: he and Catherine and Nona, a miniature replica of her mother; Ilona and George and Johnnie; Tattie, with twelve-year-old Gregory and thirteen-year-old Svetlana, very much a Borodina; Natasha Brusilova, all blushes at finding herself in such company; and Boris Petrov and Judith Stein. All his women, he thought, in one room. All George Hayman's, too. What a strange yoke they wore together.

He stood up. "To the future. May we be able to meet again, often, and may we always be similarly blessed."

A brief hesitation, and then they all stood, to sip their glasses of vodka—even the little ones, on this most special occasion.

"To have you here, for the last time, and with Johnnie," Michael said to Ilona, seated on his right. "If you only knew how much I regret what happened."

Ilona shrugged, and smiled. "I feel sorry for him. Really I do. To *want*, so very badly, and be unable . . . well—" She raised her glass to her lips.

"And if he had succeeded?" Michael asked. "Or am I being too personal?"

"How could you ever be too personal with me?" Another shrug. "Then, perhaps, I could hate him. But he didn't. Are you pleased with your son?"

"Enormously so. Even if I could wish . . ." He sighed. "But dreams are for children."

"He understands, I think," she said. "And he loves one of your people. There is a hope for the future."

She smiled at the boy, but he was not looking at her. At that moment all his thoughts were fixed on Natasha.

"I suppose I'm still confused," Johnnie confessed to her. "You know, most of my life I have been influenced to hate everything Communist, even everything Nej, especially by my uncle. Now . . . how *you* must hate *me*."

"Me?" Her eyes were wide.

"Well, my uncle murdered your parents."

"But you hate your uncle, as do I."

Johnnie nodded. "Yet you must live here, for a while."

"For a while?"

"Because . . ." He gazed at her. They had known each other so very briefly, had done no more than hold each other in their arms once or twice. They had talked, but they had never allowed themselves to dream, and he had never been sure whether or not she had been permitting him her love merely because he was a prince. "Because I love you," he said. "I would like to love you."

"Like to?"

"If you would let me."

"Oh, your excellency..."

"No excellency," he said. "Plain Comrade Hayman. Or Comrade Nej would be more accurate."

"To be named Nej is better than to be a prince, in Russia today."

He smiled. "*Touché*. Natasha, I am to be deported. Never to be allowed into Russia again, they say. But that is not to say you will never be allowed to leave. I will work for that, Natasha, if you will allow me to."

"To be with you?"

"To marry me."

Once again her eyes were enormous. Then she said, "I could never work against the Soviet, Mr. Hayman. It is my country."

"Haven't you heard?" he asked. "We're all to be friends. My government is going to recognize yours. As my father says, the future could be quite bright."

"And your Uncle Peter?"

He shook his head. "Never again. I know now that George was always right. Uncle Peter belongs to the past." He held her hand under the table. "Will you come to me, if I can arrange it?"

She gazed at him for some seconds. Then she said, "If you wish me to, Mr. Hayman."

"Then I think you could try calling me Johnnie."

Her fingers squeezed his. "Johnnie."

"Young lovers," Tattie sighed, and squeezed Clive Bullen's hand. "It is easier for them."

"Not really," he said. "They have never really loved."

"Things are more difficult for us than ever. I must come to you, Clive, from now on. But I will. I promise."

"Why not now?"

She made a move, and shrugged. "All my girls, all my young musicians. Poor Dimitri Dimitrievich... He is in deep trouble, because they think his music is reactionary. I must defend him. I must defend them all. I must make sure that they all are able to develop their talents according to their talents, and not according to the ideas of some tasteless bureaucrat. Can you understand that?"

"I can both understand and respect that," he said. "You are an amazing person, Tatiana Dimitrievna."

"I like music," she said. "And young people, and laughter. It is as simple as that. But I will come to you, Clive. I swear it. As soon as my work here is finished, I will come to you."

"And when will that be?"

"I do not know. But it will not be long now. And when it is finished, I will *know* it is finished, and I will come to you."

At the other end of the table George sat next to Judith. "If there is anything," he was saying, "anything at all..." He flushed.

"You'll never change, George," Judith said. "But really, I have a lot to do."

"In Berlin, with Joseph?"

"It is the most important place to be, at the moment."

"It is very dangerous," Boris said. "I keep asking her to come to Paris. I will be stationed there now, you know. And there is enough to be done for the Jews in Paris, without placing yourself in personal danger."

"Oh, nonsense," Judith said. "How would I feel, sitting in luxury in Paris while my people are engaged in a life-and-death struggle in Germany?"

"And supposing," George said, "that Hitler does get invited to form a government?"

"We will cross that bridge when we come to it," Judith said. "But you have to agree that he will stand more chance of being elected if all of us who know that he is in the wrong merely steal away into the night."

"That's true," George said. "But—" Like everyone else he turned his head to look at the door as the waiter came in, bearing a silver tray.

"It is a telegram," Michael said, peering at it. "For Mrs. Hayman."

"For me?" Ilona took the envelope, slit it with one glossy-tipped finger, and took out the sheet of paper. "Oh, my God."

"Tell me," Tattie cried. "Read it."

Ilona drew a long breath. "DON'T PANIC STOP MARRIED BETH TODAY STOP LETTER FOLLOWS STOP LOVE STOP GEORGE." She gazed at George. "What are we to do?"

"Drink a toast to them," George said. "He loves her. And

imagine she loves him." He stood up, glass held high. "To he Haymans. And the Nejs, of course."

Ivan Nej sat at his desk and looked across the empty office t the desk opposite. It was dusk, and there was no reason any onger to remain here, but there was no longer any reason to go home to his apartment, equally empty.

As was his life. He was Stalin's creature. He had adopted hat way of life deliberately, because he had surveyed the eadership and decided that Stalin would be the eventual win-ner. And he had no doubt he had chosen wisely. But as a creature, he could live only when his master allowed him air to breathe.

And dreams to dream. Perhaps that was it. Dreams should never come true. For just two days his had been promising to do that, to break that essential natural law, and the result had been, inevitably, catastrophe. So now he had nothing. Except hate, he realized. Because just as the dreams had been named Borodin, so the rock on which he had foundered had been named Borodin—the very thought of what the name meant, what it had always represented. And would always represent to him? There was a new dream, a better dream, surely, for the future: to destroy every vestige of Borodinism in the world. There was a task to anticipate, no matter what it cost, how long it took.

With a clanking and a groaning the train drew into the Tiergarten. Judith got up and straightened her dress. It had been washed and pressed so often during her enforced absence that it was starting to look a little worn.

"Well," she said. "There was an odd three weeks. I guess it's good-bye again, at least for a while."

"Not immediately," Boris said. "I think I'll see you safely home."

"Oh, really, Boris."

"I'm not joking." He escorted her out of the compartment and handed her down to the platform. "I don't trust Berlin anymore. I don't think anyone does."

"It looks the same to me," she said, holding his hand as they went towards the exit. "Although I keep expecting to see that dreadful Anna Ragosina lurking behind every post. How do you suppose she is faring, in Siberia?"

"Badly, I suppose," he said. "Everyone fares badly in Siberia. Judith—won't you reconsider?"

"Boris." She sat beside him in the back of the taxi. "I know that, well . . . you are probably the best man I know. But I can't just be a housewife." She smiled. "Or even a housemistress. I've—oh, God, it sounds terrible to say it, but I've been *involved*, too much. I stood on the Moscow barricades in December 1905, with Lenin—and with Ilona, come to think of it—while the Cossacks were preparing to charge. I watched Rasputin die. I was there when the tsarina and her children were arrested. And I was with Michael Nej when he beat the Whites. I *can't* just step away, now. I tried it, once, and it didn't work."

He sighed. "I understand. Although I think you are wrong. I think you would fill as important a role in Paris as here. And anyway, I think you have done enough. You are entitled to some happiness."

"No one is *entitled* to anything." The taxi had stopped, and she got out. "You have a train to catch."

"There are other trains." He got out behind her and escorted her into the doorway. The landlady stared at them as if she were seeing ghosts. "Fräulein Stein? But—"

"We left rather suddenly," Judith explained. "But we are back, really and truly." She started up the stairs.

"But Fräulein Stein," the woman said. "Fräulein . . ." She began to cry.

Judith looked down at her, and then up again, and started to run up the stairs. She reached the door of the apartment only to find it standing open. It had, in fact, been torn from its hinges. And inside was a total shambles—furniture overturned, papers scattered, books torn from their cases. "Oh, my God," she said.

Boris's hands closed on her arm, and she pulled herself free and ran to the bannister. "My brother," she shouted. "Where is my brother?"

"They came," the landlady said. "Brownshirts. I ran for the police, Fräulein, but there were none to be found. They broke down the door, the brownshirts, and they went in. I heard Mr Stein screaming, but he could not fight them. They dragged m down the stairs, and right there on the sidewalk, they beat m, and beat him, until he was dead."

"Oh, my God." Judith sank to her knees.

"And the police?" Boris asked.

The landlady shrugged. "They came, and they went again. ey asked me if I could identify the men, but if I did that . . ."

Judith raised her head. "What are we to do, Boris? What n I do?"

He held her shoulders, raised her to her feet. "I don't know," said. "I don't know. But you can't stay here." He helped r to the stairs. "There will be a train for Paris in an hour."

How good it was to lie in her own bed, after so long, and much. To know that she was safe, and more important, that the children were safe. Even Johnnie. And even George nior, she supposed; certainly they seemed very much in love.

And it was so unfair. She rolled over to face George. "That or girl," she said. "That poor, poor girl. Has she ever had e slightest break?"

"It would be difficult to find one," he agreed.

"Do you still . . . ?"

"Of course I worry about her," he said. "But not in the way u mean. I never knew how much I loved you, my darling, til last month. If you can ever forgive me. . . ."

She squeezed his fingers. "Forgive you? Oh, George, I love u. And if you love me, I'm the happiest woman in the world. r I *should* be. George. . . ." She raised herself on her elbow. want to *do* something."

"What do you mean?" He opened his eyes.

"I . . . these past few days, I've realized just how *useless* I n. How useless as well as how fortunate. I just lie back and joy life, and you, and—and everything, while everyone else s to *fight* for their happiness."

"You fought for yours," he said. "And won."

She kissed him on the nose. "That was a long time ago. I n't want to fight anymore. But I want to work. To contribute mething to life. Can you understand that?"

"I can understand it. I'm not sure I go along with the idea your getting a job, though."

"Not even if you gave me one?"

"Me? On the paper?"

"Well, I was thinking about a magazine."

He studied her face. She had obviously given this muc
more thought than she pretended.

"Go on."

"Think of *Time*. And then of *Life*. And then..."

"They're not really comparable."

"But suppose their formats were combined. The house coul
do with a magazine, George. You know it could."

"And you'd be in charge of it."

"Well... under your jurisdiction, of course. I'm not prom
ising we'd make a vast profit, but it would fill a *need*. I'
sure it would."

"And it would keep you happy," he mused. "You'll hav
to think of a name."

"Oh, I have," she said. "*You*. You can't be more immediat
than that. I'm not just going to aim at women, or certain ag
groups—I want it to appeal to everyone."

"Doesn't every publisher," he said, and pulled her dow
for a kiss. "You can have a go if you like. I've an idea there'
going to be enough news for everyone, over the next fe
years."

"What do you mean, George?"

"There's going to be a war," he said. "No matter how yo
look at it. When Hitler comes to power, there's going to b
a war."

"For all of us?"

"I'm afraid so," he said. "Just pray to God we don't let hir
get too powerful first."

"Another war," she shivered. "It's almost unimaginable.'

She was in his arms. "Yes," he said, kissing her forehead
"Let's count our blessings while we may."

An Excerpt
From
THE BORODINS
Book IV
HOPE
AND
GLORY

To Be Published in May 1982

John and Natasha's feet were soft on the grass of the lawn stretching down from the academy. Above them the moon was beginning to loom beyond the cowsheds. Tattie's dance academy in Moscow seemed a remote memory this evening. It was as though they had been here in the country, at the new academy, forever.

"I don't really want to leave this place, you know," Natasha said. "I think it is the most heavenly spot on earth. Even lovelier than Papa's farm. I suppose because it's so green."

"Yes. It reminds me of Starogan," Johnnie confessed, and squeezed the fingers which lay in his. "But you're not really sorry to be leaving, are you?"

She smiled. "Of course I am nervous. I am going to a great, strange land, about which I know nothing."

"You'll love America," he promised. "And America will love you."

"You talk as if I were going on tour." She reached the garden bench and sat down. "I am never going on tour again."

He sat at her feet and leaned back against her knees. "Does that bother you?"

She rumpled his hair. "Not as much as I thought it would. I felt quite a sense of relief when I finished my final performance last week. But that was partly because I knew you were waiting in the wings."

He turned on his knees. "Really, Sasha? Do you really mean that?"

She kissed his nose. "I am going to marry you, silly."

"Yes," he said. "I still can't believe it. I still can't believe that I'm here with you, that in three weeks time we're going to be married . . ."

"And then you will give me lots of babies."

"Oh, Sasha, I wasn't thinking of that."

She sighed very softly. "Are *you* happy?"

"Yes," he said. "I am gloriously, deliriously happy."

"Then," she said, kissing him again, "the babies will come of their own accord. And now I think we should go to bed. It is very late. I heard midnight strike in the village, and that was ages ago."

"Sasha . . ." He caught her hand as she stood up, and then he rose. "Are you . . . well . . . do you wish that we . . . ," he paused again.

She smiled at him. "Do I wish that I was no longer a virgin?" She shook her head. "Not now. Now I am glad that we waited. But you will have to be gentle with me," she said seriously. "I may have . . . what do you say in America—inhibitions?"

"Inhibitions? You won't have any inhibitions. You're Tattie's protégée. She certainly doesn't have any inhibitions."

"To be like your Aunt Tattie must be the dream of every woman," Natasha said. "I do not think many attain that dream. But with you, I will not have any inhibitions. Don't tell me you are regretting it now. Can't you wait another three weeks?"

"I can wait forever," he said. "Sometimes I think I *have* waited forever. Sasha, I do love you so. It's just that I can't believe that someone like you, so . . . well, so everything, could possibly love someone like me."

"What is the matter with *you*?"

"Well, I've no talent for anything, and I've no conversation, and I'm not at all sexy—"

"You have talent. Are you not sports editor of the *American People* newspaper?"

"Nepotism."

She shook her head. "I do not think your Mr. Hayman indulges in nepotism. Anyway, I would love you if you were the hunchback of Notre Dame."

"Tell me why."

"Why? Because you're so gentle. Because you are so kind. Because you are so thoughtful. Because I do not think you would ever hurt anybody in your life. And simply because I love you."

"Sasha . . ."

"Bed," she said firmly.

And so he went to bed, but not to sleep. For the first time he actually believed the marriage was going to take place. He had lived with a dream for too long, but now at last it was all to be his. His in a way he had not believed last year, when he had put the ring on her finger, had not even believed during all the preparations, the letters going to and fro, had been quite unable to believe when he had got to Moscow, had seen her last performance, had watched the almost hysterical adulation with which she had been bid farewell by the theater audience, the flowers and the champagne, the kisses and the cheers. She was giving them all up, to marry a sports editor.

But she loved him. At last he could believe that. She loved him.

He stood at the window, watched the great swath of moonlight cutting across the lawn, listened to the faint soughing of the dawn breeze beginning to rise, the drone of the distant aircraft, slowly and steadily growing louder.

Aircraft? At four o'clock in the morning? A great number of aircraft. He peered out his window, but could see nothing. And then he heard a series of sharp punctuations, crisp bangs, also coming closer, like the planes.

John Hyman stood absolutely still, unable to believe his ears, unable to believe what his ears were telling him—that a vast fleet of aircraft was flying over Russia, and dropping bombs on it.

A woman screamed.